My Perfect Gre

Ian Wilfred

My Perfect Summer in Greece
Copyright © 2019 by Ian Wilfred

ISBN: 9781091556478

Cover Design: Avalon Graphics
Editing: Nancy Callegari
Proofreading: Maureen Vincent-Northam
Formatting: Rebecca Emin

For Ron

Acknowledgements

There are a few people I'd like to thank for getting *My Perfect Summer in Greece* out into the world.

The fabulous Rebecca Emin at Gingersnap Books for organising everything for me and who also produced both kindle and paperback books. Nancy Callegari for all the time and effort she spent editing the book, Maureen Vincent-Northam for proofreading, and the very talented Cathy Helms at Avalon Graphics for producing the terrific cover.

Finally for my late mum who is always with me in everything I do.

Chapter 1

It's been over twelve months since that 'family wedding meeting'. To be precise it's been 384 days. How do I remember that? That was the last time, I, Cheryl Harris, ate either a chocolate bar or a single piece of cheese and how I've hated every one of those days. I was so excited, looking forward to the thought of sitting around that table with my mum Rachel, dad Dave and sister, Julie. It should have been one of the happiest times we would share as a family, but sadly it wasn't to be.

The day had started off with such big dreams. I'd left my little staff room at the Harbour Hotel in Dartmouth, caught the bus to Exeter and then in front of me on the way to Nottinghamshire I had my file of magazine cuttings. It was so exciting. My little sister, Julie, was getting married and she wanted my help to organise it. I could hardly believe she valued my input and advice. Perhaps it was because I was a catering manager or could it have been because she wanted to make it a special family occasion? I just hoped my bridesmaid dress would be a flattering colour. Julie's very stylish, so I'm sure it would be modern and certainly not a shade of peach or baby pink. As little girls we talked about our future weddings for hours. Which one of us would get married first? What would our dress look like? How many bridesmaids would we have? Gosh, that was over twenty five years ago.

Dad was at the station to meet me for the short drive home through the Nottingham countryside. He drove the long way around the village as I wanted to see the village church to visualise exactly how the big day would be – flowers around the door for a beautiful family wedding. I had so many ideas and thoughts to share with Julie.

Dad was unusually quiet. In hindsight I really

ought to have noticed that, but the excitement of my little sister's wedding had totally overwhelmed me. I couldn't wait to share my ideas with Mum and Julie. It was then I got the first hint that something was amiss.

"Cheryl, before we go in, I'd like to ask you something. You know me, I worship the ground you walk on, but I need you to promise me something," Dad stopped to say to me.

"What's wrong, Dad? Of course, I'll do anything for you."

"There's nothing wrong yet, but I'd just like this damned wedding to be over and done with. When you hear what Mum and Julie have to say, I want you to promise not to argue. It's Julie's day, and as I've said, let's just get it over with."

"It'll be fine, Dad. It's only a few hours after all. There'll be a lovely meal in the function room at the back of the village pub followed by a disco and we'll take some lovely photos to remember the occasion. Don't worry, the day will fly by. I think you're getting yourself worked up about nothing."

"Cheryl," Dad replied, "just promise me, no fighting or getting upset."

I couldn't understand what Dad meant, but I gave him my promise and headed into the house where Mum was preparing dinner. There was an awkward silence. Every time I voiced the subject of Julie's wedding, Mum gave me the same answer. "We'll wait until your sister gets here." I tried to talk about all aspects of the wedding from what she would wear, the flowers, etc, but I always received the same reply.

As usual Dad sat and read his newspaper and the atmosphere in the house was so strained, you could cut it with a knife. However, I could see he wasn't actually reading the newspaper. I could sense something was about to happen. What could it be?

We all ate dinner in complete silence. I then heard a car pull up on the drive outside. That had to be

Julie. As soon as the car door closed, Dad excused himself saying he needed to go to the next village to price up a pluming job. Mum looked tense as she cleared away the dinner plates.

"Hi, Mum. Hi, Cheryl. I'm here. Where's Dad off to in such a hurry?"

"Oh, Julie," I exclaimed. "Isn't this so exciting?"

"Cheryl, I must stop you there," Julie interrupted. It's not Julie anymore. It's Julieanne."

"You've changed your name? Why?"

"I haven't changed it. I've just added a bit on the end. I think Julieanne sounds far more sophisticated and Richard loves it too."

I looked at Mum in amazement, but she quickly looked away and finished clearing the table. Julie opened up her bag, took out some notepads, pens and a huge file and I went to get all my magazine cuttings. As we all sat around the table to start the wedding planning, I noticed Mum couldn't keep her hands still. She was constantly fiddling with her rings. Julie took a deep breath. Suddenly I became rather nervous as it was beginning to appear rather official. It seemed more like planning a funeral than a happy family occasion.

"Right, Mum and Cheryl, you'll both need to make notes because the more we can get through the better. Let's start to get the ball rolling."

I started chattering away excitedly. "You'll probably laugh at this, Julie, but I made Dad drive past the church on the way here. It's going to look wonderful. I've seen those lovely photos of flowers around church doorways. Look, I'll show you some. I've cut some out of these wedding magazines. I've loved putting this wedding file together for you. There's bridesmaid dresses, centre table decorations and so many photos of beautiful church flowers. It's going to look fabulous."

"Cheryl, stop. We're not getting married in the village church."

3

Then I remembered. Perhaps this was what Dad was referring to. If Julie and Richard weren't tying the knot in the village church, where could it be? It would be so sad if it was a registry office.

"It's so exciting," Julie continued. "Richard, my husband to be, and I are to be wed on the Greek island of Holkamos. Not just that, but on the beach with the beautiful sea behind us."

"But why, Julie? Why?"

"Because this is a once in a life time event and I want it to be special. We both want it to be perfect."

For the next two hours I sat there speechless, listening to Julie talking about the island and the beach venue for her wedding. The reception was to be held in a beach café where Julie and Richard had spent lunch times during their last holiday and apparently the owner, Vangelis, had agreed for them to hold their evening meal there. This was my role – to organise the wedding reception meal with Vangelis.

I asked Julie why she wasn't having a properly organised beach wedding like the ones you hear about in Dubai or the Seychelles, but she said it would have been far too expensive. Costs would have been at least twenty times more. Mum remained silent and I now understood Dad's unusual behaviour. The wedding would take place on a Saturday. Guests would arrive a couple of days in advance and everyone would stay for a fortnight's holiday.

I needed clarification. "So let's get this clear, Julie. I just need to email Vangelis with your wedding details, the table plans, the numbers of guests, etc? It sounds straightforward."

"Yes. I'm sure you're more than capable of handling the arrangements as you're a waitress in a posh hotel, Cheryl."

"No, Julie. I'm a catering manager in a hotel, and yes I'm perfectly capable. Now, can we move on?

4

Where we are staying, what will you want me to wear and how many other bridesmaids will there be?"

Mum couldn't get out of the room quick enough. "Cheryl, Julie, I'm going to make a cup of tea. Would either of you like one?"

I knew that Mum and Dad wouldn't want this type of wedding at all, but whatever Julie wants, Julie gets. Who would be paying for it all though? I know my parents have savings and Dad earns good money, but a two week holiday on a Greek island? Richard and Julie haven't got the money to pay for all of this.

Julie went on to explain. "Well, Cheryl, everyone will book their own flights and accommodation on the island, so they can stay as long as they want. As for bridesmaids, I'm only having two. My best friend, Clare, and her six-year-old daughter, Zoë. You're not going to be a bridesmaid."

"Why not? As children we always talked about how we'd be each other's bridesmaids. You promised me, Julie."

"We were kids then, messing around. Times have moved on."

"But why can't I? I'm your sister."

"There's no easy way of saying this, Cheryl, but you're too frumpy. To be brutally honest, you're too large and unstylish. I want the wedding photos to look just those in Hello magazine. My album will be just like the Beckham's or Kate and Will's and if you're in the middle it wouldn't look good in years to come. In due course you'll thank me for not putting you in that position. Basically everything will be glamorous and that's not a word I would use to describe you."

Stunned into silence I sat there for the rest of the 'wedding meeting' ready to explode with anger but also with sadness. Julie (and I do mean Julie, not Julieanne) explained Clare, her husband, son, and six-year-old Zoë were close friends and Dad had agreed to pay for their two week holiday. It seemed that Julie had another role for me to play at the wedding too. I would be sitting on a table with all the children, keeping them entertained and well behaved.

When I brought up the subject of money all Mum would say was that Dad would have to work extra hours at the weekends. It was little wonder he wanted to get this over and done with. Julie went through the seating plans, food, table linen etc, everything she wanted down to the last tea light holder. Everyone would be arriving by sea taxis and the path down to the beach would be lit by candles. Julie handed me Vangelis' email address and told me I had over a year to ensure everything was arranged. None of this worried me as I regularly organised weddings at the hotel. Anyway, if anything didn't go to plan, it would be Vangelis' fault. As the meeting came to a close I couldn't get up the stairs to my old bedroom quickly enough. I wasn't sure whether I was going to scream or cry.

"One more thing, Cheryl," Julie added. "Everyone has to wear white. Even Dad will have a white suit, so I thought I'd order you a size 22 white dress and have it sent to you. Do try to lose a few pounds. If ever there was a time to make something of yourself, it's for my wedding. You could get a tailor in Dartmouth to take it in for you. I also think it might be a good idea if you had a big summer hat as I know how you struggle with your hair being limp and lifeless. And one last thing, shoes. Will you please buy a pair of really high heels and practice walking in them. As for your make up and nails, that will all be taken care of in Greece."

I was fuming. I went up to my room and sent a text to the Head Receptionist, my best friend Johnny, to phone me at a given time and then went back to the kitchen and waited for the phone to ring. I walked into where Mum and Julie were still sitting.

"Oh, no, Johnny, that's dreadful. Look, I'll come back on the first train tomorrow morning. Don't panic. I'll be back late afternoon."

"What's going on, Cheryl? I thought you were staying at your parents' for three days?"

"No, it's perfectly fine. I'll see you tomorrow, Johnny."

I explained to Mum and Julie that there'd been an emergency and I had to get back to Dartmouth. Whether they believed me or not I couldn't have cared less. I made an excuse to have an early night and said that I'd need to be at the station by seven in the morning and to ask Dad when he got back if he could drop me there.

"Oh, Cheryl, you could have stayed," Dad said. "I knew you'd be upset."

"Dad, I'm doing just as I promised you. If I stayed any longer, I'd end up breaking that promise. Who the hell does Julie think she is? And to expect you to pay for it! Talk about living above her station! The whole thing is ridiculous. I'm telling you, this is going to all end in tears, but they won't be mine. You just wait and see. White suit? When did you last wear a collar and tie, let alone a suit? Surely you should have refused to go along with all of this."

"What could I do? Mum wants it as much as Julie does, and if I work hard enough it won't be overly expensive. Please, Cheryl, for my sake, just go along with it."

On the train journey back, I went through all the instructions which Julie had given me. As angry as I was with both her and Mum for encouraging such a silly idea, I was more mad with Dad for not putting his foot down. However, I was given my tasks and I would make sure she had the perfect wedding reception.

It really hurt me to think that Julie considered me to be a size 22. I'm not. I'm a size 14, possibly 16, but that's an average size, not fat. As for my hair, I'm happy with it. I'm more than happy with the way I look. She thinks that all the celebrities she reads

7

about in magazines have a perfect life and that's what she wants too. How can she be so stupid to think it's real? It's to sell magazines. My life's great. I'm very successful at what I do. I'm content. I don't have great ambitions. Life in my world is good.

I did 'Google' the island of Holkamos and it sounds beautiful. It's only a small island, near to Corfu. It doesn't have its own airport, so you fly to Preveza on the mainland and then take a ferry to the island. Then it's just a short drive to Holkamos town which looks stunning in the photos. It has a little 'U' shaped harbour with little restaurants around the harbour wall and then there's a steep narrow hill leading up to the ruins of an ancient castle. On the way up the hill there are tiny shops and upon reaching the top you can look down to a harbour view one side and the beautiful beach of Volmos the other side. The beach seems endless and both areas have many holiday apartments. I also searched online for Vangelis' beach café and as much as it hurts me to say it, I think it could look stunning when set up for a wedding. There also was a photo of Vangelis. He's very handsome, which is a bonus.

There you have it. That was 384 days ago and I've not seen any of them since. There've been hundreds of phone calls and emails about the wedding going to and fro, but in a few days' time I'll be facing them all on the island of Holkamos.

Did I have a surprise in store for them? It's none of my doing, remember. I only followed instructions.

Chapter 2

So much has happened since that wedding meeting, not just the dozens of emails between Vangelis and myself, but also here in Dartmouth. Sadly Graham, the hotel owner has died, and Suzy his widow, doesn't have a clue how to run the place. Saying that, she's never here now she's got her hands on Graham's money. She's off on holiday every five minutes, leaving the running of the hotel to the receptionist manager, Johnny, Clive, the head chef, Debbie, the housekeeper and yours truly. When we complain about the hours we have to work and not being paid for all of them, she says that our contracts state that our hours are as required. Graham would never have treated us in this way.

In less than a week's time I'm off to the Greek island of Holkamos and Johnny's coming with me. That was Julie's idea. She says that Johnny's a fun character and very camp, and every wedding needs a gay man to create a lively atmosphere. She won't be saying that when she sees what he's done with me. Today we're off to the dressmaker in Exeter to collect the two dresses which Julie ordered for me. They're both size 22. The day time one is white, and the evening dress is bright red in colour.

"Are you ready, Cheryl? I'm so excited that everything's coming together for the big day. I can't wait to see how that tent's been turned into a stunning creation."

"Johnny, if you're that excited about it, why don't you wear it? I can't believe you even talked me into this, or should I say bullied me into it. I was happy as I was. I shouldn't have to change my appearance, just to please them."

"Cheryl, I've done it for you, not them. Julie's been horrible to you all her life and I know you don't like me saying so, but your mother's treated you two girls

9

so differently. Just because you were bigger than Julie, she wouldn't let you do so many things. No dancing class, no gymnastics, not even singing lessons. What did she make you do? Learn the trumpet. No, my darling, you're special, and in a few days' time the smile will be wiped off Julie's face. You've worked bloody hard losing two stone. She's the one who wanted you to be thin for her wedding and you've done just what she asked you to. You should be so proud of yourself. Oh, by the way, I've another little surprise for you later."

I know Johnny thinks he's doing good things, and yes, I was a little overweight but that's me. Even Clive preferred me bigger, not that Johnny, or anyone else come to that, knows about mine and Clive's little arrangement. Johnny wouldn't approve of me showing affection to another male. It's only Clive and me who knows about our situation and it suits the both of us. One, out of the four of us employees, must be on duty at the hotel overnight. Some nights we're all here, but on other nights it might just be one of us. If Johnny and Debbie are off duty and not staying overnight, Clive and I have sex. Neither of us want to be in a relationship, but every few weeks it's good to have a bit of fun without any complications. No one gets hurt or feels used, it's just fun.

"What's the surprise, Johnny?"

"You just wait and see. It wouldn't be a surprise if I told you."

I'm nervous arriving at the dressmaker's. I have an idea what the dresses will look like, but nothing could have prepared me for what I can see on the hanger. This wonderful woman has taken the maxi white smock dress and turned it into a long, slim beautifully fitted creation complete with sequins and rhinestones. I really can't believe it's for me. She's transformed the red dress into a short fitted summer dress and laughed that there was enough fabric spare to make another two. Johnny's far more excited than

I am. Since all this stupid wedding business began I've really become a project for him. He used to joke that as a young boy he wasn't allowed a Barbie doll but now he has a real one to dress up. I must have been crazy to agree to all of this. We thanked the lady and as I can see Johnny checking his watch I guess we need to be somewhere by a certain time.

"Right. Come on, Cheryl, keep up. This is so exciting."

'If you told me where we're going and what's going to happen, I might share your excitement."

We've stopped outside a hairdressers. "What's the point of getting my hair done? Julie's sent me that huge white hat so no one's going to see my hair under it. Come to that, they won't see my face either."

In the salon everything becomes clear. Hair extensions! Oh, my God! I am to turn into that Barbie doll. All I need now is my very own Ken. Everything's getting out of hand now. I'm not me anymore and I don't like that. Dad was right. Let's just get it over with. Talking of Dad, I've not really spoken to him for months. Mum says that all he does is work, but that's nothing new. That's all he's ever done. Even as small children I can remember that when anyone in the village bought something new, Mum would want it too, so Dad had to work to get it for her. Sadly she didn't appreciate it, or him, come to that.

"Look at you! How fabulous is that? I'll style it for you on the morning of the wedding."

"Yes, but no one will see it as it'll be under the hat."

Back at the hotel we both got ready for the late shift. As we crossed the car park, I can see Suzy pulling into a parking space. Her interfering in the restaurant really is the last thing I need today, especially if she's had a few glasses of wine.

"Hi, you two. Could you spare me a couple of minutes in my office? It won't take too long."

Here we go. I'm in no doubt that this will be

another stupid idea which she's either seen on the television or in a magazine. What was it last time? Oh yes, the dinner time cutlery would have ribbon around it. I think that lasted two shifts

"I have a little problem," Suzy explained. "I'm going away with my sister on a little holiday. She's having a rough time of it, so I need you both to cut your holidays short as I can't just leave Debbie and Clive here alone with the staff. I know this will accrue a cost and I'm happy to cover that. I'm not asking you to miss the wedding, but I need you both back here on the Tuesday. That still gives you five days."

"Sorry, Suzy, but Johnny's only away for seven days, and I have two weeks. Could I just ask what will happen if I demand to have the full fortnight's holiday?"

"But you won't be doing that, Cheryl, because you need this job. How many jobs these days come with a home attached? I think you'll understand my predicament and come back on the day I've asked you to. Right, that's everything. I think you both need to go and start your shifts."

I could have hit her. She forgets that I'm the one who gave her a job when she arrived looking for work with all her possessions in three Tesco carrier begs. It only took her a few months to get her claws into Graham and now that she's ended up a millionaire she has the cheek to tell me I can't stay and celebrate my sister's wedding. Well, Suzy dear, I'll be accepting the consequences. I'm having my two weeks off.

These last few days have flown by. There's no chance of not being organised as Johnny has lists and spreadsheets for everything. I'm sure there's even a list of all the lists he's got. I copied Julie into all the emails I sent to Vangelis, so she knows I've done all she asked me to, and she's happy with it all. She asked whether I've had to have the dress altered and I didn't lie to her. I did say that I'd lost weight, but she wasn't interested. She mentioned that Mum and Dad had been arguing more and more over the amount of money that Mum had spent on holiday clothes. I feel so sorry for Dad, but as I said to him over ten years ago, they should split up. Mum constantly tells him that they should never have got married. I sense there'll be an atmosphere for the whole two week holiday.

"So, Cheryl, everything's sorted. All the other guests are flying from Manchester and as we're leaving from Gatwick there's no chance we will see any of them. I've checked arrival times in Greece and our flight arrives five hours after theirs. We're all staying in separate apartments around the island, so we shouldn't be spotted until the wedding starts."

"But, Johnny, don't you think it's wrong that we don't meet up the night before? It would be nice."

"What, and spoil the surprise? No, Cheryl. You mustn't be seen."

"But I need to go and meet Vangelis with Julie first thing in the morning."

"No, you don't. I can do that. I've thought about everything. You can phone Julie and tell her you've an upset stomach and you don't want her to catch any bug that may be going around."

"Johnny, I know you think this makeover and losing weight is the right thing to do. I agree my sister is a bitch and it looks like a little bit of revenge, but I'm not the woman you've created. I don't want to be her. I just want to be me."

"Oh, Cheryl darling, it's not just about the wedding. You're stuck in a rut and I want you to be happy, find a nice man and have some fun. All the hard work you've put in will pay off, I promise you."

"That's where you're wrong. Yes, the job has been awful since Graham's death, but it's time for me to move on and find something else. That might happen sooner rather than later if I don't come back when Suzy says, but my weight wasn't a problem and my hair was practical for work. I know you mean well,

Johnny, but I want to be the old Cheryl, the one who ate chocolate and dipped her cheese into a jar of mayonnaise. I could understand it if I wasn't fit and healthy, but I am. You're my best friend and always will be, but changing me is not for the good."

Johnny's not annoyed I've said those things to him because deep down in his heart he knows I'm right. In a strange way this is more about him than it is me, which is very sad. I really just want to get this wedding and holiday over with and get back to normal. Yes, that's just it. I'm Cheryl, I'm normal. Leave me alone.

Chapter 3

There's no going back now. The plane has landed in Preveza and we're now on the ferry taking us to Holkamos. The sun's shining, there's a warm breeze and my stomach's in knots. Johnny's excitement isn't helping matters, neither is it helping that I drop everything I pick up thanks to these false nails which are more like claws. Yes, they do look gorgeous, but they're not in the slightest bit practical. Thank God, this time tomorrow the wedding will be in full swing and all this silly nonsense that Johnny's put me through will be out in the open."

"Come on, Cheryl, the boat's docking. It's time to get off. This is where we need to be careful. I've brought you a hat to wear just in case someone recognises you on the coach. By the way, where's that piece of paper with the name of the accommodation written on it?"

"Johnny, it's called Maria's apartments, and it's on the street behind the harbour. The coach isn't able to get up the little alleyways so we'll have to walk about sixty yards. Don't make me panic. I'm a bag of nerves as it is."

The coach drops people off at several hotels and villas on the way into Holkamos town before it's finally our turn to get off. We seem to have more luggage between us two than the rest of the coach load put together. We make our way through the quaint little cobbled streets and finally arrive at a beautiful renovated building where the lovely Maria is there to greet us.

"Hello, and welcome to Holkamos! I'll show you to your room. I'm very sorry, but it's a twin room. Did you book a double with the tour operator?"

"No, that's fine. A twin room is perfect, thank you."

It's a gorgeous room with a little balcony. You can

just see the sea between the two buildings in front.

"Cheryl, come in from the balcony. Someone might see you."

"Oh, be quiet, Johnny. I'm tired, I'm hot, but more than that I'm hungry."

"Well, my darling, I'll put the air conditioning on. You can have a sleep, but as far as food's concerned, I'll get you some fruit. You've got a tight fitting dress to get into tomorrow."

My phone rings. It's Julie checking we've arrived, arranging to meet for dinner and to go over the last minute details. Johnny grabbed the phone from me.

"Oh dear, sorry, Julie. Cheryl's had to run to the bathroom again. What a nightmare journey we've had. The poor thing's had some sort of bug. I've told her to go to bed and stay there until the morning, but I've got all her notes and bits and bobs so I could meet you. To be honest, it will be a relief to get away from her. The last thing I need is to catch her bug."

"So you're telling me to stay in this room until tomorrow?" I don't think so. I'm on a beautiful Greek island with stunning views and some of the best food I'll ever taste. No way!"

After arguing for half an hour (which is something we never do) I've agreed to stay in the room. Johnny's gone off to meet the family and I've spoken to Vangelis on the phone for the first time. He sounds just as sexy as he looks in the photograph. Everything's in order and he's as laid back about tomorrow as I am. He said the one thing he's looking forward to the most is meeting me. I feel very flattered. Dad's also phoned to make sure I'm alright. He tells me that he doesn't believe I'm unwell and wants to come round. I've put him off, but reassured him that everything will be fine tomorrow and it will be a lovely day. Apparently Mum's been out spending money on more clothes since they've arrived, Richard and his mates are trying to drink the island dry and my grandma (Dad's mum) has complained non-stop about the heat. Oh, and Julie's hair has gone frizzy, so I'm quite glad I'm not meeting them all tonight. They're all over on Volmos, so it means that if I want to go out here in the town they won't see me. That's my cue. I'm off.

Anyway, why would I stay in when I'm on my holiday? I love these little streets where everyone's dressed up and the aromas from the restaurants are to die for. Once I get out of that dress tomorrow, I'll eat moussaka until the cows come home. I also want to see where the little water taxi that goes over to Volmos is. Apparently it only takes a few minutes, but it saves the long walk up over the hill. That's the way everyone's going to be travelling to the wedding tomorrow. I know I've moaned about all the fuss of not having the wedding back home in the village we've grown up in, but this is such a beautiful setting that I want to get on that sea taxi now. Could you imagine their faces if I arrived on Volmos? No, I'll have a quick drink in one of the restaurants overlooking the harbour and a Greek salad and then go back to the apartment. Johnny will never know I've been out. That one over there looks nice and it's not that busy.

"Hi, do you have you a table for one, please?"

"Is this one alright for you? Can I get you a drink while you look at the menu?"

"Yes, please. Half a carafe of red wine and I already know what I want, just a Greek salad, thank you."

One thing's for sure, and that's I'm not going to be saying the word salad again for a long time. It's strange, but I really feel at home here. I've visited other islands in Greece before but there's really something special about Holkamos. Perhaps it's because I've had twelve months to get to know it with all the research and emails from Vangelis. Something tells me I'm going to have a lovely holiday here.

Oh God, I've been out for over two hours. Johnny

can't be back because he would have phoned me by now. I'd really love to walk from one end of the harbour to the next, but that would be pushing my luck. Time to head back, I think. Oh no, there's Richard and his mates. What do I do? Quick, head into one of the shops.

"Hello, can I help you? Is there anything in particular you wanted to look at?"

"I'm sorry if this sounds rather stupid, and I can explain but could I hide here for a few minutes? You see, I'm here as a sort of surprise which is happening tomorrow and I've just seen some..."

"You don't need to explain anything. Go through to the back. By the way, I'm Andreas. Nice to meet you."

"Oh, I'm Cheryl. Thank you so much. You have a lovely shop."

"That's okay, but I must correct you on a couple of things. It's my mother's shop and it's not really a lovely shop. In England, I think you'd call it a load of tat, but my mother took over the business when my father died and I've moved back here from Rhodes to help her during the summer."

"That's nice of you. She must be very grateful as there aren't many people who would give up their lives to help their families."

Andreas explained that he was studying Art at a Greek craft school, specialising in oil painting. At the school there were potters, jewellery makers, textile workers, etc and the only criteria for attending was that you needed to be over thirty years of age. Most of the pupils had had enough of the rat race and wanted to fulfil their dreams. Some were in their seventies and eighties, but sadly Andreas only attended during the winter months as he had the shop to run with his mother.

The time was flying by so I explained exactly why I was here on the island and why I was hiding. Andreas thought that very amusing.

"I think that's your phone ringing, Cheryl."

"Oh no, I've been caught out. It's Johnny."

"Hi, Johnny, I can explain."

"Explain what? I've just called to tell you that I'll be back in half an hour. I'm just walking down to catch the sea taxi back to Holkamos harbour. What were you saying, Cheryl?"

"Oh, nothing. Sorry, I've dosed off. I was miles away. See you soon. I can't wait to hear all about it."

"Thank you again, Andreas. I've really enjoyed talking to you. I'm sorry to be rushing off."

"That's fine. Have a lovely day at the wedding tomorrow. I hope everything goes well. Do pop back if you have some spare time while you're here. I'll try and sell you some fridge magnets or tatty mugs. Don't forget we have every item in the world which can be personalised with your name on it – pens, bookmarks, baseball hats, as well as everyone's favourite, keyrings.

"Oh, Andreas, it could be far worse. It might not be what you and I would buy, but look at the stunning place you live and work in. Thanks again, and I promise I will pop back."

Clothes off, teeth cleaned to avoid all traces of alcoholic breath, untidy bed. What an actress you are, Cheryl. Johnny will never guess that you've been out.

"Hi, Cheryl. I've so much to tell you that I don't know where to begin. I'm so sorry you've had to stay here alone, but it was the best thing you could have done and tomorrow you'll be thanking me, I promise. Now, where do I start? As usual there was an awkward atmosphere between your parents, and your grandma didn't help the situation by saying how hard your father has had to work to pay for all of this and why would anyone want to come to this heat? Richard and his mates weren't allowed to be there as Julie, or should I say Julieanne was... I kept forgetting to call her that, which annoyed her, but... And, I've met him, my darling and he's huge. He has gorgeous tanned skin and dark eyes that just bore into you. So good looking. If you don't want him, I will."

"Who are you talking about, Johnny?"

"Vangelis, of course, and he kept asking about you. He can't wait to see you. Come to that, wait until everyone claps eyes on you! I'm so excited. By the way, Julie asked me a favour. She wanted me to make sure you looked 'half decent' and also told me that the little flower girl – I forget her name – has been told to stand in front of you in all the photos to hide your stomach. I could have hit her, my darling. There's only going to be one princess at that wedding and that's you. Twenty-nine years of revenge in one day."

"But, Johnny, it's not about revenge. This whole thing is stupid. Yes, to some people I will look stunning, but I don't want to look glamorous all made up to the nines. I just want to be me."

"You will be you, Cheryl, a new you. All you've done is what that vicious sister of yours has asked. You've lost weight and done something with your hair. Subject closed. We have a busy day tomorrow, so time for some sleep. Night, night, darling."

Oh, God. What have I let him do to me? As much as Julie has been horrible to me, she is my sister and it's her wedding, her special day. Perhaps I could take the hair extensions out, but one thing's for sure I won't be able to put two stone back on by tomorrow. I just want it all to be over and go back to being me.

Chapter 4

God, it's only 5am and I'm wide awake. Even last night's wine didn't help me to sleep and there's still fourteen hours before the wedding. Somehow I need to go over to Volmos and make sure everything's organised, but it's too early. Yet the thought of being stuck in this room with Johnny treating me like his Barbie doll all day is too much. I need some fresh air. No one from the wedding party will be up yet. A walk will do me the world of good. It's starting to get light now. I read somewhere about this fabulous bakery which is open early. Perhaps they sell coffee too. I'll be back before Johnny wakes up.

"One vanilla slice and a double espresso to take away, please. No, make that two vanilla slices."

I can't believe how many people are around. No one's talking, they're just walking around doing what they have to do. The little boats are coming and going. Sitting here looking out to sea with my pastry and coffee, it's all so perfect that I wish I could stay here all day. One more coffee, I think, and then back to wake Johnny up."

"Hi, can I have another double espresso to take away, please? By the way, the pastries were delicious."

"Cheryl, is that really you? I didn't recognise you. What's happened? If it wasn't for your voice, I wouldn't have known you. God, you look lovely."

"Hi, Dad. No, I don't look lovely. I'm far too thin, I've got someone else's hair sewn onto my head and as for these bloody nails! Would you like a coffee?"

"I think I need a brandy for shock, but at six am on the morning of your sister's wedding I don't think that's a good idea, do you?"

"Another coffee, please, and two more vanilla slices. I'm not having you eat one in front of me, Dad."

"Isn't it a stunning island, Dad? How are you feeling? I hear Mum's been nagging and spending. Promise me you'll slow down when all this is over, but more importantly you'll start to stick up for yourself. For as long as I can remember I've never heard Mum say a good word to you, or about you, come to that."

"Oh, Cheryl, she's not that bad. Anyway, let's forget about them for now. Tell me what's happened to you. You look so lovely. I'm so proud of you, I really am."

"Yes, Dad, I do look good, but it's not really me. When I got back to Dartmouth after that 'family meeting' I told Johnny all about how horrible Julie had been. I mentioned that I'd try to lose a little bit of weight and that was the cue he needed to transform me. I went on a strict, but very healthy, diet and went to the gym three or four times a week. As for the rest of me, it's all false. Johnny's worked so hard, but really all this hasn't been about me. A lot has happened in his past and for many years he couldn't be himself. Taking so many knocks from his family has an effect on him, so this isn't about taking a swing at Julie. It's more about getting back at his family in some bizarre way. We're such good friends, so how could I ever destroy his dream?"

"Look, Cheryl, you've always taken second place where your sister's been concerned and I know I should have done something about that before now. Julie's always been nasty to you and that obviously upsets Johnny, but to you it's like water off a duck's back. As your best friend Johnny's sticking up for you, and that's something you need to thank him for.

"As I said over twelve months ago, let's just get today over and done with. I don't know why you're worrying about your appearance anyway. You're not a fifty-something who has to wear a white suit! That's something I'm really not looking forward to at all. Come on, drink up. Let's go for a walk and plan how

22

we're going to spend the next two weeks. One thing I am looking forward to is seeing your mother's face when she sees you. Hope someone has their camera ready!"

That was a nice walk and chat with Dad. Him wearing a white suit really will be a sight to behold. It's time to head back to the apartment and begin preparing for this momentous day.

"Where have you been, Cheryl? I thought the nerves had kicked in and you'd got the first flight back to England?"

"No, Johnny, don't worry. I've come this far and I'm not chickening out now. So what's the plan of action? We've nearly ten hours before we need to be on Volmos. I personally think the most difficult part of the day will be avoiding my family. Surely Julie will want to talk to me at some point."

"That's all organised, my dear. I've sent Julie a text to say that you've been up all night, but you're feeling better now. You're going to sleep all day and we'll see them at the sea taxis later. Oh, one other thing. Seeing that you aren't well, I'm going over to check everything with Vangelis. My little treat of the day!"

Thank God he won't be here. I imagined having to go through a day of hair, makeup and whatever nonsense he'd include. But a whole day to myself is sheer bliss!

"Right, darling, I'm off. See you in three or four hours, depending on how long Vangelis wants to play with me."

"In your dreams, Johnny. In your dreams."

So what am I going to do with myself for the next four hours? Stay here in the apartment and twiddle my thumbs? Not on your life. A little disguise – I think a baseball cap, dark sunglasses... Perfect. Oh, you are pushing your luck, Cheryl. The little streets are getting busy now with everyone off to the beaches or boat trips to other islands. A boat trip would be lovely, but could you imagine what would happen if I didn't get back in time for the wedding? I don't know who would be more angry? Julie or Johnny? I'm sensing it would be Johnny.

"Morning, Andreas. How are you? Thanks so much for last night. You were a life saver."

"So, Cheryl, today's the day of the big reveal. Are you excited?"

"No, not in the slightest. I just want the day to be over with so I can enjoy the rest of my holiday."

"I'm making a coffee. Fancy one?"

He's right about what he says about this shop. It reminds me of something from the 70s when it was a novelty to take gifts bearing the place name of where you'd been back to family and friends. It wouldn't be too difficult to move with the times and buy some new stock though, things which customers would actually want. God, there'd be so much to get rid of. There must be at least a couple of hundred magnets with Holkamos printed on them.

"Hi, here's your coffee, Cheryl. What are you smiling about? Please don't tell me you find the jokes on the mugs and T-shirts funny. You'll go right down in my estimation."

"No, I was just thinking... Oh, it doesn't matter. Thanks for the coffee. Now tell me more about yourself, the art school and how you came to be there."

"Where do I start? How long have you got?"

"Four hours, so please start at the beginning as it will take my mind off the wedding."

"Okay. Well, I was born here on Holkamos, as were my parents and grandparents and that was twenty-eight years ago. My parents had high hopes for me, which was lovely. They knew that if I wanted to make something of myself I'd have to leave the island so they encouraged me to study in extra classes after school. They weren't like some parents who push you in a certain direction, but once I'd chosen something I enjoyed, that's when their real encouragement started. I loved drawing and painting, so cutting a long story short I ended up studying to be an architect in Athens. I loved it and did so well at it that I could have progressed much further, but unfortunately I had no ambition. I was and am a plodder. Why are you laughing, Cheryl?"

"I'm not really laughing. That's the word that describes me, plodder. I've got myself into a bit of a rut and just need a kick up the backside to get me to stop plodding and to do something else. So how did you get from architecture in Athens to Art school in Rhodes?"

"That sort of happened overnight. Someone I grew up with, who was the same age as me, had a heart attack and died. I suddenly thought that could have been me. I came back to Holkamos for the funeral, chatted to my parents and explained that I'd saved a bit of money. If I sold my flat in Athens, that would be enough to fund me to go to Art school. Plus I had a home back here with my parents and within a few months that's what happened."

"That's very brave, Andreas. How did your parents react?"

"They didn't have a problem with it at all, because they said if things didn't work out I could always go back to architecture."

Then my dad died and I've been coming come back here from April to October, which isn't a problem. Well, it is as nothing sells. My mum doesn't like change as it was my dad's shop and she'd feel guilty if we didn't keep it going just the way he did. It would cost a lot of money to restock everything and that's money we don't have, but the biggest problem would be what to do with all of this."

"But the good thing is that you're doing what you love. It might only be for half the year, but how exciting is that?"

"Not as exciting as what's happening today, Cheryl."

"What do you mean? What's happening?"

"It's your unveiling to your family."

"Oh, shut up! I don't want to think about it. It's not exciting, it's a nightmare and talking of that, I'd best make my way back to the apartment. Thanks again for the chat and coffee."

"It's been great talking to you again. Please promise me you'll come back and tell me how it's all gone."

"Well, if you like, why don't you pop over to Volmos tonight for a drink? We're at the restaurant until very late. There'll be fireworks at eleven-thirty. That's actual fireworks in the sky, I mean, not fighting. It's at restaurant Vangelis."

"Oh, Vangelis' place."

"Do you know him?"

'Yes, Cheryl. We all know Vangelis, some better than others."

"What do you mean by that, Andreas?"

"Oh, he's a nice lad. We were in the same year at school. Let's just say that throughout the years Vangelis has broken lots of hearts, normally every two weeks when one plane leaves and another arrives."

"Well, what can I say, apart from poor Johnny. Thanks again, Andreas and please, if you can come over as my guest, I'd love to introduce you to all these crazy people I've been talking about."

Now back to the apartment, or should I just do a runner and sail off to one of the other islands? On a more positive note, after today I'll be back to my normal happy self. I won't be as glam, but I will be me.

Chapter 5

5-4-3-2-1... Wait for it. I can hear him coming up the stairs. Please God, make this day go quickly.

"I'm back, Cheryl. It's so exciting that I don't know where to start. Everything's under control, so you don't have to worry about a single thing. I did make some changes to the seating plan though, not that anyone will notice. I know you didn't do it on purpose, but my place was facing a wall so I wouldn't have been able to see what's going on.

Your mum doesn't know which one of the three outfits she's brought along would be best to wear. I can see where Julie gets her bitchy side. Do you know what your mum said to me in front of several people? Could I tell you to keep your hat on and not to show Julie and the family up. It's Julie's day so it has to be special. Julie's worked so hard to make everything happen.

"I nearly told her that Julie's done nothing apart from give you instructions. You're the one who's organised everything. Sorry, I think I've gone off on one there, haven't I? Oh, and I did tell them that there's no way you're going to look after the children's table and that the best solution would be to have the children sitting with their fathers. I didn't give them any choice in the matter but to agree, so now you're sitting on the top table. One of the best men is with his children anyway. Why are there two best men? One is sufficient.

"Your grandma's a lot happier now as I've fussed over her hair and hat. I've also seen your dad's white suit and I actually think he'll look quite smart in it.

"Well, that's about it, my dear, but you were missed. Vangelis was so disappointed that you weren't there. He said to say how much he's looking forward to meeting you tonight."

"I bet he is."

"What's that supposed to mean, Cheryl?"

"Oh, nothing. So what's first on your list, Johnny? Let's get this over and done with."

"Don't be like that, Cheryl. Let's enjoy this part. We've always had fun getting ready to go out. With a bit of Kylie on the iPod and a couple of glasses of something sparkly, what's not to love?"

"Right, so we need to be down in the harbour for six-thirty. There're three sea taxis booked. The first one will be taking all the relatives. The second one is for your mum, the bridesmaids, and you and me. Once we're all on Volmos as darkness draws in, your dad and Julie will arrive. Then four hours later it will all be over with and we can start to have a proper holiday."

"Yes, my dear, that might well be the case, but before all that I need to turn you into a princess. Well, you're already a princess. I just need to make you into a special princess."

There's half an hour to go and this dress is so tight. I suppose that's what the three vanilla slices have done. Anyway, I do feel special although I know that Johnny wouldn't allow me to look anything but good. I've done exactly what Julie asked me to do. I've lost weight, I'm wearing the hat and the dress she ordered for me and I've also sorted out my limp hair. There's only one thing to say...

"Johnny, it's showtime! Let's get this circus on the road. Are you ready? Gosh, I feel so silly, walking to the harbour dressed like this. Thank goodness it's not very far. Come on."

"Don't rush me, Cheryl. I just need a little more glitter on my hair."

"Are you serious? Oh, my God, you are, but it does look great. I think your little plan won't work, Johnny. Everyone will be looking at you rather than me. How fabulous you look. We are actually Barbie and Ken. Oh my God."

You didn't think that I wouldn't make an effort,

did you, Cheryl? Now come on, otherwise we'll be late. Just remember two things – tits and teeth. Yes, girl, work that body. Tits and teeth."

"Here we are, but I can't see Mum or the bridesmaids. Oh, no. Johnny, we've forgotten the suitcase with our change of clothes for later. You'll have to run back for it. I can't in this dress and shoes."

"I'll go and get the case, Cheryl, but I won't be running. I don't want to turn up all hot and sweaty. Stay there, I'll be two minutes."

Two minutes turned into ten minutes and I still can't see any of the three boats with ribbons on. Oh, God, they've gone, even the one with Dad and Julie on. We'll either have to get another sea taxi or try and get a normal road taxi.

"Johnny, look. There's one with the ribbons on coming back from dropping them off."

"Leave it with me, Cheryl. I'll get him to take us over. It only takes five minutes."

This shouldn't be happening. Julie should be the last one to arrive. It's not like arriving late to a church and slipping in at the back. Everyone's going to be looking at us when we pull on to the jetty. I can see Dad and Julie getting off the boat now. Perhaps we can work our way around the side and then stand at the back. Oh, no, everyone's looking.

"Here we go, Cheryl. It may not be quite the arrival I'd planned for you, my dear, but this is far more exciting. Just remember, tits and teeth, girl. Tits and teeth."

"Johnny, why you ever talked me into all this I'll never know. Mum and Julie are going to be fuming. I just know it, they'll kill me."

"It's not life or death, darling. We're just a little late for a wedding and you've done everything Julie wanted. You've lost weight and you're wearing the dress she ordered for you. Oh, no, Cheryl, quick, the hat! The sea breeze has taken it. It's too late. It's in the sea."

I need to take a deep breath and face the music. Everyone's looking at me now. Grandma's clapping with excitement and Dad's started to cry. Come to that, so is Julie. Actually, I don't think they're tears of joy, but more like tears of anger and Mum's face says it all.

"Come on, Johnny. Help me off this boat and let's go around to those empty seats at the back."

The service is now over and hopefully there's enough time for people to forget about my grand entrance. I'm feeling better now as there're lots of smiles from Dad and that's helped. Thankfully, all I can see is the backs of Mum and Julie's heads. Everyone else is looking at the bride and groom. They do look beautiful together. I can see a few smug smiles from Richard's friends. I remember one of them from a Christmas party a few years ago. He tried karaoke singing while very drunk and when he'd finished he shouted out, "Cheryl, who ate all the pies?" That created a room full of laughter, but sadly, at my expense.

Now for the horrible part. I can hear it already. Look at all the weight you've lost, Cheryl, and how have you grown your hair? I do feel better now that hat has floated away as it did feel quite hot underneath it. I know it's not my own head of hair, but for the first time since it's been sown in, I'm quite enjoying it. Here we go... Who's going to be the first?

"Hi, Gran. What a lovely service. You look wonderful. Johnny's done such a great job with your hair and your hat suits you. I love the colour."

"Oh, Cheryl. I'm lost for words. You look beautiful."

"You might be lost for words, Grandma, but I'm certainly not. Cheryl, what do you think you're playing at? I'm the one who should be the centre of attention. You arrive late looking stunning. What a horrible, spiteful thing to do. You've ruined my wedding day."

"Excuse me, Julie?" No one's spoilt your wedding day at all. Cheryl's done exactly what you've told her to, and yes, I do mean told. You told her, you didn't ask."

"What are you talking about, Johnny?"

"Correct me if I'm wrong, but did you or didn't you tell her to lose weight, grow her limp, tireless hair and wear the dress you chose. Okay, yes, the hat blew away, but she's done everything else you said."

This isn't how things should have gone. Time to check on the reception and finally get to meet Vangelis, but first I think I need a large gin and tonic. I'll leave everyone chatting and congratulating the happy couple. Where's the bar?

"Just a minute, young lady. Don't you walk away, I want a word with you. What do you think you're playing at, ruining Julie's special day like that? She's worked so hard to plan the perfect wedding and you turn up looking like..."

"Looking like what, Mum? Tell me, what do I look like in the dress Julie ordered me to wear? My hair's not dull anymore, so tell me, what have I done that's so very wrong? Here comes Dad. Let's hear what he has to say about it."

"Your father thinks exactly the same as I do. You've come here to upstage your sister."

"No, Rachel, she hasn't, and having paid for all this, I won't have any arguing or fighting. It's a very special family occasion and we're all going to enjoy it. It's not about dresses or even this island. It's all about family and friends being together, and if anyone thinks otherwise I want them to leave right now. Do I make myself clear? Now I think it's time to talk to all these lovely people who have travelled to Greece to celebrate Julie and Richard's wedding, don't you?"

Well, in all my years I've never heard Dad put his foot down like that. I'd better make that gin and tonic a double one as we're in for a long evening.

31

"Hello, you must be Cheryl. I'm Vangelis. It's so good to meet you in person at last. You're not a bit like I imagined you to be. Would you like to come and check the tables before everyone takes their seat?"

"Yes please, and I'm really sorry I haven't come over before. Oh, Vangelis, everything looks wonderful. What a fantastic job you've done. It's far better than I could ever have dreamed possible."

"Thank you, Cheryl. I'm really pleased with it. Have we forgotten anything or is there anything else I can do?"

"Well, if you don't mind, there is just one thing. Could you please take your hand off my bottom."

Judging by the look on his face, I don't think he'll do that again. This lady won't be leaving with tears in her eyes. The room does look stunning and I couldn't be more happy for Julie as her dream has come true. It's time for everyone to relax and enjoy the happy occasion with great food and each other's company.

"Cheryl, I've been looking for you. By the way, Julie's fine. I've calmed her down and she agrees that you've only done what she asked of you. I saw you talking to Vangelis earlier. He's gorgeous. Didn't I tell you so?"

"Yes, he is, Johnny, but somehow I don't think there'll be any romance between us. Come on, let's take our seats. It looks like the food's about to be served."

This food's not the easiest to eat with these fingernails. They'll be coming off tomorrow. I think I'm secretly enjoying all the looks I'm getting from Vangelis. He probably doesn't get put in his place very often. I can tell he hasn't given up though, probably thinks I'm a bit of a challenge.

Dad's speech was lovely, not a hint of anything unpleasant, just happiness, and even Mum's kept a smile on her face. Not that she means it, and God help Dad later for having the courage to stand up to her. Now I ought to mingle with the guests and I'm also going to tell Johnny that I shan't be changing into the red dress. One shock is enough for my family.

"So, Cheryl, I agree. You've done everything I suggested, lost weight and I do love your hair. I can't thank you enough for organising such a fabulous reception, but most importantly, can I ask you something? What's it like to feel normal? It's a shame you've had to wait twenty-nine years to look so good. What a waste of time when you could be having fun."

"Normal? Julie, there's nothing normal about the way I look. It's all false. Anyway, it's not about the hair, makeup and nails. It's what's inside that matters. Do you know, I'm glad I've done all this for you as I've now experienced both sides of the coin, and I'm telling you this, Julie, my previous style was far more realistic. Yes, I needed to make some changes to my working life, but it wasn't about losing weight and having false hair.

"I should be thanking you for being so rude about my appearance because if you hadn't, I wouldn't have realised how important it is to be yourself in life. I'm glad you're happy with the reception. I've loved organising it, not just because it's been a success, but because you're my sister, I love you and all I want is for you to be happy."

"Oh, thank you, Cheryl. I am happy, and I know that people think I should have got married back home in the village church, but I do think I've done the right thing coming here. Don't you think so too?"

"Yes, this island is very special and I'm looking forward to spending the next two weeks here. Look, they're clearing the tables away for the dancing to start."

"Yes, and no doubt you've had the red dress taken in for the dancing. I can't wait to see it and I really mean that."

"No, Julie, I'm not wearing the red dress tonight."

"Cheryl, Julie, it's time to change for the disco. Come on, I'll help glam you both up. Wait until you see my new shirt, my dears, I'm going to sparkle like a Christmas tree."

"No, Johnny. Cheryl says there's no red dress tonight."

"That's what she thinks. If she doesn't wear it tonight, she never will."

"Why won't I?"

"Because you know as well as I do with all you've had to eat and drink today, you'll never get into it again."

"Go on, Cheryl, it seems a shame not to wear it."

"Okay, but I want you both to promise me one thing. You'll never get me to look like this again. Barbie I'm not. I'm Cheryl, the old Cheryl, and from tomorrow she's coming back. She might be flawed in your eyes, but one thing she is and always will be is herself.

Chapter 6

Thank goodness there isn't as much fuss over the red dress and I'm pleased Julie likes it. She does look beautiful in her evening outfit, a real princess, and she's loved all the attention she got from Johnny. I still can't believe how he's put me through all of this for the last twelve months and to think it was all for just a few hours. I can tell Mum's still angry, but I'm not really sure what about. Is it because I kept everything a secret from her or because I upset Julie? No doubt by the end of the holiday she'll have her say.

"Hi, Cheryl. You do look lovely! That shade of red really suits you. Are you pleased with how things are going?"

"Yes, thank you, Vangelis. I'm more than happy with it all. You and your staff have done a wonderful job. My family and I couldn't ask for anything more. You should be very proud of yourselves."

'Thank you, but it's down to all your organisational skills. The details you gave me were very clear, so all we had to do was carry them out."

"Vangelis, I think it was teamwork. We both did a great job. Oh, if you will excuse me. I think my date has arrived."

Oh, look at Andreas. Hasn't he scrubbed up well and did I notice just a hint of jealousy in Vangelis' eyes? I'm quite enjoying the attention. I know Andreas arriving here might cause tongues to wag. Cheryl, do you really want to go back to the old you?

"Hi, Andreas, thanks for coming. Let me introduce you to the family."

"Hi, Cheryl, how did it all go? Seeing as you're still alive, I presume everything went to plan."

"Well, sort of. It's all a bit of a farce really, but it's all behind me now. All I want to do is have a lovely holiday and discover what the beautiful island of

Holkamos has to offer."

"Well, I know where you can go and see some stunning fridge magnets. Oh, and not forgetting personalised keyrings."

"You never know, I might end up buying a few. Now come and meet Johnny. I'm sure you haven't come across anyone like him before."

"Johnny, can I introduce you to Andreas? He's got a lovely gift shop on the island. Excuse me, I think that's my phone ringing. Chat amongst yourselves for a minute."

I'm glad I didn't answer it. I only listened to the voicemail message. Who does that woman think she is? That was Suzie just checking that Johnny and I will definitely be back on Wednesday. I don't think so because the holiday forms were signed off by Graham. I can't speak for Johnny, but I'm willing to take the consequences although I know she won't sack either of us. Where would she find anyone stupid enough to do our job for the money? Plus, how would she manage until they're fully trained up? She isn't capable of doing either of our jobs.

"Looks like you've lost your date, Cheryl. They both seem to be getting on very well. Of course, Andreas has never married."

"Sorry, Vangelis. What did you say?"

"I said how well Andreas and Johnny seem to be getting on."

I'm not going to even bother to reply to that. There's Dad down by the edge of the sea. He does look nice in his white suit, not at all silly. It's strange how we both thought that coming here wasn't a good idea, but something tells me we are in for a nice holiday. It's nearly time for the fireworks now. Grandma's dosing off. It's been a lovely day.

"Penny for your thoughts, Dad?"

"Hi, sweetheart. How are you doing? Red really suits you."

"Thanks. It's been a nice day. No, actually it's been

a special day, and those are words I never ever thought I'd say."

"I know. It's strange really, but I think we were the two who were least looking forward to the day and it's turned out that I've enjoyed it so much. Why do you think that is, Cheryl?"

"I'm not sure, but Julie's had the best day ever. Everyone's happy. What more could we ask for?"

"But are you happy, Cheryl?"

"Yes, Dad, I think so. Well, once I've got rid of these bloody nails, I will be. How about you? Will a white suit feature more in your daily life when you get home?"

"Actually, I did feel very smart in it, but the answer is no. It's been lovely to wear it today, but I'm not going to be carrying this look over to my working life."

"Time for the fireworks, Cheryl. What a perfect end to a beautiful day? Best go and find your Mum before she kicks off again. Are you coming?"

"No, I think I'll just sit on this rock for a while watching the little waves lapping to and fro while the firework display is on."

This is beautiful. Even the fireworks are perfect as they aren't that loud and brash. They're silver, white and pink, so not too much colour. Just perfect.

"Excuse me, Cheryl. You invite me here on a date and then leave me to fend for myself. Johnny's very funny. He thinks a lot of you and your family, but he did ask me some personal questions. I didn't answer him, just kept changing the subject. Somehow I was expecting the evening to be different to this. I think Vangelis has done a superb job with the restaurant and the atmosphere is perfect. Are you happy with everything? Are you glad you've let Johnny...?"

"...create this monster of a Barbie doll? I suppose it's made him happy and that's very important to me, but really, I haven't changed. I've only put on a costume. I'm still Cheryl, and my looks and weight

37

aren't things which needed changing."

"What do you mean?"

"It's my life that needs changing, not my appearance. I work seventy hours a week and that's not right. I'm in a rut, and I suppose getting away from the hotel for a short time has showed me that there's more to life than working three shifts a day for seven days a week. Since Graham, the owner of the hotel, died, Johnny, Clive and I have been working so hard because we didn't want to let him down and see the hotel fail. Getting away from the place makes me realise how stupid that is. We should have realised that the whole essence of the hotel died when Graham passed away. It's a totally different business now and it's time for others to step in. Sorry, Andreas, you didn't need to hear all that."

"That's fine. This island makes you think like that. When I returned here for my friend's funeral, being back on the island made me realise that I had to be true to myself rather than how other people wanted me to be. I do think some people fail to realise that you only get one go here on this little earth so you need to make the most of it. I'm so glad that I understood that before it was too late. Now, Cheryl, it's your turn. It's time for you to fly, enjoy life and be who you want to be."

Oh no, Andreas just kissed me on the cheek. Yes, it's my time to fly, but where to, I really don't know yet. Dartmouth's been a special place for me, but now it's time to say goodbye and hello to somewhere new.

Chapter 7

The holiday really starts today, but saying that, yesterday was a very special day which I wouldn't have missed for the world. I think Julie's forgiven me now the initial shock of my weight loss has passed and the excitement of her day took over. It's now time to relax, have some fun, go to the beach and sample all the fabulous restaurants, but most importantly, explore this beautiful island.

There's just one thing I'm waiting for and that's the inevitable showdown with Mum. She's given me disapproving looks already, so I know it won't end there.

"Morning, Cheryl. How are you feeling? What a wonderful day we had yesterday."

"Hi, Johnny. Yes, it was very special, and I'm feeling the best I've felt for twelve months. Do you know why? Because I'm me again. The first thing I've done this morning is get rid of those false nails. They're gone for good. I'm not saying I won't have nicely painted nails again, but they certainly won't be those claws."

"Enough about the nails, darling. We've other things to talk about, my dear. Where did Andreas come from, and how and when did you meet him? Okay, he hasn't got Vangelis' looks, but he's very nice. Talking of Vangelis, from what I could see I think he was jealous. You know me, I'm not one to miss anything, and you both did seem to be getting on famously."

"I met him a couple of times here on Holkamos."

"But I don't understand, Cheryl. You haven't been here before."

"You didn't really think that I'd be sitting in the hotel room just twiddling my thumbs while you were over at Volmos checking the seating plan, did you?"

"What would have happened if someone saw you

though? Anyway, enough of that. Tell me more about Andreas. Are you going to be seeing him again? I need to know."

"Oh Johnny, you're so funny. I'm glad you came to the wedding. No, I've not made any plans to see Andreas again, but I expect I'll pop into his shop from time to time. I do enjoy his company and we did have a giggle together last night. Before any of that though, what are we going to do about Suzie? Neither of us can afford to lose our jobs, but I'm going to be staying for the full two weeks. What about you?"

"She won't sack us both because that would leave her in a right mess. Personally, I think we should stick to our plans. I'm staying here for a week and when I go back I'll face the music and we'll take it from there. Right, that's enough of work talk. We're on holiday! Let's go and have some fun. There must be dozens of Greek men on this island in need of a kiss, so let's go find them. Well, that's if you've not kissed one already."

"Very funny, Johnny. I haven't kissed anyone, but that's not saying I won't. Come on, get yourself ready. I'll text my parents and tell them we're going to the beach if they want to join us."

"I hope your grandma comes. She's nearly as sharp tongued as I am, and as for your mum, when she starts, her face is a picture."

No sea taxi today. It's a lovely stroll through the town, up the hill to the castle and then down the other side to Volmos beach. It's a hot day, but we can take our time. Shall I introduce Johnny to the lovely bakery? I think I will, but we won't be going past Andreas' shop. It's early morning and he won't be ready for the full singing and dancing Johnny. That's best left for another time.

Dad sent a text back to say that they were tired after yesterday and so wouldn't be coming to the beach. They also wanted to say their goodbyes to several people who'd be leaving the island today and thank them for travelling all this way to Julie's wedding. So it's just me and Johnny, which will be nice. Hopefully, we'll be back to our old selves with no talking about dresses, hair and makeup. That's all in the past, thank goodness.

"Here, Cheryl. There's two sunbeds on the front row. Perfect for seeing who's walking by."

"You're dreadful, Johnny. What am I going to do with you?"

"Nothing, dear, but if we go to Vangelis' restaurant at lunch time, he can do whatever he likes with me."

Johnny's so funny. He's been like this all the years we've been friends. Only once or twice has he let the cracks show. He knows that I realise how everything's an act with him and how it's always showtime. In Johnny's words, it's tits and teeth. No one will ever see the real him. He's like an actor. People only see the fabulous characters Johnny creates, but I sometimes wonder whether he's happy and contented. What happens when the day's over and he's all by himself? I'm not sure he's so happy then.

The beach is beautiful. Looking out to sea from my left, there's the ruins of the ancient castle and over to the right it looks like the beach continues around the rocks. I can see why Julie and Richard fell in love with Holkamos.

"Cheryl! Oh, I'm so glad I've found you. Your dad said you'd be here somewhere."

"Hello, Grandma. How are you today? Are you by yourself?"

"God, yes. I did enough smiling and being sociable to everyone yesterday. Another day of all that would drive me mad, but saying that, it was fun. Isn't Johnny with you, Cheryl?"

"Yes, he's just gone for a walk along the beach. You know what he's like, he can't keep still."

"You wiped the smile off a few faces yesterday, Cheryl. No one expected you to look like that."

"It won't be happening again, Gran. I can reassure

41

you of that. I only did what Julie told me to do."

"What did your mother have to say about it? I don't expect she was too pleased."

"She hasn't really said anything, Gran."

"No, that's because she hasn't had time. Since we arrived here all she's done is nag your father. He can't do right for doing wrong, but it's no different from being at home, I suppose. I'm sorry, Cheryl, I know she's your mum, but your dad is my son and throughout the thirty plus years they've been together, it's always been the same. When they first started going out together, she was at him every five minutes. I've made no secret of the fact that I didn't want them to marry, but if they hadn't, I wouldn't have you and Julie, would I?

"What does your mother want out of life? Your dad works every hour God sends to be able to give her everything she wants. I've lost count how many times the rooms have been decorated and she doesn't seem to appreciate any of it. At one time I thought she must have some kind of hold over him. It was just as if he'd been naughty and got caught out, but he assures me that wasn't the case. I don't know if anything will ever make her happy, and that's so very sad.

"That's enough about them. Tell me about that lovely Greek man you were talking to last night."

"Hi, Margaret. Did I just hear you ask Cheryl about her Greek admirer? Well, did you know she has two? If we aren't careful we might have another wedding to go to before the end of this holiday."

"Shut up, you two. It's nothing of the sort. Vangelis is the chap who I organised the wedding with and Andreas owns a little gift shop. Now drop the subject please. Why don't you both go and get yourselves an ice cream? I'm trying to sleep. I don't know which one of you is the worst."

"Come on, Johnny. Let's go and have some fun. She's turning into her mother. Sorry, Cheryl. I'm only joking. I would never let that happen."

Saying that, it is quite nice to have all that attention, and I do feel that I've got to know Vangelis really well over the last twelve months. However, I can see that he's got quite a reputation and no, I don't need a holiday romance, thank you very much. What was it with Andreas and that kiss? It was just the one and nothing happened afterwards, but did I want anything to happen? Did he expect me to make a move? Who knows, time will tell.

Dad sent me a text thanking me for looking out for Gran for the day and that most people had now gone home. Julie and Richard are spending the next couple of days by themselves, so Mum suggested we do our own thing tonight and not meet up until tomorrow. That suits me fine. Johnny and I can go out for a few drinks, have a meal and a few laughs. That's if we can get rid of Grandma.

"There's your ice cream, Cheryl. Eat it quickly before it melts. If we promise to keep quiet, can we join you for the rest of the day?"

"You two, keep quiet? That's impossible. There's more chance of it raining champagne."

"Oh, by the way, Cheryl. I've sent Suzie a text telling her I shan't be back until my week's holiday's over, and I haven't had a reply yet."

"I'm not going to bother even doing that. Before I left, I told her I'll be away for two weeks. Anyway, when I do go back, it won't be for very long. I think it's time to move onto pastures new. I don't have a clue where yet, but I'm going to enjoy this holiday first. What do you fancy doing tonight? It's just us two, unless you want to come out on the town with us, Gran?"

"Oh no, my dear. It's an early night for me. You go and have some fun. I might go and annoy your parents for an hour or two. That's more my idea of fun."

We had such a lovely day on the beach. Once my

grandma and Johnny get together there's no stopping them. They're both as bad as each other. I'm so pleased that I chose this restaurant overlooking the harbour. I think Johnny likes it, but he's very quiet tonight. He's drunk more wine than usual, hence him keep having to go to the bathroom. I think it was me telling him that for me, Dartmouth's had its day. We're a team and have been so for many years, but all good things come to an end at some point. Anyway, it's time Johnny had some new challenges too.

"Are you alright, Johnny? Do you want to go back to the apartment?"

"No, not yet. I fancy a coffee, and to be honest, I don't want to take my eyes away from the view. This place is all about looking at the twinkling lights of the town. It's just so beautiful. Do you know, Cheryl, there's no one else in the whole world I'd want to share this with? We're good together, aren't we?"

"Yes, and perhaps I shouldn't have said all that I did today. It sounded as if I'd just flipped out, but we both know how we've worked our fingers to the bone since Graham died, and it's all been for nothing. Suzie doesn't appreciate anything we do. Anyway, it's not just that. It's coming away to a different environment and even the environment. You did make me look good, but it's not about that either. It's about me being me, not the person my mother wants me to be, and not the member of staff who Suzie wants to own. It's about doing what I want to do and you've helped me to realise that, Johnny. You know more than anyone else, how your father and uncles made you live the life they wanted. I think that's horrible. No one should ever go through that."

"I know, Cheryl, but happily I'm here to tell the tale. I've been thinking about those years a lot recently and actually your makeover these last twelve months was more about me than it was you. I know that sounds stupid, but when Julie was nasty to you, that's bullying, and God, do I know how that feels?

44

When people talk about their childhood memories, mine are about being bullied. How sad is that?

"I remember being at my grandparents' house one Sunday afternoon. I suppose I could only have been about five or six years old. My cousin was there with her dolls and I was so excited to be playing with her in the hallway. Then my dad came out to see what we were up to and when he saw me with a doll, he went mad, shouting that I was never to play with them again otherwise he'd slap me. I didn't understand why. It wasn't as if we were running around making a lot of noise. We were only playing, but as I got older I realised that to him a doll was a girl's plaything. I think that must have been the first time I realised that I was different.

"Then things got worse. I'm not saying that I was abused or not loved, but I just had to be a boy. I was sent to cubs which I hated and also had to join in with traditional boys' sports like football, rugby and boxing. Luckily that only lasted for a couple of weeks. My uncle took me to the boxing club and there I was, this twelve-year-old boy, standing in the boxing ring and expected to fight. I was old enough to understand that the boxing club wouldn't allow me to be killed, so I just stood there and didn't do anything at all. I took a few smacks, but I didn't return them. Eventually they gave up on taking me there.

"Then, when I was sixteen I had to go to the pub with Dad. There was a snooker table in the back room and I remember thinking that at least it wasn't a cold, wet football pitch. I did try to play snooker, and although they thought I was enjoying it, I wasn't very good at it. The real problems started when I had to leave school and get a job. My dad wanted me to get an apprenticeship in something useful like carpentry, plumbing or electrical work. He would have killed me if he had known that I really wanted to be a hairdresser. While I was still at school I managed to get a job washing dishes in a hotel. My dad was proud of me for getting myself a job and not hanging around on the streets. The job wasn't a good one at all, but I loved being at the hotel and having a laugh with all the bad tempered chefs. It was there that I discovered all these funny gay waiters and this was my way out. I realised that a lot of hotels had staff accommodation, so it would be perfect to get a hotel job as far away from home as possible."

"And that, my darling Johnny, is how you met me, and we've never looked back. There's been fun, laughter, and lots of wine. More than ten years of wine!"

"Yes, but now it's coming to an end."

"No, Johnny. Only the working part of it is. Our friendship will last forever. We both know we'll always have each other."

"I know, Cheryl, but it's still sad."

"It's not sad, my darling. It's time we moved on. Our disco days are over and it's time to fall in love and settle down rather than continuing to stay in bloody hotel staff rooms. We're nearly thirty. It's time to be responsible adults. We'll still meet up, drink lots of wine and dance to Abba and Kylie though. I expect we'll still be doing that when we're in our eighties. What do you say?"

"I'd say that I've got the best friend in the world. How many people would go through all you have over this last year just to please your friend? That's exactly what you've done with me because I've made you starve, exercise and wear so much makeup. You did look fabulous though."

"Come on. Let's pay the bill and head off. I love you, Johnny. Thanks for being my friend."

Chapter 8

So the dreaded Wednesday has arrived. Here in Greece the time's two hours ahead of the UK, so I suppose it's a bit early to be hearing from Suzie. Mine and Johnny's shifts are due to start at three o'clock, but that won't be happening as we're both still here on Holkamos. She'll shout and scream and to her, it will be the end of the world, but it won't be for us. We're having a fabulous holiday.

The last three days since the wedding have been lovely. We've been to the beach in the daytime, out to dinner in the evenings and it's all been very relaxed. Tonight might be a bit different though as Julie wants me, Mum, Dad and Grandma to all go out together without Johnny and Richard. In her own words she wants it just like the old days.

I'm not sure tonight will be that much fun, especially if Mum has a dig at Dad because Grandma's not just going to sit there quietly and that's not what we need on a family holiday. Sadly, I've had to turn down Vangelis' offer of dinner. It's his friend's birthday and a group of ten are going out for a celebratory meal. Vangelis invited both Johnny and I, but when I declined the offer Vangelis couldn't really tell Johnny that he wasn't invited. So Johnny's going as he loves a birthday party.

"Morning, darling. Have you had any text or phone call from Suzie yet? I haven't?"

"No, me neither. What do you fancy doing today? Remember, you'll need to get back early as you have to preen yourself for tonight's party."

"Oh yes, but I'm slightly concerned that no one will speak English, and I only know Vangelis a little bit."

"You'll be fine. Just use sign language. It's always worked for you in the past."

"Very funny, my dear. Come on, get yourself ready.

Let's go and top up the tans. After we've been to the bakery, that is."

Volmos beach is quiet today as lots of planes must be leaving. I'm so glad that Julie and Richard decided to get married here and every day I've sent her the same text – 'thank you for bringing us to Holkamos'. I have to laugh, every time Johnny gets out of the sea he brushes his hair and then parades along the edge of the beach for half an hour. He uses the excuse that he's drying off, but no, he's looking at hot Greek men. Not that he's met any yet. One day perhaps!

So what am I going to do with myself after the holidays are over? I love Dartmouth but there aren't any job opportunities there. I'm not going back to the Midlands. I think I should start looking in the catering magazines and online for jobs in Devon and Cornwall. I'd miss living near the sea if I went anywhere else, I think.

"Have you dried off, darling, and is the beach any busier down the other end?"

"Yes, I've dried off, and there are a lot of families playing around the jetty. Some of the men are quite cute, but sadly there're single, rich holiday makers waiting to entertain me."

"Oh dear. You'll just have to put up with my company. I'll entertain you, Johnny. Would you like me to sing or should I do a little dance?"

"Very funny, Cheryl. Somehow I don't think that's the entertainment I'm looking for. Oh dear, my phone just made a noise and I think yours did too. I wonder who could be sending us text messages."

An hour later and after a lot of shouting from Suzie, she calmed down and realised things are about to change. We've fallen over backwards for her and the hotel since Graham's death, but now things will be different. Both Johnny and myself know that there's no way Suzie would sack us as she's unable to cope without us. She'll just have to manage for a couple more days without Johnny and another week without me. I'm sure that when we do get back to the hotel there'll be loads of things to put right and sort out, but that's all in the future. Back to today...

There's no sea taxi back into Holkamos harbour, so it's time to walk off all those pastries and set off up the hill to the castle. As Johnny hates the hill, I'll let him look in the little shop on the way down the other side. Talking of shops, I must look in on Andreas as I've not seen him since the wedding on Saturday. I hope he doesn't think I was offended by him kissing me. Perhaps when Johnny goes back to the apartment I'll call in on him.

"Cheryl, these leather belts are lovely and so cheap at only four euros each. I think I'll get a brown one and a black one. Have you seen these bags? The leather's so soft. Come and feel it."

"Yes, that's lovely. Really nice, Johnny."

"Oh, Cheryl, say it as though you mean it. I know you hate shopping, so just humour me. It's not like walking around Debenhams. This is holiday shopping and it should be fun."

"I'm sorry. Yes, I agree they are lovely bags and at that price the belts are a real bargain. Would you like to see Andreas' shop? I'm sure there'll be things on sale there that will interest you."

"Not just me, I don't think! Lead the way, Cheryl, but I can't be much longer as I need to do a face pack. I want to get all the sand and salt water out of my pores. I need to glow next to all those Greeks with their beautiful tanned bodies."

"Glow? My dear, you'll positively shine. Trust me."

I could tell by the look on Johnny's face that Andreas' shop wasn't his type of place, but thankfully he was very polite and bought four fridge magnets. God knows who he's going to give those to. He did make a quick exit when I told Andreas what Johnny needed to get done before the night out. He laughed, but did say he would probably have a good time as Vangelis and his friends are real party people.

49

We were just about to talk about the wedding when an older, quite serious looking Greek lady came in, and Andreas introduced me to his mum. I was shocked as she wasn't how I imagined her to be. It was obvious that he hadn't discussed me or the wedding with her. His mum looked sad and exhausted. Andreas fussed over her, getting her a chair and a glass of water, but I could tell she was very suspicious of me. I said my goodbyes although I didn't want to. I really wanted to ask them how I could help. There must be something they could do to help make this shop take some more money.

Please let Johnny be gone now. I've stayed out long enough and I just want half an hour to myself before I have to get ready to meet the family. Yes! He's gone! Judging by the smell in this apartment, he's used a whole bottle of aftershave. Sorry, I mean cologne. I do hope he has fun tonight as tomorrow is his last day here. It's back to England for him on Friday. Somehow I think he'll stay working at the hotel in Dartmouth. He likes it there and he's really the manager. He does everything to do with the computers, bookings, paying bills, etc, and I'm sure Suzie realises that. If I stay in the Devon area we can still meet up from time to time. Now, girl, get yourself ready for hopefully an evening of laughter and no arguments.

"Sorry, I'm late. I fell asleep in the chair on the balcony. Have you all had a nice day? What have you been up to?"

"Hi, Cheryl, that's okay as we haven't ordered yet. Take your time, there's no rush."

"But if you'd been on time, Cheryl, we might have ordered. You know Julie wants this to be a nice family evening and you're late."

"Oh, it doesn't matter, Mum. Don't worry, Cheryl. Like Dad says, we're on holiday."

"Yes, but..."

"There are no buts, remember. I'm the

grandmother and the oldest one here. I'm the head of the family and I'd just like to say one thing. I've been really looking forward to spending the evening with the four of you, so please can we stop the bickering?"

God, Gran, that knocked the smile off Mum's face. None of us dare look up from the menu. Swordfish for me, I think, and just a Greek salad to start with. I know I said I wouldn't have salad, but with the olives and a huge chunk of feta it doesn't look like a boring salad.

So far so good. Most of the conversation is about the wedding with no mention of me and the weight. Lots and lots of chat about Holkamos and how beautiful it is, and to my surprise no nasty digs at Dad from Mum.

"Oh, by the way. Richard and I thought that we'd catch the ferry over to Corfu next week and have a three-day honeymoon. If you don't mind, that is."

"Of course that's okay, darlings. We don't mind at all, do we, Rachel? It'll be nice for you to spend some time away from the rest of us."

"I would have loved a honeymoon, but your dad wouldn't let me. Yet again he said that we didn't have any spare money."

"Rachel, that's because we were buying a house. We couldn't have everything we wanted and a home was more important."

"You just had to spoil the evening, didn't you, Rachel? I wondered how long you'd last before having a go at my son. We've come out for a lovely evening together with good food and wine, which I will add, your husband has worked so hard to pay for. You just have to have a dig at him."

"Margaret, all I said was that I'd have loved a honeymoon. I wasn't having a dig."

"While we're all here, and seeing that you've ended the evening like this, Rachel, I've got something to say. It's something that I should have said many years ago and it hurts me to say it. I think you two

51

should split up, go your separate ways and sell the house. You keep saying that you regretted marrying David. He can't do anything right in your eyes, so while you're still fairly young why don't you just move on and find someone else?

"There, that needed to be said, and now if you don't mind, I'm going back to the apartment. Would one of you mind coming with me?"

"Come on, Mum. I'll walk you back."

"Julie, Cheryl, what did I say for her to attack me like that? All I said was that I wished I'd had a honeymoon."

"I'm sorry, Mum. I know my wedding should be a happy family occasion, but perhaps Grandma's right. Maybe you should sell the house and buy yourselves a smaller property each. Before we came here for the wedding you did say that your marriage was like a prison sentence."

"Yes, but, Julie, most of the time I'm only joking. That's how married couples are. Everyone bickers."

"Well, if you're right and that's what I've got to look forward to with Richard, I want out now. I don't want my marriage to be like yours and Dad's. He works so hard and you don't appreciate any of it."

"Look, Mum, Julie, enough of this arguing. We've had a lovely evening, so let's make our way back to the apartment. We'll see you tomorrow, Julie, when everyone's calmed down. Night, night. Love to Richard."

I need all this like a hole in the head and by the time I've walked Mum back to her apartment you can guarantee all of this would have been my fault. I can hear it now.

"Mum, how do you fancy a coffee down in the harbour? It's not too late and it's such a lovely evening. I don't think you should take any notice of Gran. You know what she's like. Dad's her son, so he'll always be perfect in her eyes. Everything will blow over by the morning. I think it's just been the

52

worry and excitement of the wedding."

"Yes, the wedding day; and you were the one who spoilt that turning up late and taking the attention away from Julie. You really had to make it your day with your 'Look at me, I've lost so much weight. How do you like my long hair?' Yes, Cheryl, it was you, you, you."

"Mum, is that really what you think? You think that I purposely set out to spoil Julie's wedding day? What can I say?"

"You said it all when you stepped off that boat looking like a million dollars."

"I'm not arguing with you, Mum. There's been enough of that tonight already. Now, would you like a coffee or not?"

I really don't know why I suggested a coffee as we've been sitting in silence for the last half an hour. Mum does look upset and all this rubbish about me spoiling the wedding isn't true. It was Julie's day and she was happy. I didn't spoil anything.

"You know, Cheryl. I made a mistake marrying your dad. I knew beforehand that it was the wrong thing to do."

"So why did you go through with it. Mum?"

"Because I was greedy. There was this other chap, Kevin. Oh, he was lovely. He thought the world of me, but he was lazy. Always in and out of jobs, he didn't really want to work in the pub every night and was always borrowing money off me. I knew he'd never change and one night I met your dad who was hard working and had a really good job. I knew he'd treat me well, so it was goodbye to Kevin. I'm not saying I didn't like your dad because I did. I still do, but liking someone isn't the basis for a happy marriage, is it?"

"I don't know what to say. It's just so sad for both of you. Does Dad know any of this?"

"Of course he does. For as long as I remember I've told him that I made a mistake in marrying him, and the stupid twit has just let me carry on. The thing is,

53

it doesn't matter how horrible I am to him, he still says he loves me."

"Mum, I don't know what to say, but surely you must have been happy for a while. It couldn't have been that bad."

"Yes, of course I was happy. I had you and Julie who brought me a lot of happiness, but once you became teenagers and didn't need me anymore I felt lonely and unwanted. What a bloody mess I've got myself into."

"Come on. I'll walk you up to the apartment. To be honest, nothing that's happened or been said tonight changes anything, but the ball's in your court. Dad's not going to do anything, is he? Gran's opinions and remarks are the same as they've ever been, and as for Julie and me, we just want you both to be happy."

"Cheryl, I'm sorry what I said about you spoiling the wedding. You didn't and you had a right to keep everything a secret. Both Julie and I were very cruel to you about the way you looked and that was wrong. I know I've not been a good mother to you. It was just that Julie was…"

"Julie was pretty and you just wanted to live the life you never had through her. I realise that and it's not a problem as far as I'm concerned. I'm happy and that's nothing to do with how I look and it never has been. Come on, let's get you back. Tomorrow's another day. It's time to put all this behind us."

Chapter 9

I've gone from one bit of excitement to another. Last night it was all the palaver with Mum, Dad and Grandma, and this morning it's a text from Johnny sent at 2.am. He says he's had a lot to drink, so he's staying at a friend's. Over the years I've had many texts from him all saying the same thing, and no doubt it's always the same reason. He's met a man. I'm pleased for him and can't wait to find out all about it, but I won't be waiting around here for him to get back as I'm off to the beach.

This holiday lark is hard work; first, a coffee and vanilla slice down in the harbour and then I might pop into the shop to see Andreas. Hopefully his mother won't be there. I suppose I should also text Dad to find out how things are with him and Mum. Perhaps I'll use the excuse that it's Johnny's last day here to give me a day away from them all. It's not as warm today. Perhaps it won't be as nice on the beach. I'll have my coffee first, and then hopefully the day will brighten up.

"Good morning, Andreas."

"You're up early, Cheryl."

"That's because of that lovely bakery. It's the first thing on my mind every morning I wake up. I've brought you a vanilla slice from there. Sorry, I didn't get you a coffee, but there's just so much to choose from and I was bound to get it wrong. Here's your slice."

"Thanks, Cheryl. Now tell me all about your holiday. What have you been up to?"

"That's easy. I've lain in the sun on the beach and gone out at night for something to eat. It's been a perfect holiday, but Johnny goes home tomorrow so life will be a lot less fun. That said, I'll spend more time with my parents and Grandma."

"That will be nice."

"That's not quite the word I'd use, Andreas, but that's another story. It was good to meet your mum yesterday."

"She's not the friendliest of people, but her heart's in the right place. Oh, excuse me a minute, Cheryl."

"Hi, can I help you?"

"Yes, I was looking for the owner."

"That's me. How can I help?"

"Well, I'm an artist and I'm looking for somewhere to sell my paintings. I'm not asking for you to buy them, but if you did manage to sell any, you'd get commission. Can I show you some of my work?"

"Sorry, but we aren't that sort of a shop. Good luck with it anyway."

"Andreas, that's the answer to your problem. God, how simple is that? Back in the UK it happens in all the little coastal towns during the summer."

"Sorry, Cheryl, but I'm not following you. What have I missed?"

"Your shop! Why not get all the artists you know at the school in Rhodes to display their art in your shop? You won't need to buy it, so there's no outlay for yourself but you take a commission if anything sells. It's a perfect idea, and then just thin out all the stock and put it on one small area.

"Once your Mum sees the money coming in, she'll soon let you get rid of all the old stock. Most importantly though, you'll be selling items you really love – pottery, paintings, jewellery, etc, and the thing is that no one else will be selling the same things. It's not mass produced Chinese stuff, but traditional Greek crafts which the holiday makers would love."

"Slow down, Cheryl. It's not as easy as that."

"Yes, it is. Just email all your friends and ask them to send you the stock. Once it arrives, put in on the shelves and sell it, job done. Andreas, why are you laughing at me? It's not funny. I'm being serious."

"Oh, Cheryl, I do like your attitude to life, but here on Holkamos your ideas would be discussed for years before anything actually happened. The stumbling block here is my mum, she wouldn't agree to it."

"Yes, she would, I'm sure. Once you tell her all about it, she'll be encouraging you to get on with it straightaway."

"How can you be so sure?"

"Well, you'd be so successful selling your paintings that you wouldn't need to go to Rhodes in the winter, and since you have a very successful studio here on Holkamos... Well, I'll leave all that with you, but when I come back I'll expect to see some progress."

"But, Cheryl, you haven't even seen my paintings, so how do you know they're good enough and that people would want to buy them?"

"I know they're good because you're a good person. Actually I think they'd be very good. See you later, Andreas, and remember, I'll be wanting to see progress. Have a lovely day."

Now to text Johnny and see what's happening. No reply, but it is only 11.30am. The sun's coming out now, but I think I'll stay on the town beach instead of going all the way over to Volmos. I know it's busier, but it will make a nice change. Also, it's the other side of the harbour, which I've only walked to once. Perhaps I'll have another coffee before I settle down on the sunbed. I'm quite looking forward to a day by myself with time to mull things over. So much has happened this week. Oh, at long last, there's a text message from Johnny.

"Still with my NEW friend. Hope you don't mind. I do feel bad that we aren't spending my last day together on the beach, but I'll see you at the apartment around 6pm. Loads to tell you. Lots of love. Xx."

What's he like? Of course I don't mind. It's his holiday as much as it is mine. I wonder if I'll be doing the right thing leaving Dartmouth as I love the job, the staff, and even the customers who come back year after year. Johnny and I work so well together, but then there's someone else I'll miss too and that's Clive. I'll miss the excitement of not knowing when Johnny and Debbie won't be staying in the staff accommodation and the sex is very good. Not that I really know any other sex apart from with Clive, but that little arrangement is something I look forward to and relish.

Perhaps it's time for that to come to an end before it starts to get boring and routine. I know I said I wouldn't worry about looking for another job until I get home, but maybe I should get my phone out today while I'm on the beach and see if there's anything online.

"I'm back, Cheryl. Sorry about today. What have you been up to? I've got so much to tell you, I don't know where to start. I'll pour us both a glass of wine. Anyway, where are you?"

"If you'd let me get a word in! I'm in the bathroom having a shower. Give me a few minutes and I'll be out."

"Okay, but hurry up because we need to be ready to go to dinner in two hours and it's going to take me ages. God knows what I'm going to wear."

"Thanks for the wine. Now start at the beginning. Who is he and where did you meet him?"

"Okay. So I turned up at the restaurant for the birthday party and Vangelis and his friends made me very welcome. By the way he was so disappointed you weren't there, but that's another story. Everyone spoke English, which was good. There were nine of us plus one empty chair at the end of the table, opposite me. I didn't think anything of it, just thought someone wasn't coming. There was lots of wine and then food started to be served. Everyone was laughing and joking and the birthday girl was lovely. The waiter cleared the starters away and we were waiting for the main course to come when in he walked."

"Who's he? What's his name, Johnny?"

"Hang on. Don't rush me. You said to tell you everything, so be patient. There were lots of hugs and kisses and then Vangelis introduced me. It was Nico.

"Oh, Cheryl, he's so handsome, his eyelashes are to die for. He quickly ordered some food but I was all fluttery. I could tell he was gay and surprisingly he sussed out that I was too. No need for any sarcastic comment, Cheryl. I can come across as straight if I have to, but this wasn't the occasion.

"Well, the food was served and we couldn't keep our eyes off each other. Everyone was having a good time and the food was delicious. As the evening continued, and more drink was consumed, all the other guests started to leave. Nico just looked at me and without any hesitation said... 'Johnny, are you ready? It's only a short walk to my apartment'. "Talk about brazen, Cheryl. I thought it would have been rude not to go."

"Oh yes, Johnny, as if that was going to happen! I think you need to leave the story right there. I don't need to know what happens when you get to Nico's apartment."

"Paradise, Cheryl. PAR-A-DISE, that's all I'll say. Anyway, enough of all that as I need to get ready. Now, what do I wear?"

"Surely you don't need me playing gooseberry tonight, Johnny. Go and have a nice meal, just the two of you."

"Oh, it's not going to be just me, you and Nico. There'll be plenty of others there. Anyway, it's my last night here on Holkamos, but I'm telling you, the way I'm feeling now I could quite easily phone Suzie and tell her to stuff the job as I'm moving to this Greek island. Just one word, Cheryl. PAR-A-DISE."

"What are you like? I'll come as long as you promise me there'll be others there too."

"Oh, yes, Cheryl. There'll be someone else there. Trust me."

*

Walking up to the hill towards the castle I can tell that Johnny's nervous. This isn't at all like him. He really must be taken with this Nico. It's such a shame he didn't meet him at the beginning of the holiday. I'm going to miss him when he goes back to England. There's a week of family fun in store for me, I don't think! But I'll go and do things with Grandma and leave Mum and Dad to do their own thing.

"Oh, Johnny. Look at those shoes in that window. Can we just pop in?"

"There's no time for shopping, Cheryl. I need to get up this hill and find the restaurant before Nico gets there, so I can mop myself down. I'm sweating like a pig. Come on, best foot forward."

Johnny not wanting to look in a shop? That's a first! He really must be smitten with this Nico. One quick look over the harbour from the gate of the castle. It's a rule. Once up the hill, you have to look down onto Volmos one side and Holkamos town on the other. I love these little streets, especially at night with all the lovely aromas coming from the little restaurant. I've not seen this part of Holkamos, it's so quaint with all the tables outside on the pavements. This part looks nice. It's very busy and a bit upmarket with all the vines and Bougainvilleas over the canopies. Yes, I do like this.

"Oh, no, Cheryl. Nico's here before us. He'll see me all sweaty."

"I'm sure it's not the first time he's seen you sweat, Johnny."

"There's no need for that smutty talk, Cheryl. Now come on, follow me. I'll introduce you and then go to the bathroom."

"Hi, Nico. What a lovely restaurant. Can I introduce you to my best friend, Cheryl? Talk among yourselves while I just nip to the bathroom."

"I'm sorry, Nico, but I thought Johnny said there'd be other people here too. I don't want to play gooseberry, but it's so nice to meet you."

"And it's good to meet you too, Cheryl. Johnny's talked so much about you. Don't worry, my brother's joining us so you won't be a gooseberry. He should be here soon."

Well, I do like Nico and my first impressions are usually very accurate. He's good looking, but best of all, he's not full of himself. I can see why he and Johnny have hit it off. Johnny's on his way back now, all tidied up. Nico's face lit up when he saw Johnny coming. How nice is that? I wish Nico's brother would hurry up as the last thing I want to be doing is sit here and watch these two drooling over each other. I'll only be able to look at the menu for so long.

"So, have you two been getting to know each other? I hope you haven't been telling Nico any horrible stories about me, Cheryl. Anyway, we know that would all be lies. I'm a nice person, I don't have a vicious bone in my body. Neither of you need to comment on that!"

"Here comes my brother."

"Oh, it's Vangelis. Johnny, you didn't tell me that Vangelis is Nico's brother."

"I thought I had, Cheryl."

"Hi. Sorry, I'm sorry I'm late. Nice to see you again, Johnny, and it's really lovely to see you, Cheryl. Are you having a nice holiday? I thought you might have popped over to Volmos for a chat or have you been spending all your time popping into Andreas' shop? By the way, have you all ordered yet?"

"No, we've only just got here, Vangelis. We've only ordered a litre of red and a litre of white wine."

I can't see this being much fun. Perhaps Johnny conveniently forgot to tell me Vangelis is Nico's brother because he knew I wouldn't have agreed to come otherwise. I can't leave now though, and no doubt I'll have to chat to him the whole evening while these two love birds stare into each other's eyes. As for Vangelis and his sarcasm about Andreas' shop, perhaps I could wind him up and tell him that I've been there a lot.

Right, back to the menu. Feta in filo pastry with honey sounds great for a starter, and my favourite main is swordfish in garlic sauce.

"Cheryl, I didn't tell you that Nico owns the hairdressers in town. If those hair extensions really get on your nerves you could go in and have them taken out. I told him how it was me who persuaded you to have them."

"I don't think persuaded is the right word, Johnny. I'd say 'forced'. Anyway, they're not too bad really, not that it will ever happen again."

Vangelis is very keen to keep filling everyone's glass, the food is lovely and I'm loving all the stories about their life here on Holkamos. Now I need to start thinking of a way to make my escape. The last thing I need is for Johnny and Nico to leave and for me to still be here with Vangelis. Too late, I sense Nico looks like...

"Right, if you'll excuse us. I want to take Johnny down the hill to my favourite ice cream parlour as he hasn't had ice cream since he's been on the island. Why don't you two stay and finish the wine? It's still early and you can chat about catering or whatever restaurant people talk about. Come on, Johnny, you can't waste too much time. You have a plane to catch tomorrow."

"I could walk down with you as well."

"Oh, Cheryl. Don't spoil their fun. Stay and finish the wine. Actually, there's something I'd like your opinion on, and no, it's not anything related to catering. I'll say goodbye to Johnny because I won't see him before he leaves, although I get the impression he'll be visiting Holkamos again."

"I'm not sure about that, Vangelis, but I do like the island. It has a lot of attractions, some of which are very special."

"What time's your flight, Johnny? If I'm out and about, I'll be back at the apartment before you leave for the airport."

"It's not until the evening, Cheryl, so I'll need to be at the airport for 4pm. Bye for now. Have a nice rest of the evening, you two. Love you lots, Cheryl."

"Aren't they funny, Cheryl? They do make a nice couple and I've not seen my brother this happy for a very long time. It would be great if something came of it but it's very early days yet and obviously Johnny thinks the world of you."

"Yes, we're good friends, but we're both in a bit of a rut at the moment. Anyway, whatever happens, we'll always be friends, I'm certain of that. Now, Vangelis, what did you need to pick my brains about? You're the businessman. I don't know how I can help you with anything?"

"That's where you're wrong, Cheryl. First, let me top your glass up. I want to ask you about the wedding. I think it was a huge success. I treated it as a one-off, but during the week I've had people come into the café to enquire about bookings.

"I've given it some thought and while I didn't make a lot of money because I wasn't sure how to price it properly, I'm sure it could be a success. You were very clear with your instructions and basically gave me a checklist to work from, so I wondered if you could give me some advice on how to be a wedding co-ordinator. I don't have the time or the patience to work it all out for myself."

"Yes, Vangelis, it was a great success and I'm sure your restaurant would be a real hit if you decided to hold wedding receptions as Volmos beach is a perfect setting. To be honest, it was cheap. You could have charged a lot more. Weddings are the most important days of people's lives, so adding an extra fifty euros here or a hundred euros there would have been easy. I think you could be onto a winner with it."

"I agree, but how I do I get started?"

"Well, you need to set up a website with stunning wedding photography. I'm sure Julie and Richard would be happy for you to use some of theirs. Then you need to work out costs, how much profit you want to make after making deals with suppliers. If you haven't got time to organise everything yourself, you could hire a wedding co-ordinator. I really do think that if everything's done correctly, you could be very busy and of course, the more you do, the easier it all becomes."

"So, Cheryl, when can you start being my wedding co-ordinator?"

Chapter 10

I've been in bed for four hours, I can't sleep and my head's ready to explode. I wish Johnny had come back tonight as he would have been able to make sense of things. No, actually he wouldn't, because I'm the sensible one.

I shouldn't just be lying here getting all confused. I should get up, have a coffee, and work out a list of pros and cons. On the positive side, I could easily be a wedding co-ordinator. I've organised hundreds of weddings back in Dartmouth and I'd love to live and work on this beautiful island. That's two reasons to take the job.

On the downside, I've never ever considered living and working in a different country. Would I want to work for Vangelis? Could I leave my family? Do I have the courage or the confidence to do it? Oh, never mind coffee, is there any wine?

God, what's the time? I must have fallen asleep in the chair. I can remember going to bed. Oh yes, for a brief couple of seconds I forgot all about Vangelis' job offer. It's now 7.30am and I feel rough. I've had too much wine. Perhaps a shower, coffee and vanilla slice would do the trick, although it won't resolve the issue. Actually, it's not really a problem. My life hasn't changed overnight. All that's happened is I've been offered a job, which I can accept or refuse. Come on, Cheryl, get your act together. You're not a child.

"Could I have a large espresso and two vanilla slices to take away, please?"

What a lovely morning! I think it's my favourite part of the day here on the island as everything comes to life and a new wave of holidaymakers are going out on trips and heading to the beach. The local people are off to work, and although a lot of them didn't finish until late last night, it really is a fantastic place to work. If I worked for Vangelis I could be one too.

65

Well, for part of the year, and that's something I need to consider. What would I do when the season's over? There'll be no weddings from October to March, but I suppose I could go olive picking with the locals.

"Hi, Cheryl. What gets you up so early? You're on holiday and should be having a lie in."

"Hi, Andreas. I love this time of day, but yes, I couldn't sleep, although that's quite another story."

"I'm just going to the bakery to get a coffee. Would you like another one? We can sit on the sea wall if you have time as I don't need to be in the shop for another couple of hours."

"Yes, that would be lovely. A double espresso, please, but no pastries as I've had two already."

"There you go, Cheryl. One double espresso."

"Thank you very much."

"Well, you haven't asked me. I thought that would be the first thing you'd do."

"Asked you what, Andreas?"

"Oh, Cheryl, you're really not with it, are you? The changes to the shop. Surely you want to know if I've done as you suggested. I thought you'd be knocking on the door wanting to see what's new."

"I'm sorry. Of course I'm interested, it's just that..."

"You don't have to explain, but I've acted on some of your ideas today. My friend, Maria, who lives in Preveza, is a potter, and she's bringing me some of her pottery. She's also bringing some silver rings and bracelets that a friend of hers makes from ancient cutlery. I've cleared about six foot of space near to the window and given the wall a fresh coat of paint too."

"How exciting. I'm so pleased to hear that, Andreas, but what does your mum say about all these changes?"

"She's happy with it because Maria is the daughter of one of her good friends. I think I'd probably have had more of a problem convincing her if it was just the artist from Rhodes, but one step at a time where

Mum's concerned, I think. Hopefully, if we can sell some of the pottery and jewellery, she'll be fine about getting other people's work into the shop."

"That's fabulous news. I'll come and buy some pottery before I go home."

"You don't have to do that, Cheryl, but it's a lovely thought. Does Johnny go home today?"

"Yes, he's flying back to England tonight and I'm going to miss him. Perhaps I could ask you something, Andreas? You know that the reason we're all here on Holkamos was for my sister's wedding. How do you think it went?"

"Well, from what I saw of it, it was really enjoyable. I thought it was a wonderful setting for such a romantic special occasion. Who wouldn't want to get married on such a beautiful beach on a stunning island? Also, I think if Vangelis has his head screwed on, he could do more. It's the perfect use for his beach restaurant. Cheryl, why are you laughing? Have I said something funny?"

"I'm not laughing at you. It's just that you've answered something before I've even asked the question. Come on, let's walk to your shop and I'll explain everything on the way. I want to see the changes you've made and with any luck the pottery may arrive while I'm there."

So, Andreas didn't make any comment. I really thought he'd say "Oh, don't work for Vangelis. He's a ladies' man and you'll be doing all the hard work while he's out having a good time." It would have been nice if he'd said, "That would be great because we could see more of each other." I wish I hadn't even mentioned it, and I don't think I'll say anything about it to Johnny when he comes back to pack his case. I'm going to keep this to myself. I don't want anyone telling me what I should be doing. It's made me cross because it hasn't answered my question. What should I be doing? Working seventy hours a week for Suzy in the hotel in Dartmouth or moving here and work for

Vangelis?

"Hi, darling, I'm back, but oh, I really don't want to go back home to England. I want to stay here with Nico. Please say I can stay, Cheryl. We've had such a great night."

"I don't need to know about your night, Johnny, and you know you have to go home. There's nothing to stop you coming back for holidays to see Nico though, but you know as well as I do that holiday romances are about having fun before returning to the real world. You've had a lot of holiday romances over the years, haven't you?"

"Yes, Cheryl, but this is different, very different. There's more to it than just the obvious. What should I do?"

"You need to go home, start back to work and then see how you feel in a week or so. I'll be home in another week and we both need to decide where our future lies. We can't continue to work all the hours we do for someone who takes us for granted and doesn't appreciate us. When Graham died we both knew it was time to move on, so perhaps our future does lie here on Holkamos. I mean, your future, Johnny.

"Come on, get that case packed. The fun's over, but you never know what's ahead for either of us."

Chapter 11

It's been a whole 24 hours and I've not spoken to a single person since Johnny left apart from just the odd pleasantry in the shops, and it's been lovely. Perhaps I need to find a job where I don't have to communicate with anyone.

The silence will soon come to an end as I'm going out to dinner with Grandma tonight. It will be good not to have Mum there bickering with Dad. Should I mention the job offer from Vangelis? I'm not sure. One thing I do know is that I'm going to do exactly what I want to do and not what other people expect me to do.

"Hi, Gran, this is nice. Where do you fancy going to eat? It's your choice. Is there anywhere you've been with Mum and Dad that you'd like to go back to?"

"I really don't mind where we go, Cheryl. I'm starving hungry, so I'll eat anything. I've been asleep beside the pool for most of the day, so let's hit the town, have some pre-dinner cocktails, a lovely meal and then dance the night away. I'm only joking with you, Cheryl, but I think it would be lovely to go somewhere in the harbour and sit and watch the people after we've eaten. Don't you agree?"

"Yes, that would be great. Let's go and eat at the harbour instead of one of the restaurants near the castle. We can look in the shops and have the cocktail you were talking about too."

Three hours later and I'm slightly tipsy. I've eaten too much and I'm tired, but Grandma's still going strong, chatting to anyone who has a British accent. She's really on a roll tonight, and I'm so pleased as she's spent most of the holiday defending Dad and having to put up with Mum moaning about everything. She's really let her hair down tonight.

"Was that your phone I heard ring, Cheryl? I hope

it's not your mother checking up on me. If it is, you can tell her where to go."

"No, Grandma, it was a text from Johnny telling me how much he hates being back at work at the hotel as everything's in a mess. Suzy has caused so many problems and has left him to sort everything out. I feel bad about not replying, but I'm not going to because the conversation will go to and fro for a long while and I'll end up having to sort things out by phone."

"Good for you, Cheryl. You've given too much of your life over to that hotel. It's about time you put yourself first and have some fun while you're still young. In my day we didn't have the opportunities you have today. Yes, Cheryl, spread your wings and fly. What are you laughing at?"

"Nothing really. Yes, I know it's time to leave the hotel and find some new challenges. Perhaps I could find a job here and become a beach babe."

"That's a very good idea, darling, although not the beach babe thing. Holkamos would be a lovely place to live and work and I could come over for holidays."

I think that's as far as I'll go with that conversation. I won't mention Vangelis because if Grandma had her way she'd have me working here from tomorrow and I wouldn't be a bit surprised if she'd decide to move in with me. Actually, that could be fun.

"Right, Gran, it's eleven thirty. Are you ready to go back to the apartment or would you like to move on somewhere else for a coffee?"

"Eleven thirty, Cheryl? The night's still young. Of course we can go somewhere else, but it won't be for coffee. Where would you like to go?"

"You choose, Gran, and I'll try my best to keep up. God knows where you get your energy from. I think that's my phone again. Not another text from Johnny."

"While you answer it, Cheryl, I'll nip to the ladies

and put a bit of lippy on."

It's not Johnny, but Vangelis to see whether I've thought about his offer and do I have any questions about it? He'd like to chat about it again tomorrow if I have time to spare. Actually, I would like to chat about and I'll think up lots of questions between now and then.

"Come on, Cheryl, put that phone away. It's time to party. You never know, we might find ourselves a couple of chaps."

I can't believe it's nearly 3am, and if it wasn't for the restaurant staff wanting to go home and close up, I'm sure Gran would still be out. One thing's for sure, she's going to be tired tomorrow.

Talking of tomorrow, I'm going to start writing a list of things to talk over with Vangelis. Wages and accommodation are top priority. Oh, am I doing the right thing? Am I being over ambitious? What happens if people don't want to book their wedding here? What do I do then? Do I really have the courage to take this gamble? But I know I'll never get such an opportunity again. If I don't take it, will I regret it for years to come? I'll sleep on it and make that decision tomorrow.

Chapter 12

"Hi, Cheryl, thanks for coming over to Volmos. Can I get you a drink or something to eat?"

"Thanks, Vangelis, an espresso would be lovely."

"Okay, just give me a few minutes. I need to pop upstairs and get some paperwork which I'd like to show you for advice."

Right, Cheryl, keep this professional. Stop staring at him even though he is looking so sexy today. I guess he's done that deliberately because he knows I fancy him. Or do I? He's a ladies' man and I don't want to fall for his charm. I'm here to discuss a job, my future. If we did get friendly and later fell out, I'd still have to work for him, so no, Cheryl, just pretend he's ugly. This conversation is all about work, but I do need to know whether he's taking this wedding co-ordinating seriously. I don't want him to suddenly revert back to only having the beach café and no wedding receptions. There's so much to think about and my decision needs to come from the head, not the heart.

"Sorry, Cheryl. I've got paperwork all over the place. I'm so excited about this new venture, but first of all I want to ask your advice about the website. I've got a friend who will create it for me, but I want to get it right. I've spent hours looking at wedding websites and although they're all basically the same, some are vague on what they offer and the costs involved.

"I was thinking that since we're only a beach café, we won't be able to cater for more than thirty to forty guests, and we don't have any accommodation. On the plus side, we do have the beach and few overheads. I don't want to give out the impression that we're cheap and cheerful, but neither do I want to emphasise the fact that we aren't expensive."

"You've really thought this through, Vangelis. I'm impressed, and agree with you. I think where you could make some more money is through the little extras, the flowers, table arrangements, drinks packages, etc. If people realise that they don't have to accept all these extras, they'd be keen to book the café as a wedding reception venue and then nearer the big day they'd give in and order them.

"Yes, keep the website as simple as possible. The selling point will be the beach. I'm very excited for you, Vangelis."

"Excited for me, Cheryl, or do you mean for us? Would you like to be part of this new venture or not? Sorry, I shouldn't put you on the spot like that as you've probably got lots of questions you'd like to ask me about it.

"I've thought of the things you might be concerned about and I'll just go through them. Firstly, what happens in the winter? Well, obviously we close down. Most of the people who live and work here take holidays to work on the olive plants, but the website would still receive enquiries so hopefully we could come to some kind of pay agreement if you worked on that during the winter. If the job didn't take up too much of your time, you might be able to work in the café during the day too, although the wedding part would take priority.

"If you were to take me up on the job offer, where would you live? Well, Nico and I have a little block of ten holiday studios. They're not very large, but they are modern and I could rent you one of those. What do you think is a good salary? I'm not saying I'd be able to pay it, but it gives us a starting ground for discussion. So, Cheryl, what would you like to ask me? While you're thinking about it, I'll get us another coffee. I'll save the wine until we have something to celebrate!"

He's thought of everything and more besides. Now this is looking serious, plus there was no flirting which I'm slightly disappointed about. It was strictly business, even down to where I would be living. Apart

73

from how much I would be earning, I don't have any questions. Come on, Cheryl, think. You need to ask him something. Show some interest quickly before he comes back. God, I want this job more than ever and to think I'll be on this beach nearly every day. He's coming back. Come on, pull yourself together.

"Vangelis, you've been very honest and transparent with everything. I'm sitting here trying to think of questions, but you've answered them already. I can't think of anything else I'd like to ask. I'll take the job, but we need to talk about timings as I have to go back to England and hand in my notice at the hotel. Anyway, it's going to take some time to set the website up. It's now early June. Would people still book weddings for the rest of this season? Is it better to delay coming here until next year when hopefully the diary will be full?"

"The website will be up and running next week. My friend owes me lots of favours, so he's already started on it. I've also dipped my toes into social media and I have three enquiries for September plus a confirmation from a couple in Preveza for August. It's all beginning to come together, so you can start whenever you wish. Do you really need to go back to England? Can't you just stay here?"

"No, I'm afraid I do need to go back to work to hand in my notice. I'm not one to let people down and it is polite. I managed to organise Julie and Richard's wedding from England in a month to six weeks. I could do the same if that's alright with you."

"That's fine with me, and now all the fine details are settled, it's time to celebrate. "What would you like to drink? Champagne, I think, don't you, Cheryl?"

"Could we leave the celebrations until I get my first booking, Vangelis? Let's have a look at your ideas for the website and your pricing structure. Then we need to set up Instagram, Facebook and Twitter accounts for the business. By the way, what are you going to call this new business?"

"I've not thought about all that. Can we sort that out later? You haven't even started work yet. You're still on holiday, so how about going somewhere nice for something to eat? Let's call it a mini-celebration."

"Vangelis, I want this wedding venue business to work. I'm giving up everything to come here, so it must succeed. I think we need to start as we mean to carry on. You're the boss and I'm the employee, so perhaps going out for meals and drinks isn't a good idea. Why don't you show me where I'll be working from. I presume it will be above the restaurant?

"Can I make you a list of stationary and things I'll need? Oh, and I'll also need the email address of your friend who's building the website? What do you think about calling it 'Holkamos Weddings?' I'll also go through Julie's wedding album and see which photos would be best for the website."

"So, Cheryl, what you're saying is it's all work and no play. I was hoping we could get to know each other a little bit before we start work on this."

"The thing is, Vangelis, you're the type of chap that would soon get bored. I reckon your type of fun would last about two weeks, if you know what I mean?"

"Who's been talking? That was in my younger days when I was a teenager. We were all like it, all the waiters."

"You mean one plane's taken off and another's about to land. Just in case you feel like being a teenager again, I think we should keep things professional so we both know where we stand. Now, Vangelis, where's this office I'll be working from?"

What a day! My whole life changed in just that one meeting. Why was I so stupid in telling him to keep things professional? God, I wanted to see those eyes more closely. What I would have given for him to kiss me, but instead I'm sitting here in my hotel apartment with a coffee and a book, preparing myself for an evening of Mum, Dad and Grandma bickering. I suppose I'd best make the most of it because I won't be seeing much of them once I move here.

Can you believe it? Me, Cheryl Harris, a wedding co-ordinator on a Greek island! Who would have thought of that? Not Julie, that's for sure. What was it she told me? I'm boring, doing nothing with my life. Well, eat your words, Julie. I might not have the right hair or be a size 8, but I'll be living on a beautiful island making people's dreams come true.

Chapter 13

Why haven't I pressed 'send?' I've written and rewritten this email for the last three hours. I want the job here on Holkamos. If I don't take it, I'll regret it for the rest of my life. I don't owe Suzy anything. It would be different if it was Graham. Anyway, I've told Vangelis that I'll take the job as his wedding co-ordinator. Here goes. 'Send'. Now to wait for her reply, which will probably be a phone call. I'd best phone Johnny before he hears my news from her.

"Hi, Johnny. Can you talk? Yes, it's very hot. No, I've not seen Nico and of course I'm missing you, but there's something I need to tell you. I think you need to sit down."

"Who's died? What's happened, Cheryl?"

"No one's died. I've just got some exciting news. I've handed in my notice to Suzy because I'm coming here to work."

"What? You're going to live on Holkamos? Have you found yourself a fella?"

"No, no fella. I'm going to work for Vangelis as his wedding co-ordinator."

"Oh my God. Look, I'm going to have to call you back as someone's trying to contact me. Oh, it's Suzy. Speak to you later when I finish my shift. Love you lots."

That was perfect timing. Now to tell the family. I really don't know what their reaction will be, but first of all I'm going for a walk. I might even celebrate with a large gin and tonic by the harbour. Seeing that it's such a special occasion, I think I'll make it a double. I also need to find some books on the history of the island as the more I can read and learn about Holkamos the better. Perhaps in amongst all the junk... No, I mean, gifts, that Andreas has, there might be something. Oh, that's something else I need to do, tell Andreas my news.

"So, Cheryl, how exciting! Vangelis is a good businessman. He's invested his earnings into property and I think the wedding business will work well. I'm really pleased for you. It will be great having you living here on the island."

"That's enough about me, Andreas. Your shop looks great now. I love the pottery and jewellery, and what's this over here? Paintings! They're wonderful. Am I right in saying your name's on them? How is it all going?"

"It's going really well, Cheryl, especially the pottery. I've sold almost half of all Maria brought in. In fact, she's bringing more over tomorrow. My only concern is that she won't be able to keep up with demand and I've also sold two of my paintings."

"I'm delighted for you, and how's your mum been with all the changes?"

"Oh, she's been acting like a totally different person. When I told her how much we'd made, she started to talk about new furniture for the house. I think she's forgotten all about the sentimental side of things. Can you see how I've reduced the amount of tat in here? No, I really mean the old stock, it's gone down to next to nothing now. Isn't it exciting, Cheryl? A new start for the both of us."

"Yes, although I'm nervous as well as excited as I haven't told the family yet and I'm not sure what their reactions will be. Oh, by the way, you don't happen to have any books on the history of Holkamos amongst your old stock, do you? I think it could help with the social media side of the business."

"No, I don't have anything here, but there's loads of things at Mum's. If it's any help to you, I could go through it all. How about we meet up tomorrow night after I've locked up the shop and we take a look?"

Date number two with Andreas! That's something to look forward to, but first I need to get tonight over with. At least I can tell all the family at the same time because Julie and Richard are back from their mini-honeymoon. Now for that gin and tonic and to make a list of questions for Vangelis about all the things he won't have thought of. Perhaps I should drip feed him the questions a couple a day rather than all at once. Otherwise he might get fed up with me even before I move here. Perhaps I should also email his friend who's creating the website and suggest what needs to be included, or would I be talking myself out of a job? No, probably not. Vangelis only sees the euro signs.

"Hi, everyone. Sorry I'm late. How was your mini break away, Julie?"

"Oh, it was lovely, wasn't it, Richard? A real little mini-moon."

"A what, Julie?"

"It's what couples have before the honeymoon, a couple of days called a mini-moon."

"Well, I've never heard anything so ridiculous. Your grandad and I had two nights in Skegness when we got married and the weather was so bad that we couldn't even see the moon with all the mist and fog. But we did have a very nice time, if you know what I mean."

"We don't need to know that, Margaret, thank you very much," Mum chirps in.

"So what have you all been up to while we've been away? Now let me guess. Lots of sunbathing, eating and drinking, no doubt."

"Yes, darling. Also, I think your sister and Grandma had a late night out. Margaret woke us up when she got back."

"Oh, I'm on holiday, Rachel. We were having fun, weren't we, Cheryl? It was a real laugh, and I think I'll do it again before we go home on Sunday. Would you like to let your hair down for a change and come with me, Rachel?"

Here we go, the bickering's started! I suppose it makes a change for Mum to be having a go at Gran rather than Dad. Actually, he's very quiet tonight. I expect he's had a telling off before they came out. I need to pick the right time to tell them all my news. Perhaps I should leave it until just before it's time to go back to the apartment.

Oh, an email. I only sent the questions to Vangelis two hours ago and he's already answered. He's more on the ball than I ever imagined he'd be. How serious he's taking this is a very encouraging sign.

"Cheryl, you're miles away. You know the rules, no phones at the dinner table. I expect that's Suzy asking you lots of questions. Tell her you're still on holiday."

"Actually, Julie, perhaps this is a good time to tell you my news. It's not Suzy. It's an email from my news boss. I've got myself a new job and I'm moving away from Dartmouth."

"What, you're going to be waitressing in another hotel?"

"No, Julie, I'm delighted to announce that I'm going to be a wedding co-ordinator, doing exactly as I did for you, organising everything from the food to the flowers. It's so exciting."

"It's one thing doing it for my wedding, but do you really think you're capable of such a responsible job, Cheryl. We all have our limitations."

"Well, Vangelis seems to think I'm perfect for the job. That's the other bit of my news. I'm coming here to Holkamos to live and work."

Chapter 14

They all seem to have taken my news well. Julie was excited until I told her that I would only be living in a studio so she and Richard wouldn't be able to come over for free holidays. Mum's comment was that she'd never see me. Well, that wouldn't be much different to when I was in England. Grandma's comment was the funniest. As long as I've got a double bed, she'll be able to come and stay for months at a time. To be honest, that wouldn't be a problem. Dad was the only one who didn't say much, although he did look rather upset. He said he was pleased, but I don't think he really meant it and that worries me.

I think a little walk down to the bakery for a couple of vanilla slices is called for before I go through the emails from Suzy. I see there's also an email from Vangelis asking to meet up and talk about the website content to accompany the wedding photos. I'm surprised there's not been any calls or messages from Johnny. He normally has so much to say.

Then I've got my second date with Andreas to look forward to. Who am I kidding? They're not really dates, are they? Firstly, I invited him to the wedding out of politeness and tonight he's helping me to find out more information about the island. A date would be going out for a nice meal and drinks, and then perhaps a little more... but apart from that kiss he hasn't showed any more interest in me. Enough of those thoughts, the bakery calls...

Oh, there's another text. Ah, it's from Clive with just four words... 'I will miss you'. Well, that's not something I ever thought he'd send. Yes, our little evenings were very nice, but I didn't think it meant anything to him. Maybe I was wrong.

The email from Suzy is just as I expected. She's hoping that I'll reconsider and has even offered me a pay rise together with a shorter working week. I've been polite and told her that I'll be back late Sunday night and will work as per the rota schedule on Monday. There's not been a reply. Probably that's because she's away on yet another holiday.

I haven't answered Clive's text as I don't really know how to respond to him. No word yet from Johnny, but on a positive note the Twitter account I've set up for 'Holkamos Weddings' now has lots of followers, and there's been interest on the photos of the island and Julie and Richard's wedding. I've had contacts from people in England, Norway and Germany, which is surprising. I just presumed it would be people from England. It's all getting very exciting!

I need to get ready to meet Andreas now. I'm feeling nervous or is it excitement?

"Hi, Cheryl. I've just got to close the shutters and lock the shop up for the night. Have you had a good day? What was I thinking? I haven't eaten and there's a little restaurant just up that side street where many of the shopkeepers go when they close their shops. It's small, but the food's lovely. I've also brought some books that might be helpful to you."

"That would be lovely, Andreas."

It's beginning to feel like a date! We're going out for a meal, Andreas has gone to the trouble of finding me the books, and I'm sure he's dressed differently today. He looks smarter than usual, and I'm sure I can smell aftershave. He must have put some on when he went to the stock room. If he's trying to impress me, I'd say it's working.

This restaurant is lovely, it's so quaint and rustic, just like stepping back in time. Andreas knows everyone and I recognise some of the locals now. That's weird, we've not ordered anything yet, but the owner's just brought a carafe of red wine to our table and given us our cutlery. We haven't even seen the menu.

"Every night's a surprise here, Cheryl. Stenos gets here in the morning and then whatever he decides to cook is what everyone has. No one complains and we all love it. It reminds me of when I used to come home from school and Mum would put food in front of me. How many restaurants do you go to where you can't decide what to eat? This takes the decision making away. I hope it's something you'll enjoy."

"I'm sure I will. There's not much I don't like. Tell me about the shop. When's the stock from the artist in Rhodes coming in?"

"It's not just the new stock I have to tell you about, Cheryl, but the old stock too. You know I reduced it all down to a ridiculously low price. Well, the owner of the little gift shop on Volmos knows me very well, and when he saw the price I was selling it for he said that he could easily get more for it. So he's taking it all off my hands and he'll give me fifty per cent of the proceeds. From next week all of it will have gone – not a fridge magnet in sight!

"But that left me with a dilemma as I wouldn't have any stock left in the shop. So I've emailed all the craftsmen and artists I know in Greece to ask if they wanted to display their work for a thirty per cent fee. I've had so many replies that there's too many to go through. I've chosen the ones I think look best and will complement other pieces well. So once the old tat has gone, I'm going to close for a day while I redecorate the whole shop. I've got you to thank for this, Cheryl, as it was all your idea, and I'm so thrilled with how the pottery's selling that I've invited two more potters to display their work too.

"Mum's happy now, as I explained to her that the commission we made on three pieces in just one day was more than a week's takings from the old stock. Anyway, that's enough about the shop, tell me more about your new job. When do you start?"

"I'm going back to England on Sunday to work out

my month's notice period and then I'll come back here. As the business is online, I've already started working for Vangelis as several enquiries have come through.

"I've told all my family about it and they're quite happy about it although I think they're concerned about what I'll do in the winter. However, that's five months away and I do have some savings to fall back on. The worst thing that could happen is having to go back home to my parents and getting some waitressing work at Christmas in restaurants or hotels. It's a busy time, so I'll be able to find some work somewhere."

"You seem to have everything well organised, Cheryl. I really am delighted for you and I'm sorry I didn't show my enthusiasm when you first told me about it. It's embarrassing for me to admit it, but I was jealous of you working for Vangelis. I wish it was me you'd be spending so much time with. Oh, here comes the food. Thank you, Stenos. What delights do you have in store for us tonight?"

Oh dear, where did that come from? He likes me far more than I could ever have imagined. I hope I'm not blushing. If so, I'll blame the hot food. Thank goodness it arrived when it did as it saved me from having to reply.

My life's changing so fast. First, a new home and job, and now I could have a boyfriend too. Everything seems too good to be true. I hope it's not a dream and I wake up to being back in Dartmouth working three shifts a day.

"That meal was delicious, Andreas. Thank you so much for bringing me here. This island just gets better and better, and I'm so happy to be coming here to live. You don't have to be jealous of Vangelis at all as I'm not going to be another woman he charms into bed. I'm working for him and that's as far as it goes. He needs to save all his charm for all the mothers of the brides. They're the ones holding the purse strings to their daughter's weddings. All he needs to do is flutter his eyelashes at them. If he chats up any of the brides and the weddings get called off, I'll kill him."

"No, he's not that daft, Cheryl. Vangelis knows which side of the bread is buttered. He's a businessman and he knows how to make money. Would you like some more wine or a coffee?"

"A coffee would be nice. Let's go and get one from the bakery and take it down to the harbour wall to sit and look at all the little boats."

"Yes, we'll do that. You know when the bakery opened and the owner said he was going to be open twenty-four hours a day, all the locals laughed? Well, I'm telling you it's the busiest business on Holkamos. Both the locals and holiday makers love it. Everyone goes there on their way home to buy pastries for their breakfast the next day. Have you tried one of their baklavas? They really are to die for."

"What did you say they were called, Andreas? I think they're my new favourite pastry, but don't tell the vanilla slices as I don't want to upset them."

"They're called baklavas, and I don't think you could eat them for breakfast as they're very rich. There's no need for the vanilla slices to get upset! Do you fancy a little walk around the harbour now?"

"That would be lovely. I'm so amazed at how different Holkamos is at night compared to the day time. In the mornings everyone's rushing around going on the boat trips and catching the sea taxis over to Volmos, and then at night it's so special. Everyone's dressed up and there's flickering lights on the sea and wonderful aromas as you walk by all the little restaurants. I think I've fallen in love with your beautiful island and even if Vangelis hadn't offered me a job here, I would have made my way back one day."

"I know exactly what you mean, Cheryl. When I was in Athens I really missed this place. Rhodes is beautiful as well, but when I get on the ferry at

Preveza my heart misses a beat and I get so excited. I'm very lucky to have been born and brought up here. Talking of my heart, it's been feeling quite different since you've arrived, Cheryl. It's not just my business that's changing. Since you've been here, I've changed too. I like you a lot, Cheryl. In fact, more than a lot. Since that first night when you came into the shop to hide, I've not thought of anything else. I'm so happy you're coming to live here. Would it be alright if I gave you a kiss, Cheryl?"

"Oh, Andreas, I was beginning to think you never would!!"

Chapter 15

DARTMOUTH

I'm back in my little room and no one's here except Debbie the housekeeper. Apparently, Johnny's visiting friends and Clive's off to his parents for a few days. I suppose that could be a good thing. I can handle the Johnny situation, but Clive, that could be awkward.

I'm missing Holkamos already and it's not been twenty-four hours yet. I think I'm missing Andreas just as much too. Three days of kissing that lovely man has got me wanting more of him. I want him and I know he wants me but we've got a whole four weeks to wait. In the meantime there's so much to organise here. The hand over book says that Suzy will be back next week and from what Debbie's told me she hasn't advertised my job because she's convinced I'll be staying. Well, sadly she's mistaken.

To think the last time I was in this room Johnny had tried to turn me into a different person, someone who'd look good in a celebrity magazine shoot. I was off to a wedding I didn't want to go to. How life changes in just a couple of weeks. I'm shattered. It's late and time to get some sleep before a long eighteen-hour shift tomorrow. I'd best check my phone first though.

A text from Dad to say they're all home safely and one from Vangelis saying he's keeping his fingers crossed that no one will change my mind and I'll want go back to Holkamos, and a final one from Andreas with just five words 'I'm missing you so much'. How sweet is that! I'll text back '28 more sleeps'. God, that seems so strange. Just 28 more days and my life will change. I'm so nervous and excited.

*

It's 6am already and I don't seem to have been asleep for more than a couple of minutes. It's time to face the day. No doubt there'll be lots of questions from the staff. I'll miss them as they've all become my family in the last few years, so let's get the worst bit of the day over with. A quick chat with Bob, the night porter. He's someone I won't miss, always moaning and complaining. How he's had to hand keys to guests, put newspapers outside bedrooms and, oh dear, someone ordered a ham sandwich at midnight. I don't think he'll mention that he fell asleep behind reception for five hours.

"Morning, Bob. Anything to hand over? Has anyone checked out yet? How many residents are booked in for breakfast?"

"It's a full hotel. I've not stopped all night. I've not had time to hoover the lounge yet as guests were still sitting there at two am."

"Yes, but they're on holiday, drinking and spending the money that pays your wage. Was that everything? I suggest you get off now as you must be so tired. Home for a sleep or are you doing your painting and decorating job today?"

"I don't know what you mean, Cheryl."

"I think you do, Bob. What is it, sleep here all night instead of doing the jobs you're supposed to and then go off and work a day job. Thank God I'm leaving."

"If you don't mind me saying, Cheryl. You're like a different person since you came back from your holiday and I don't know whether I like it. I'm off by the way. Clive's phoned and he's not feeling very well. He won't be back until later in the week."

"Thank you. Have a good day and I'll see you tonight, Bob."

Clive's sick? In all the years I've known him he's never been sick. How strange. I'd best check the chef's rota and see if one of the others can cover his shifts. Talking of rotas, I'd best see when Johnny's back. Right, Cheryl, you're in for a very long day, but only 27 more once today's over with. Thank God!

I can't believe it's 5pm already. Where's the day gone? In a way it's been good that Johnny hasn't been here as I wouldn't have got as much work done. He'll be back tomorrow afternoon though. As for Clive, it was as if he knew he'd be off sick. All the orders for the week's food deliveries have been done and he's covered all the shifts. This has something to do with me leaving, but he was the one who wasn't interested in a relationship. He was the one who went back to his room once the sex was over. There were plenty of opportunities to become a couple, but all of a sudden I'm leaving and he says he'll miss me. Sorry, Clive, but I'm going. I don't just have a job waiting for me, I also have Andreas.

"Hi Cheryl, How was your first day back?"

"Okay, so far. Just the dinner shift to cope with and it'll be over. The first day back is always the worst, isn't it? How's housekeeping been today, Debbie?"

"All fine, thanks. Most of the rooms have been stay overs so quite an easy one really. Can I ask you something, Cheryl. Are you definitely leaving? You're not going to change your mind, are you, because Suzy's convinced you will. She said the Greek islands have a short summer season so come October you'll have to come back and find work here."

"Yes, I'm definitely leaving, but she's correct about the islands. Everything does close the second week of October. I'll cross that bridge when I get to it. Can I ask you something too, Debbie? It's about Clive being off sick. It's very unusual, so not like him at all. Was he unwell when you last saw him? It's just I'm a little concerned."

"You're right, it's not like him at all. Actually, he was acting rather oddly the day after you handed in your notice. The other chefs and the waiting staff said he was in a foul mood, snapping at everyone and banging pans around. Someone said he was worried about who would take over the role of Catering Manager because his life could become difficult if he didn't get on with them."

"Is that what you think the problem is?"

"Well, I think it's obvious that he likes you. He's always fancied you. Everyone in the hotel knows that by the way he looks at you as you enter a room. He's not man enough to tell you, so I think the real reason he's gone sick is because he can't face you."

Midnight and the first of the twenty eight days is over. My feet are killing me and I'm tired, but there's one more thing to do before I switch the light off and that's send Clive a text. What should I say? I don't want him to get the impression there could be something between us, but I don't want to come across as uncaring either. Oh, never mind. Just five words will do. 'Clive, we need to talk'. No kiss at the end, just 'Send'. God, that was quick, he's already replied. Oh, no, it's not from him, it's from Johnny. 'Very excited. Loads to tell you. See you tomorrow, missing you tons xx'. I wonder what that's all about.

Day two and what a surprise! The hotel is shining like a new pin. I sense our night porter was feeling a little guilty. The paperwork's been done, the registration cards for today's arrivals have all been printed and all the public areas have been hoovered. For the first time he's even emptied the bins. Perhaps I should have said something years ago.

There's no text from Clive. I'll give it until tonight and then send him another one. There's more enquiries for weddings on Holkamos and one of them is from a couple who are on holiday there at the moment. I'll forward that to Vangelis and he can show them what's on offer, but the best thing is all the photos from Andreas showing me the new stock in the shop. I can't wait to go back and see it for myself.

Right, a morning of paperwork for me because once Johnny's back this afternoon I won't be able to concentrate on anything. I wonder what he has to tell me and I'm also interested in where he's been for the last few days. So many secrets!

"Hi, Cheryl, I'm back. I've so much to tell you, but let me go and get changed into my uniform first. See you in ten minutes."

There goes peace and quiet, Johnny's back! But he is the heart and soul of this hotel, the staff all love him and so do the guests, especially the older ones. If he's not on shift they're so disappointed. I remember Graham saying hundreds of times that Johnny's the reason the guests return year after year. It's like he is on a stage. Every time he walks through the service area door for a new shift you can hear him shout 'Showtime'. Even when he's not quite his normal chirpy self, the minute he hits reception he switches it on. It's such a performance.

"Right, what have I missed? How many check-ins are there tonight? Let's get this shift on the road. I'm only joking, Cheryl. I couldn't give a damn about tonight's shift really. I'm so excited! So much has happened. I didn't tell you what I was up to just in case you tried to put me off. I also wanted to make sure I could do it and enjoy it and the answer to both questions is I can and I do. I'm so excited, Cheryl."

"I'm completely lost with all this so far. I'll go and make us a coffee and then you can start explaining everything. By the way, did you know Clive's off sick?"

"Yes, I know. It's because he's so in love with you, he doesn't want you to leave. Surely you realise that, Cheryl."

Why oh why didn't you tell me that yourself, Clive? Everyone else seems to know it apart from me. For the last couple of years we've kissed and had great sex, but once it's over you switch off. Why didn't we even cuddle? I'm so mad with you. The sooner you get back to this hotel, the better. Now calm yourself down, Cheryl. Make the coffee and go and find out what exciting things have been happening in Johnny's life. He's obviously forgotten all about Nico. A question of being out of sight and out of mind, a holiday romance which was great while it lasted.

"Right. Now start at the beginning. Oh, and seeing that you haven't asked, yes, I had a nice holiday and I'm still leaving the hotel. Now go for it."

"Well, I've been in Bath for the last three days staying with my friend Cleo who has the hair salon. I've been working in her salon. Well, not actually working, more like training. The thing is Nico wants me to move over to Holkamos with him and says that I won't need to work as he earns enough to keep us both. But you know me, I'm not a scrounger and I do like to be a little independent, so I've told him I'd like a job there. He said 'Come and work in the salon'. I thought about it, but wasn't sure I'd like it, so I've been at Cleo's learning how to wash hair, massage people's heads and all the things apprentices do. She did say that all the towels on the shelves have never looked so tidy. I've learnt so much."

"I don't know what to say? Have you told Suzy you're leaving? You're the heart and soul of this hotel."

"Yes, I'm the heart and soul but being paid for forty hours and working seventy, the heart will end up packing up. No, I've not told her yet. I wanted to see whether I liked the hairdressing first, so I think once everyone's checked in I'll put together an email to send her."

"Oh my God. She's going to be devastated, Johnny. You do so much for her, the invoices, the wages, everything."

"Yes, and I only get paid a head receptionist's

wage. Ask me if I feel guilty and the answer is no. Right, I've got four weeks to get sorted and then I'm off. Do you know, apart from the gorgeous Nico, one of the best things about living on the Greek island of Holkamos will be being there with you, my best friend in the world. This is exciting for both of us, Cheryl. Actually, it's more than exciting. It's very special. I love you, lovely lady, I really do."

Chapter 16

"You can't do this to me. It's just not fair after all Graham did for both of you too. He treated you just like family and would have done anything for you. I'm so upset. Surely you can see that I've flown all the way back from being on holiday with my sister. One of you leaving is bad enough, but both of you! Well, I'm telling you this. It's not going to happen. What do I have to do to make you stay? The way you're treating me isn't fair. You can't leave me in the lurch like this. I've no head chef either, as apparently Clive's off sick with his nerves. Well, one of you speak, say something."

"It's like this, Suzy. I'm only speaking for myself, but Graham wouldn't have treated us like this. We would never have been told to work seventy hours a week. I have so much to thank him for as he taught me everything I know and I'll always be grateful for that, but it's now time for me to move on for a new start. I'll leave everything up to date for you. What more can I say? Perhaps the reason Clive's off sick is because of the hours he's made to work too. Have you thought of that, Suzy?"

"Oh don't throw that at me, Cheryl. The reason he's not here is because of you deserting him. He loves you, but then you know that. Don't think I haven't sussed out what goes on over in the staff bedrooms. I'm very aware how close the two of you get."

"Don't be silly, Suzy. There's nothing going on between Cheryl and Clive, and to be honest you're going the wrong way about trying to make us stay. You should be thanking Cheryl as if it wasn't for her, where would you be? She gave you the job here the day you arrived with all your possessions in a carrier bag. You never would have wormed your way into Graham's affections and ended up owning this hotel if it wasn't for Cheryl. So think again, lady, before you start letting off steam."

"Get out of my sight the pair of you, and by the way you'll both be hearing from my solicitor. This matter isn't over yet."

"Well, Johnny, that was fun. If we hadn't truly made up or minds to leave, after that, we certainly would have."

"Forget that, have you and Clive been more than work colleagues? No, that's a load of rubbish. I know he fancied you, but surely you've never... You would have told me, wouldn't you?"

What a day! Hopefully Suzy has calmed down. I'd love to be a fly on the wall when she speaks to her solicitor, and as for Johnny he's too excited about moving to Greece to get angry at me for not telling him about my nights of passion with Clive. There's still no text or phone call from Clive, so there's nothing more I can do but the best bit of news is I'm off tomorrow and I'm going to be looking over the new website for any errors or corrections that need sorting out, and then Vangelis can launch it. That's when the real work starts. Fingers crossed for lots of enquiries to be converted into bookings.

I'll miss Dartmouth. I've been happy and very contented here and the staff have been great to work with. There've been lots of laughter and a few tears too, but it's been good.

The future's exciting though. The wedding enquiries are coming in and as the time to leave gets nearer, the more I'm looking forward to moving to Holkamos. I can't believe where the time has gone. In just four days I'll be in Greece. At last Suzy understands we're both leaving. Surprisingly, neither Johnny or myself ever did get a letter from her solicitor and she's been interviewing candidates for our jobs.

Today's going to be nice. Dad's coming to collect

everything I'm not taking to Greece with me, winter clothes, books, CDs and the television. It will be great to see him as I haven't really spoken to him since we all came back from Holkamos. He's the only one who hasn't made comment about me moving away. I don't know if he's happy for me or not, but I'm so pleased he's coming over by himself.

"Morning, Dad, you're early and you've brought the van rather than the car. I don't have that much stuff. It's only a little staff room I've been living in."

"Hi, Cheryl. I wasn't really sure how much there'd be so I thought I'd bring the van over just to be on the safe side."

"It's all packed up, just needs loading. Why don't we go for a walk and something to eat? You can spare a few hours, can't you?"

"Of course I can. You know how much I love Dartmouth!"

"How's everyone at home, Dad? How are Julie and Richard settling into married life? Gran must still be tired as she didn't stop for the whole two weeks in Greece. I'm so happy she enjoyed it."

"Yes, she's looking forward to going back and staying with you, which I think will be nice as long as she doesn't get in your way. You've not asked about your mum, Cheryl."

"What's there to ask, Dad?" It will be the same old moaning and complaining, wanting you to work harder so she can have new carpets, curtains and sofas."

"Actually, Cheryl, that's where you're wrong. She's been very different since we've been back, very different, and extremely quiet. In the last three weeks she's only snapped at me once and that was over Julie wanting me to decorate her and Richard's spare room, or as Julie calls it 'her dressing room'. When Julie asked, your mum's words to me were, 'Dave, you need to start saying no to people. Life's not all about work. People can't expect you to drop everything and run'."

"Oh, my God, what's all that about? Do you think it's something to do with the way Gran snapped at her?"

"I'm not sure, but she has something on her mind. Perhaps it's you moving to Holkamos, but I keep thinking it's the calm before the storm. There must be a reason behind it."

"Dad, you've not given me your opinion about my move to Holkamos. Everyone else has had their say, yet there's been no word from you and you're the closest person to me. Are you happy for me? Do you think I'm doing the right thing? You must have some thoughts about it."

"Come on, Cheryl. Let's get something to eat. I know it's just a river here in Dartmouth and not the sea, but let's have seaside fish and chips and a nice cup of tea. Lead me to the pub."

So he does have something to say. I know he won't stand in my way, even if he doesn't think I should go. I wonder what all this is with Mum. I've never ever not known her to nag and moan. Why is all this happening just before I leave? Thinking about it, she was a bit odd the last time I spoke to her on the phone. There was none of this 'Julieanne this', and 'Julieanne that'. If anything, she was a little negative about Julie and Richard. Perhaps she's having a mid-life crisis.

"There you are, Cheryl, large cod and chips. Look, there's a table in the garden overlooking the river. What more could we ask for? I shall miss coming to Dartmouth when you go and not just for the chips. It's a lovely calming place to come and visit."

"Yes, Dad, you're saying all the right things, but I need your advice. Am I doing the right thing in moving to Greece? Do you think it's all above me? You heard Mum and Julie. They think the only thing I'm good at is being a waitress. Am I going to fail and

97

have everyone laugh at me? Please say something, Dad."

"Oh, Cheryl. You're not going to fail. The job is perfect for you. You could do it standing on your head with your eyes closed. I'm so happy for you in one way, but in another way it will break my heart because this time you'll fly with so much success that I'll lose you. You won't need me again and I won't be able to pop down here for lunch with you.

"Darling, this is your time. You won't be in the shadow of your sister any more. You proved your worth when we were on holiday. I've always been so proud of you, but this time is different. It's your chance to shine, Cheryl, and I'll miss you so much."

Come on, Cheryl, hold it together. There's been enough tears over lunch, so smile and wave goodbye. Let him see that you're okay, although you're not. If it wasn't for Dad sticking up for me over the years when Mum and Julie bullied me... Of course, they wouldn't call it bullying. To them it was just their way of telling me how to live my life. It just went on and on, but Dad was always there to fight my corner. I'm sorry I won't be there to do the same for him when Mum and Julie nag him, but it does seem that Mum has changed. There must be something behind it. Like Dad says, the calm before the storm.

Chapter 17

So this is it! One hour and the plane will be landing in Preveza, a slightly different arrival to my last time here with all the worry about Julie's wedding because hopefully this time it's going to be about hundreds of weddings. Anyway, it's not just about the job as in one hour's time Andreas will be at the airport waiting for me. Whoever would have thought it would be me working in Greece. I was the one who never seemed to shine at anything, the girl who no one had any hopes for.

I'm so pleased for Johnny too as he's going to have a lot of fun on this island. I don't know whether the hair salon is ready for him, but they'd better be – he'll be here in two weeks' time.

Now I need to organise myself. The strange thing is it's not really like starting a new job as I've already been doing it for the last four months. The only difference is I'll be on Holkamos and that's very exciting.

Right, let's start a list. The most important thing between now and September is there's nine weddings already confirmed and another four enquiries. There's also several couples arriving with a view to booking next year. Vangelis has told me that the little office is ready for me with a desk computer and filing cabinet, but the best bit is the wonderful sea view. How fabulous is that? Even more exciting is that I'm going to be spending time with Andreas.

That's a bit of luck. My suitcase is one of the first on the carousel. Oh, I love this airport. It's so small and friendly. Andreas has sent a text to say he's waiting for me here. But what's this? Another text? Oh, it's from Vangelis and he's waiting for me as well. Surely they've seen each other as it's such a small airport. What shall I do? Whose car should I go in? I know Vangelis has the key to my studio, but this wasn't quite the arrival I'd planned. Come on, Cheryl, face it head on. If Johnny was here he'd say 'Come on, tits and teeth. Let's see the smile'.

"Well, this is nice. My boss and my boyfriend have both arrived here to greet me."

"Oh, so Andreas is your boyfriend is he, Cheryl? I didn't realise that. Of course, I knew you were friends but..."

"I'm sorry, Vangelis, but I thought you knew. This is a bit awkward for me now. Whose car do I go in? Andreas, do you mind if I go with Vangelis? We have lots of work to talk about and I will be living in an apartment he owns? Once I've unpacked, I'll come to the shop. I'm so looking forward to seeing all the new stock. The photos looked fabulous."

That was embarrassing, but Andreas seems happy with the situation. Poor Vangelis though, he looks like he's had the wind taken out of his sails but I did explain to him about keeping things professional. Better send a quick apology text to Andreas.

"Are you, alright, Vangelis? You're very quiet. Does this have anything to do with Andreas? Come on, cheer up. We've got some exciting times ahead. Lots of weddings means plenty of money. Tell me about the couples you've shown around. Have they booked for next year? Mark's made such a fantastic job of the website."

"Yes, the website's great. Cheryl, I am excited about the business and I've also been looking forward to you coming to live on the island, but..."

"No buts, Vangelis. For a start I'm not your type and another thing, you'd get bored with me. Come on, cheer up, there's lots of lovely girls who have just arrived for their holidays and looking for a little Greek romance."

"What if those days are over for me, Cheryl? What if I need more than just two weeks of fun? Perhaps it's time for me to settle down."

"Vangelis, there's plenty of time for all that. Now

come on, let's have a fabulous summer turning couple's dreams into reality. You're onto a winner with this wedding business, so let's enjoy it."

I've had years with no interest from fellas. Now I'm excited about having fun with Andreas; Vangelis thought we could have a good time together, and poor old Clive's left it too late. Thank goodness for the new job. My life's going to be 24/7 romance and that's not even taking Nico and Johnny's relationship into consideration. I really hope Vangelis snaps out of this. The thought of him moping around is enough to drive anyone mad.

"I know what I need to ask you, Vangelis. I've had a strange request from someone about dividing the beach up so that members of the public aren't able to see into the restaurant. Is that possible? Initially I said no, but they've come back to me again with it. The other strange thing about it is that the request hasn't come from a wedding couple, but a PR agency. I've told them I'd get back to them by tomorrow. It's all very odd."

"It's a public beach, Cheryl, so we can't stop people walking by. We could put plants and things in front of the restaurant so no one can look in, but if anyone's worried about privacy perhaps we're not the right venue for them. We're nearly there, Cheryl. Are you looking forward to your new apartment? I've already taken your suitcase there and filled the fridge with a few essentials. Here we are. I'm sorry that it's the back of the building and doesn't have the sea view."

"That's not a problem. I'm very grateful you've let me rent it. Lead the way, Vangelis."

"Here you go, Cheryl. Welcome to your new home."

"It's lovely, thank you. I'm going to be very happy living here for the summer. Oh, there's some flowers with a card: 'To Cheryl, thank you for being part of my dream. Love Vangelis'. Thank you very much. I just hope I'll be able to help bring your dream to life.

Let me pay you for all the food in the fridge and the champagne. Come on, let's open it and celebrate."

"Not now, Cheryl. I'll get going and let you settle in. I expect you'll be very eager to get off to see Andreas, so I'll see you tomorrow at work. Have a lovely evening."

"Thanks for everything, Vangelis, and I don't just mean the apartment and the job. It's far more than that. You're one of the few people in my life that's ever had faith and confidence in me, and that means so much that I'll always be grateful to you. Now go out and see the young ladies who have arrived today and have fun because tomorrow we've got a lot of work to get through."

Oh dear. I would have given him a hug and kiss, but that would have been rather awkward. Cheryl, this is it your new home for the rest of the summer and it's fabulous. It might not have the sea view, but does have a lovely little terrace and as it's at the back, no one can look onto it. The kitchen's adequate and there's plenty of storage. What more do I need?

Right, I'll get on with the unpacking later. Off to see Andreas' shop and more importantly, to see him.

Chapter 18

I can't believe I'm awake so early. It's only 5.30am. I'm excited about the new job, but I don't have to be there until ten o'clock. I even had a late night last night. Andreas was fine with Vangelis bringing me to the apartment and as for his shop, I'm so pleased for him. It's so different from anything else here on the island. Instead of customers spending a couple of euros on a tea towel or a fridge magnet, they're now buying pottery at nearly sixty euros and even paintings costing a couple of hundred euros a time. It's so exciting for him and his mum.

Talking about Andreas' mum, initially she was friendly to me, but I'm not so certain now. She was very odd last night and there was no way she was going to leave us by ourselves. It was like she was acting as Andreas' chaperone. Yes, she was pleased that I encouraged him to refurbish the shop and she's loving it and thinks that her husband would have approved, but she was adamant about coming with us for something to eat after closing the shop. It was a nice evening and Andreas and myself had a giggle about it all.

But today's another day. Dare I switch on my laptop and check the website enquiries? First, I'll email the PR agency and tell them we aren't able to separate the beach off, and then I'll write a 'to do' list for the day. I need to show Vangelis I mean business and every hour counts. Top of the list will be a wall planner so I can plot weddings in red and enquiries in blue, so we both know exactly what's going on. The other thing I've forgotten to do is tell the family I've arrived safely. I clean forgot about that. I'll do it later as it's still a bit early now. Shower, dress, bakery, a little sit in the harbour before work – let's start as we mean to carry on, and what better start than a vanilla slice?

This office isn't very big but that's fine as it won't be used as a wedding dumping ground. I have everything I need here and the Internet is very fast, far better than back in Devon. The wall chart's finished. Now to print off all the files for the confirmed bookings. Also, before the end of the day I think I'll create some sort of checklist we can all use with dates, number of guests, whether they need a cake or flowers, etc. Yes, that would be good.

"Morning, Cheryl. You're early. Didn't we say ten o'clock?"

"Hi, Vangelis. I couldn't sleep. I just wanted to get stuck in and there's so much to do. Did you have a nice evening?"

"Yes, thanks. I had dinner with Nico. He's really looking forward to Johnny arriving."

"I'm not sure the island's ready for Johnny yet, let alone the hair salon."

"The island may not be ready, Cheryl, but Nico's more than ready. By the way, did you and Andreas have a nice evening? Oh sorry, that's not really any of my business."

"The three of us, Andreas, his mother and I, had a funny sort of evening. It was different!"

"Oh, Cheryl, Greek mothers and their sons! They can get very protective of their little boys whatever age they are. Good luck with that one."

It was good to have Vangelis back to his old self, even though I did see him staring at me a few times throughout the day. Those eyes are to die for, but no, Cheryl, don't complicate things. It's good we've achieved so much and we both understand what our roles are in this new business. Now we just need to get the first wedding under our belt and we'll all feel more relaxed.

One last job before going home... saying that sounds funny. Holkamos is home now and I can't stop smiling. Where's the day gone? It's now 7pm. Here's to the last email of the day and the fourth from this silly PR company. What more can I tell them and how many more questions will they have? Perhaps I should just say the date they're looking at has been booked, only it hasn't and we need every wedding booking we can get. What was their last question? How many metres is the restaurant from the sea and what time does it get dark? Right, 'send', switch off laptop, back home to unpack and then hopefully to see Andreas without his mother.

"Hello, you're okay, Cheryl, she's out having a nosey around the harbour. Someone had new tables and chairs in their restaurant and on this island it's a major event. They'll be discussing it for weeks. Come out the back, I want to kiss you. I've missed you so much."

"That was lovely. I've missed you and those gorgeous lips of yours too. Is that someone in the shop? I thought I heard something."

"Oh, hi, Mum. Is the new furniture nice? Cheryl's here, she's just looking at the new paintings in the stock room. I'll just call her. Cheryl, Mum's back."

"Hello, Mrs Galanis. I just popped into to say thank you for a lovely evening last night and to tell Andreas about my first day at my new job."

God, if looks could kill! Vangelis was right. This Greek mummy isn't letting anyone... well, me, anyway near to her beloved son. Thank goodness these customers have come in. So much for spending some time alone with Andreas, that's not going to happen here tonight. In a way it's quite funny. You could understand it if we were both teenagers, but were nearly thirty.

"Right, I'd best get off, lots of paperwork to do. Thanks again for a lovely evening. We must do it again some time."

"Yes, that would be lovely, Cheryl. We'd like that wouldn't we, Mum?"

Oh dear, Andreas looked so sad, but it's not my job to stand up to his mother. So much for a romantic evening. I'm hungry, best get used to spending my evening alone. I'll take a walk along the harbour and find a nice quiet restaurant for a big bowl of pasta, I think. Oh, I'm so lucky to have moved here. It's paradise and I can quite see why we've had so many wedding enquiries. Who wouldn't want to get married on such a beautiful island as Holkamos?

"Hi, Cheryl. Not out with Andreas tonight?"

"Hi, Vangelis. No, let's just say 'Greek mummy'. I'm off to find myself a big bowl of pasta. Where would you recommend that's not too busy so that I can reply to emails while I'm eating?"

"You've not moved here to work all hours, and I know the perfect place for pasta. It's in the back streets, no sea views, not many visitors, mostly only locals, and if it's alright with you, I'll join you. We could call it a staff outing if you like, purely business."

"Why not? Lead the way, Vangelis, and we can talk business. I've got some ideas for next year."

"That pasta was lovely. I'm full. I think this is likely to become my favourite place on Holkamos, after the bakery of course. We haven't talked about work and there's so much to discuss. All we've done is chat about our childhoods, but it was nice. I've really enjoyed myself, thank you. Now, before I go home we must quickly talk weddings."

"That's very upfront, Cheryl. We've only known each other a short while and you want us to get married already. I'm sorry, but that look on your face said it all. Just in case you're interested, I also have a Greek mummy watching my every move."

"Vangelis, you don't miss a trick, do you, but I suggest you save that charm for all the future brides and their mothers. I want to talk about the wedding that PR agency keep emailing about. I've done virtually everything to put them off, but I did think that seeing as they're so insistent, I should just put the price up and they might go away. Something tells me they'd be a nightmare client."

"I think you'll just have to carry on telling them it's a public beach. If it's someone famous and they're noticed, it will all be on social media within seconds and everyone will be down on the beach taking photos on their phones. Good publicity for us, but not a happy wedding day for them."

"Yes, I'll get on with that first thing in the morning. It's been a lovely evening, Vangelis, but it's time for my bed. No need to comment on that, just say goodnight."

"I don't know what you mean, Cheryl. I was going to ask whether you'd like to go somewhere for another drink. The night's still young!"

"No, sorry Vangelis. I have work tomorrow and my boss is very strict. I wouldn't want to get on the wrong side of him."

"Ha, ha, it's been a nice evening, Cheryl. We must do it again, and by the way I don't give up that easily."

"Goodnight. I'll see you tomorrow, and thanks again."

I don't think I should have kissed Vangelis goodnight. Was it the wine or his charm that made me do it? I suppose it was only on his cheek, but it was a lovely evening and I'm glad he now knows more about me. I don't know whether he sees me as being more vulnerable or more confident, but I can't see him being able to stop flirting. It's part of his character, and if I'm honest I wouldn't want him to change. I think I like his little smiles and gestures.

So that's my first working day on Holkamos over with and it's been a really good one. I think I'll feel more relaxed that things are going well once the first wedding's over. The only thing I haven't done is phone home, but I can do that tomorrow.

Chapter 19

The week has flown by. I can't believe I've been here a week already and that means there's only another seven days until Johnny arrives. I'm so pleased to have achieved everything I set out to do. It seems like I've been doing the job forever, although it's six days to the first wedding. The good thing is it's a very similar wedding to Julie and Richard's, so at least Vangelis and his team have had experience.

The wedding couple want their reception to be very relaxed and informal. We're aiming to create that type of atmosphere for all the weddings we hold here. We aren't really catering for couples who are looking for grandeur and a master of ceremonies. We're just a little beach restaurant where you'll get sand on your feet and children play outside on the beach. It's family friendly and laid back, that's what weddings on Holkamos are like.

It's been a lovely week here on the island. The only disappointment has been not being able to spend time with Andreas. I know it's difficult for him to get away from the shop as it's open for fourteen hours a day, but I feel as though his mum has some kind of tracking device. The moment I get anywhere near him, she pops up. Hopefully, tonight will put paid to that, as once Andreas closes the shop he's coming round to my apartment.

The only other problem I've encountered this week is with the PR agency. I still can't shake them off, but that might happen on Tuesday when I go to Preveza airport for a meeting. They're flying in and out again on the same plane, so I have time in between cleaning and the plane being refuelled to meet them in person. Why they can't come all the way here, I don't know. Right, a quick call home and then I must get ready for Andreas.

"Hi, Dad. How are things? Is everyone okay? I

miss you all."

"Oh, hello, Cheryl. How's things going with you? Still loving the job? Hope you're not working too hard. Everything's great here. Your gran keeps asking when she can come out to visit you. I've told her to give you time to settle in first. Everything else is okay...ish."

"Why are you whispering, Dad? Should I ask the questions and you just say yes or no?"

"Yes, Cheryl. That would be ideal."

"Is Mum there with you?"

"Yes."

"Is she still behaving strangely?"

"Oh, yes, very much so."

"Has she started nagging and picking on you again?"

"No, far from it. Actually, the complete opposite for some unknown reason. Oh, Cheryl, your mum's here. Would you like a quick word?"

"Not really, but if you insist, Dad."

"Hi, Mum. How's everything?"

"Oh, everything's fine here, darling. Are you enjoying yourself and having fun?"

"Yes, I'm fine. It's busy, but I'm loving it. I'm going to have to rush off now as I have a wedding couple to chat to. Give my love to everyone. Bye."

She called me 'darling'. That's something that's never happened before and she's still being nice to Dad. I wonder what's caused that. Perhaps it's me leaving England and she wants free holidays, but after all these years why has she stopped nagging at Dad? I can't see that lasting.

Right, what shall I wear tonight for Andreas coming round? Something comfortable, but easy to take off. That's a naughty thought, Cheryl. Oh, I need to set out the chairs outside on the patio and surround it with candles. I'm glad I bought new cushions and throws as it now looks less like a holiday apartment and more like a home.

I'm not ready, but that sounds like a scooter pulling up. If that's Andreas he's early as he doesn't close the shop until 11pm and it's only just gone 10pm. It is him. I can hear footsteps. Oh no...

"Hello, you're early. I've only just got out of the shower, but do come in."

"I'm sorry, Cheryl. Would you prefer it if I came back later? It's just that I thought I'd close the shop earlier tonight."

"Don't be daft. Come in."

"What are you looking for, Cheryl?"

"I'm only teasing, Andreas. I was looking to see if your mum was behind you."

"Don't joke, but no, she isn't."

"Go through to my little patio and I'll get us a drink. Red or white, I've both here?"

"Red, please. This is a great little studio. You must be delighted with it."

"Yes, I'm really lucky. Now, tell me all about the shop. What exciting things have you had in and is everything selling well?"

"It's really good, but the best part of it is I'm loving going to work. Okay, I miss the painting but I know I can start that up again come the first week in October. I just need to decide whether to go back to Rhodes or stay here on Holkamos, but I've a few months to think about that. Tell me about the wedding business, Cheryl. How it's going? Have you got lots of bookings coming in?"

"The wedding business is going well, as is your shop, but enough of all that. Just kiss me, Andreas. I can't wait any longer."

"Talk about getting right to the point. I've missed you, Cheryl. Come here."

Well, where did the next four hours go? If I ever had any doubts about moving here, I'm now sure I've done the right thing. How lucky am I to have found Andreas? It was his shy nature which first attracted me to him, but what's just happened has completely changed my view of him. He's far from shy. How lucky am I? If only he could have stayed all night!

Oh, Cheryl, what have you done to deserve all this good luck? A fabulous job on a beautiful island and a fella who can't get enough of you. The way he touches me! I'd forgotten what it was like to make love. All those nights with Clive I thought were passion, but no, what's just happened was passion, love and fulfilment all rolled into one.

Chapter 20

So, today I'm off to Preveza to meet this PR representative and hopefully find out about the people who want to have their wedding on Holkamos. Both Vangelis and I have tried everything to put them off, so they must really mean business if someone's willing to fly here for an hour just to talk about it.

One thing's for sure, I've spent hours emailing them with information, so I'm not leaving that meeting until I find out who they are. I don't care if we get the booking or not, I just want to know why it's so important to them to get married on the beach here. Vangelis thinks I'm wasting my time. He can't be bothered to come with me, but no, I'm on a mission, and I won't be browbeaten on this. Here goes, one bus ride, one ferry trip and then a taxi to the airport.

"Hi, good morning. Can I have a large espresso and two vanilla slices, please?"

"Good morning. So it's today you're off to Preveza, Miss Marple."

"Hi, Andreas. Less of the Miss Marple, if you don't mind! Anyway, how are you today?"

"Actually, now you ask, I'm exhausted because I've got this gorgeous new girlfriend who's worn me out for the last three nights. I think I'll end up a shadow of my former self."

"Oh, if that's the case, perhaps you should go straight home when you close the shop tonight, instead of going round to your new girlfriend's apartment."

"Ha, ha, no, I don't think so! Have a lovely day and I hope you get to the bottom of your mystery. See you tonight!"

Up till now I've never really appreciated just how beautiful the island is. I've always travelled by car and spent the journey chatting to the driver, but now taking the short bus ride from Holkamos town to the ferry, I've noticed everything – the olive tree lanes heading down to little coves, and lots of people saying their goodbyes at the ferry. They all repeat the same words – 'See you next year'. Even if meeting the PR representative today ends up being a total waste of time, I've enjoyed the day.

Now, where's the arrival board? It looks like the plane's scheduled to arrive on time, so I just need to wait for them to land and get the phone call. I might as well find somewhere quiet so we can chat. To be honest, I'm beginning to agree with Vangelis. If I'm going through all this just to talk about a wedding, can you imagine the fuss involved for an actual wedding? We don't really need all this hassle. It's just my curiosity which has brought me out here.

"Hello, Miss Harris. Thank you for coming to meet me. It's much appreciated. My name's Carla. Can I get you a drink?"

"No, I'm fine, thanks, and please call me Cheryl."

"Thank you, Cheryl. I'll get to the point as I've not got long before I have to get back on board the plane. My clients don't want to get married anywhere else apart from Holkamos beach. Their reasons are personal and private, and believe me I've tried to persuade them to change their mind. They completely understand that it's a public beach and although that's far from ideal, they're okay with it. The date is perfect for them too.

"It's to be a very informal wedding with only twelve guests. I've had a look at the photos you've emailed me and I think that with a clever placement of plants, it could be made a little more secluded.

"I'll be honest, Cheryl, if this had been some really big, exclusive wedding held behind closed doors for five hundred people, it would be a lot easier all round. I would imagine you're fed up to the back teeth with the amount of time I've taken up, but my clients are more than happy to pay over the odds. Is there anything you'd like to ask me? Here's a copy of the itinerary for the day, which I've put together. It includes everything you need to know from table arrangements, food, time schedules, etc. Perhaps you'd like to have a read of it while I nip to the ladies."

Oh, my goodness, I don't need to do a thing. They've thought of everything – flowers, taxis, the lot. Basically, all we need to do is let them have the restaurant. Staff will lay the tables, flowers and bring all the crockery, candles, plants, etc. All they want from us is the venue. I think Vangelis will suddenly become very interested in this booking when I tell him it's for 10,000 euros.

"So, Cheryl, have you managed to read through it? Do you have any questions?"

"Not really, Carla, just where will the guests be staying?"

"They've rented Villa Volmos for the week."

"I've never heard of it."

"I suggest you ask anyone on this island about it. They'll know all about Villa Volmos. Do you have any more questions, although I can't talk about the couple getting married. However, I'm sure that the amount they're paying for their day, will help to take away any thoughts you may have on that."

"Carla, I'm sure Vangelis, the restaurant owner, will be more than happy to take this booking without enquiring after the client. I'm the curious one. I'm intrigued and I have to say, slightly frustrated, to be going back without even knowing their names."

"I realise it must be annoying for you, but on the day, Cheryl, you'll understand why you've not been told. I've been in this business for more years then I care to remember and dealt with events costing millions of pounds, but this has caused me such a headache because of the privacy issues that I really do appreciate all you've done, Cheryl. So you go back, have a chat to Vangelis and by the time my plane lands in England I suspect I'll have an email confirmation from you. On a personal level, I'm so looking forward to visiting Holkamos. I feel as if I know it already. Thanks again, and I'm sorry it's been so difficult. I'll see you in seven weeks and it will be far less stressful then."

"Everything will be fine, Carla, I promise you. We'll have a drink and laugh about the amount of time it's taken for one meal for twelve people."

"That makes it sound even scarier, Cheryl. Bye for now."

I like Carla but what a stressful job! I'm disappointed that I'm no closer to finding out who the wedding couple are, but on the plus side there's a huge chunk of commission for me. Now to go back and wind Vangelis up.

"Why do I have to sit down, Cheryl?"

"Because, Vangelis, I need to tell you all about my meeting and the little bit of business we've just turned down. Before all that, tell me about Villa Volmos. Where is it, I've never heard of it

"Villa Volmos is about a mile up the hill. It took about five years to build. Lots of the residents on Holkamos know it well, but no one knows who owns it except that whenever they arrive they come from Athens by helicopter. When people have tried to find out the owner's name, it's just registered as a company name. The staff who live in the quarters are often in town or on the beach but they never say who they work for. Everyone who's been up there says Villa Volmos is just like a palace. It does get rented out, but no one ever sees who to as the gates and wall hide everything. Anyway, why are you asking about Villa Volmos?"

"That's where the wedding party would have stayed if we had agreed to the booking, but as you've said, 'no', I presume they won't stay there. I'm only joking! I've taken the booking without asking you because I'm sure you'd agree. They're paying 10,000 euros for five hours at the restaurant."

"Are you serious, Cheryl? Oh my God! Who are they and what have we got to do for that money? Can't they have it for ten hours at double the price?"

"Don't be greedy, Vangelis. So can I email Carla and confirm we'll take the booking?"

"Yes, now, straight away, Cheryl."

"So I presume you're glad that I didn't take your advice and not go to the meeting."

"Thank you, Cheryl. I think you've just earned your first ten per cent commission fee for going against the wishes of your boss."

Chapter 21

The excitement of the mystery wedding meal has died down, contracts have been signed and we hand over the restaurant on the morning of the wedding. Vangelis is more than happy about it, but before all that we've got other weddings to think about, ones where we know the names of the couple! It's only 48 hours until the first one, and in three days' time Johnny will be here. Nico is like a cat on a hot tin roof. He's ready to explode.

Our first ever bride and groom arrive tomorrow to run through everything. This will also be a very informal event, so as long as Vangelis and his team are well prepared it should be straight forward. Seeing that I'll be here all day on Saturday, I'm taking today off. No emails, no office, just the beach and as Holkamos is my place of work I'm off to one of the little coves on the other side of the island. Andreas has one of the artists running the shop for him, so he's coming with me. My picnic bag's packed. I've got plenty of sun cream. How lucky am I?

"Oh, I thought we were going on your scooter, Andreas, but you've brought the car instead."

"Well, I thought we'd struggle with the picnic things on the bike. Sorry to disappoint you, Cheryl."

"It's not a disappointment at all. What time do you need to be back?"

"Tomorrow! Oh, yes, Cheryl. I can be out all night. I just need to be back to open the shop in the morning."

"Can I have that in writing, please?"

"Less of the cheek, Cheryl. Where's the bag of food? Let's head off before the day gets taken up with other things."

What a beautiful, unspoilt beach! This is turning out to be the perfect day. Well, that was until Andreas fell asleep. He looks so calm when he's sleeping. How lucky am I? I know that I said no emails, but I could catch up with texting the family as I have rather switched off from them all since I've been here.

"Dad, how are things with you?"

"Johnny, are you packed and getting excited?"

"Gran, do you know when you want to come and stay?"

"Julie, how's married life?"

And my final text has to be to Clive. "How are you feeling?"

"Ha, Cheryl. I thought you said there's be no work, but you're on your phone."

'So you've woken up then, Andreas! No, it's not work. Just a few texts to the family back in England, but I'll read any replies later. How about another swim?"

"Do we have to? Let's just lie here and relax."

"No, because you'll fall asleep again. Okay, I give in. You stay here while I go for a walk along the sea shore."

I really think I've worn him out. I've lost count how many times we've been in and out of the sea. He does deserve another nap as he works fourteen hour days for seven days a week. Everywhere I go on this island becomes my new favourite place and this is the latest! It's so quiet with no holiday makers and only a few of the locals. It's the first time since arriving here that I've been able to really switch off, yet one problem persists.

What am I going to do when the season ends? Vangelis will pay me a small wage for manning the website and organising next year's weddings, but where will I do that from? I know I can move back to England to my parents' but after the freedom of living here I'll get suffocated. I could go and live with Grandma, but I don't know how many hours the wedding business will take up and where else my income would come from. More importantly, will I still be seeing Andreas by October? He might have become bored with me by then.

"Cheryl, your phone's been going crazy for half an hour. You seemed miles away sitting there on that rock."

"No, not miles away, just here on Holkamos. Now Andreas, I'm not taking no for an answer. In the sea now, before I drag you in."

"What's that on the side of your face, Cheryl? Come closer and let me rub it off."

So there was nothing on the side of my face at all. He just wanted to kiss me again and again, but I wasn't complaining. It turned out to be a very kissy afternoon and would have led to lot more if there hadn't been other people on the beach. He makes me feel so special and at 29 years of age, no one apart from Dad and Gran has ever been able to do that.

Dad always told me I was special and that one day I'd realise it too. Just because I couldn't be good at all the things Julie took part in, didn't mean I was a failure. What a few months it's been, losing the silly weight, which happily is going back on slowly, and when it does I still won't be fat, I'll be normal. I hated the hair extensions, but I'm loving growing my hair and most of all I'm happy being me. I always was happy. I may have come across to others as boring, so everyone thought they knew best for me but I was stupid enough to believe them.

"That's a lovely shower you have, Cheryl. I'm clean now and ready to cook for you."

"I've poured you a glass of wine, and I'm going out on the terrace to read all these text messages. Shout if you need any help."

The first one's from Johnny. He's packed and ready to leave. Suzy hasn't employed anyone yet and has succumbed to using agency staff. She's also learning how to work in reception. Good luck with that!

The next text's from Julie to say that married life isn't any different. She's not enjoying her job as much as there's been lots of changes and her manager has left. She also mentioned that she doesn't know what's happened, but Mum and Dad seem to be getting along better. That leads me onto Dad's text.

Apparently Mum's stopped nagging and spending, but the biggest thing is that she's got herself a job. I've never known her to go out to work. She gave that up when she was expecting me. Dad's told that her she doesn't have to, but she wants to work. It's a part time job in the tea room of the village garden centre.

There was no text from Clive. He's still not back at the hotel.

"Andreas, what's that noise I can hear? Oh, it's you singing."

"Yes, I always sing while I'm cooking. I hope you're hungry as I seemed to have cooked an awful lot. Can I get you another drink?"

"No, don't worry. I'll come in and get one."

"This has been such a perfect day. I've had seven hours on the beach and now you're cooking dinner for me. I'm so spoilt. Thank you, Andreas."

"You can thank me later, Cheryl, but you might not like what I'm cooking and then I won't get thanked."

"Oh, I'm certainly going to thank you. How long does it need to simmer for? Let's say, an hour."

"Why would it need to...? Oh, I understand. You're thinking that while it's simmering we could... Just a minute, I need to wash my hands and turn dinner down to low."

"I think very low, don't you, Andreas?"

Chapter 22

"Come on, Andreas, it's 9.30am and you need to have the shop open in half an hour. No doubt your mum will already be there waiting."

"Five more minutes, Cheryl. Come on, come back to bed. I don't think you've thanked me enough for the meal I cooked you last night."

"I think you'll find I thanked you until 3am. I have to get going, as I'm meeting a bride and groom in an hour's time to talk through the final arrangements for the wedding tomorrow."

"Okay, two minutes."

"No, I really do have to go. Please can you lock the door behind you, and who knows, if you're lucky I might find time to thank you again when you close the shop tonight. Bye for now, and yesterday was very special, thank you."

So here goes. Although this part of the job's new, it's something I did every Friday in Dartmouth. The bride and groom would arrive excited for their wedding and then there would be the bride's mother, which is where I'm hoping Vangelis' charm will come into play.

We can't show them how the restaurant would be laid out yet, as today it's a beach café, but they can see photos of how we'll arrange it as well as photos of Julie and Richard's wedding. This time we've arranged for flowers and a disco, but no fireworks. I admit I'm not too confident about it all, but I'm not letting Vangelis and his restaurant staff know that. I don't want them to get nervous too, but I do want them to understand that this is one of the most important days in the bridal couple's life, so nothing but one hundred per cent is required from them.

I love this walk to work of a morning. It's just when Holkamos comes to life for the day. Oh, there's a text just come through from Andreas, thanking me for yesterday and saying that he thought it was special. Oh, bless him. It was very special indeed.

"Morning, Vangelis. How are you today?"

"Fine thanks. Ready to charm the wedding couple."

"No, your job is to flirt with the mother of the bride and show her your Greek charm, even if she's seventy. Imagine she's a young lady arriving for her first holiday without her parents."

"I really think you've got me all wrong, Cheryl. You've been listening to all the gossip. It's not true what they say about me. Well, not all of it. By the way, how was your day off? What did you do?"

"We went to the beach, sat on the terrace and had dinner. It was lovely, thanks."

"I noticed a car parked outside your studio this morning when I drove by. I expect Andreas left it there last night as he had a few drinks and didn't want to drive home. Far better to walk."

"Vangelis, come closer as I don't want to shout, but no, Andreas stayed the night and there wasn't a lot of sleeping, if you know what I mean!"

"Oh, I wasn't being nosey. I just thought..."

"I know what you thought."

"Cheryl, I'll say just one thing. Does his mother know about it, because I've told you before that Greek mummies are very protective of their little boys?"

"I'm up in my office if you need me, Vangelis. Give me a shout when the bridal couple arrive. They're called Sue and Dean and the mother's name is Doreen."

This Greek mummy lark is very annoying, but I expect Vangelis is right I wonder if Andreas told his mother where he was staying last night. Anyway, let's get straight on to the emails. Hopefully there'll be a few more enquiries for this year although I'm beginning to think that most will be for next year.

I think I need to get a wall planner up for the next two years and let Vangelis see it in black and white.

Another text. What now, Andreas? Oh, no, it's Dad, asking whether I can phone him this afternoon. It's not urgent, but if I have a minute or two.

"Well, Vangelis, that was great. I knew you'd be able to charm her. They're so laid back and said that tomorrow will all go fine, but I'm telling you one thing, that marriage won't last."

"I don't understand, Cheryl."

"Didn't you notice how he was ogling all the women on the beach? He wasn't remotely interested in his own wedding. You could have told him anything and he'd have agreed to it."

"Cheryl, you're so cynical. He could have just been looking at the beach and the boats moored out to sea, for all you know."

"No, no, Vangelis, it's a shame, but you mark my words. Just watch him tomorrow and see if I'm right. There goes my phone. See you later, Vangelis, and just remember, keep your eyes on the groom."

"Hi, Dad, are you alright? Is anything the matter? Are you there? I think I've lost you."

"Yes, Cheryl, I'm here. Your mother's told me that she doesn't love me and she never has."

"Oh, Dad, she doesn't mean it. You know what she's like, take no notice."

"Cheryl, I need to get things straight in my head. Would it be okay with you if I came over to Holkamos next week for a couple of weeks?"

"Of course, Dad, that would be fine. A break from each other will do you both the world of good."

That was difficult. Dad seemed gutted, but why after all these years has Mum told him that now. What does she have to gain? Should I phone her, but then it will all be my fault No, I'm not to take sides although it's far easier said than done. Now to find him somewhere to stay. It's peak season so it won't be easy. Perhaps Vangelis or Andreas might know of somewhere.

Now who's texting? Oh, it's Andreas. He wants me

to call him when I get a minute.

"Mum's not well, so I think I'll go straight home after I close the shop tonight. I'm sorry, Cheryl."

"That's not a problem. Give her my love and tell her I hope she feels better soon. By the way, my dad's coming to stay next week. It's a long story and I'll explain it when I see you."

"I've got to go as there's a customer in the shop. I'll call you later when you get back from work. Miss you tons."

So is Andreas' mum really poorly or did she find out about last night? This Greek mummy thing is starting to play on my mind. Perhaps it's time to clear the air with her and let her know we're seeing each other before we get too serious. I know one thing, I'm not standing in the way of a mother and her son.

Another text. Who's it this time? Oh, what a surprise, Clive! Short and to the point – 'thank you for thinking of me'.

Chapter 23

"What are you doing working at the computer at this time of night, Cheryl? Can't it wait until tomorrow? There you go, one very large gin and tonic which you've most definitely earned. So, we've got the first wedding under our belt and if they all go as smoothly as that, it will all be fantastic."

"Yes, Vangelis. It's been a great success and I'm delighted with how it's all gone. It's been a long day, but a lovely one. How did the bar go? They seem to have drunk champagne as if it was going out of fashion. I can't believe how quickly the day's gone. It's 1am already. I've nearly finished here, just posting some of the photos on the social media accounts. A few hash tags Holkamos will get people interested."

"Don't stay working too much longer. Get home and have some sleep. Johnny arrives tomorrow. Well, actually, today! Anyway, I expect we won't see much of him and Nico for a few days. Yes, I think we priced the food and drink perfectly. We aren't a large wedding venue, so we can't compete with them, but we do offer good value for money, and will still make a very healthy profit out of it."

"It was so lovely to see everyone so happy, and even the bridegroom seemed to be taking an interest in his wedding day, Vangelis."

"You were right about him though. He was chatting up one of the waitresses on his wedding day. Can you believe it, Cheryl? Right, I'm off to help turn this wedding venue back into a beach café for tomorrow. Don't work too much longer. Get back home to Andreas, and thanks again for everything, Cheryl."

Well, I'm home but not to Andreas. I'm home alone, but that's probably a good thing as I'm exhausted but still on a high. Deep down I knew everything would go well, but there was always that niggling doubt whether Vangelis had done the right thing by opening up the café for weddings.

Talking of Vangelis, what was the kiss all about? I know it was only a quick peck on the cheek, but it made me go all tingly and I'm sure he noticed that I blushed.

Anyway, it's great to have got the first wedding over and done with. I've made notes on how we can improve things for the next time, but that can all wait until tomorrow. I'll have a quick shower and enjoy a glass of wine on my terrace, I think.

Three texts from Johnny telling me how excited he is and one from Dad to say he's booked his flights, but there's nothing from Andreas although I've sent him three texts today. Perhaps his mum has got worse. I think I'll pop over to the shop before I go to the restaurant in the morning as an excuse to see him.

That's better. I can't believe how hot it was today and it's still warm here at 2am. Perhaps that's because I had the shower too hot I love this little terrace and I'm so pleased that it doesn't have a balcony on the front. This apartment at the back is so private.

I only posted those new photos on the wedding Twitter account an hour or so ago but they've received so much interest already for next year. That's so encouraging, Vangelis will be pleased. I think one of the reasons today has gone so well is because everyone did their bit and didn't interfere with each other's jobs. Vangelis is the perfect host. He just switches on the charm and everyone loves it, but why did he kiss me? Time for bed, I think.

"Good morning, Andreas. I've brought you a present, but you'll guess what it is by the bag. It's a vanilla slice."

126

"Hi, Cheryl, it's good to see you. How did the wedding go? Was it a big success and has Johnny arrived yet?"

"Slow down, Andreas, so many questions. I think you're forgetting something."

"What have I forgotten?"

"Come in to your stock room and I'll show you with my lips."

"I've missed you, Cheryl, and thanks for that kiss. It's made me feel so much better."

"Why? Aren't you very well either?"

"It's Mum. She's in a strange mood. She's not poorly, but..."

"The but, Andreas, we both know, is about me. I've arrived on Holkamos and shown an interest in her beloved son. Firstly, I'm not a nice Greek girl, and secondly, she thinks that because I persuaded you to change your business, I'm also trying to change you. By the way, I'm not. I like you just the way you are, but that doesn't change the fact that your mum sees me as a threat."

"You're not a threat to anyone, Cheryl. It's just that she doesn't want to see me get hurt again. That's another story, but enough of that for now. Can I see you tonight?"

"Of course, and maybe you'll tell me the story. Oh, there goes my phone again. You know what that means. Johnny's arrived and the peace and quiet of Holkamos will be gone forever. Oh, and by the way, my dad's arriving next week and that's another story too. Looks like we'll be busy telling each other stories tonight."

"We will be busy, Cheryl, but it won't be with telling each other stories, I can assure you of that."

"I'll keep you to that, but now I've fed and kissed you, I need to get over to Volmos and do some work. One more kiss before I go. That damned phone again, this time it will have to wait."

"That was nice. I'll see you at eleven tonight for

more! Have a good day, Cheryl. Missing you tons. Just answer your phone to Johnny and say hi from me."

"Yes, Johnny, I know you're arrived and are very excited about it, but I'm trying to work."

"But you aren't at work, Cheryl, because that's where I am."

"Okay, I'll get the sea taxi over. See you soon, and welcome to Holkamos. I'm really glad you're here."

How many people can say they go to work on a sea taxi in the Greek islands? How blessed am I? So what was all that about Andreas getting hurt? I knew his mother wasn't impressed with me, but I've no intention to use him or hurt him. I feel it's getting a little complicated, but time will tell. That's his problem, not mine.

Is that who I think it is on the jetty? I didn't think they made clothes like that anymore – a bright orange track suit! Oh, Johnny, you look like a Cadbury's chocolate orange. I really don't think the island's ready for you, and this is before you even start on customers' hair.

"I'm over here, Cheryl."

"I know, that's why I'm avoiding you. Where, oh where, did you get the outfit from?"

"Don't you like it? It's the perfect outfit to travel in."

"But you're not travelling now, you've arrived. Johnny, please promise me it won't see the light of day ever again. Promise."

"That's not very nice, Cheryl. I've put a lot of effort into my appearance. By the way, this is only a quick hello and goodbye as Nico and I have so much to catch up on."

Well, it was good to get his arrival over with. I knew Johnny and Nico wouldn't hang around for very long. Right, it's nearly twelve o'clock, so emails up to about four pm and then a debrief with Vangelis about yesterday's wedding on how we can improve things for the next one.

There's a lovely email from yesterday's bride thanking us for making their day so special, and also an email from Julie who wants to talk about why Dad is leaving Mum and why am I encouraging him to come to Greece? Sorry, didn't Mum tell him she's never loved him? There's no time to talk to her today, I must get my act together with all this work. Cheryl, stop looking out the office window at the very inviting sea, and focus on the computer instead.

It's surprising how much you can get done when you put your chair the other side of the desk and just look at a blank wall. Right, Vangelis should be here soon. Where's my list of things we need to talk about, plus next year's bookings? The good thing is I've got so far ahead that I'm taking tomorrow off and catching one of the little boats to another island. There'll be no Internet or phone calls, just me all by myself, and I'll be able to give some thought to what to do when Dad arrives. I'm going to ignore Julie's text. Another text from Andreas.

'Sorry Cheryl, can't make tonight. Mum's got visitors and I have to drive them home when I close the shop. How about tomorrow? Andreas xx'.

I was so looking forward to seeing him; because once Dad arrives I won't have much spare time. I wonder whose idea the visitors were?

"Hi, boss, how's it going?"

"You're the boss, Vangelis, not me. And it's all going fine, thanks."

"Only joking, Cheryl, but it does seem strange you organising my life for me. I've never had that before."

"I'm only organising the weddings, not your life. You're quite capable of doing that yourself."

"Don't say that. I'm quite enjoying being told what to do. What do we need to talk about? Not weddings, please not more weddings."

"Yes, Vangelis, weddings. First of all, I think we

129

just need to tweak a few things for the next ones. We need to ensure we have plenty of candles. It was a bit touch and go whether they'd last the whole evening. Also, I think the flowers were a huge hit. Shall we try and do a better deal with them if we say we'll put them on our website? Also Nico's hair salon? How would he feel if we could introduce him to the brides with some sort of package? That's about it. Do you have any thoughts about any of this?"

"Oh, I like it when you're all official, Cheryl. I'm not saying I don't like you at other times, but there's something very sexy when..."

"That's enough of that, Vangelis. I've got something important to show you. It's a calendar for next year, and I can't believe how much interest there's been so far and the number of people coming over to Holkamos this summer to have a look at what we have to offer. I've created a diary for you, it's a kind of hand over book. Promise me you'll check it every day, as you'll need to meet some of these people if I'm not around or where I think things would sound better coming from you."

"Okay, whatever you say, Cheryl. I've not let you down yet. Now is that everything? Why don't we go and get something to eat to celebrate our first official meeting, a staff outing?"

"Vangelis, you seem to have a reason to celebrate anything. No, I want to finish up here as I've got a few more wedding files to set up and then I'm taking tomorrow off."

"Oh, that's good. Where shall we go, Cheryl?"

"We're going nowhere, Vangelis. I'm having a day to myself."

"Not with Andreas?"

"No, he'll be working."

"By the way, I know it's not really any of my business, but how are the three of you getting on?"

"Just now you said I was the boss and the two of us are getting on fine and as for the third one in the relationship, well, I'm not so sure but you did say that Greek mummies are very protective."

"Yes, Cheryl, and I expect that Andreas' mother is even more protective as a result of what's happened in the past."

"What was that, Vangelis?"

"Oh sorry, Cheryl, I thought Andreas would have told you. It's not my place to speak about it, but you should ask him."

"Well, as a very responsible employer who takes a great interest in the welfare of his staff, I think you should tell me. Please don't leave anything out because I want to know everything. Vangelis, I too, can play your games."

Chapter 24

Vangelis knew I didn't have a clue and couldn't wait to tell me, although he didn't mean to do it in any negative kind of way. I'm so pleased he told me, so at least when, or if, Andreas does mention it, it won't be such a shock and I'll know what to say. It does explain why his mum behaves how she does, and who could blame her? I'd be exactly the same if I was a mother. Oh, poor Andreas, it's not only the embarrassment and the hurt, but how do you move on from that and trust anyone ever again? And to have it reported in the local Preveza newspaper as well. Vangelis told me to Google it and read about it, but now that he's told me I don't know if I want to read it. Perhaps it's not as bad as he's made out. No, I'm not going to look, but then again...

"The wedding of Andreas Galanis of Holkamos to his bride Elpis Piccolos came to a sudden halt last Sunday in front of three hundred guests. After walking down the aisle with her father, Stenos, Elpis started to cry and then turned to face the man she was going to marry. With that Andreas asked her whether everything was alright and she replied that it wasn't. She couldn't go through with the marriage as she was in love with someone else. She then ran out of the church followed by an unknown male."

Oh, poor Andreas. Somehow it seems worse seeing it all in print. What a bitch! How could she have done that? Surely if that's the way she felt, she shouldn't have left it until the last minute to tell him. How do you ever get over such a thing? More to the point, how will his mum get over it?

I wonder why he hasn't mentioned it to me yet. He must have known that Vangelis would say something about it at the first opportunity. Perhaps he prefers to block it from his mind, The most difficult thing will be how I'll be able to tell him that I do know all about it, and I'm not just showing him affection because I feel sorry for him.

Oh, look at the time. The boat for Dissinos leaves in ten minutes. I can make it if I hurry. I need a day away as I seem to have more problems than I did in Dartmouth when I ran the hotel. Look at that view! Devon is beautiful but this is something else.

"Welcome aboard this little boat, everyone. Well, all seven of you. Not many visitors go to Dissinos because there's not much there apart from one long beach, a little café and twelve homes which are only lived in during the summer months. If you're looking for tourist shops for gifts you're out of luck as there's no shops. The other thing about Dissinos is there isn't a real jetty, so you may find yourselves having to paddle a few metres to get onto the beach.

Now the positive bits. It's paradise! I say that because my wife and I run the cafe, and that's why half the boat is full of groceries. Enjoy the ride, everyone. We should be paddling in about twenty minutes. Make sure you don't miss the boat back as there's only a few trips each day. There's a return trip at 5pm and one at 6.30pm, so enjoy your day on our lovely little island."

When he said 'little' island, he really meant it. Standing on this hill I can almost see around it. As for the homes, they're more like little shacks but very beautiful. Now to find a stretch of beach to spend my day on. One last look at my phone and then it will be switched off for the day.

There's only two texts. One from Johnny which just says – 'How lucky are we? Love you lots.' The other is from Andreas after I text him to say where I was going today. 'Cheryl, you've gone to my island! It's my favourite place in the whole world. Say hello to Rhea in the café for me xx' Right, phone switched off.

I really didn't realise I was so tired. I slept for three hours. Thank goodness I covered myself in sun cream. It's time for a dip in the sea now. It's very hot, but that cool sea breeze is so welcoming. I can't believe all this is on my door step. What a place to come and spend my day off! I thought that the clear blue water on Holkamos with all the fish around your feet was special, but this is just so clear and clean.

"Hi, are you on holiday? My husband and I have been coming to Holkamos for more than twenty years. We didn't know this island existed and we're so upset to have missed it for all those years."

"No, I'm not on holiday. I've just moved here to work and it's the first time I've been here. I think it will become my go-to place for days off though. It's paradise, just like the boat owner said."

Time to dry off. Hopefully the café will have ice creams. You can't go to the beach and not have an ice cream, can you?

"Hello, how can I help you?"

"A very large ice cream, please. I'm spoiling myself as it's my day off."

"So you aren't on holiday then? Do you live on Holkamos?"

"Yes, I've just moved here. I'm working on Volmos organising weddings."

"Oh, yes. I've heard all about it. My husband and I agreed that it's such a wonderful place to get married. So you're working for Mr Charmer himself, Vangelis?"

"Yes, I am, but the flirting and fluttering eyes don't do anything for me. I'll leave that for the holiday makers. By the way, are you Rhea?"

"Yes, why?"

"Oh, Andreas said to say hello."

"Do you mean Andreas, the artist?"

"Yes, when I told him I was coming here today, he asked me to say hello to you."

"He's a lovely chap, so completely different from Vangelis. They're like chalk and cheese, those two. I went to school with both of them. Vangelis hasn't changed a bit, but Andreas has as he used to be far more outgoing. Here's your ice cream. Why don't you sit here in the shade and eat it before it melts."

"Thanks, what an enormous ice cream! So Andreas changed when the wedding thing happened, or didn't happen?"

"Oh, so you know all about that. Well, yes, it was about eight or nine years ago, but I was actually happy about it because Elpis wasn't right for him. She only wanted to marry him because his father owned a business. To be honest, she's still a tart."

"Is she still on Holkamos then?"

"Yes, and no. Her family live there and she moved to Athens when Andreas did. She only comes back a few times a year. She has no friends on the island as they all took Andreas' side, and to be honest, when she does come to visit her family she keeps herself to herself until she hits the wine and then she's a different woman. That's when you need to keep an eye on your husband or boyfriend. The greater the challenge, the more she loves it."

"Oh, dear, it's a bit of a mess, isn't it?"

"Yes, but it could have been a lot worse if they had gone through with the marriage and then started a family. Tell me about yourself. What brought you to the Greek island if it wasn't Vangelis' charm and eye lashes?"

"Excuse me, but I'm taking the last boat back to Holkamos. Are you planning to catch it too, as you've only got five minutes?"

"Oh, my goodness, is that the time? I must have been chatting to your wife for hours. I'll be right with you."

"Gosh, where has the time gone? Cheryl was just telling me how she's just moved to Holkamos and working for Vangelis down on Volmos. She's friendly with Andreas too. It's been lovely chatting with you, Cheryl. I can't believe we've been at it for over two

135

hours. You must come back and bring your dad when he visits and next time you must have something to eat with us. Oh, and tell Andreas it's about time he gave us a visit."

"No, actually we need to go and visit him at his shop. Everyone's saying how good it is now he's changed the pottery and art work. It's lovely that at last he's displaying his own paintings, and I'm pleased that his Mum allowed him to do that. She can be a bit stubborn. Right, Cheryl, I'm going to have to hurry you along as there's a few others waiting to go back on the boat."

"Thank you, Rhea. It was lovely to meet you and I think you might be seeing a lot more of me on my days off. It's worth the boat ride for the ice cream alone."

"Thanks, Cheryl. See you again soon, and please do give my love to those two men in your life. Make sure you don't mix them up."

"No fear of that, and I won't be falling for the fluttering eyelashes. I promise you that."

"All the women say that, but give in eventually."

What a really lovely day I've had. Rhea and her husband, Moisis, are so nice. Hopefully I'll finish off my day with a visit from Andreas, but if so I've got two hours to shower, eat, check my emails and down the best part of a bottle of wine. Perhaps I should send him a text to check he's still coming round.

"Are we still on for tonight? Xx"

"We are. I'll see you about 11.15pm. The harbour is very busy with holiday makers so don't want to close too early. Can't wait to see you, Cheryl xx."

That's great, but I'm not counting my chickens yet. There's still time for his mum to throw a spanner in the works. Oh, a message from Johnny asking if I'll be a guinea pig in the hair salon tomorrow. He feels that if he could just get the first few done, he'll gain confidence. I really can't believe he's going through with this hairdressing thing. Also, I'm not sure that he and Nico working and living together is a good thing either. At least this time it's my own hair and not those stupid extensions.

Another text from Julie and again I'm going to ignore it. I'm not even going to look at the fourteen work emails either. More wine, a little bit of music, and light my candles. Shall I tell Andreas that I know what happened to him in the past? No, I'm going to wait until he tells me himself. If he wanted me to know, he'd have told me already.

"Hi, Cheryl, how are you and what did you think of Dissinos? Did you meet Rhea?"

"Come in, I've got a bottle of wine out on the terrace. I've missed your kisses, Andreas, and I've missed you too."

"That's nice. Did you have a nice day?"

"Yes, I love Dissinos, and not just for the fabulous ice cream. Rhea and Moisis are really nice. They said it's about time you popped over to see them. I was thinking we could go together if you could get your potter friend to run the shop for a day."

"Yes, I'll see what I can organise, but enough of future plans, what have you got in store for tonight?"

"Well, like I said, there's wine out on the terrace and then perhaps we can have a little lie down."

Now that was a lovely end to my day off, although it was spoilt by the fact that Andreas had to go home. I understand it all now, and I wish there was some means of convincing his mum that I'm not out to hurt him. I know he would have stayed if he could. Lights off, early start at the hairdressers in the morning, but one thing's for sure. I'm not going to be talked into having a hairstyle I don't want. Oh, no, not this time I won't.

Chapter 25

"Morning Cheryl, and welcome to the salon. Take a seat and my new assistant, all the way from the United Kingdom, will be with you shortly."

"Hi, Nico. I can't believe I've been talked into this. Please promise me that he only washes my hair, and there's no scissors or hair dye involved along the way."

"No, just wash and shampoo. Well, for today anyway."

"Hello darling. Isn't this exciting? You're my first client here on the island. You know you can go online and give me a five-star review for my shampooing skills, don't you?"

"Yes, Johnny, and I can also go online and put a one-star review, so no messing about. I just want a straightforward wash."

"If madam would like to walk this way. Can I take your coat? Oh, you don't have one. There you go. Make yourself comfortable and I'll begin."

"Less of the madam, Johnny. It makes me sound like someone who runs a brothel or an old person, and I'm neither of those. How are you settling in with Nico?"

"Cheryl, it's wonderful. I know I'm loud and over the top and that annoys some people, but Nico doesn't have a problem with it at all. He's so kind and thoughtful. I'm very lucky. I do know my place here and I'm not going to get all grand and bossy. I'm here to wash hair and help out as much as I can.

Now, tell me how you're doing. Oh, by the way, Nico was telling me how you've organised Vangelis. He says that you're the first person to ever do that and also said that he thinks Vangelis fancies you. Just imagine! We could be dating two brothers. How strange would that be!"

"That, Johnny, is never going to happen. For one, I

don't fit the profile of the type of women Vangelis goes for, and secondly... Well, there is a secondly, but I can't think about that yet. Now, concentrate on my hair if you want your five star review."

"Oh, that's another text from Suzy. I can't believe how many she's sent me since I've arrived here, Cheryl. She really has no idea what's she's doing. Last night I had to phone her and talk her through how to do the banking. Debbie, the housekeeper, phoned me to say the hotel is in chaos. She's got bookings on pieces of paper instead of the computer and she's forgetting to order things. It's a complete mess."

"But Johnny, she didn't worry while we were working seventy hours a week and she was off on cruise ship holidays every five minutes, did she?"

"I know, but in some ways I do feel sorry for her. Your hair's finished now. If you'd like to come this way, we'll start the next stage of your experience."

"Experience, Johnny? I did say no scissors or hair dye."

"No, it's just a blow dry. That will give it a bit of volume."

"So, Cheryl, do I need to sack him on his first day or are you pleased with all Johnny's done?"

"Done, Nico? That's not the word you should be using. I've created a work of art for Cheryl and that's what she'll say in her review, won't you, darling?"

"Johnny, why don't you help me out by writing and posting the review?"

"Well, I can if you like, but it's not really the done thing."

"Right, thank you for my work of art. I have to go to work now, so have a lovely day both of you. We must plan a night out, just the three of us. No blind dates or matchmaking, thank you, promise me."

"We promise, Cheryl, don't we, Nico?"

"Yes, and thanks for coming in today, Cheryl."

I'm exhausted and the day hasn't even started for me yet. I can see that Johnny's going to love being in the salon. Although he's only washing hair, he'll make the job the most important one there. God help Nico and the rest of the team.

Enough of all that. I need to get some work done. There's loads to catch up on after yesterday's day off. First, the sea taxi or the hill? I know which one it should be, but I think the easier option would be the boat ride.

"Morning, Cheryl. Did you have a nice day off?"

"Lovely, thanks, Vangelis. There's loads to catch up with though. I've just glanced through my emails and notice one from the mystery wedding PA, Carla, with the table lay out. She's also ordered some screens to go around three sides of the restaurant which will be installed first thing in the morning before all the other things arrive and she's slipped something else into the email. I don't know if it's by accident or on purpose, but there'll be six security guards constructing a false wall to create a little room. This is becoming more bizarre by the week. Look, Vangelis, you know everyone on this island. There must be some way of finding out who's staying at the Villa. Just the surname would do."

"Do you think we could ask them for more money for the inconvenience caused, Cheryl?"

"No, Vangelis. They're paying well over the odds for renting the restaurant. All we have to do is open the door for them to do everything themselves. No, what I was thinking was, if for some reason the name of the wedding couple leaks out, the publicity would be out of this world. Everyone will want to get married here. I really do think we need to be prepared for the media turning up, although before photographers or journalists are able to get on the island, the wedding will be over and he mystery guests will have gone to the Villa."

We can't say anything on Facebook or Twitter because we've signed a confidentiality clause. But what if someone else with a Twitter account just happens to take a photograph from the beach and post it. Surely we can't be blamed for that?"

"Exactly, Vangelis, but all I'm saying is we need to be prepared. Have you had any famous people in the restaurant? Is there anyone who keeps returning because Volmos is meaningful to them?"

"God, yes. We've had many famous Greeks and Italians here over the years. I'm not too sure about any famous English guests though. I doubt I'd know them anyway."

"Oh well, we'll soon find out on the day. Right, I'm off to do some work in the office. Is there anything you need from me, or anything else I should know about?"

"I don't think so, apart from the fact that some chap came in yesterday and asked after you. He was English, in his thirties, wouldn't leave his name but he said he'd pop back at some time."

"Was it to do with a wedding?"

"No, Cheryl, I don't think so. I got the impression he knew you, but he did seem rather nervous and shy."

"Oh, that's a bit strange. I'm up in the office if he comes back. See you later."

How odd. I wonder who that could be. Must get on with some work now, and first on my list is an email to Julie explaining that I haven't taken sides and it wouldn't be a problem if it was Mum coming over and not Dad.

Next a quick text to Dad. He's arriving next week and I need to tell him that his accommodation is booked and it's just around the corner from me. At last I can get stuck into some wedding work. Everything's ordered and arranged for the next wedding, which is a lot bigger. Vangelis will have to get more involved as it's a Greek family with a lot of demands. It shouldn't present any problems to him though.

A quick reply to Carla. I've nothing to lose, so I'm going to be cheeky and ask her who the mystery couple are. I don't think she'll tell me outright, but she could give us a hint. Now for the boring jobs, setting up the files for new enquiries.

"Hi, Cheryl, how are you doing? It's nearly six pm now, and you didn't come down for any lunch. Just to let you know the chap who asked after you has just turned up again. When I told him that you were here, he blushed. I think you've got a secret admirer. Perhaps Andreas and I should be worried."

"Why would you be worried, Vangelis? I've told you time and time again that we only work together and that's exactly how it's going to stay."

"You might say that, Cheryl, but that's not the way you want it to be. I'm just biding my time until you give into these beautiful eyes."

"In your dreams, Vangelis. Now let me go down and see for myself who this chap is."

"Hello, Cheryl."

"Clive!"

Chapter 26

I need this like a hole in the head. Why is he here? Well, I know why, but to just turn up out the blue. I'm pleased that I made an excuse to be working and had phone calls to make, but now I have to face him and hear what he has to say. What do I wear and where are we going to go to eat?

Thank goodness Vangelis believed me. Well, I wasn't exactly telling a lie. We did work together and he's on holiday, but do I tell Clive about Andreas? I know I ought to, but Clive's fragile and upset. He was part of my old life though, the life I lived when I was pleasing everyone else. I'm different now and Clive isn't my problem. Oh, God. I've not thought of Johnny. And what he'll have to say. Come on, Cheryl, best foot forward. It's nearly time to meet Clive in the harbour. If only he'd have come next week when Dad's here. They could have done things together.

"Hi, Clive. So you found it okay. What do you think of this beautiful harbour? Well, come to that, do you like Holkamos? I've yet to find anyone who doesn't fall in love with this place. I thought we could have a little walk and then get something to eat. We can walk the entire length of the harbour in about half an hour. I just love the lights reflecting in the sea and the gorgeous aromas from the restaurants, and you never know, we might bump into Johnny. He's loving his new job at the hairdressers."

Oh, Cheryl, just be quiet and let Clive get a word in. Actually he's got that look on his face, just like a lost puppy. Keep walking, I think. It's so busy here, the atmosphere is so vibrant and exciting. Do we walk back past the hair salon and see whether Johnny's there? Do I just be honest and pop into Andreas' shop to introduce them both? Oh, this is so awkward. The thing is, I don't really know what I ever saw in Clive. He's a nice chap and I enjoyed working with him, but we were in that hotel bubble and I've moved on.

"Clive, from here you can look up to the castle on the hill and from there it's such a wonderful view down to the harbour. There's some lovely restaurants up the top by the castle. From some of them the view is the opposite direction, to Volmos."

"I'm sorry that I've come over to Holkamos, Cheryl. I can see all this is a problem for you because you're just babbling on. Perhaps I should catch the next plane home. This was such a bad idea."

"Don't be stupid, Clive, it wasn't a bad idea at all. Now that you are here, let's enjoy the time. Let's get a drink and then we can chat about things."

"Cheryl, when I first called round, the chap at the restaurant told me it was your day off and you were probably spending it with your boyfriend. Is that true?"

"Well, it's true that I'm kind of seeing someone, but it's not as straight forward as that. Actually it's all a bit complicated. Come on, let's find somewhere to have a drink and I'll tell you about everything that's happened since I've moved here."

So that's why Clive has the lost puppy look. Vangelis has stirred it up a little. I'll have to explain everything but the most important thing is to make it clear that I've moved on from Dartmouth and not to let him think there's any chance we could become a couple.

"Sorry, Cheryl, there was a long queue for the toilets, and I got talking to someone who asked me if this was my first time on the island. Everyone's so friendly here. When I said that it was my first time here, he told me not to talk about it when I got home as it's one of Greece's biggest secrets and no one wants it to change."

"I don't think the restaurant and shop owners would agree with that, but it's very special here. I'm very lucky to be able to live and work here."

"I've been so stupid, Cheryl. My parents don't

understand why I'm not at work and moved back in with them. The doctors have diagnosed me with depression as I'm not coping well. It's the small things I struggle with, things like making a cup of tea or deciding which clothes to wear. The big things, like coming here, I'm great with. It's just that when you said you were leaving Dartmouth and the hotel, my whole life seemed to collapse. I know we weren't a couple, and oh, this is so silly."

"No, Clive, it's not silly. It's okay, just take your time."

"I know I didn't give you the impression that it was anything more than just the nights of sex together, but I really did live for those nights. That's all I had in my life. It was so special."

"But why didn't you tell me this before? You had plenty of opportunities, and one other thing I don't understand is that afterwards you always went back into your own room as if it had never happened."

"I thought that's what you wanted, and I felt guilty and so ashamed with myself that I was using you and treating you badly."

"We both used each other, Clive, but it was a mutual thing, something we both wanted to do and we both enjoyed it greatly."

"So, Cheryl, you're telling me you enjoyed it and didn't do it just to please me?"

"Of course, Clive. I enjoyed it very much and really looked forward to our nights together, but it did hurt my feelings that afterwards there were no cuddles or chatting, which would have been nice and made it even more special."

"So you're saying it was special?"

"Of course, Clive. I wouldn't have done it just for the sake of it. I looked forward to those nights just as much as you did."

"All that time and I didn't even realise it."

"Now that little matter's cleared up, let's have a drink and go for something to eat. I'm starving and you're on holiday."

Have I made things worse? Surely he knew I was having fun, but have I done the wrong thing in telling him that or will he think there's more to our friendship? I hope I haven't encouraged him or led him to believe we could have a future together. This evening is turning out to have such peaks and troughs. Before the night's over I need him to understand that we don't have a future together, not now or ever, and I know exactly the way to do that.

"Come on. I know of a restaurant part way up the hill that serves beautiful seafood. This way. I just need to pop into a shop around the corner for two minutes."

"Hi, Andreas, how are you? Can I introduce you to a friend of mine from England? We used to work together. This is Clive and he's a chef. By the way, don't I get a kiss and what time will you be around tonight?"

"Sshhhh, Cheryl. Mum's in the back. Nice to meet you, Clive. I hope you have a nice holiday on Holkamos. Have you come by yourself or are you with a wife or girlfriend?"

"Hi. No, I'm by myself."

"Okay, let's get off before... Well, before you..."

"Before my mum comes out. Sorry, Cheryl."

What a disaster! Now Clive knows that Andreas' mum doesn't approve of me, so that's another thing to explain. Thank goodness I wasn't with Vangelis. He would have loved a situation like that. I can hear him now, saying "Never come between a Greek mummy and her son."

"That fish was beautiful. Can you see down there in the harbour, Clive? That's the boat that caught it today. How fresh is that?"

"So, Cheryl, your relationship with Andreas is a bit like ours, carried out in secret?"

"No, Clive. It's nothing like ours. You don't know

the full story. It's difficult for Andreas as his Mum just doesn't want him to get hurt. Anyway, she's coming round to the idea, so we just need to not rub it in her face."

"Sorry, I didn't want to upset you."

"You haven't upset me, Clive, but let's just drop the subject. Tell me about your plans for the future."

"I don't have any plans, but I do know that it's something I need to think about as I've nearly got through all my savings and won't be able to live off my sick pay. One thing's for sure and that's I'm not going back to Dartmouth to work for Suzy again. I feel the same way that you and Johnny do. The hotel's just not been the same since Graham's death. We've slogged our guts out and for what? Graham certainly wouldn't approve of the way Suzy's treating us, and if she's got any sense at all she should sell the place. No, I'm moving on. Coming here to see you is all part of that process, I think."

"Yes, it's sad about the hotel, but we have to just look back at all the happy times when Graham was there and how we worked hard and enjoyed it. Graham taught us all so much. With your qualifications, Clive, you could easily walk into a job anywhere in the UK."

"Yes, Cheryl, but not just the UK. I could get one anywhere in the world."

What an evening! Thank God I'm home. I'm quite pleased that Andreas isn't coming over tonight. I just need to clear my head and unwind. If someone had said to me six months ago that I would be living and working here on Holkamos with three blokes fancying me, I'd have laughed in their face, but that's is the reality of the situation.

Vangelis only wants me because I've rejected him, which isn't something he's used to. Then there's Clive who apparently was in love with me, but didn't think I was interested in him even though I was, now there's Andreas, who's been hurt so badly in the past.

147

Perhaps he'll always have it in the back of his mind that I might hurt him if we were together. It's all happening here on this little island. Time to sleep, Cheryl, and when you wake, one thing's for certain and that's that these problems won't have gone away.

Chapter 27

My office door's going to be closed all day as I really don't want to talk to anyone. Normally the thought of eight hours of paper work would drive me mad, but not today. Bring on the emails! Vangelis has gone over to Preveza to get some stock, so he won't be popping up the stairs every five minutes, but it does mean I'll have to go down and get my own coffee. It's a hard life!

It's surprising how many local businesses want to get involved since the success of the weddings we've held here. Perhaps I should compile a list of suitable types of accommodation to send to bridal couples enquiring about the weddings instead of them having to research it all on the Internet for themselves. I think we're also missing an opportunity with somewhere to eat the night before the wedding. I'll ask Vangelis whether he and his chefs could put some wedding eve dinners together.

Emails answered, wall chart up-to-date, daily contact with PA Carla done. Even I'm starting to lose interest in this wedding now and I'll be so glad when it's all over and done with. Today her enquiry was about the number of plug sockets in the restaurant and to get an extension lead. How many do they need? I'm beginning to get more and more sarcastic in every reply. I know it can't be easy for her, but the sooner she realises Holkamos is not closing just for them, the better.

That's it, I've done my hours. Just a quick diary print off to leave for Vangelis and that's me heading home. I can't believe I've gone all day and not spoken to anyone, no phone calls because my phone's been switched off. On the walk back home I'm going to have the biggest ice cream I can find and then a bottle of wine on the terrace with my book. The perfect end to the day.

The only question is when's best to switch my phone back on as that's sure to be when the day gets spoilt. Should I play a little game and guess who's sent me a text? Julie? Clive? Johnny? Andreas? Dad? Vangelis? No, this game can wait until I'm half way down the bottle.

I'm drinking slowly because I don't want to get to the half way point, but here goes, got to be done. It's nearly nine o'clock and there's lots of missed calls, but no voice mails. Nothing from Julie, Andreas or Dad, but a couple of texts. One from Clive. 'Thank you for last night. It was lovely to see you and I'm so glad we cleared the air. I realise how stupid I've been all these years. Clive.' Another text from Vangelis. 'Your phone's been off all day. I wouldn't normally bother you, but a friend of mine who's got a restaurant in the harbour wants to know whether that friend of yours is reliable because he's been in to look for a job.'

Oh no! I was only thinking that it's only a few more days before Clive goes. What's he doing looking for work here on the island? What can I say? It would be lying to say he's unreliable as he really is a good worker. I'm going to have to make it clear to him that nothing's going to happen between us and he needs to go back.

Another text from Vangelis. 'Cheryl, ignore the last text. My mate has taken on your friend for the rest of the season. Have a lovely evening. See you tomorrow.'

I don't know about finishing this other half bottle of wine, I think I'll need a bottle of gin! I'm just going to ignore him being on the island. There's nothing between us and what he does with his life is his own business. Now what? Who's that at the door? If it's Clive... No, it can't be Clive as he doesn't know where I live.

"Hello, Cheryl. I was hoping you were in."

"Hi, Andreas come in."

"I've brought some wine as I think we need to talk. I've got something to tell you which I probably should have done weeks ago."

"There you go. I'll warn you, I've already drunk quite a bit and perhaps it's time for me to tell you something too, Andreas. I have to be honest with you, I think I know what you have to say. It's about Elpis and that day. I've not been snooping around and no one has told me in a nasty way. It was only out of kindness to you and as for your mum, I'd act in much the same way if I was her. She doesn't want you to get hurt again."

"I thought someone might have said something, Cheryl. It was a few years ago now, but hardly a week goes by where someone doesn't look at me in that sympathetic way. Me, I feel the complete opposite about it. I had a narrow escape. God, could you imagine if I'd gone through with the marriage? I'd have had to endure years of misery. There's always a but though, and my poor mum can't get over what see sees as the shame. I don't see it as a shame, more of an embarrassment, but certainly not shame. If I had a euro for everyone who popped their head in the door those first years and said, "Oh, it's poor Andreas", I'd be a very rich man indeed."

It didn't take me too long to get over Elpis, but it has made me very wary of relationships, although I don't feel that way with you. For a start, when we met you were being very open and honest about hiding in the shop. No, Cheryl, you don't scare me. Actually, I think that's the wrong word, but you know what I mean, don't you?"

"Yes, Andreas, I do, and it was Rhea over on Dissinos who told me. From that moment I realised that our friendship wouldn't be easy because of your mum and who can blame her? Come here and kiss me."

"But you said you had something to tell me as

151

well."

"Oh, that's not important. It can wait. At the moment I've got other things on my mind and I'm hoping you have too."

Andreas looks so peaceful when he's asleep. I'm so glad we talked about his marriage that didn't happen. What was so lovely was when he said how he felt different with me than in his other relationships. That makes me feel so good, but it doesn't solve the problem of his mum. I need to win her round if we're going to continue seeing each other, and that's not going to be easy. I have to convince her that I'll never hurt her son.

Well, it's four in the morning and I reckon Andreas is staying the night. It will be lovely to wake up together in the morning. Well, in a few hours! Oh, Cheryl, you're so very lucky.

"Good morning. I must have fallen asleep. So sorry, Cheryl. Oh, you're up. What's the time?"

"Oh, it's still early! Only seven-thirty. What time do you need to leave? Shall I make us some coffee?"

"No, the coffee can wait. Come back to bed as I want to tell you something."

"What's so important that I need to get back in bed, Andreas?"

"I think this little habit of mine is turning into something else. I think I'm falling in love with you, Cheryl."

Chapter 28

I really hope Andreas didn't realise how shocked I was. I'm still trying to process it. "I love you, Cheryl." No one apart from my dad has ever said that to me. I'd given up hope that anyone ever would, but Andreas meant it. How happy that makes me feel! I didn't come to island looking for love or anything at all really. I'm a different person now to when I arrived here, and I don't just mean the stupid hair, nails and skinny body. Okay, I haven't put all the weight back on, but it's not that. I'm a new Cheryl. I'm the person I always wanted to be and not the one people expected me to be.

All those years thinking I wasn't good enough and Mum asking me why I couldn't be like Julie, popular and top of the class at school. She told me that I'd never stand out at anything, and that was even at ten years old. It's a miracle it didn't screw me up for life, but it wasn't just mum. The teachers were no better, seating me at the back of the class because I was slower at understanding things.

It wasn't that I wouldn't put my hand up to answer a question because I was shy, but that I just didn't know the answers. I didn't have any friends and I had no interest in anything because I wasn't encouraged to have hobbies except from playing the trumpet, which I hated. I wasn't even allowed to practice it at home because it made too much noise. Then at weekends I had to sit in the car for hours as Mum drove Julie around the country to take part in dance competitions or singing contests. If I moaned about it, it was just a case of, "Cheryl, you don't have any dreams, so don't spoil your sister's."

While we were driving around to all these silly events, Dad was working every hour God sent to pay for it all as Julie needed different outfits for every competition. Sometimes she'd only wear a dress for an hour. Oh, no. she couldn't be seen in it twice. Thank goodness that the older I got, the more I was allowed to stay home by myself while Julie and Mum travelled around. Once I reached the age of sixteen I had to go and get a Saturday job. Mum got me a job washing dishes on a Friday and Saturday night in the local pub restaurant and to be honest that was the nicest thing she ever did for me, because that's how Graham came into my life. He didn't just teach me the ins and outs of the catering trade, but gave me confidence and encouragement.

There's been two pivotal days in my life while working for Graham. The first was when I'd only been working for him for about six months. One of the waitresses had left to have a baby, and one night as I was mopping the kitchen floor, Graham handed me my wages and said, "From next Friday, Cheryl, I'd like to train you up to work in the restaurant. I'm not expecting you to learn everything in one shift. It will take a while but I know you're going to be really good at it."

God, I was scared all week, but I needn't have been. I loved it, but more than that I was good at it, the customers liked me and at last I had found something I could do.

But that was only the start of it. After leaving school I worked there as a waitress full time. I was very proud of that, but it wasn't good enough for Mum and Julie. Oh, no, years of comments about "You should do something with your life. Anyone can be a waitress." Well, not everyone can. I've seen hundreds over the years who think they can do the job, but can't as they lacked common sense. As for Julie, we never did find out how she got promoted so many times in the insurance company, but she did use to go out for dinner once a week with the Chief Executive of the company and I don't think his wife went with them.

One day - and up until coming here it was the best

day of my life – Graham called me into the office to tell me he'd sold the pub and he was moving to Devon. I felt so very sad about this as we'd worked so well together. However, that wasn't the end of it. He wanted me to come and work for him there as the Restaurant Manager and I'd get to live in the hotel? Was I interested? What do you think? Leave behind a nagging mum and a bitchy sister, move to a beautiful part of the country and be independent. Of course I wanted the job and the rest, as they say, is history.

So, Dad loves me, Graham had faith and confidence in me and now Andreas tells me he's falling in love with me. This is a whole new thing! But do I love him? And what will happen if I think I do and then realise I was wrong? I don't want him to be hurt for a second time. I do like him very much and I get butterflies in my stomach when I see him. When we have sex, it's more than that, it's making love.

Oh, Cheryl, think it through, but am I overthinking? Should I just go with the flow? What's going to happen at the end of the season when I have to leave the island? I can't stay here as I won't have anywhere to live. More importantly, I need to earn a living. Yes, Vangelis will pay me a little for sorting out all the wedding enquiries. Talking of Vangelis, I'm not in the right mood for him today. I'll send him a text with an excuse. I'll text Johnny to see if he's at work.

"So, darling, what's so urgent? I've had to leave the wash basins at the salon! Don't worry, I'm only joking. I'm off today and I was actually going to surprise you and turn up down on Volmos with some pastries. But now you're here that's spoilt that little surprise. Shall we go for lunch? Where do you fancy?"

"Can we go for a walk first? Why don't we walk up to Creakos away from the town and the beach. There'll be somewhere up there to eat."

"Are you alright, Cheryl? You don't seem yourself. Has something happened?"

"Yes, Andreas has said he's falling in love with me."

"Oh, how wonderful! I'm so pleased and excited for you, but just a minute. Why the sad worried face? Surely you're happy about it?"

"I don't know how I feel. No one's ever said anything like that to me before. Oh, Johnny, I want to run away. I'm scared."

"Scared of what? Falling in love with someone who wants to be with you, love you and take care of you? How is that scary? Oh, Cheryl, come on, it's the final piece of the jigsaw. You live in a fabulous place doing a job you love and now a man has come into your life. Why on earth would you ever want to run away? Grab it with both hands darling, and enjoy it."

"You make it sound so easy, Johnny. Andreas has been hurt badly once. I can't do it again to him."

"Why would you hurt him, Cheryl? I'm starting to get annoyed with you now and the subject is closed until you can talk about it sensibly. Right, come on. Let's walk up to Creakos and have a lovely lunch with some wine. Everything will seem that much clearer this afternoon."

Clearer? Well, that was seven hours ago and although Johnny and I had a nice walk up to Creakos, a lovely lunch and, as always a good laugh, I'm still not right in my head about Andreas. On top of all that I've had a text from Clive asking me if I would meet up with him as he has something to tell me. Well, I feel like texting back and telling him I already know and it should be me asking him why he's decided to come and work on Holkamos. So, no, I won't be meeting him today. I'm going into the office, throw myself into my work and switch off from men for the rest of the day.

"Hi, Cheryl. I didn't think you were coming in today."

"Yes, I've done all I needed to do, Vangelis, but I wanted to print some things off the computer? Did you see my note about guests needing meals the night before weddings?"

"Yes, I'll put a sample menu together and you can email it to the bridal couples. All they'll need to do is give us the number of guests we'll have to cater for."

"Thanks, Vangelis. Oh, by the way, I've got something in common with you! I'm fed up to the back teeth with this celebrity wedding. They've had me counting plug sockets, and I'm just waiting for the email asking us to change the colour of the sand on the beach. There'll be one, I just know it. Don't laugh! Every day it's something different. Wait till they tell you to dress in traditional Greek clothes, you won't be laughing then. Right, was there anything else? I need to get on with some work."

"Well, Cheryl, there is something actually. It's very nice and you'll enjoy it. We're going on a little staff outing to Corfu. Sadly it's only a day trip, but a cousin of mine who lives on the island runs a beach café. He was wondering if we could go over and help him and his wife set up a wedding business like ours, so I thought we could go and take a look at the café. You could show them how you take the bookings."

"I suppose that will be okay. When are we going?"

"In a couple of days' time. I thought that would give you enough time to put some samples together."

"Yes, I can do that. Now I need to get on. Was there anything else?"

"No, I don't think so. Oh, my friend said that the chap from the UK is a really hard worker. He's thrilled to bits with him."

"Oh, that's a shame. I was hoping he'd have got the sack. No, I don't mean that really. It's just complicated that's all."

"So, Cheryl, you were in a relationship with him and that's why he's come to Holkamos and it's a little difficult now you're seeing Andreas."

"You've got it wrong, Vangelis. Clive and I have never been in a relationship apart from a working one."

"But I get the impression, Cheryl, this Clive chap would like to be in a relationship with you. It's a very difficult situation all round. I'll have to let you know which day we'll go to Corfu."

Corfu! That will be nice, something different, and it's not as if it's just going to be me and Vangelis there. I'm looking forward to it, but why did I let slip about Clive? How stupid was that? Knowing Vangelis, he won't let it drop either. The day's just getting worse. Thank goodness it's nearly over, and on top of all this Dad will be here in a few days, which brings more problems. Time for home, I think, Cheryl, and a bottle of wine on the terrace.

Chapter 29

"So, Vangelis, let me explain what I've put together for your cousin. I've copied every form we use, from the original enquiry to the feedback once the wedding's over and I've also printed things off our website that might help. The one thing I haven't done is the menus we offer. Can you think of anything else? By the way, how long does this boat take to get there? I know we can see it in the distance from Holkamos on a clear day but it seems to be taking forever."

"Oh, calm down, Cheryl and enjoy the journey. We're in for a nice day, it's not a business meeting! I think you've done a fabulous job putting all the information together. They'll really appreciate it, so chill out and we'll have a fun day."

"To be honest, I don't know why you haven't come by yourself. You are capable of explaining everything to them. You don't need me there."

"I want you to be there, Cheryl. You have to take all the credit for getting our wedding business off the ground. If it had been left to me, so much would have been missed. So sit there and enjoy the ride. It will only be another twenty minutes."

I've just realised Vangelis is loving this. He knows I don't need to be here and he also knows he has me all to himself for the day. Chilling out isn't easy. I still haven't spoken to Clive, and more importantly I haven't mentioned Clive to Andreas, which is something I should have done. Not that it's a problem with me, as Clive means nothing to me, but this whole situation has screwed me up and it's only a matter of time before Vangelis brings it into the conversation.

However, I'm looking forward to visiting Corfu and the beach café sounds lovely. Very different to ours on Volmos, and a much smaller beach.

"Right, we're here, Cheryl. Are you ready? You

were miles away, day dreaming, but then I suppose you would be as you're on a date with me."

"It might not be a business meeting, but it's certainly not a date either, Vangelis."

"So what is it then, Cheryl?"

"Hi, Bemus, can I introduce you to Cheryl, my right hand women and the first female in my life to organise me and tell me what to do?"

"Nice to meet you, Cheryl, and thank you for coming over today. You must be very special if you've sorted Vangelis out. Many women have tried and failed, so what's your secret?"

"No secret at all. I've just pointed out how much money he can earn and that will give him more to spend on his lady friends. We both know how much he enjoys having fun with the holiday makers."

"That's a bit harsh, Cheryl. You know I'm not like that, Bemus, don't you? Stop laughing both of you, it's not funny. I can't help it if a few visitors every summer want to spend time in my company. Anyway, it's not pick on Vangelis day. We're here to see the beach café, so lead the way to your car, cousin!"

Well, that put him down a peg or two. I think I've got the upper hand plus Bemus is on my side so I'm starting to enjoy my day after all. Bemus seems really nice, not a bit like Vangelis but more of an Andreas kind of chap, a little shy but very switched on. I'm looking forward to meeting his wife.

A quick check on my phone. There's a text from Johnny saying "Have a nice date." it's not a bloody date. Andreas is asking what time we'll be back because his friend, the potter, can cover the shop from five o'clock. There's nothing from Clive. Perhaps he's got the message that I'm not interested in him, but there's the daily email from PA Carla.

"Vangelis, Carla has emailed her daily question and it's one for you. The bridal couple want to know if you'll be there on the wedding day as they said it would be nice to see you again. So, Vangelis think.

What famous people do you know? Perhaps you knew them before they were celebrities."

"I'm telling you, Cheryl, I don't have a clue who they are. Email back and tell her the price will go up if they want me there."

"Don't be greedy. I'm not doing that. Oh, is this where your restaurant is, Bemus? What a fabulous view?"

"You haven't seen anything yet, Cheryl. We need to leave the car here and just walk a little way through the olive trees and then you'll see the magic."

"Hi Vangelis, it's lovely to see you again. Thanks for coming over, and you must be Vangelis' new friend. By the way, I'm Arianna."

"Hello, yes, I'm Vangelis' friend, but I'm his employee and nothing else. You both have a fabulous setting here. It's perfect for weddings. You must be so excited!"

"Yes, we are, aren't we, Bemus? Hopefully you're both going to help us get the business off the ground."

"Cheryl can go through all the computer stuff and forms with you, Arianna, and I can show Bemus how I would lay the tables out to maximise the amount of people you can seat. We can also have a chat over a beer."

"As usual, but I'm telling you both not too many beers. I know what you're both like once you get together. I'll get Cheryl and me a bottle of wine. It will make the computer go faster! Red or white, Cheryl?"

"It's a bit early for me. Could I have a coffee instead, please, Arianna?"

"No, it's your day off, Cheryl. If they can drink booze before eleven in the morning, so can we. Red or white?"

"Well, if you insist, Arianna. Red please."

*

I don't think Arianna should be opening a second bottle, but saying that, we've nearly finished going through everything. She's obviously spent time looking at our website and has put a lot of things in place already. I'd never say it to Vangelis, but the setting for their weddings is a lot better than ours. No, that's wrong, it's different. They're both beach settings, but I think they might struggle getting things to the restaurant and I do wonder whether people would be prepared to walk through the olive groves to get to the restaurant.

"Here you go, Cheryl, and thanks for coming over to Corfu. You'll have to come back when we do a wedding and tell us what we're doing wrong. One more thing, how far in advance are people booking weddings?"

"Well, Arianna, this has been a great surprise. We've had an enquiry for five years' time, although I'm not taking that one very seriously, but generally people are enquiring for three years' time. Another thing we're discussing with bridal couples is pre wedding evening meals and brunches on the day after for guests. It almost turns every wedding into a three day event."

"I hadn't thought of that, but it's definitely something to think about. Well, that's about it. Why don't we take the wine outside and join the boys. You can tell me how you fell for the charms of Vangelis. I bet it was the eyelashes."

"I'm sorry to disappoint you, Arianna, but I only work for Vangelis. I have a boyfriend on Holkamos. The eyelashes do nothing for me whatsoever."

"The beach is busy today. There's a lovely youthful vibe here during peak season as there's students here from all over the world. The staff we have helping in the café this year are really good. We've given them incentives. The more they sell, the more they earn. We're very lucky to have them. Now where are those two?"

"We're over here. I see you've got another bottle of wine, Arianna."

"If I were you, I wouldn't mention it. I hate to think how many beers you two have had. Well, Cheryl and I have been sweating over a hot computer, so what should we do now? The staff will be fine running the café, so shall we drive somewhere for something to eat?"

"Oh, that would be nice, but unfortunately Vangelis and I have to get back to Holkamos."

"No, we don't, Cheryl. We can catch the later boat back. It will be nice to finish our day off with something to eat. Lead the way, Bemus."

I knew coming here was a bad idea. Vangelis didn't need me to go through everything, he could have done it all himself. Okay, they're lovely people, but oh, I don't know what's wrong with me. Just try and relax and have fun. It's not like it's just a social trip. We have talked business.

"Did you enjoy that, Cheryl? It's one of our favourite restaurant's here on Corfu. We've been coming here for years, haven't we?"

"Yes, and because it's on the other side of the island, it's a completely different view from that of our little bit of beach. On a really clear day you can see Paxos in the distance."

"Right, we need to start making a move if we're going to catch the last boat back to Holkamos. Are you ready, Cheryl?"

"Yes, it's been a lovely day and I've really enjoyed it. I've eaten too much, drunk too much, but it's been lovely. I'm so excited for you both with the café. I think you're definitely onto a winner with it, don't you, Vangelis?"

"Come on then, we'll drop you back at the harbour. Actually, would you mind if I get you a taxi because I think I've had too much to drink. You can drop us off on the way. We'll leave the car here and pick it up tomorrow."

I'm ready for home. They were nice people and I've had a good day, but I'm looking forward to my evening with Andreas. Come on, Vangelis, just pay the taxi driver. Why is he standing there chatting? I'm going to start walking down to the jetty. It's starting to cool down now. There'll be a nice breeze on the journey back to Holkamos. Perfect for clearing my head of all that wine."

"Wait a minute, Cheryl. We've got a slight problem as I've misread the boat timetable. We've missed the last one back and now there's not another one until the morning. We'll have to find somewhere to stay. Look, the taxi hasn't gone yet. We could get the driver to take us into Corfu town."

Count to ten, Cheryl, and keep your mouth shut. It's all very strange that the taxi didn't pull off. What a bit of luck he's still there. It's almost as if this whole thing had been planned. I could swing for Vangelis, I really could, but I'm not going to let him see I'm angry or upset. I'm just going to take it in my stride. He's not the only one who can play games.

First of all I need to phone Andreas. What will he think? And what are we going to do here for the rest of the evening? One thing's for sure, it won't be what Vangelis would like to be doing.

"Cheryl, I've got some friends who have a little hotel on one of the streets which leads off the square. If we get the taxi to drop us off there, and they don't have any vacancies, I'm sure they'll know of somewhere that has. Is that alright?"

"Yes, that's fine with me. Then you can go and show me around Corfu town. I've heard so much about it and as you've been coming here all your life, you're the perfect tour guide. We'll get something to eat, go back to our own rooms and then the first boat back to Holkamos in the morning. I just need to phone Andreas and let him know. I don't want him turning up at my apartment after he's closed the shop to find I'm not there."

164

So here we are at the hotel and it's very obvious they're close friends as they are extremely friendly with all their kisses and hugs. They do seem to be a lovely couple, but I'm one step ahead of Vangelis, I reckon that once the hugs are over, he'll come back to me and say they've only have one room available, so would I mind sharing? My answer will be no, and I've got the perfect solution to the problem. So, I think it's countdown time, five - four – three- two - one and here he comes.

"Cheryl, they do have rooms. Well, they have one room, if you don't mind sharing it. It's a twin."

"Perfect, Vangelis. I'll have the room and seeing that these people are such good friends of yours I'm sure they won't mind you sleeping on their sofa. Is that the key? I'll just go and freshen up and meet you back down here in fifteen minutes and you can give me a tour of Corfu town."

Well, that took the smile off his face. I presume the next stage is a lovely romantic meal with wine and brandy, his last chance to woo me. There's no reply from Andreas and I don't think he'll be that pleased as he knows exactly what Vangelis is like.

"God, my feet are killing me, Cheryl. We must have walked miles. Can we stop the sightseeing now and have something to eat? There used to be a lovely little restaurant on this street. I don't know whether it's still here, but I think it was a few hundred metres in this direction, if that's alright with you."

"Yes, no problem. You're better at judging where to eat than I am. Sorry your feet are hurting, but thanks for showing me around. We'll both sleep well tonight after such a long day."

I actually feel sorry for Vangelis. If he's planned all this, what a complete waste of a day! I'm very tired, but the walk has given me an appetite. There's still no reply from Andreas. Surely he trusts me or does all this go back to his wedding to Elpis which didn't happen?

"Well, you were hungry, Cheryl. It's a bit daft to ask you whether you enjoyed it. There's nothing left! Now, dessert or coffee?"

"A coffee would be lovely, Vangelis, and the food was beautiful, thank you very much. How about a couple of brandies with the coffee to finish the day off? It's been a lovely day and I enjoyed meeting Bemus and Arianna, and even though it was unexpected, it's been great to spend the evening here in Corfu."

"I think my charm must have stopped working. Well, on you, anyway. You're not silly, are you, Cheryl?"

"No, sorry, Vangelis, but I figured that out back at the taxi driver stage. Don't apologise, just put it down to needing to try harder next time."

"But, Cheryl, I..."

"But nothing, Vangelis. You're a very handsome man and I'm flattered you find me attractive and perhaps, and it's only a maybe, but if I came here on holiday for a week and those long gorgeous eyelashes fluttered in my direction, sex, with your experience, would be very exciting. But I'm not a holiday maker. I live here and you're my boss. More importantly, I've got a boyfriend who I suspect because he knows of your reputation, isn't overly happy with us being here together. So why don't we enjoy our coffee and then head back to the hotel?"

"So, Cheryl, you are saying if you were here on holiday ...?"

"I'm not saying anything more than I love my job and working with you. I'm looking forward to seeing what the next few years has in store for us in a business sense only though."

"You know, Cheryl, I'm not going to give up. I really do fancy you and I've always known you've fancied me too. The first time we met at your sister's wedding you blushed when we talked, the attraction was there and I think it still is. Can I ask you something and I really don't mean it in a horrible way, I'm just very curious. What attracts you to Andreas? He's quite shy and not very outgoing, almost boring in fact."

"Oh, Vangelis. Let me think, what excites me about him. I love him being quiet, and his shyness is attractive too. One other thing, when it comes to going to bed Andreas is far from being boring, if you know what I mean? Now shall we finish off our coffee and head back. We both need a good night's sleep as the boat sets off for Holkamos at seven-thirty in the morning. Joking aside, Vangelis, I've had a really lovely day. I know it hasn't turned out the way you wanted it to, but I hope you've enjoyed it as much as I have. If I'd have finished off the day having sex, it would have spoilt it.

Chapter 30

I've been back from Corfu for two days now and still not seen Andreas. The couple of times we've spoken on the phone has been like pulling teeth. He obviously wasn't impressed with me staying on Corfu with Vangelis, but I know I've done nothing wrong. I'm not Elpis, so he should be able to trust me. He also knows that my dad arrives tonight, so all my spare time from work will be spent with him.

The good thing is that I'm up to date with all my work. The enquiries for weddings has virtually stopped for this year, so we know exactly how the rest of the season is going to pan out. Once Dad's gone back to England, we're right into the celebrity wedding. What shall I do with Dad for two weeks, apart from go to the beach and go out in the evenings? I hope he's feeling positive and thought about what he wants to do with his life, but before all that I have the problem with Andreas to resolve. I'm not having that hanging over me for a fortnight.

"Hi, Andreas. I thought I'd come and say hello before I head off to the airport to pick up Dad. There's something I need to ask you. What have I done wrong and why are you avoiding me? If it's to do with staying on Corfu with Vangelis, nothing happened between us. You'll have to believe me."

"Hello. Let me lock the door, Cheryl. Anyway, there aren't many people around. As it's so hot, they're all on the beach. Would you like a coffee? I was just about to make one for myself."

"Yes, thanks. You don't need to close the shop."

"I think I do. Firstly, I know nothing would have happened between you and Vangelis. He may have tried it on, but you're far too clever to fall for all his charm. Also, you love your job too much to spoil it by having a relationship with the boss. No, Cheryl, Vangelis isn't the problem. What's upset me is Clive.

When were you going to tell me he was here working on the island and where does it leave me?"

"Clive! How do you know about him, not that he's a secret? I was going to tell you about him but you fell asleep and we haven't been together since. You have to believe there's nothing between us."

"But why is he here, Cheryl? You might not think there's anything between you, but he sees it completely differently."

"What do you mean?"

"Clive's been in here in the shop and he's told me that he's here on Holkamos to win you back. You both made a mistake splitting up and now he's hoping you'll have him back."

"We were never a couple, Andreas. Yes, we worked and lived in the same place and had sex a few times, but there was never any emotional attachment. He also knows that I'm angry with him for coming to Holkamos and I don't want anything to do with him. Anyway, how does he know about you and this shop?"

"Cheryl, you have your boss to thank for that, and perhaps I should also be thanking Vangelis because if it wasn't for him I might not have found out about Clive until it was too late."

"What do you mean 'too late,' Andreas? Now you're talking rubbish. Clive means nothing to me, and whatever he has told you he's lying. As for Vangelis, you know him better than most. He doesn't like the fact that we're seeing each other. He's jealous of you. Yes, he's always flirting with me, but he doesn't stand a cat in hell's chance of getting anywhere with me. When I see him tomorrow, I'll be giving him a piece of my mind, and as for Clive, I'll rip his head from his shoulders when I get hold of him."

"But why would he say such a thing, and give up a life in England? He really must want you, Cheryl. You seem to mean an awful lot to him."

169

"He didn't have much of a life in the UK. He was signed off work with his nerves and had years to tell me how he felt about me. The times when we did have sex, and that's all it was as it wasn't love, he was out of the room the second it was over and it was never discussed. Not once did he tell me how he felt. He only mentioned it after he turned up here on the island for a holiday.

Andreas, what you and I, have together is very special and I wouldn't jeopardise that for anything. You have to believe me. I don't want Clive, Vangelis, or anyone for that matter. I want you and only you. I don't know what else I can say. I can't make you trust me. That's something you have to sort out in your own head. I need to go and catch the bus to the airport to meet my dad, and whether you believe me or not, Andreas, I love you. I really do."

Vangelis, you won't want to see me tomorrow. I hope for your sake I've calmed down because if I haven't I won't be responsible for my actions. As for Clive, he's just delusional. But what upsets me the most is Andreas. Why doesn't he trust me? He knows what we have between us is special so why would I throw that away? The ball's in his court now as I can't make him trust me and if we did have a relationship that lasted would that always be in the back of his mind? If so, that's not good for any couple. In a way I'm thankful Dad's coming over. It will give Andreas some time to sort his head out, but one thing's for certain and that's I'm not chasing after him. He knows where I am, so it's up to him.

"Over here, Dad."

"Oh, Cheryl, it's so good to be here. You're looking well."

"Yes, and it's all me! I'm not that stick person with the false nails and someone else's hair. I'm back to being the real me. The appearance may have changed, but I'm still me, perhaps with a bit more go, and a lot more attitude and confidence."

"I much prefer this Cheryl than the one at Julie's wedding. That was all a bit odd, but I did secretly enjoy her wiping a few smiles off the faces of certain people."

"Enough of that, Dad, you're on holiday and it's time for a rest and some fun. We'll get a taxi to the harbour and then the boat over to Holkamos, followed by a bus ride and by then it'll be time for something to eat, don't you think?"

"That sounds perfect to me, Cheryl. Do you know, the bit I'm looking forward to the most is sitting down for dinner with you and not having any bickering!"

"That sounds great to me, Dad, but I suppose there is something I need to ask. How's Mum and what's happening between you both?"

"There's so much to tell you, darling, but not today. We've got a fortnight to discuss all that. Now, I'm waiting to get on that boat and start my holiday properly."

Oh, what a day! I'm exhausted and I've not even been to work or answered any emails. I'm pleased that Dad likes his little studio and also glad that he wanted an early night. He still hasn't mentioned Mum or Julie, but he will in his own time. I think he's looking well though and seems very happy. Something's obviously happened before he came here, but I'm determined to give him a lovely holiday. It would be just the same if Mum had come here by herself, so whatever Julie thinks, I'm not taking sides.

So, that's Mum and Dad's domestic situation. What about mine? I knew there wouldn't be any call or text from Andreas. He needs time to think through all I said to him and to analyse the whole situation. I was right though. I can't make him trust me. He has to be able to do that himself. As for Clive and Vangelis, I realise that a shouting match isn't the answer, but I'm not going to drop it. Both of them need to realise how angry I am.

Right, Cheryl, time for bed. You've got a lot of catching up to do tomorrow before meeting up with Dad in the afternoon.

Chapter 31

Oh, what a surprise! Before I've even sat down there's an email from Carla. What will be today? Can we control the speed of the sea breeze? Can we make sure there's no sea birds on the beach? Surely there can't be much else left to ask. Gosh, no questions! And, for the first time, the email is addressed to Vangelis and myself rather than the company.

'Dear Cheryl and Vangelis. This comes from me, myself, and not my clients. I'm so very sorry for all I've put both of you through. No doubt, by now you'll be wanting to get this wedding over with. I really would like to tell you more about the people who will be there on the day, but I am not permitted to do this. I'm truly sorry, but will say that on the actual day of the ceremony you'll realise why I haven't been able to divulge the details. Thank you again for your patience, politeness and most of all, discretion. Lots of love. Carla. Xx.'

"Morning, Cheryl. Did your Dad arrive safely? It's not too hot here now? It was so much cooler when he was here for your sister's wedding."

"He's fine, thank you, Vangelis. The only one who's hot around here is me, and do you know why that is? Clive. You told Andreas all about him, didn't you? Now, I'm going to tell you something once and for all, so let it sink in to that ego of yours. Even if Andreas and I split up because of all the gossiping you've been doing about Clive... Are you listening to me? You and I will never get together, Vangelis. Am I making myself clear? Now if you'll excuse me, I have work to do. Please shut my office door on your way out."

"But Cheryl, I've..."

"Door, behind you, Vangelis, shut! Now goodbye."

Well, I think he got away very lightly. I felt like hitting him. Somehow I don't think he'll be back in a hurry. It's a shame it's had to happen today because it's a little milestone for the wedding business. We have a confirmation on our thirtieth wedding. It may be over a year away, but it's very exciting. I remember how Vangelis, Nico and I celebrated when he hit the twenty mark. That was such a lovely evening.

It's less than three weeks until the celebrity wedding, but there're two more to do before that. They're both very straightforward. One's a lovely young Norwegian couple with thirty guests, and the second one's a couple in their fifties from the UK who are just renewing their wedding vows with ten friends and family. I'm really looking forward to that as it's their silver wedding anniversary. I know every wedding we do is special, but I'd like to go the extra mile for that one.

I don't seem to have as much work to do as I thought I would. Perhaps that's because I haven't been interrupted every five minutes by Vangelis and I've been able to sail through it so much faster. I've got a couple of hours before I meet Dad. Perhaps I should get the situation with Clive over and done with and give him a piece of my mind, although to be honest I haven't got the energy. Perhaps he'll give up and leave the island if I ignore him. I know, I'll go and see whether the hairdresser of the year can spare half an hour for a coffee and a gossip. Perhaps it's time to tell him about my predicament too.

"Here you go, Cheryl, one gin and tonic. Now, tell me what's up. You knew it would be difficult having your dad here by himself. Your mum probably thinks you're taking sides, and I know you'd never admit, it but if you had to take sides it would have to be his. Darling, I think you'll just have to grin and bear it for two weeks. Fingers crossed, your mum doesn't turn up here on Holkamos.

"Now, let me tell you my exciting news. Well, as you know I'm loving the salon. It's not like work, it's fun. Talk about being on the stage, I'm in my element! The problem is because I'm not trained, all I do is the wash people's hair and do a couple of blow dries. However, my gorgeous Nico is going to let me train to be a proper hairdresser! I'm going to go to college over in Preveza for two days a week and then one of the lovely stylists is going to do the training in the salon. Nico thinks that by the start of next season I'll be able to start cutting and colouring. How fabulous is that!

"Come on, Cheryl. Be a little more pleased for me. Is something the matter? You weren't really paying attention to me at all."

"Oh, Johnny, the whole situation here is turning into a nightmare. I can handle Vangelis, but now Clive's here, Andreas doesn't trust me. Well, it's not that he thinks I'll go off with Clive, but Clive's told him that we had a thing going on and he's come to Holkamos to win me over. Vangelis is loving the situation. Oh, Johnny, what can I do to convince Andreas that it's him I want?"

"Three guys fighting for your attention! Once upon a time I'd have killed to have had one wanting me, but that was before I met Nico. The solution's easy, Cheryl. We just need to get rid of Clive one way or the other. If he isn't going to leave the island, we just need him to find another interest."

"What do you mean?"

"A girlfriend, Cheryl. We need him to fall in love. Surely it can't be that difficult."

"The way I'm feeling at the moment, Johnny, I can't even look at him, let alone talk to him."

"Leave it to me. I'll speak to Nico and I'm sure we'll be able to think of something. Now, put that smile back on your face and have a lovely two weeks with your dad. Andreas will come around eventually, and if he doesn't, he obviously isn't the man for you, and that will be his loss."

"Oh, Johnny, I'm so pleased you've come to Holkamos. Can you believe how our lives have changed in just a few months? We're so lucky."

"I know, darling, but the thing I'm most proud of is how confident you've become, and I don't think it's because of all that silly nonsense at Julie's wedding. For the first time in your life you've started to think of yourself. Throughout your childhood your whole life revolved around Julie and keeping her happy. Then there was Graham and the hotel. I know he was a good boss, so unlike Suzy, but he worked you to the ground. He knew the hotel was your life and you would do anything and everything for the place, and that was wrong. He didn't encourage you to make a life outside of it. He only made you feel special so that you'd give it your all. But, my darling, those days have gone. It's now your time to live. Have fun!"

"You're right. Taking away the Andreas and Clive situation, I've never been happier. The job's fabulous and I know Vangelis appreciates it. Sometimes I think he works for me, rather than the other way round, but I'm making money for him and that takes away the worry of the winter months when he doesn't have any income."

"Yes, Cheryl. Nico says that Vangelis has never been so well off financially and he does think the world of you. Aren't you just slightly tempted though? He's gorgeous and very experienced by all accounts. The number of girls and women who come into the salon and ask Nico about him"

"Johnny, you've said it all. He's experienced, and that means he's had loads of practice. I don't want to be another one in his fan club, if you know what I mean."

"I do, Cheryl, but those eyelashes are just to die for."

"Enough of this Vangelis worshipping, Johnny. I need to go and meet my dad. Thanks for the chat and advice, but most importantly, thanks for being the best friend in the world. I love you."

"Have a lovely evening, Cheryl, and give my love to

your dad. Now, leave that little problem of Clive to me and Nico."

I'm feeling better even though the problem hasn't yet been resolved. I'm so happy for Johnny and Nico as although they're like chalk and cheese, they are suited to each other. Now, let's see where Dad is. He should be back from the beach and at his holiday studio. I want to take him somewhere quite busy with a lot of atmosphere. A nice meal, some Greek music, a little too much to drink and no talking about Mum.

"Hello, trendy young man! I was expecting my dad. Who are you?"

"Do you like my new clobber? Your mum bought it for me to come away with. She said I needed a new look. I think it's all a bit too young for me."

"No, it's not too young at all, Dad. I think you look very smart, but I wonder why she's done that now, after all these years. It's all a bit bizarre. Anyway, let's go and have a good night out. I know a lovely restaurant down in the harbour. It's very busy and the food's fabulous. Make sure you tuck a napkin in your shirt as we don't want you dropping any food down that new shirt."

"Lead the way, Cheryl."

I can't believe the time! This must be the fifth or six time Dad's been up on the dance floor. Talk about letting your hair down! We've not mentioned Mum or Julie once. I know mine and Johnny's lives have changed, but that's nothing compared to what's going to happen with my dad. Oh, Mum's a survivor, but I can't see him living by himself, coming home from work to an empty house, cooking a meal for one. No, he isn't going to cope with that at all.

"Fancy some more wine, Cheryl, or a brandy perhaps?"

"No more alcohol for me, thanks. I'd love a coffee, but can we walk along the other end of the harbour to somewhere quiet? Let me settle the bill."

"No way, Cheryl. I'm paying for this. It's my treat

as I'm on holiday. I'm just going to the toilet and then I'll deal with it."

"Okay, thanks Dad. I'll wait for you over by the harbour wall."

"Hello, Cheryl. Why haven't you been answering my texts or calls?"

"Well, me not answering you should tell you all you need to know, Clive. You're a lovely chap, but I like you as a friend and nothing more. You shouldn't have come to Holkamos and certainly not stayed. When I found out that you'd been to see Andreas, I could have happily ripped your head off. I'm sorry if I've upset you by moving here, but I don't feel the same way about you. I'm sorry, I truly am, but that's how it is. You see, I'm not the same Cheryl you knew back in Devon. When I left Dartmouth I left her behind, and she won't be coming back."

"All paid up, Cheryl. Lead me to the coffee. Do you think there'll be any Greek dancing? By the way, who was that? He looked rather familiar?"

"No Greek dancing. Just a quiet coffee. He's just someone who needs to sort himself out and move on. Once upon a time he was very familiar, but not anymore."

Chapter 32

It's been four days and I've not seen Vangelis to speak to. Obviously he feels guilty about stirring up the situation between Andreas and Clive. Every time I catch his eye he seems to find something to do, but it's nearly the weekend and we've got to discuss Saturday's wedding. The bride and groom arrive today to go over the last minute details, so do I apologise to Vangelis for having a go at him? I don't know. The last thing I ought to do is create an atmosphere in front of the happy couple.

The good thing is there's not been any calls or texts from Clive. Perhaps he's finally taken the hint. The bad thing is there's not been any contact from Andreas either.

I thought that I would struggle to entertain Dad while he's been on holiday, but it's been the complete opposite. He's seen more of the Greek islands in the few days he's been here, than I probably ever will, going on boat trips all over the place. I'm pleased for him, but we will have to talk about his future. He can't keep avoiding it. The holiday will come to an end and he'll be back with Mum, the woman who's told him she doesn't love him. Anyway, that conversation can wait. I need to bite the bullet and find Vangelis before the situation gets out of hand.

"Good morning, Vangelis. I've brought the wedding file for you to have a quick look at before the couple arrive in a couple of hours' time. Do you have any questions? Is there anything I've missed out? By the way, it's a good job we didn't celebrate that thirtieth booking, as I've just had a cancellation. A young couple booked in for next year have split up, so I'll release that date on the website. Hopefully it will soon get snapped up, and then we can celebrate. This time it's my treat."

"Apart from the weddings, are we friends again,

Cheryl?"

"Of course we are. It was only a tiff. I'm sure we'll have many more over the years to come, but we're both adults so we'll get over them, won't we, Vangelis?"

"I'm sorry, Cheryl. It's just that..."

"Enough said. It's over with, and time to move on."

Well that went better than I expected. At least he said sorry. He looks even sexier when he's sad than if he's flirty and happy. How I didn't cuddle him, I don't know. The bridal couple seem very happy and all should be very straightforward. It was nice to see such an easy going bride and groom and no interfering from the bride's mother either.

A text from Dad to say that he won't be back from his trip until late, so we won't be able to meet for dinner. I have a free evening now. I wonder if this is an omen. Should I pop into Andreas' shop or should I just stay in and mope? No competition! It's time to start to fight for the man I want.

The harbour's really busy tonight. I keep forgetting it's the height of the season. It's very strange, as much as I don't take any of this for granted, you do seem to live day by day and week to week. Is that wrong? Should I be treating it as a six month holiday? It's not as if I'll be here in the winter after all. Just a few more yards and the shop will be in sight. Quick glance at my reflection in a window. Not bad, go for it girl. Five-four-three-two-one.

"Hi, Andreas. The shop's looking lovely. I see you've got some new pottery. Oh, hello, Rhea, I didn't see you there."

"Hello, Cheryl. Yes, Moisis and I have come over from Dissinos for a night out. Well, no, that's not quite right. Moisis is out on the town with a few of his mates and I'm doing what I do best, shopping. Enough about me, Cheryl. How's everything going?"

"Good, thanks, Rhea. The weddings are in full swing. Yes, everything's fine."

"If you'll excuse me, Cheryl. I need to chat to this couple about some paintings. I'll catch up with you later."

"I sense an atmosphere. Have you two fallen out?"

"Sort of, but it's a long story."

"Well, why don't we go out for drink? Have you eaten yet?"

"No, I was just... Well, I don't really know why I've come here, to be honest."

"Cheryl and I are going out, Andreas. We're going to go for something to eat. We'll meet you after the shop's closed. Hopefully Moisis will be back by then. We're staying here for the night as there's no way I'm getting in a boat at night after he's had a drink. Text me and I'll let you know where we are."

"That meal was really good. I always say that we'll try different restaurants when we come over to Holkamos, but I always end up here as the food's so lovely. I always sit at the same table too, so I can see everyone walking by.

"So, Cheryl, from what you say, you're in a bit of a pickle. One thing's for sure, Andreas knows you would never go off with Vangelis, but for this Clive chap to give up his life in England and follow you here, he must really want to win you back."

"But that's the stupid thing. He didn't have me in the first place, Rhea. I've gone through most of my adult life without a man in tow, and perhaps that's how it should stay. My little world was far simpler then."

"Don't give up, Cheryl. Fight for what you want. Both you and Andreas are so suited to each other. When I speak to him on the phone he sounds thrilled to bits with the way you've encouraged him with the shop. Winning him back is the easy bit. You can do that. However, the difficult bit will be getting his mum on your side, but if you can do that, you'll have a wonderful future.

181

"Now, come on. Let's leave all that to one side, go for a walk and find somewhere to sit and soak up the Greek holiday atmosphere."

I've had too much to eat and drink, so I'm walking home to try and work off some of the calories. It was a lovely evening. Rhea's so lovely. It's such a shame that she's not over here on Holkamos more often. Moisis is funny. I can see why they're staying the night. I think he'd probably fall asleep steering the boat.

Andreas didn't turn up after closing the shop, but I'm not surprised as deep down I didn't think he would. I'm not going to give up though. Rhea's right, I need to fight for him. As for his mum, I'm not going to get worked up about her. One step at a time.

I can't believe it's still so hot as it's nearly two in the morning. Where's my key? I can hear my bed calling me.

Oh, what's that in front of my door? Looks like flowers. They're beautiful and there's a card attached with just one word on it 'sorry'. I wonder who they're from. If it had been in Greek, it would either be Andreas or Vangelis, but seeing that it's in English, it could also be from Clive. They're lovely flowers, but not what I need before I go to bed. Just something else to worry about.

Chapter 33

"We've done it again, Cheryl. Another successful wedding! The bride and groom are over the moon with everything."

"All I did was take the booking and order the things in. You and your fabulous team of chefs and waiters made it a success, Vangelis."

"Yes, but you're a big part of that team, Cheryl."

"You may say that now, but you know what this means. We're just one wedding away from the big one, the celebrity wedding. After that you'll be wishing you'd never employed me let alone set eyes on me."

"The first half of that sentence could be right, but me setting eyes on you? Now that's something I'll never regret. You haven't just made my business a success, but you've taught me about myself and..."

"Enough of this, Vangelis. Come on, there's a couple more hours left of this one. Let's check whether any of the candles need replacing and make sure the chap knows what time to set the fireworks off. These people are having an amazing day, so let's make sure it ends on a high."

"Okay, boss, whatever you say. See, that's the thing with you, Cheryl, your attention to detail and the professionalism you bring to everything, and that's another thing you've taught me."

My feet are killing me. Thank goodness I've got tomorrow off to spend a day on the beach with Dad. I can't believe he's been here a week already. Enough time to switch off and enjoy himself, but I'm afraid it's time to discuss the future. That's one of the reasons he's come here, to think about his life and what he wants to do. Sorry, Dad, but tomorrow's the day to face up to your demons.

"Morning, Dad. I thought we could go onto the town

beach today instead of Volmos. I never seem able to relax properly with the restaurant behind me."

"Yes, that's fine with me, darling. How did the wedding go?"

"It went well, thanks, everyone was really happy with it. The next one's a very small one, the couple are just renewing their vows. It's their silver wedding anniversary, but it's the one after that I'm worried about. Anyway, that's enough about weddings. Let's stop off at the bakery and get some pastries to take with us. I can't believe you've been here a week already."

"Tell me about the vow renewal? What does that consist of and why would they want to do it?"

"Oh, this couple didn't really have a special wedding. It took place in a registry office and they were in a queue of other wedding ceremonies. Now they've got a little bit more money and it's their twenty-fifth wedding anniversary, they want to do something special. We've got quite a few of these booked. All the couples have different reasons for doing it. Some have been seriously ill, others want to share the day with their children, others have been through difficult times for all kinds of reasons.

"Here we are at the bakery. I want you to pick something full of fat and sugar. I'm having a vanilla slice and one of those bacon croissants. Actually I might have two. It's my day off."

"I'll have the same, Cheryl, and some of those biscuits in case we get peckish during the day."

"You're worse than me, Dad!"

"Yes, but I'm on holiday and you're not!"

Right, I need to broach the subject of Mum. With all the conversation this morning, there's been no mention of home. He's chatted about anything and everything and if he mentions the boats moored out there again, I'll scream.

"Look, Dad. You've one more week here on Holkamos, so let's get this over and done with, and then we can relax."

"It's so hot, Cheryl. Let's have another swim, or do you fancy an ice cream?"

"Enough, Dad, we're going to have a talk now, and then you can go for a swim or do whatever you want to do. What's going to happen when you go home? You can't just ignore the problem? Have you discussed the future with Mum, and what does she want to do?"

"We've not discussed the future at all, just the past. She told me that she didn't love me when we got married and the guilt she feels about making me work every hour God sent. The only good part about those years was having you and Julie, but then she says other things."

"What other things, Dad?"

"Oh, just things."

"Dad, please tell me."

"Cheryl, don't upset yourself because none of this is your fault. Your Mum loves you so much, but she tried to live the life she wanted through Julie. She admits now that neither you nor I ever came into it, but now she knows how wrong she was."

"It doesn't upset me at all, Dad. I've known all that for years. As a child I didn't understand it, but once I became a teenager I just accepted it. I was never jealous of Julie with all her singing, dancing and special outfits. I was just thankful that it wasn't me. I would have hated being Julie, and to be honest even now I wouldn't swap places with her."

"Yes, but it was wrong. Your Mum should have treated you both equally."

"Dad, you're wandering off the subject. All that was the past. What's going to happen when you get back to England? You can't carry on like this. Something needs to be resolved."

"I know, darling, but things are different. I can't remember the last time she nagged me or asked for something. If anything, it's the other way around

185

now. She's telling me to take days off from work, the shopping bill's cut right down and that's something I would never have believed would ever happen. She loves her little job too. She's different, believe me, Cheryl."

"But, Dad, she doesn't love you. Why would you want to be with someone who doesn't care for you?"

"I really don't know what to do. I thought coming here would help the situation, but the problem is that I've had too much time to think. I've loved being here on the island with you, Cheryl, but I'd give anything to go back to my old life even if it was with your mother nagging. I really do miss that life."

"Oh, Dad, I'm so sorry. I don't know what to say or what I can do to help the situation."

"There's nothing anybody can do – only your Mum and I can sort things, and that's something I'm going to have to come to terms with."

Well, I've messed that up. As much as I wanted to help and find out what was going on, I seem to have made things worse now. Perhaps I should go back to the UK for a couple of days and talk to them both together. Really I think they just need to split up and go their separate ways, but more importantly start to build new lives for themselves.

"Here's your ice cream, Cheryl. I hope it's okay. There wasn't much choice so I ended up with two plain vanilla ices. See, my darling, I can't even make my mind up about an ice cream, let alone my marriage. It's all a bit of a mess."

"Now, come on, Dad. Things will sort themselves out soon, I'm sure of it. You've got another week here to think things through before you go home, so how do you fancy some more Greek dancing tonight?"

"Not really, Cheryl. All that rushing around I was doing was my way of avoiding talking about everything."

"Well, we've discussed it now, Dad, and there's nothing you can do while you're here on Holkamos, so why not just make the most of the week here and enjoy your holiday? See how things are with Mum when you get back and talk about what she wants to do.

"As for Greek dancing, you may not want to, but I do. Let's go out tonight and have lots to drink and plenty of laughs. I'll meet you on the jetty at eight o'clock sharp. I'm off to do some paperwork first, and by the way, make sure you've got some comfortable shoes on. We'll be on our feet all night."

Chapter 34

I'm pleased that Dad and I had a chat, but it hasn't been mentioned again since. It's for Mum and Dad to sort out when he gets back to England. The good thing is we've had such a lovely time. Today he's going over to Paxos on a boat trip and I've got the final preparations for the silver wedding couple's big day. I also need to pop over to see Johnny as he's got some news about Clive. He did tell me not to get excited, Clive hasn't left Holkamos.

The mystery of the flowers I found left on my door step hasn't been resolved. I've seen Vangelis' handwriting, but I don't think it's his. Who's to say someone in the florists didn't write it? Anyway, they're beautiful flowers, whoever sent them.

Another email from Carla to say she'll be arriving on the Thursday before the celebrity wedding and would like a meeting at the restaurant. I wonder if this will be when we'll get to meet the bridal couple. I'd love to meet them before the big day. You never know, I might never have heard of them, and that would be embarrassing. Enough of that, let's go and see Johnny before going to the office.

"Good morning, all. How's everyone today? I must be the only person who keeps coming into this salon and walks out looking the same!"

"Hi, Cheryl. My new assistant can give you a makeover, if you'd like. What do you say to that?"

"Nico, I'll say, 'Been there, done that, never again' thanks very much'."

"Well, Cheryl, yes, granted it wasn't the Cheryl I love, but you did look fabulous and it did wipe the smiles off a few faces."

"And put the fear of God into me that I'd never look like the real me again."

"Right, I've just got one lady's hair to wash, so why don't I meet you down by the bakery in ten minutes?

Could you nip in and get us a coffee and a cake, please?"

"Okay. See you in a bit. Bye for now, Nico."

I think just being in the salon on a bad day would cheer you up even without having your hair done. It's too early for Andreas to be opening his shop. Let's have a quick look in the window. It's looking so fresh now, and I just love the window display. The sage green pottery is stunning and I'm pleased to see he's put three of his paintings in the other window. They're very different from his usual landscape style though. Very abstract and with rather strange titles – 'Can't smile', 'No smile', and 'Never smile'. How sad is that? He must have painted them after his wedding episode. Oh dear, perhaps he just wants to sell them to get rid of the memories.

"Hi, Cheryl, do you like them?"

"Hi, Andreas. Yes, I love the paintings. I could see them all grouped together on a large white painted wall. If I'm honest though, I'm not sure about the titles. They're a bit sad, aren't they? The actual paintings are very happy, the colours and freshness just bounce off the canvas."

"Thanks. I painted them over two nights last week, and that's the first words that came into my head."

"Andreas, I don't want you to be sad. I want to see your smile. Can we talk, please?"

"Hi, Andreas. Come on, Cheryl. I've only got half an hour before my next appointment. See you, Andreas."

"Hi, Johnny, and yes, Cheryl, I'd like that. See you later."

"Haven't you got the coffees yet? Come on, I'll come with you."

Of all the times to have to meet Johnny. Andreas must be really upset to have given the paintings those titles, but I've done nothing wrong.

"Come on, here's your coffee and cake. Let me sit over there on the harbour wall."

189

"Thanks, Johnny. So, what's the news on the Clive front? By the way, he's stopped phoning and sending me texts, so that's a good thing."

"Well, my darling, I told Nico all about the situation and he came up with an idea. Nico knows a girl called Mimi who comes into the salon to get her nails done. She's a waitress in the restaurant where Clive works. She told Nico that after work Clive goes straight home instead of going out partying like a lot of the restaurant workers do. Nico asked Mimi to persuade Clive to go out with them, introduce him to some girls and if he eventually finds himself a girlfriend, he'll let her have her nails done for free. Mimi jumped at the chance. She even said she'd date him for free nails, but I think she was only joking."

"I suppose if he goes out socialising more he'll enjoy himself even if he doesn't find himself a girlfriend and that should take his mind off me. Thanks, Johnny, and give Nico a big thank you hug from me. Whatever would I do without you, Johnny?"

"Like the song says, Cheryl. 'That's what friends are for! Now, tell me, are you and Andreas back on speaking terms? It looked like it to me."

"Not quite, but I'm working on it. I just need to wait until Dad goes home on Sunday. Then we have the big celebrity wedding to contain with."

"Oh, yes, the wedding, but I still don't understand why it's to be held at the beach café and not at the big villa. Apparently, one of the cleaning staff was telling our cleaner at the salon that the security guards have already been assessing the villa for risk. It's all a big mystery. The villa looks more like a prison with all the security measures so no one can see in, yet Vangelis' café is open for all the world to see. I know one thing and that's I won't be washing anyone's hair when it starts. I'll be there on a sunbed right in front, even if it's the evening, I'll just bring a blanket.

"Oh, and another thing, two huge black Range Rovers with blacked out windows have been hired and are already up at the villa."

"To be honest, Johnny, I just want it over and done with as I can see it being a complete shambles. This was supposed to all be a secret, but all of Holkamos seems to be mentioning it to Vangelis now. I think the beach will be packed. I'm looking forward more to this weekend's wedding, small, quiet and very special to the couple and their family."

"Right, my darling. I'll have to love you and leave you. My public await me back in the salon. Well, just Karen from the ice cream shop. Have a lovely day, Cheryl. Why don't you go back and chat to Andreas?"

"I don't think so. I need to get to the office now. Thanks again for everything, Johnny. Love you lots."

I wish I'd taken the day off and gone to Paxos with Dad instead, but saying that I need to get on top of my work. The lovely anniversary couple arrive today and are popping in at six o'clock. I think I'll text Dad and get him to meet me at work and then we can walk up to Creakos for a meal. He hasn't been up to the hill town yet. Right, let me check their file. Ten guests plus the wedding couple, the menu is straightforward. Arrive at 5.30, eat at 7.00. Drinks until 12 with just background music. No disco. Everything's sorted.

"Morning, Vangelis. You haven't forgotten that the wedding couple are coming in at six o'clock, have you? It's not a problem though. It's very straightforward and I can deal with it if you've got other things you need to be getting on with."

"Yes, I was going to pop over to Preveza to get some alcohol, but that can wait until tomorrow."

"No, you go. I'll be fine with them. I won't be saying that next week. Oh, I'm dreading it. Apparently, they have security guards up at the villa. It will be fun if they come down here. There's no privacy whatsoever."

"Yes, but we've told them all the negative things and tried to put them off. Please stop getting worked up about it, Cheryl. It is what it is, and I'll see you later."

Vangelis is right. Perhaps that's the attitude I need to take. I wish I could get Andreas' paintings out of my mind though. I hope someone buys them. Perhaps then Andreas will paint three happier titles. I just want things to return to how they were before all this Clive business.

Right, enough of the daydreaming. Back to the paperwork.

"Hello, it's Mary and Bob, isn't it? I'm Cheryl, welcome to Holkamos and Volmos beach. We're so looking forward to your special day."

"Thank you, Cheryl. Yes, now we've arrived here on the island, it's getting very real and exciting."

"I have your file upstairs in my office. Give me two minutes to go and get it. Oh, hello, Dad. Have you had a good day? I'll be about half an hour if you want to get yourself a drink from the bar."

"I'm so sorry. That two minutes was more like ten. I had to take a call from a very annoying PR person. Now, here we are. I'll just go over the checklist."

"No problem. We've been chatting to your Dad. He's been telling us all about his holiday and we've told him all about our reason for being here. It's been lovely."

"Here's the file. There's nothing else I need to know from you. Do you have any questions for me? Is there anything you'd like to change?"

"No, Cheryl. Bob and I are very happy with everything. We just want the special occasion to arrive now. It's getting exciting. Twenty-five years behind us and hopefully another twenty-five years ahead of us. It's going to be lovely. Thanks again for everything, Cheryl."

"Are you ready for a walk, Dad. It will take about three quarters of an hour to walk up to Creakos, but you can see for miles once you get to the top. Are you hungry?"

"Yes, I'm starving. All I've had is a sandwich. They seemed to be a nice couple, Cheryl. What a lovely thing to be doing. I really hope they have a great day with their family."

"If you're that hungry, Dad, you need to step on it a bit. Come on, best foot forward and all of that."

Dad seems very quiet. I know the walk up in the heat was difficult, but he's quite fit and he easily managed it. He seems distracted though, and when he did chat to me over dinner he kept mentioning the couple he met in the restaurant. I suppose it's sad that they're renewing their vows and he's going to be getting a divorce. That must be horrible for him.

"I thought you must have been flushed away in the toilets. You've been ages, Dad. Is everything okay?"

"Oh, sorry, Cheryl. Yes, I was talking to a couple who had a pair of binoculars. They were looking at a property down the hill where's there's a kind of a marquee being put up. The owner here explained that the villa must have someone famous coming to stay. The tent thing goes up so the paparazzi can't take any photos. It seems all very exciting."

"That's not the word I'd use. Now are you ready for the walk back down to Holkamos?"

"Yes, I can manage it, thanks, Cheryl. I hadn't eaten much all day, but I've certainly made up for it tonight. The food was lovely and Creakos is a beautiful little village. I'm so glad we came up here. I know what else I was going to ask. The wedding couple for this coming weekend. Is it costing them much? I know you said Julie's wedding was very good value and since then Vangelis has put the price up."

"No, it's not overly expensive. They're paying twenty-five euros per person for the food and the drinks. Flowers and bits and pieces are extras and that's where we make more money with all the add ons. Anyway, why do you ask?"

"I'm just interested in your job, Cheryl, that's all. Now come on. I'll race you to the bottom. Last one down buys the wine."

"I won't be running anywhere, and I don't have a problem buying the wine. It's been a lovely evening, Dad. You were very quiet to start with, but you've perked up now. Let's see how you are when we get to the bottom."

"I'm feeling good, thanks, Cheryl. I'm really pleased that it's been such an interesting holiday. I came here to think things through, and I really think I've been able to do that."

Chapter 35

"Hi, Moisis."

"Hello, Cheryl. Are you coming over to Dissinos? Rhea will be so happy. I don't think she'll get much work done once the pair of you start chatting. Hop on board. How are things going?"

"Fine, thanks. I've just seen my dad off to go back to the airport. He's been here on holiday for two weeks. We had a lovely wedding at the restaurant yesterday, but I'm gearing up for a nightmare week, so I thought I'd switch off from it all for one day and come over to Dissinos."

"Good for you. We won't be leaving for a few minutes, so take a seat and enjoy the early morning sunshine."

"Thanks, Moisis."

Well, I'm tired, but it's been a lovely couple of weeks with Dad. I really think he's enjoyed himself and hopefully the holiday's given him time to think about what he wants to do when he and Mum split up. It's a new start for both of them. I wish he'd have let me go to the airport with him, but I suppose he's right. It's a long way by taxi boat just to say goodbye for five minutes and then have to travel all the way back. He realises I'm tired after yesterday's wedding.

I knew the wedding would be lovely, although different, and it was better than I could have imagined because all the guests wanted to be there to see Mary and Bob renew their vows. That made their day, and it's a special thing to be doing. What a way to celebrate 25 years of marriage than to show your other half how much you still love them? And for their children to witness it, that's just wonderful!

"Cheryl, we're ready to go now. Not too many people on board today as Sunday's are always rather quiet on Dissinos. By the way, how's that naughty Vangelis? Is he still breaking holiday makers hearts or is he concentrating on the wedding business?"

"A bit of both, I think. Deep down he's a good guy, but he just has a bit of a weakness for the young ladies. I hope he settles down before it's too late. He needs to start thinking about finding a more stable relationship rather than trying to keep up with the eighteen-year-old lads."

"Dare I ask how Andreas is?"

"Oh, Moisis, don't ask. Nothing's really changed between us. We did have a quick chat the other day, but Andreas knew that my dad was here, so I think he stayed out of the way. Perhaps now Dad's gone back home, I might see a bit more of Andreas, who knows?"

"I'm sure it will sort itself out soon, Cheryl, but today just switch off from everything, have a day to yourself and enjoy the beautiful island of Dissinos."

"I will, thanks."

Yes, Moisis is right. I need to switch off from everything, Andreas, Dad, Clive, and most importantly weddings, just for one day. There is something I can't get out of my mind though and that's where do I go at the end of the season? I won't have a job or anywhere to live. The last thing I want to do is go back to Mum and Dad's. I don't even know whether they'll still be together or will have separate homes by then. Grandma's little place only has one bedroom and no Internet connection.

That's something else I need to consider as I'll have weddings to organise still. I know Johnny and Nico would let me stay with them for a while, but they need their space too. No, I need to find a short term contract catering job somewhere. As soon as I get this damned wedding over and done with I'll start applying for jobs which offer accommodation. However, today's a day of pure indulgence: sun, sea and ice cream.

"Hello, hello, what are you doing here, Cheryl?"

"Hi, Rhea. I needed a day away from everything

and where's better to come than Dissinos?"

"Away from everything or someone in particular?"

"Well, yes you're right, but not just one person. Anyway, that's another story. How are you?"

"I'm fine thanks, but I'm feeling even better now you're here to chat to, Cheryl, although you might just want to relax and lie in the sun."

"Oh, a chat and ice cream on the beach. My perfect day! First of all though I'd like to go for a swim. I'll catch up with you later, if that's alright."

It's like getting into a warm bath, yet I'm the only one here. I can't believe how special this place is turning out to be. It's my perfect summer! When I think back to my time in Dartmouth, it was such a stunning part of the UK to live and it was a great job, but if it wasn't for that I'd never be doing what I'm doing now.

I've got so much to thank Graham and the hotel for. It's just such a shame that the place is in such a mess now. I don't really blame Suzy. I know she doesn't have a clue how to do things, but Graham shouldn't have spoilt her. Why didn't he teach her how to run the business properly and why didn't she want to be with him working together rather than out spending all the profits? Perhaps if I hadn't given her the job in the first place, all this mess would have been avoided. Now she's there with three of her management team having left. I do feel slightly guilty about that, but I needed to move on. I need to find the real me and well, what a place to come to!

How lucky I am, and to think it all started with Julie wanting me to be a size six with long flowing locks and a face full of makeup. That was the last time I'm ever going to look how anyone else wants me to. No, these last few months have taught me to be myself. I'm not that catering manager in Devon running to everyone's beck and call. I'm not that sister and daughter who just keeps agreeing with everything to keep them happy. No, I'm me, Cheryl

Harris, the girl who's taken 29 years to find herself. Now that I've found myself, I'm certainly not going to let that go.

"Hi, can I join you, Cheryl? Moisis is looking after the café. It's very quiet today, so he'll spend his time with his head in a book. Did you enjoy your swim?"

"Yes, Rhea, it was so lovely that I didn't want to get out of the sea. Volmos beach is quite special, but I think Dissinos is paradise. You're so lucky to live here."

"Yes, we know that and never forget it. I count my blessings every day. Now, tell me what's happening with you and Andreas."

"Nothing, nothing, nothing. All I know is that he's sad. Not that's he's told me that exactly, but I've seen a few of the pictures he's painted these last few weeks and I feel bad. He's been through enough over the years."

"No, Cheryl, you shouldn't feel bad at all. None of this is your fault. Andreas needs to realise that, but if it's all over with he needs to man up. That's what I tell him every time we meet up. I think the real problem is his mum. She won't let him forget it. There's no shame on his part, but she can't see that if it wasn't for the death of his father, Andreas would never have come back to live on Holkamos and that might have been a good thing. That said, if he hadn't returned, he wouldn't have met you and you're exactly what he needs in his life.

"I really could slap him, Cheryl. He'll never find anyone as special as you, and both Moisis and I have told him so."

"That's kind of you, Rhea. I don't know if I'm special, but I'm different from most I suppose. I really did think we could make a go of it. Well, I'd like to try."

"That's the right attitude to have, Cheryl. Now, how's the other man in your life, Vangelis? Is he still trying to get you into bed? Please tell me you haven't,

198

as you'd go right down in my estimation. Saying that though, I can't talk as I once did that myself."

"You had sex with Vangelis?"

"Yes, but we were young at the time. It was more than twenty years ago now. It was winter time and lots of silly things happen on the Greek islands when everything's shut down. We have to find ways of entertaining ourselves until the holidaymakers return in the spring. Alcohol was involved, so that's my excuse, and it was only the once."

"So was it good? Are all the rumours about him true?"

"Cheryl, they're more than true. It was fabulous. Vangelis was good, very, very good."

"I'm shocked, Rhea. Does Moisis know about it?"

"Yes. We were all mates at the time and it was years before Moisis and I got together. Like I said, I don't think we were even out of our twenties. Things like that happen on a little island like this. No one gives it much thought afterwards, it's all part of growing up, and I can assure you it wouldn't happen with Vangelis again, even if I was single."

"Oh, Rhea, you've such a lovely life here in Greece. I'm so jealous."

"Don't be silly, Cheryl. You could also have a lovely life here. All you have to do is convince Andreas and his mum that you're the right woman for him. It's as simple as that."

"Piece of cake, I don't think. Anyway, that's enough of all that talk. I've had a swim and a chat. Now for the ice cream. Shall we walk up and see if that handsome husband of yours will sell us one."

"He is handsome and very special, but I don't tell him that too often in case he gets big headed. I don't want him turning into Vangelis, otherwise I'd never know what's going on in that boat of his."

That was a lovely day on Dissinos, but it's nice to be back on my little terrace with a bottle of wine. Rhea and Moisis are such a nice couple and it's so good to think I'm the right person for Andreas. I know they wouldn't say it if they didn't mean it. Rhea's an angel.

I knew the rumours about Vangelis had to be true and that it's not just the eyes. Anyway, I'm certainly not going to become another one in his fan club. No, we'll just keep it as employer and employee. Better than that, we'll stay friends. As for Andreas, I'm beginning to realise that it's nothing to do with Clive. Clive's just some sort of excuse or obstacle that Andreas is putting in the way. I just need to make him see it's about us and no one or anything else.

It's really been such a lovely day not having phones ringing. Would you believe it, the minute I think that, the phone rings. It's okay, it's Dad.

"Hi, Dad. Are you back home now? How was your flight?"

"It was good thanks. Yes, I'm back, but I just wanted to thank you for a lovely holiday. It was just what I needed. You live in a gorgeous part of the world and it's done me the world of good. I really feel as though I've cleared my head and I do realise that I need to sort things out with your mum. Time for a fresh start."

"I'm glad you're alright with it all now. You know you're welcome here anytime, Dad. I've enjoyed having you here so much. We always were a good team, you and I."

"Yes, Cheryl, and we'll continue to be a good team, always there for each other whatever happens. I love you, Cheryl."

"I love you too, Dad, and whatever you decide to do now I'm behind you one hundred per cent. I feel there's exciting times ahead for both of us, and do you know something? We both deserve it."

"Yes, we certainly do. Night, night, darling, sleep well, it's a whole new day tomorrow."

"Yes. Night, Dad, love you lots."

Chapter 36

After what seems to have been years in the planning, the celebrity wedding will take place in a few days' time. PR Carla is arriving tomorrow and seems more stressed than I am. All my other paperwork is complete until next week, so in two hours' time after I've eaten three vanilla slices, drunk two large strong coffees, I'll make my way to work. That will keep me occupied until the day's over.

A quick hello to Nico and Johnny and my social life will then switch off to become celeb, celeb, celeb.

"Morning, guys, how are we today?"

"Just the person we want to see. Johnny said he was going to text you. Johnny, Cheryl's here."

"Hi, darling. Are you getting excited? I am."

"Excited about what, Johnny?"

"Well, the big wedding of course. I can't wait! Apparently staff have arrived up at the villa doing all sorts and I've been told by a very reliable source that they're staying for a week. Go on, Cheryl. Ask me how I know that."

"Johnny, how do you know that?"

"I'm glad you've asked me that, Cheryl, because a large cruise boat has been booked for a week and a huge speed boat will bring them here from Preveza. By the way, if you knew who the mystery celebrity couple were, you wouldn't keep it from me, would you? We've never had secrets from each other, have we?"

"I don't know and to be honest, Johnny, I don't really care anymore. It could be the Royal family for all I'm bothered."

"Oh, don't be like that. It will be fun, as well as being great for the wedding business."

"I know, of course it will, and I'll be over the moon to see this famous couple in all the magazines and newspapers.

"Right, I'd best get myself over to Volmos. Do I look alright to face the paparazzi hiding in the trees? I'm joking! See you both at some point and I promise the minute I know who the happy couple are, you'll be the first to know. Love you lots."

"Oh, Cheryl, before you go, I've got some news regarding your little problem, and I'm sorry to say that it's not good. When Clive went out with all the staff the other evening people were asking him why he was working here, and he gave everyone the same reply that he was here to win you back. Sorry, darling, but like Nico said it's early days. We'll get there eventually, just not as fast as we'd hoped."

"That's the least of my worries for this week, but thanks, anyway. Love you both. Bye."

No sea taxi today, but a nice walk up to the castle and then down the other side to Volmos. It's really hot and the beaches will be busy. I'd love to be going over to Dissinos and see Rhea for the week and then come back when it's all over, but like the boys said, the publicity will do the wedding business the world of good. Also, people may want to book week day weddings. They don't have to always be weekends, we can cater for weddings any day of the week.

There's a text from Julie saying she'd like to have a chat as Dad's come back from his holiday very happy. I'll send a quick text back, "Sorry, can't talk. Just eating three vanilla slices." I'm lying to her as I've only eaten one. I'm saving one for later and the third one's for Vangelis. It will be interesting how he plays this week. Although he doesn't have any patience with all this messing around and the planning, he will realise that this could lead to big business which means more money in his pocket.

From up here at the castle I can just about see the roof of the villa, but I can't see where they put that tent thing up. I'd kill to be able to look around and get some clues as to who the wedding couple are. Perhaps I'm getting a little bit excited, just like

Johnny.

"Morning, Cheryl. How are you today? I'm so glad you're here as I'm so nervous. What happens if it all goes wrong and we get the blame for it?"

"Vangelis, you're normally the laid back one and I'm the worrier. Now get us a couple of coffees as I've brought you a present. I'll go and sit in the shade and wait for you."

I need Vangelis to calm down. At the end of the day they're only renting the premises from us, we're not supplying anything, so really we shouldn't be getting worked up about any of it."

"One coffee for madam. Now, where's my present?"

"I wouldn't get too excited. It's only a vanilla slice."

"Thanks, Cheryl, you know the way to my heart. Well, one of the ways to my heart."

"Enough of that. This isn't the time to be messing around. I've had my daily email from Carla and she seems to be very stressed. She'll be here tomorrow evening, so we need to make sure the place is shipshape. Are you listening to me, Vangelis? Who are you staring at?"

"That couple walking towards us, Sharon and Brian. They've been coming here every year since I can remember. They eat lunch in the restaurant every day. We've been out for dinner lots of times and their daughter... Oh, no, I think the penny's dropped."

"What are you saying, Vangelis?"

"Hello, welcome back to you both. It's so lovely to see you again. It doesn't seem five minutes since you were here. Can I introduce you to Cheryl? Cheryl, this is Sharon and Brian, my two best, and loveliest customers here in the restaurant."

"It's really nice to meet you, Cheryl. Are you Vangelis' girlfriend? We've been telling him for years that he needs a nice girl to settle down with."

"Sorry to disappoint you both, but no, I only work for this handsome chap. We best make him feel good,

Sharon."

"So it's your first day. Let me guess. Two half of lagers and two club sandwiches, am I right?"

"You're spot on, Vangelis. You know us too well."

"Right, I'll go and get someone to sort that for you. Excuse me a moment."

"You obviously know the island very well, and this restaurant too."

"Oh, yes, we came here on our first holiday together and then when our daughter was born we came here all the time. It's such a beautiful island and so safe. You wouldn't catch us going anywhere else. Well, we do pop over to America from time to time, but not coming here for a holiday every year would feel very strange."

"Here we go. Two half lagers and I've brought us one as well, Cheryl."

"Thank you, Vangelis. So how long are you here for, Brian."

"Two weeks. Yes, we always come for a fortnight twice a year, don't we, Sharon?"

"Yes, Brian, but this holiday is very special for us."

"Oh, that's nice. Where are you both staying?"

"Oh, that's part of it being very special. We're in a villa up the hill. To be honest, it's not our type of thing, but as our daughter's paying for it we don't like to tell her that we'd sooner be in one of the little studio apartments behind the beach."

"Is your daughter with you?"

"Well, yes and no, she's coming in a few days all the way from America."

"That will be a nice family holiday."

"Yes, but it's a bit more exciting than that as we're here to get married. You see, we've never bothered about it before, but our daughter, Bella's been on about it for years. She organised everything. All we have to do is turn up. We'd only want something small, but she's organised everything up at the villa, wedding reception everything."

"Oh my God, it's their wedding and the famous person is their daughter. They obviously don't know it's taking place down here in the restaurant and that's why it has to be here as it's their favourite place in the whole world. It's all making sense now. But who is the daughter?"

"Sharon, Brian, if you don't mind me asking, but is your daughter famous and would I know of her?"

"Yes, if you like opera you'd know her. She's Bella Lacywhite. That's her stage name though, not our surname."

"You mean, your daughter's the world famous singer who's one of the greatest singers of our time? Oh, that explains everything now."

"Sorry, what explains everything?"

"I was getting slightly confused about things, but am I right in saying that your daughter's boyfriend is none other than Riven Raven, one of the top American actors?"

"Yes, that's right, and we're so excited, aren't we, Brian, because Riven's flying over with Bella to be at the wedding."

Chapter 37

I don't know whether I'm angry at Carla for not telling us or I'm sorry for the nightmare she's had to organise. I'm so glad I met Sharon and Brian yesterday as at least we now understand what's happening. I'm still not too happy with Vangelis. How many times over the last few weeks have I said to him that he must know who these famous people are, and surprise, surprise, he did know that Sharon and Brian's daughter was a world famous opera singer. If he'd mentioned that it would have only taken me a second on Google to find out who her partner was. We might have got it wrong in thinking that it was them getting married rather than her mum and dad, but at least we would have had names.

So do I email Carla and let her know that I know all about it or should I be kind or sarcastic? No, the poor woman has a nightmare week coming up. I'll be very gentle.

'Hi, Carla. Looking forward to meeting you later today. Vangelis and I had a lovely couple of hours yesterday with Sharon and Brian. We didn't let the cat out of the bag and they have no idea about the wedding taking place down on the beach. It's going to be such a lovely surprise for them. Have a safe journey. Looking forward to meeting you this evening. Love, Cheryl xx'

Sent. That's all done. Now to think of ways in which we can capitalise on this wedding. I think the first thing we need to consider are prices for anyone who enquires. It's good that we don't have Bella and Riven on the website, and even better that we don't have a celebrity couple getting married. We just need a couple of photos of Bella and Riven with a named caption saying they're attending a wedding on Volmos beach, wedding venue. Something along those lines. Also, if we can get people to take photos on their phones and send them out on social media with the hashtag of Volmos beach...

An email back from Carla with just two words and a kiss –'Thank you x'. I'm sure we can help her to keep calm. I would imagine she has enough to worry about up at the villa. I'd love to be a fly on the wall up there. I know what I have forgotten, I promised the minute I find out who the celebrities are, I'd let Johnny now. He will die when he finds out. I need to hear his reaction, so I'll phone him and perhaps have a laugh at his expense.

"Hi, Johnny, how are you? I've found out who they are."

"Oh? I'm all ears. Who?"

"Well, it's rather strange actually, as they're only guests at the wedding."

"Tell me."

"So it's Sharon and Brian who are getting married."

"Cheryl, you're winding me up. Tell me who they are."

"It's Sharon and Brian's daughter who's the famous one and her boyfriend."

"Cheryl, stop teasing me. I'm waiting to hear their names."

I think I can make him even madder. What if I make a noise when I actually say the names? A toilet flush should do the job. I'm wicked, but he knows I'm only joking, so here goes.

"Oh, the famous people's names, Johnny. Well it's... how fabulous is that?"

"Now I know you're taking the piss, Cheryl. You're playing games with me. You know I didn't catch any of that."

"I'm sorry, Johnny, but I just wanted to have a bit of fun with you. Are you sitting down with something to hold onto? Drum roll... Bella Lacywhite and Riven Raven. Are you there? Johnny?"

"You're joking. You mean, Riven Raven's coming

to Holkamos and I'll be meeting him?"

"Sorry, how are you meeting him?"

"Didn't I tell you, Cheryl? I'm volunteering to work for free that day as your PA."

"Do I need a PA? You're so funny, Johnny. Of course I do, it's exciting, isn't it?"

"Exciting? It's bloody fabulous, darling. After I tell Nico, I promise I won't say a word to anyone, Scout's honour. Got to go now. Speak later. Now to think about what to wear for the big day."

What's he like? It is rather exciting though, and to think that Bella could have chosen anywhere in the world for her parents' wedding, but she chose the one place that her mum and dad love; a place which means so much to them. How lovely is that! What wonderful daughter she must be. I get the impression she won't be a diva. I really think it's going to be a beautiful few hours on the beach.

Enough of the sentimentality, Cheryl. It's your job to sell weddings and this is the greatest bit of publicity you'll ever have. Vangelis needs to give them a wedding present. He's known them for years, but I bet he hasn't thought of that. It has to be something made on the island of Holkamos. I know, a painting of Volmos. Now I wonder where I could get one of those from? I think this is called killing two birds with one stone.

"Hi, Andreas. How are you?"

"I'm fine, thanks. I've spoken to Rhea and she said you'd been back over to Dissinos. I'm so jealous. I don't get to go as much as I would like to. It's such a lovely place."

"Yes, it really is special, and I love it there.

"I was wondering if you could help me, Andreas. You know we've got this big wedding. Well, I need a gift for the happy couple. They've been coming to Holkamos for many years as it's their favourite place in the world. Would you have a painting of Volmos beach? By the way, you won't believe who the two famous guests are. None other than Bella Lacywhite and her boyfriend, Riven Raven."

"So, they're going to be here on Holkamos. That would explain all the comings and goings up at the villa. Apparently loads of things have been taken up. How exciting is that!"

"I know! I'm beginning to think the whole day will be taken out of our control, but that's certainly not a problem and we need the publicity. The more weddings I can sell, the more successful the business becomes and the most important thing...'

"Vangelis makes more money."

"No, Andreas, that's not it at all. What I was going to say was... the longer I'll be able to live and work on this beautiful island because I feel it's becoming my home and I want it to be a forever home."

"I'm sorry, Cheryl. I didn't really mean that. I was just being stupid. I do have a few paintings if you want to have a look at them, but not many of Volmos. Actually, I do have some at home. They're not framed, but that wouldn't take too long to do."

"How about you choose one you consider to be appropriate, Andreas, and I'll come back when it's ready. I do need it for Saturday though."

"Okay, I'll go through some, and I'm sorry I said that, but it's just that I miss you and wish I was the one spending time with you, not Vangelis."

"You could be spending time with me when I'm not working. What you have to remember, Andreas, is that this was your doing, not mine. You're the one that's screwed up about Vangelis and Clive. Let me get this wedding over with and then I'll have more time to give you. Andreas, I miss you very much."

"And I miss you too, Cheryl, I really do. Give me a few days and I'll get the painting ready. Hope this week goes well for you and Vangelis and I do mean that."

"Thanks."

Little steps and you might get there! Andreas

seems to be warming to me again. Well, I really hope so! Enough of that, now to get ready to meet Carla. If Vangelis can switch on the charm, that may calm her down.

"Hello! It's Cheryl, isn't it?"

"Hi, Sharon. Are you getting excited? The sea taxi back to Volmos shouldn't be very long. Where's Brian today?"

"Brian's on the beach. I've just come over to go to the jewellers as I wanted to get something for Bella. It seems silly really when you think of all the expensive jewellery she has, but I want her to have something as a remembrance of this special week."

"I'm sure Bella will make the week very special for you with lots of surprises, but if it was your choice to plan a special day here, how would you do it?"

"I know exactly what I'd do. It wouldn't be in some fancy hotel or restaurant with posh tables. I'd want somewhere on the beach. Yes, Vangelis' beach restaurant and have one big round table with everyone sitting around it so they don't have their backs to each other. In the middle I'd have a fabulous flower arrangement with scented candles. I'd have Bella's CDs playing in the background and some beautiful Greek food and lots of local wine. None of that fancy sparkly stuff that makes you belch. Very informal. Yes, that would be perfect for me and I know Brian would like that too. When we've been to big posh functions with Bella he gets so nervous and anxious as we're very low key people.

"Here comes the sea taxi, Cheryl. Don't you just love this little ride, or sail or whatever you call it? It's best at night when all the lights are twinkling in the water. This is a magical place. You're so lucky to live here."

"What's stopping you and Brian coming more often? Without being rude, surely you could now that Bella is so famous."

"Brian's what's stopping us. He won't let Bella

spend her money on us. Even when she puts money in our bank account, he won't spend it. The only thing he's allow her to pay for is flights to and fro from America to visit her and take us out for meals. He's so stubborn. The only way he agreed for her to pay for the wedding was if it was held here on the island."

"Whatever your daughter's planned for you will be special and you'll both have a lovely day."

"Yes, you're probably right, but I'd just prefer it not to be too posh because we really aren't that type."

Oh dear. We haven't got a circular table. Everything's very formal and the complete opposite to what Sharon wants, but that's what her daughter has requested. Poor Carla is only carrying out Bella's instructions. Should I throw that spanner in the works and tell her what Sharon said? If anything it would save money, but then money isn't the issue here. I won't mention any of this to Vangelis though. I'll just see how things go with Carla first.

I have a few hours before Carla arrives, so I'll call Julie. I'm fed up with all her texts but she might have some news about Mum and Dad.

"Hi, Julie. Sorry I've not got back to you. How's everything?"

"How would I know? You're the one who's spent two weeks with Dad? I don't know what happened over there in Greece, but all I get from him is that he's thought things through and there are going to be changes. What changes, Cheryl?"

"I don't know what you're talking about. I've done nothing apart from giving Dad a nice holiday."

"Well, you must have said something. Do you know what he's been up to?"

"No, but are you going to tell me, Julie, or do I have to play a guessing game with you?"

"There's no need for sarcasm. He's viewing houses. He spent two whole days looking at properties, so what's all that about?"

"I don't have a clue. He didn't say anything to me about that. Now, was there anything else you want to shout about before I get back to work?"

"No, apart from the fact I liked the old Cheryl a lot better. I really don't like the way you've changed."

"Oh, you mean the old Cheryl, who spent her life playing second fiddle. No, we can't do that because Julie has to go here, there and everywhere. Can't you see Julie needs these things? Julie this, Julie that. Well, I put up with it for years. You were spoilt by Mum from day one and now you're clicking your fingers and poor Richard is at your beck and call. I suggest you start thinking of others before yourself and your needs, Julie."

"That's nasty, Cheryl. I do think of Richard. I've agreed he can go out with the lads one night a week and play snooker instead of being at home doing DIY."

"Oh, isn't he lucky! Right, I must go. As for Mum and Dad, whatever they decide to do with their lives is their business and I'll support both of them. I suggest you do the same. Goodbye, Julie."

Well, do I feel better for that? Not really. Although I know what I said was true, I shouldn't have said it to her. Now back to work. Let's see if I can put an alternative plan on paper for Sharon and Brian's big day. What do I need? Table seating, food, flowers, music. Oh, God, I need to get all of Bella's CDs ordered. They'll be here in a day. It would also be nice to have the restaurant as it was when Sharon, Brian and Bella first came here. I wonder whether Vangelis has any photos. This could be fun actually. Get rid of all the muslin and rustic chic. Think Cheryl, think.

"Vangelis, I need a very quick favour. This needs to be sorted out immediately. I need photos of how the restaurant looked when you first opened it. Please call me back."

"Hi, why didn't you come down to the restaurant and ask. You didn't need to text, Cheryl. What's the great panic? I thought we were leaving any other enquiries until this wedding is out of the way."

"Sorry, Vangelis, but I'm just a little bit anxious and uncertain about something."

"How can I help? As for photos, I've got loads. They're ones which either visitors take and send me or they're photos we've taken ourselves. They're all in that big box over there. What's the urgency?"

"Bear with me, Vangelis. How large a circular table would fit in the restaurant and what number of people would it seat? Also, do you have a list of the top Greek food dishes? Oh, I need a cigarette and I haven't smoked for fifteen years."

"Enough of all this, Cheryl. Now take some deep breaths and calm down before you give yourself a heart attack. Right, I'm your boss and I'm telling you to go downstairs, walk the length of the beach for twenty minutes and on your way back up here get yourself a large gin and tonic. I'll have everything you need on your desk waiting for you. Now go before I have to physically remove you."

Well, what was all that about? I've never seen Vangelis act like that before. I know he's right and I do need to calm down, but I actually found him very sexy and attractive. I can't believe I've got into such a panic over something that might not be necessary. It just shows that all the time I think he's so laid back and not taking everything in, it's his way of letting me get on with things. He really must trust me, although he could see that I needed help and became my knight in shining armour. Perhaps I should play the innocent maiden more often.

Oh, don't be stupid, Cheryl. Pull yourself together. Vangelis is Vangelis and could never change from being the charmer. He's not what I need, but saying that he's given me goose bumps.

"I'm back. No gin though. I've brought us up two coffees. I'm sorry, Vangelis, but I really don't know what came over me. I just felt as though I couldn't cope for a minute or two."

"Not a problem, Cheryl. Here's the things you need – photos of the restaurant, top Greek starters, main courses and desserts. At a squeeze we could fit a sixteen-seater circular table in the restaurant, but it would be more comfortable with less seats. Was there anything else?"

"No, that's all, thanks, Vangelis. We're a good team, aren't we? I'm so happy here on the island and a big part of that is working here with you. I really do appreciate all you've done for me. Thank you."

"No, thank you, Cheryl. We're a really good team, and if only you could realise we could be a far better team if..."

"Don't spoil it, Vangelis. We work well together and we're best friends, but that's it. Right, I need to get sorted as Carla will be here soon."

Right. We can do this, but I just need to convince Carla and then she needs to persuade Bella.

"Hello, Carla, so nice to meet you in person after all the emails. Welcome to Holkamos."

"And you, Cheryl. You left something out! There's been hundreds of emails. I'm sorry about that."

"No need to apologise. Now, I'll find Vangelis and we can sit in the restaurant. Choose something to eat and we can go over everything."

"I've just met Vangelis. He helped me with my bags when I got out of the taxi. He's very handsome, isn't he? Oh, I am sorry, I shouldn't be saying things like that to his girlfriend."

"Oh, no, Carla, we're not a couple. He's my boss, but also a very special friend."

"That's good, but lots of couples start out as being friends, so you never know! Plus, you two being in the wedding business every day it must be all hearts and roses apart from the one this weekend. That's just stress and frustration."

"No, it's nothing of the sort, Carla, but we might have a little problem. Ah, here comes Vangelis."

"Did I hear you say problem, Cheryl. I thought everything was under control."

"Well, it's like this. I caught the sea taxi back from Holkamos town with Sharon and she happened to mention the type of wedding she and Brian would really love and I'm sorry to say that it's not the one Bella has in mind."

"Oh, no, it's too late to change everything. Bella had a set thing for her parents and that's what's going to happen with no changes. It's far too near to the big day for all of this. Sharon and Brian will love it as it's the wedding their daughter wants for them."

"Yes, Carla, it might be what Bella wants, but it's not the wedding Sharon and Brian would love to have."

"So, Cheryl, all those things you asked me about earlier were to do with what Sharon and Brian want. Well, we can do that, no trouble. I know this puts you in a very awkward situation, Carla, but I know Bella. All she wants to do is please her parents. Perhaps you should phone her and tell her that Sharon was talking about the kind of wedding she's always dreamt of. I'm sure Bella would love to make their dreams come true, but first of all, Cheryl, explain exactly what Sharon and Brian would really like for their wedding day."

"Vangelis is right. What would happen if they weren't happy with the day and Bella found out? I'm sorry, Carla but she can't kill you. It's not your fault, you've only carried out her instructions, so why don't you give Bella a call? Vangelis knows her, so perhaps it might help if he speaks to her. Here's your meal, so why not sit and think about it while you eat? We'll leave you alone, but do call us if you need anything. I'll be up in my office."

Oh dear! I wonder if I've done the right thing in mentioning it. Vangelis doesn't see any reason why we can't pull all the new ideas together in a couple of days. It's not the type of wedding we've done before, but I really think it will be very special.

"Hi, Vangelis said I should just come up. I hope you don't mind."

"How was your meal, Carla? Can I get you anything else? Do take a seat. Sorry, that it's rather small and cramped up here, but the staff in the restaurant seem to dump everything here."

"Oh no, I'm full, thanks. It might be small, but what a fabulous office view! There can't be many as good as this."

"I know. I'm sure I'd get far more work done if I didn't have that view. Have you had any more thoughts about contacting Bella?"

"Yes, I've emailed her and received a reply. She'd like to have a chat with you."

"I think she'd be better talking to Vangelis. She knows him, and I don't really feel comfortable chatting on the phone with Bella Lacywhite."

"Sorry, Cheryl, but she wants to talk to you as you're the one who had the conversation with Sharon. Bella's busy for a couple of hours and she's aware it will be late but could she call you at around midnight? That's Greek time not New York time."

"I'm regretting mentioning this. How do I talk to a superstar?"

"Just the same as you're talking to me. Don't worry, she's lovely, Cheryl, she really is. All you have to do is go through the points Sharon mentioned and Bella will agree or refuse them. I'd suggest having the wedding file in front of you. She's got her own copy, but just one other thing. She's said that seeing her parents get married is going to be one of the most important days of her life."

"So, no pressure if I mess it up then, Carla!"

Chapter 38

Please just ring! I haven't been so nervous about anything in my whole life. I want a drink, but I daren't. I really can't believe that in just over half an hour, I'm going to be talking to Bella Lacywhite on the phone. She's Riven Raven's girlfriend, how scary is that!

Calm down, Cheryl. It's all going to be fine. She's only human, and just wants to chat about her parents' wedding. Was that the door? Oh, please don't tell me she's here. No, don't be stupid, she doesn't know where I live. She could have found out though. God, I look scruffy and the place is so untidy. Deep breaths, and go and open the door.

"Thank goodness it's you, Andreas. Come in. I need to sit down."

"What's wrong, Cheryl. Who were you expecting? Shall I go?"

"No, I'll explain everything."

"I've brought the painting to see whether you like it, and I've also got a bottle of wine."

"I don't know whether I should, but thanks. I'm expecting Bella to call from New York, and my heart's in my mouth. What do I talk about? I'm just Cheryl from England."

"Yes, Cheryl, and at one time she was just Bella from England. To be honest, she only wants to talk about her parents' wedding and you've got all the answers for her. Cheryl, you're a professional, you're the most confident woman I know."

"Thanks, Andreas, that's so kind of you to say, and thanks for bringing the painting. Can I unwrap it?"

"How else are you going to see it?"

"Oh my God, Andreas! It couldn't be more perfect! Sharon and Brian will love it."

"Right, I'm glad you like it. I'm really proud of that. I painted it so many years ago when I was in a

217

really happy place. I was young and had the whole world ahead of me. It was an exciting time and then it all went wrong."

"But, Andreas, you can still have exciting times to look forward to. You make it sound as though your life's over. Look at me! I walked away from my job, home and country, and now I'm the happiest I've ever been."

"Perhaps I ought to go and let you take your call. I'll see myself out. Bye, Cheryl."

"Hello, Cheryl Harris speaking."

"Hi, Cheryl, it's Bella. Thanks so much for taking my call. It's lovely to hear an English accent. Like me you're living in a different country. I hope you're having as much fun in Greece as I am in America. Carla's told me you've had a chat with my mum and she talked about her wedding. I was wondering what she had to say. By the way, congratulations on catching Mr Gorgeous! I had such a crush on Vangelis when I was fourteen. Those eyelashes were to die for. Do you have any little Vangelis' yet?"

"No, I'm not married to Vangelis. I'm not even his girlfriend. We just work together."

"Oh, I'm sorry, Cheryl. I just thought the wedding business was a husband and wife thing. Is he still as gorgeous?"

"Well, I suppose so, and he's still breaking holidaymakers' hearts, but I haven't told you that, Miss Lacywhite."

"Okay, nothing changes there then. So, Cheryl how would my mum like her wedding to be, and more to the point is it possible to arrange it all in such a short time?"

"It's not that they wouldn't love all you've planned for them, but I think they're both overwhelmed by the villa. They do appreciate everything but..."

"But I've gone over the top, haven't I? They just want something simple. I know exactly what you mean, Cheryl, and in the back of my mind I knew it all along."

"Well, sort of, yes. I'll explain what your mum said to me."

"You don't have to, Cheryl. If it's possible to arrange it all in the short time you have, then please just go ahead and do it. I want them to have the wedding they want, not what anyone else thinks they should have. I don't care how much it costs, Cheryl. If you can do it, I'll be so thankful."

"But, Miss Lacywhite, don't you want me to tell you about your mum's ideas?"

"No need. I know you'll do a fantastic job and it will also be a lovely surprise for me. If there's anything you need, just ask Carla."

"If you're sure, Miss Lacywhite, but would you like me to email you the details?"

"No, Cheryl, just surprise me on the day, and another thing, please do call me Bella. I'm so looking forward to coming back to Holkamos as I've not been there since my life turned crazy. I'm also excited to see what Vangelis looks like. It might keep Riven on his toes. Thanks again, Cheryl, and anything you need just ask Carla. See you the day after tomorrow. Bye for now."

Wine, where's the bloody wine! I can't believe I've been on the phone to Bella Lacywhite who's just told me to plan her parents' wedding without her even knowing the details. Isn't this all a bit crazy?

There won't be a moment to spare. I hope Vangelis is up for this because this wedding's the icing on the cake for us this summer.

Oh, God, cake... I need to know whether the sort of cake Bella's ordered will look right? Is it something that Sharon and Brian would have chosen?

First things first, emails to Vangelis and Carla: 'It's all go. Bella agrees to changes. Meet you both in the restaurant at 8.00am sharp. We have three days to organise a wedding'.

Chapter 39

"Good morning, both of you. Sorry I'm late. I just needed to check on something before I left the apartment. Getting straight to the point, Bella wants her parents to have the wedding they want rather than one anyone else thinks they should have."

"Yes, but what if it all goes wrong, Cheryl?"

"It's not going to go wrong, Carla. Cheryl will make sure of that. We'll make it the perfect day."

"Yes, we will. Now, just a couple of things, Carla. We only need you from Friday afternoon and that's to make sure that Sharon and Brian don't come anywhere near the restaurant until the wedding day."

"That may sound easy, Cheryl, but it won't be as simple as it sounds. You know how much they love the beach."

"Yes, but by then Bella will have arrived, so they'll all probably stay up at the villa. Between the three of you, Carla, I'm sure it won't be a problem."

"Right. So, Vangelis, top of your list will be to recreate the restaurant into how it was before you modernised it. Do you think it's possible to give the wedding guests a menu on the day? Remember Vangelis, there's enough money to hire another couple of chefs in to help. My morning will be spent interrogating Sharon or Brian without them guessing what I'm up to, so Carla go and see what the beautiful island of Holkamos has to offer."

"You're both so kind, you really are. As much as I worry about everything, I know that you're fully in control of everything you're doing for the wedding day. I was dreading all of it, but now I'm so excited. Thank you both so much."

So where's my beach bag? I have to be prepared to lie on the beach for the day if that's what it takes to find out how the bride and groom want to have their wedding day. I still have to pinch myself when I think

Hollywood actor Riven Raven is going to be at a wedding I've organised.

I can see them. They always have the same two sunbeds. No, it's only Brian. That might not be too helpful as he's not really one for talking. He leaves all that to Sharon, but here goes.

"Hello, Brian. Getting excited about the wedding? Where's Sharon today?"

"Hi. She'll be down later. She's tidying up before the staff arrive. She can't help it. Yes, I'm looking forward to getting married. We should have done it years ago but I'm not really looking forward to the day. It will be nice to see Bella and the rest of the family, but I don't know, I always feel like a fish out of water at those type of things I'm getting a bit more used to this type of life since Bella's become so famous, but deep down this is the real me. Put me in a corner with a glass of wine and I'm happy."

"It will be a lovely day. I'm sure Bella realises that and I expect there's lots of corners up in the villa to sit in."

"The villa's the problem. Have you ever been up there? It's so posh. I even feel nervous sitting at the kitchen table, never mind the dining room."

"So if you were planning your wedding, what would you do, Brian?"

"I don't know. I've never really thought about the actual day. A good meal to keep everyone happy, but most importantly the people attending would want to be there rather than feeling that they should be. Yes, I think it's all about making people feel comfortable. It's not nice if you aren't relaxed in the surroundings. If I had my way everyone would be in shorts and t-shirts, but I think that's where Sharon would put her foot down."

"Oh, no, for a wedding you have to dress up and that's not just the bride and groom. Your guests would want to feel special too. Brian, would you have any music?"

"Of course, but it would have to be Bella. I don't listen to anything else really."

He's not given me anything else to go on. It was a bit like pulling teeth. So we have the ceremony on the beach. I can't change that, and to be honest I don't want to. He wants everybody to be happy. This is so much harder than I thought. Come on, Cheryl, you need to pull this out of the bag. There must be one special thing to finish off the day. Fireworks?

"Hi, Cheryl, how are you? I'm a bit late getting down here, but I like to make sure everything's left just so. Don't want people thinking we don't care less."

"Right, well you two have a chinwag. I'm off into the sea for a swim."

"How's it going, Sharon? Still excited for the big day? I was going to ask, have you had any input into things you want on the special day?"

"Yes and no, Cheryl. Bella did ask me and I said that we didn't want too many people there, just our very closest family and friends. Everything else I've left to Bella."

"Have you seen the cake? Do you know what it looks like?"

"No, but I'm guessing it will be over the top knowing Bella. As long as we don't have it as dessert. I like a nice ice cream. We've got a little ritual that whenever we're here on holiday we go for a nice meal and then go for a walk and have an ice cream. We finish the evening off with a hot chocolate and look at the stars from one of the restaurants. We've have been known to make a flask of hot chocolate and come and look at the stars down here on the beach. We bring a little packet of biscuits with us. Yes, we do have some funny little habits when we're on the island."

"I don't think they're funny, Sharon. They're special to you and Brian and I think it's really nice. I need to get back to work now. Have a lovely day and I expect I'll see you and Brian again before the big day."

"Oh, yes, Cheryl, don't tell anyone, but the more time we spend down here and not up at the villa the better. I'm not one for pools. I love to see the sea."

"Yes, with your sun cream during the day and your hot chocolate at night, that's the perfect holiday, Sharon."

"You forgot the biscuits, Cheryl."

"No, I haven't, Sharon. I've not forgotten anything. See you later."

Chapter 40

A world class opera singer and a Hollywood superstar arrive on the island today and as I guessed the secret's out. There are a few strange people walking around with big cameras and apparently there's even more up at the villa. That's not my problem though, and to be honest I don't have any problems. Well, not work related ones.

Not that I've been able to give personal problems much thought, but they're more from Andreas' perspective. Anyway, he knows this weekend is a matter of life and death for me. There's just one thing I need to speak to Carla about which hopefully might help her situation, apart from that as long as my many parcels arrive today I'll very happy. It's strange that all the local people I've had to get involved with over the last few days are very excited, but they're not fazed by anything. They just want to make the day special. It's not just Vangelis and his team making things happen, it's a little Greek island all coming together. How lovely is that!

"Cheryl, are you up there? There's a delivery of boxes. What on earth have you been buying?"

"It's alright, Vangelis. It's not the restaurant's money I've been spending. I'll come down and get them."

"Don't worry, I'll bring them up. It's like Christmas down here. Whatever have you bought?"

"I'll help you, Vangelis but I just need to answer my phone. One minute."

"Are you alright, Cheryl? You look like you've just seen a ghost. Don't tell me something's not arrived."

"I've not had a chance to check everything off yet, but we've been invited to have dinner with a Hollywood actor at the villa tonight. I've tried to make excuses, but Bella won't listen. I even said that Sharon and Brian would find it odd, but no, Bella says that you've been a friend for many years and I'll be there as your guest."

"Fabulous, Cheryl. I'll get to meet one of my favourite actors in person. How cool is that!"

"It's scary, Vangelis. What do we talk about? Bella's going to make an excuse to show me something and we'll go off and talk about the wedding. I'm nervous, Vangelis."

"Don't be so silly, Cheryl. They're only people, just like us. It will be fun. Now, sort out your parcels, go home, have a nice shower and doll yourself up. I'll pick you up in a taxi. What time are they expecting us?"

"Any time after eight, as dinner will be served at nine. This is getting slightly out of our league, Vangelis. It's okay to be doing weddings for Mr and Mrs average on the beach, but we're talking Hollywood royalty here."

"Look, Sharon and Brian are Mr and Mrs average, and they want their wedding to take place in my restaurant. Okay, they don't know the details and we mustn't let that slip, but we're a great team offering five star weddings. Now get yourself home and sort yourself out before that prince comes to pick you up and takes you to the ball."

Now let's have a look in my wardrobe. The red dress from Julie's wardrobe would be perfect if I was a stone lighter, not that I'd ever want to be that thin again. Loose cotton beige trousers with a nice top and sparkly sandals. That's about all I've got that's smart enough. I'm going to have to buy something new for the actual wedding day. I've got the look I feel comfortable with but I need the confidence to go with it and that's not going to happen tonight.

"Hi, you look nice, Cheryl. Actually, you look lovely. Just relax and be the smart, fun woman you always are."

"You've scrubbed up well yourself, Vangelis. You're quite the gentleman, and I'm very proud to be your date tonight."

"So this is a date, a real date like I've been trying to get you to do for months."

"Of course it's a date, a dinner date. We're going out, we have a meal and then go home separately. What's all those flashing lights? Don't tell me the paparazzi are there. Well, they're going to be very disappointed when they see their photos later and it's just me."

"Smile, Chery[, we could be in the Hollywood papers tomorrow."

"I'm nervous enough, Vangelis. Don't make it any worse than it is."

"Hi, Sharon and Brian. You're both looking lovely. Have you had a good day in the sunshine? It's been really hot today."

"Lovely thanks, Vangelis. We actually had a few hours in the shade. What can I get you both to drink? Bella and Riven will be here soon. They're just getting ready."

"Anything for me, Brian. I'm so nervous."

"Don't be like that, Cheryl. How about a gin and tonic with lots of ice and lemon. That's all I've been drinking. I miss my red wine, but imagine the mess it would make if I spilt it. Gin just looks like water so it won't stain."

"I can hear them coming. These stone floors make such a noise."

"Hello. Oh, Vangelis, you've not changed a bit. Still got those eyelashes that women would kill for. How long's it been since I last saw you? Five or six years, something like that. Let me introduce you to Riven."

"Hi, nice to meet you. Bella's told me so much about this beautiful island. I can't wait to go and explore."

"Lovely to see you again, Bella and meet you..."

"It's Riven, just plain Riven. Look, if it will help, I'm just the same as you. The only difference is I'm on the cinema screen. I'm here on holiday, and for this weekend I'm not a celebrity. The only stars here are Sharon and Brian. Isn't that right, Bella?"

"Yes, darling. I'm sorry, you must be Cheryl. I'm so pleased to meet you. Thank you for coming up."

Thanks for inviting us. It's very kind of you. How do you like being back on Holkamos?"

"I'm loving it, thanks. It's not until I look at that view that I realise how much I've missed it. I was a little disappointed with the start of the journey as we went to the ferry port in Preveza. You might think this is funny, but I wanted to get on the little ferry. We came over on a flash looking boat, but it wasn't the same. This villa makes a lovely change from a studio apartment we stayed in. I know Mum and Dad won't agree as they love their little apartment, but this is more practical for the weekend."

"Has everyone got a drink? It should be champagne, but I love a beer. I remember filming in the UK a few years back, and going to some of those micro brewers. I've been hooked ever since. Please raise your glasses to Sharon and Brian and a very special weekend!"

"Dinner will be in about an hour and a half, and no, Mum, the chef and the housekeeper do not need any help. Relax. You're getting married in a couple of days, so enjoy all the fuss. I promise you, once the wedding's over, you can go and clean to your heart's content if it makes you feel any better. Now, Cheryl, come with me and let me show you the view from the balcony. I'll pour us another drink first."

"Thanks, Bella, the view is amazing. Are we out of ear shot?"

"Yes. I can't thank you enough for all this, Cheryl. I'd have got it all wrong, I must say that Carla told me your idea to keep the press out of the way and on the wrong trail is brilliant. Both Riven and myself are used to publicity, so if they do turn up at the restaurant it won't be the end of the world."

"Well, everything's organised. Your dad gave me a

few more ideas and it will be a lovely day."

"Do you need me to do anything? I don't want to know everything, but if I can help with anything I'm happy to do so."

"There is one thing I need to run past you. If your dad had his way, everyone would be dressed in beachwear, but after talking it over he thinks it will be nice if everyone dressed up. But what I was thinking was... As it gets dark, and before the fireworks start, one of the surprises would be... Well, I'll show you on my phone, Bella, but if you think it's a stupid or tacky idea, please say. I just thought it would please your dad and be unique to their day. If you like it, I think it would be better if you orchestrated the situation."

"It's brilliant, and it's just my dad down to a tee. You're so clever, Cheryl. You don't fancy coming back to the States and running my life for me, do you? Oh, I know you can't as you have to stay here and fall in love with Vangelis. You do make such a beautiful couple, and the way he looks at you!"

"Sorry, there'll be no falling in love and he looks at all women like that. I'm not saying it's not nice, but where Vangelis is concerned, there are lots of buts."

"Mark my words, Cheryl, you can't live on this island and not fall in love and have a fabulous romance. Holkamos was made for it."

"Ladies! Dinner is served."

"Thanks, Carla, we're on our way."

What an evening! My little studio apartment feels so small now. I think some of the sofas up at the villa were actually bigger than this place. I can't believe I got myself into such a state of nerves over it.

Riven may be a Hollywood star but he's so laid back. It was quite funny when he said he was only in it for the money. Surely that's the reason why we all go to work. It was nice to see how he brings Brian into the conversation. There was no corner for him to hide in, but both he and Sharon had a lovely evening.

It's all quite bizarre, but exciting too. Yes, I'm really looking forward to Saturday's wedding. Vangelis was different tonight too. I think I've seen the real him rather than the one who tries to flirt with the women. Tonight he was far more mature, and that's something I found very attractive.

Chapter 41

Everything's ticked off. I've not missed a thing, but I'm still checking it every half an hour. That's bad enough, but what's even crazier is that it's only six in the morning. I've been up for two hours and the wedding is still twelve hours away. I'm excited for Sharon and Brian because they don't know what's ahead of them, but I'm not nervous any more. I think going up to the villa to meet Bella and Riven helped a lot.

We've achieved so much, and I can't believe how different the room looks with all the traditional bits and pieces. The only thing to do is to set up the huge circular table and for the chefs to prepare the food. Vangelis has worked so hard pulling everything together to get the right look. I wouldn't have known where to start with any of it.

These last few days have seen a real difference in Vangelis. It's so stupid to say, but he's more grown up. The laid back carefree chap has disappeared. Yesterday, while transforming the restaurant, adding pictures and terracotta plates, I swear it must have been the first time he wasn't distracted by all the girls in bikinis on the beach.

Now I need a plan of action for the actual day. I don't really need to be at the restaurant until midday as all that will be happening will be in the kitchen. I need to buy something to wear and I'm hoping Johnny will come with me to choose it. I need to go and pay Andreas for the painting and I expect there'll be a dozen or so emails from Carla. All she has to do is make sure everything at the villa is running smoothly and I'll worry about everything in the restaurant.

There goes my phone, a text already and it's not even 6.30am. What on earth can she be wanting to know at this time of the morning? I take that all back, it's not Carla but Johnny to say he's not needed in the salon today and he's booked me an appointment for my hair and nails as a thank you for letting him help in the restaurant tonight. That's nice, but and it's a huge but, I'll dictate how I look. Come to think of it, I've not had my nails done since Julie's wedding and those were dreadful. More like claws than nails. That won't be happening today, and as for my hair as long as it's my own and not someone else's sewn in, they can do what they like. I want to look like me, Cheryl, not a Barbie doll.

But before all that, a walk in the harbour with a coffee and pastry is the order of the day. The bakery is one of the places on the island that makes me feel like I live here. I walk in and don't even have to tell them what I want. That makes me feel good. Talking of home, it's not that long until I go back to England. I need to think about what I'm going to do financially during the winter. I don't need to earn a lot as my commission here on Holkamos has been really good and as for Sharon and Brian's wedding, Bella's been more than generous. Let's just get today over with, get back to a normal routine and then start to plan everything.

"Hello, you're up early. I love coming down to the harbour before anyone else is around. I was the same back in Dartmouth, sitting by the ferry and looking over to Kingsway. I've missed you, Cheryl, and in one way as much as it's lovely here I wish we were both back in Dartmouth in a relationship rather than that silly routine we once had."

"Clive, there were many opportunities for that to happen. You knew that was what I wanted, but no ifs and buts, that was the past and this is the future. We both need to move on. I have, Clive, but it's time you did too."

"Okay, Cheryl, but we don't have to go back to Devon. We can go anywhere, I just want to be with you and..."

"No, Clive, the answer is always going to be no. Even if things don't work out for Andreas and me, it will still be a no. I'm sorry, I really am and as much as I want to scream and shout at you for messing things up, I can't. Clive, please find someone else and start again somewhere else. Leave Holkamos and more importantly, forget about me."

"I'm sorry, Cheryl, but I don't think I can."

I hope the rest of the day doesn't go like this. What a bad start, but Clive really needs to get over it and move on just like I have. It's still not even eight o'clock. The salon won't be open for another couple of hours. Another coffee and a little walk.

"Hello, you're up early, Cheryl."

"Oh, Bella, sorry, I didn't recognise you for a moment."

"Yes, that was the intention. I thought I might get away with not being spotted if I pulled a baseball cap down over my face. I just wanted to experience Holkamos in the way I used to. Nowadays I travel to exotic countries and receive five-star treatment, but my heart is in two places, back home in England and here on this island. I've got a beautiful house in America, which I really love, but it's really only just a base."

"I know what you mean. I will really miss it when I leave."

"So stay. Why do you have to go?"

"The summer season will be over soon and there'll be no jobs here until next spring. I'll come back then as the wedding business in the restaurant has really taken off and I love it. Every day is just like a holiday, I'm so lucky to have such a wonderful job."

"Yes, and a fabulous boss, Cheryl. I can tell Vangelis thinks the world of you. You're more than just an employee. The other night up at the villa when you were talking at dinner, you should have seen the look on his face. He's in love with you, Cheryl, surely you can see that. Why not give him a chance?"

"I know what you're saying, Bella. At first I was a bit of a challenge to him, but as time's gone on, he's been far more caring and respectful. Our working relationship is perfect, but I don't want to mess that up, so I think things are best left as they are."

"Mark my words, Cheryl. One day you'll look back on this and wish you'd given in and fallen for those deep dark eyes and firm, fit gorgeous body. Oh, dear, enough of that. I should be getting back, I have a wedding to get ready for, plus a few white lies to tell Mum and Dad. They still don't know that we're heading down to the beach for the ceremony and wedding breakfast. I'm delaying telling them that until the very last minute."

"Yes, it's going to be a lovely day, I'm so looking forward to it, Bella."

"I think I'd best make a move. My security chap is getting a little twitchy over there as more people are getting up and milling around, but what do you have to lose by giving it a go with Vangelis? What a lovely end to the summer it would be and you never know, you might not need to go back to England for the winter. See you later, Cheryl, and thanks for everything."

She's so lovely, and to think that all the times I've seen her on the television singing and being the fabulous diva Bella Lacywhite, she's just like the rest of us. We all have issues of some kind, whether they be big or small. Right, time to get the mini makeover and although I wouldn't tell Johnny or Nico, I am quite looking forward to it."

"Morning, guys, how are we today? I hope you have a lot of patience. Trying to sort my hair out will be a challenge."

"Cheryl, tell us everything. Have you seen them yet?"

"Seen who, Johnny?"

"Stop it. Bella and Riven, of course."

"Oh yes, Vangelis and I had dinner with them a

couple of nights ago. What colour should my nails be?"

"Never mind your nails, Cheryl. Tell us about them. Is he as gorgeous in real life as he is on the screen? Did you speak to him?"

"Yes, I said we had dinner together. It would have been very difficult not to talk to him as there were only six of us there."

"Oh my God, how lucky were you!"

"He's handsome and so down to earth. I've just been chatting to Bella down in the harbour too. Now, the important thing. The other night I wore the outfit I was planning to wear for the wedding, so I need one of you to come shopping with me and help me find something else."

"Let's get started with the hair wash. The nails can be done at the same time as the hair, and I promise you, Cheryl, this will be nothing like the last time you went through this. When we've finished you'll still look like Cheryl, but perhaps with a little twist. By the way, did Riven smell nice?"

"Yes and his lips are so soft, I've not washed my cheek since. No, I'm joking, but I did get a kiss. Now come on, work your magic on me before I change my mind."

Is that my refection in the shop mirror? Haven't they done a great job! I look half human. Right, I've got twenty minutes to see Andreas before I have to meet Johnny up at Elenora boutique. Do people still use that word? Never mind, it's a clothes shop.

"Hi, how are you?"

"I'm good, thanks, Cheryl. You look lovely. It reminds me of the first time we met."

"I hope not, Andreas. I had someone else's hair then, but I know what you mean. Johnny and Nico didn't trust me to do my own make up so they've done that as well as the hair and nails."

"So is everything set for the wedding of the year? I see you went up to the villa with Vangelis for the evening?"

"News travels fast."

"Yes, there's a photo in the Preveza times showing you two getting out of a taxi."

"Oh how does it look?"

"Here, I've got a copy. You both look very nice. I think the photographer must be looking over the wall. You can just see Vangelis holding your hand and helping you out the car."

"We had a nice time, thanks. I've come to pay for the painting. It's perfect and Sharon and Brian will love it. You must come over tonight and meet them. They're such a lovely couple. The fireworks are going off at 10.30pm and there's about ten times the amount that we normally have for weddings."

"I'll see what I can do. I really hope everything goes well for you and Vangelis today. I know how important it is for both of you."

"Yes, it is a bit special and hopefully the publicity will bring more business. That would mean I'll be able to stay on the island as all I want to do is make it my permanent home."

"That would be nice. Perhaps when this weekend's over, we can get together for a drink and something to eat and we could..."

"Come on, Cheryl. Time is of the essence. There're clothes to try on. I'm not letting you buy the first thing you see. I know what you're like."

"I'm sorry, Andreas, but I need to go. Please come over tonight as I'd really like Sharon and Brian to meet you, and I also want to see you too."

Well, that was painless and I've proved Johnny wrong as I've bought the first thing I tried on. I'm over the moon with it, lovely white linen trousers, a pale blue top and some fun holiday jewellery. Now to get showered without getting my hair wet. Easier said than done. I think. I really hope Andreas comes over to Volmos tonight. I think it will do him the world of good to hear people praising his work. He should be so proud of himself.

Is that the door? A visitor's the last thing I need. Perhaps it's a holiday maker asking if I want a drink on their balcony."

"I won't be a minute."

There's no one there, but someone's left another bouquet of flowers with the same writing as the previous one.

"You are very special."

Chapter 42

"Look at you! How stunning do you look, Cheryl?"

"Likewise, Vangelis, you've scrubbed up well again too. This is becoming a habit. I'm just going to nip up to the office and get my file for the timings. How's everything coming on with the food?"

"There's far too much, but that's better than not having enough. We're making so much money on this that we can afford to suffer some waste. To be honest, Cheryl, this is turning out to be one of the easiest weddings we've done because the staff from the villa are coming down to serve and organise all the drinks. We don't have a lot to do. I'm not putting the cake or anything to do with the wedding out until the last minute because people just think it's a normal day in the restaurant."

"That's a good idea. I'll see you soon, I just need to sort out a few things in the office. By the way, I've found a little job for Johnny later on tonight, but I haven't told him yet. He'll either love it or hate it. He should be here soon, so be prepared to be asked a million questions about Riven."

Deep breaths. Everything's sorted. I don't need to worry about the food. I just need to explain to the staff about the hot chocolates and biscuits. The ice cream's in the freezer and Johnny's outfit is ironed. Andreas' painting is wrapped, candles need to be lit twenty minutes before they arrive. The priest is organised with the little service and I don't need to get involved with that. No sea taxis to worry about as all the guests are staying on Volmos and my little secret is looking good. I just hope they all fit. I just need to check the table and make sure that the flowers aren't blocking anyone's view. Talking of flowers, why did I receive some more today, and why doesn't the sender sign their name. There's only one thing for it. Once all this is over, I'll ask all three of them who's sending them.

"Hi, darling, I'm here. It's so exciting! I can't wait to see Bella and Riven. I really don't know what I will say. Do I have to bow?"

"No, you don't, Johnny, and please remember that it's Sharon and Brian's wedding. They're the ones who need the attention. No, I need a little favour. Hopefully you'll like it. It's more of an acting job really, but I'll tell you all about it later."

"It's very strange, Cheryl, but there aren't any paparazzi around. I thought the place would be full of them, and to be honest they'd stick out like a sore thumb on the beach."

"Yes, and fingers crossed, Johnny, Carla and I have come up with a little plan to keep them off the scent. Firstly, the restaurant doesn't look like a wedding reception venue, but more like an old Greek tavern. We've given a small group of family and friends access to the pool up in the villa. A coach with blacked out windows will drive up there. The paparazzi will be able to see people moving inside it, but not recognise their faces. Bella's huge car with blacked out windows will follow the coach into the villa, but the car will stay. Wedding music will play in the grounds so the paparazzi won't be able to hear it. Staff will bring cold drinks out to them and in the meantime all the wedding party will crouch down in the coach and be here by the time anyone gets wind of it."

"That's very clever."

"There's also a bit of a false wall, so if things get out of hand, Bella and Riven can take a bit of a breather, but saying that, as long as Sharon and Brian are alright, I think they won't mind about sightseers. They're used to it by now. Come down to the restaurant. I want to check the table and explain your secret task."

I think I did that right. Told him about his special job before he's seen what I want him to wear. The table looks stunning, the candles are lit and the music's ready. All we need now is the wedding party and knowing Carla they'll be dead on cue, not a minute early or late. I do hope she enjoys herself as she does need to relax a bit. There's nothing more to be done today. I hear the coach arriving. Here we go, show time."

"Are you ready, Vangelis. It's time to welcome the wedding party and let them see that beautiful charm of yours. Just be your normal self and remember, Sharon and Brian are old friends and it's their day. I'm in control of everything else, and Johnny, please don't scream like a little girl when Riven gets off the coach. Try and be tactful. You've got all evening to drool over him."

I knew Vangelis could do it. It's nothing he hasn't done all his life, welcoming people to his restaurant. Everyone's really gone to town with the outfits with so many bright colours and the men with their brightly coloured ties. Saying that, Bella has played it down. She's very conscious of not wanting to take the attention away from her mum and dad, and if you didn't know Riven, he seems like just another guest. Sharon and Brian are over the moon looking at how the restaurant is decorated.

"Come here, young lady, I've a bone to pick with you."

"With me, Brian? I don't know what you mean?"

"I think you do, Cheryl. You asked me what type of wedding I'd like and you've created mine and Sharon's perfect day. Thank you so much."

"You're more than welcome. Now go and get married and then we'll feed you. By the way, can you see what I've placed in the corner for you? Look over there. It's a chair. Isn't that what you required?"

"Thanks, but I don't think I'll be needing it today, do you?"

"Even if you wanted to, Brian, I don't think you'll be allowed to sit on it. Everyone's calling you now, it's time for the ceremony."

The ceremony will take no more than thirty minutes. Then there'll be time for some photographs and another drink before the food is served and a quick tidy up. If we can get through this bit without the paparazzi arriving, I think we'll be alright. It will just look like a big family meal. Vangelis is in his element with the guests. The women just love him and from where I'm standing, one woman can't take her eyes off him. Yes, I've noticed, Carla, but I don't think he has."

"Cheryl, he's gorgeous."

"Yes, I know. He's scrubbed up well he's handling all the guests and making them all feel as if they're the most important one here."

"Sorry, Cheryl, I'm talking about Riven. Who did you think I meant? You just said Vangelis is gorgeous. I knew it from day one when we set foot on this island. I knew you'd fall for him. I told you so. Oh, I'm so pleased. I can't wait to tell Nico and as well as best friends, we'll be kind of related."

"No, Johnny, I haven't fallen in love with Vangelis. He's lovely looking and he always has been very easy on the eye, but no, he's not for me. Our working relationship is brilliant, but that's as far as it goes. We won't be related, Johnny, but we will always be best friends."

The people setting up the fireworks are ready and Vangelis has arranged for some food to be sent over to them. It's now eight o'clock, so they should be sitting down. It's time to play some of Brian's favourite music. The waiters are ready to take the food orders, but there's no sign of Bella. Oh, I can see her on the beach now the sun has gone down.

"Hi, Bella. Are you alright? Is everything going as you wanted it to?"

"Cheryl, it couldn't be better. I can't believe what you've done for my parents. It's the happiest day of their lives and I'm so grateful."

"It's my job and none of it would have been possible if you hadn't had the dream to come back here for the wedding. It's you who should take the credit really."

"Let's just say we've done it between us, Cheryl."

"I'm sorry to take you away from the view but you need to go and order your meal."

"Okay, and thanks again for everything."

We've done it! A wedding ceremony and photos on the beach without a single paparazzi photographer in sight, but more surprising than that not one person has spotted Riven or Bella. I'm so surprised. Hopefully this will continue for the rest of the day. To be honest, the beach is very quiet as everyone's off to Holkamos town as it's Saturday night.

"Everyone's eating, Cheryl, and they're all happy. We've done it. After all these weeks of worrying and not wanting this booking, it's our most successful wedding to date. Are you pleased?"

"Yes, Vangelis, I'm more than pleased, but I must say something. I know you'd like our relationship to be more than just a working one, but if it was we wouldn't be so good together at the business."

"You say that, Cheryl, but I feel we would be better, and another thing, I'm not giving up. I want more than a boss and employee relationship. I want to hold you in my arms, kiss you and never stop. It will happen and I know you want it as much as I do. I'd best go and check the wedding party are alright."

That's not what I wanted to hear, and today's not the day to ponder on it all. Come to that, no day is the right time. It's not going to happen.

"Cheryl, I'm ready. How do I look? Please tell me I look like a handsome Italian ice cream salesman."

"Yes, Johnny, you do. Now the chefs should have the cart loaded up with ice-creams, so once all the main course plates have been cleared away you can get on the bike and start performing."

"Sorry, bike? Performing? Am I missing something here?"

"Didn't I tell you, you'll ride in pulling the ice cream cart and then explain the flavours and toppings. It will be fun, you'll be the centre of attention and remember tits and teeth, tits and teeth, darling. It's show time."

Once they've all had the ice cream, it will be time for the speeches, but they'll only be brief because Brian doesn't want any fuss. Bella says she wants to say a few words and Vangelis will present them with the painting. Before the fireworks and hot chocolate, they'll have an hour or so to mingle and look at my little surprise. Look at him, he's in his element. I can hear it for years to come. He's the one who served Riven Raven ice cream. Johnny's claim to fame.

"Thanks so much, Cheryl. It's the perfect day. Bella's told me that this is all your doing. I really can't thank you enough."

"I only carried out Bella's instructions, Sharon. I'm so pleased you're happy with everything, but I think they're getting ready for the speeches now."

"That won't take long, Cheryl. All Brian will say is 'thank you'."

Sharon was right. Brian only said, 'Thank you very much to everyone for coming and helping to make this a very special day'.

Now it's Bella's turn.

"Thanks, Dad. I know I can speak for everyone here by saying thank you for letting us celebrate your special day. Before I continue, Vangelis has something for you."

"Sharon, Brian, on behalf of myself, Cheryl and all my team, I have a little gift for you."

"Oh, look, Sharon. It's a painting of the restaurant like it used to be. Thanks so much. It's beautiful and so kind of you. I don't know how we'll get it on the plane but we'll manage it somehow."

"How fabulous is that, Mum and Dad. What a

gorgeous painting! It brings back so many memories of when I first came here as a child. Perhaps I can help with the little transport problem because I don't think you'll want to take it back to the UK."

"What do you mean, Bella? Of course we will. It will look lovely above the fireplace in our lounge, won't it, Sharon?"

"But, Mum, Dad, how about it goes above a fireplace here on Holkamos? My wedding present to both of you is a little apartment just behind here with three bedrooms because I know you'll always have visitors. You'll be able to come here whenever you like. I'd love to go and show you it now, but sadly it's not finished being built until next spring. By the way, when you're on your balcony, you'll be able to see the sea through the trees."

Everyone's in tears. Brian and Sharon are shocked. I know how independent they both are and how they find it difficult to spend Bella's money, but somehow I think they won't have a problem with this. What a lovely surprise.

"We don't know what to say, do we, Brian, apart from I'll get next year's calendar out before you all go and just put your names against any dates you'd like. You're all welcome at any time. Today is certainly a day of surprises and we're both so thankful to all of you."

"Talking of surprises, I think Cheryl has another one for you, but we need you two to nip upstairs to the office and change into something. Don't open this until you get up there. Cheryl will explain everything."

"Thanks, Bella. When I had a chat to Brian about his perfect wedding, he said that he wished that everyone could be in shorts and T-shirts. I explained that you'd want to dress up smartly and quite rightly too, but I've tried to carry out his wishes and had some T-shirts printed. Sharon's says 'Bride' and Brian's 'Bridegroom'. The rest of you have T-shirts

243

with letters on which spell their name. Bella, yours has a big heart on it.

"When they come back, I want each of you to stand in line in the order where your T-shirts will spell out 'We heart Sharon and Brian'. The T-shirts are very large so they will go over your clothes. I've also got some sparklers for you all to wave. So, here are the T-shirts, pick whichever one you want apart from the one with the heart on, that's Bella's. It might be quite fun if you all face the other way and then when they come back, you each turn round one by one. What do you think?"

"I think it's a brilliant idea. How clever of you, Cheryl. It will make my dad's day to be in a T-shirt. Let's get ready, and no peeping when Riven takes off his shirt and tie. I have my eye on you, Mr Ice Cream man, he's mine."

"I'm so pleased they're all up for this. Now, I'll see how Sharon and Brian are getting on and once Vangelis shouts up the stairs to me, they can come down and the fireworks can start."

"Ready when you are, Cheryl."

"There you go, Sharon. You follow Brian down the stairs. I must say you look good."

"Yes, and I feel so much more comfortable than I was in that suit. I suggested to Sharon that we should wear each other's T-shirts, me with the bride one and her with the bridegroom, but she wasn't having any of it."

"They've all got letters on the T-shirts, Sharon. They spell out something as they turn round."

"That's so lovely. You all look fabulous. What's that noise? Oh, are those fireworks for us. Look at the colours."

"What a lovely touch, Cheryl, the fireworks are spectacular. I wonder what else is going to happen as it's been one surprise after another."

"No more surprises, Johnny, just hot chocolate with squinty cream and homemade biscuits to finish the day off."

There would have been one more surprise, not for the happy couple, but for me. Unfortunately, it didn't happen but if Andreas had come down to Volmos it would have finished the day off beautifully. Something told me he wouldn't come, but hopefully I've got other nights to look forward to.

I can't believe it. It's nearly three o'clock in the morning and I'm still on a high with all the excitement. We actually got through the whole day without one photographer anywhere near. The only wedding photos that the world will see are those which Bella chooses to release and I get the impression they'll be the fun ones and hopefully not the one with the guests spelling out rude words with the T-shirt letters. It didn't cross my mind that might happen.

Time for bed after one of the loveliest days I've had on this island.

Chapter 43

It's been four days since Sharon and Brian's wedding and the island is buzzing with photographers and journalists everywhere. I've not seen or spoken to them, but our part is over.

Some of the newspaper stories are a little farfetched, some are saying that Bella and Riven have got married even though they both posted pictures on their social media sites of Bella with her parents. They've both been very helpful posing for photos when they've gone from the villa to the boat.

I'm exhausted. I can't remember when I last slept for so long. Today I have to deal with all the emails that have come in, all thanks to Bella thanking us for the perfect wedding for her parents. You could not put a price on the publicity this has given us. We've got enquiries from all over the world.

But first things first, a large coffee on my terrace and time to answer the texts which I should have done yesterday. There's one from Johnny: 'Need to speak to you Xx', one from Vangelis, saying, 'I have an enquiry for the day before we close, nothing booked but need to talk about it' and one from Rhea over on Dissinos asking whether I'd like to come over for the day before the season ends and why not stay the night. Oh, there's the phone.

"Hi, Vangelis. I thought I'd work from home today and try and get through all the emails. I've just seen your text. If you give me the people's emails, I'll contact them.

"They don't have Internet or do emails, Cheryl."

"Oh, alright, I'll phone them."

"It's okay, I can deal with it. You just need to make a note that it's a wedding blessing for no more than a dozen people. They've just asked if we could do whatever we think is appropriate and special."

"I don't understand that, Vangelis. Are you saying

we just arrange something and they turn up for it? I really think I ought to speak to them. What are their names?"

"Just put it in my name, Cheryl. Just plan something you'd like to go to. I've got to go now. The press are here again looking for some more stories. It's good that Carla comes down from the villa to deal with them as I don't know what I'd say."

That was odd. No name and just turning up? I smell a rat somewhere, Vangelis is up to something, but it must be special so I'll arrange something beautiful. Anyway, it's a while off, so I won't worry about it yet.

There goes the phone again. Another text from Johnny, "Did you get my text? It's urgent."

"Morning Johnny, what's wrong."

"Nothing's wrong, Cheryl. It's just that we have a visitor coming to Holkamos and they want to meet us for dinner tonight."

"Who? And why is it so urgent?"

"Are you ready for it, Cheryl? Suzy's coming over and she wants to meet up with you me and Clive. It's obvious that she wants us to go back once the season's over and I was thinking this might be a way of getting rid of Clive."

"I haven't got time to meet her and the last thing I want is to sit down for a meal and be sociable with Clive."

"I think you're wrong, Cheryl. We need to listen to what she has to say. You never know, this might be the answer to your problem about staying here for the winter. If Suzy's desperate for staff, she might pay well even if it's just for the Christmas period. I'll meet you outside the salon at eight o'clock."

I suppose Johnny's right, and if Suzy's here we might as well get it over with. One thing's for sure, I'm not going back to Dartmouth for the winter regardless of how much I'll need a job.

Right, back to work and to get these emails sorted.

It's quite funny really, there's genuine ones and some which only mention Bella and Riven. Those can wait. I'll have to write a standard reply to them.

I can't believe it's six o'clock already. I've got so much done and by this time tomorrow I'll be on top of everything. I could do without Suzy arriving though. I know Johnny said that she's here to get us to go back, but perhaps she's just having one of her many holidays and already has a new team working for her. It will seem strange. She was my boss the last time I had anything to do with her, and now she's my equal, but if it wasn't for me she'd never have been the owner of the hotel.

"Hi, are you ready for this, Cheryl. I'm sorry to be stroppy about this, but let's just meet her, have a nice dinner and accept her apologies."

"Okay, Johnny, but I won't be staying late. I'm tired and have another busy day tomorrow. By the way, did you see that Bella posted an Instagram photo of you serving ice creams at the wedding?"

"Yes, I saw that, and I don't look too bad, do I? Nico joked that I should have it on show in the salon and instead of coffees I should serve ice-creams."

"Come on. Let's get up the hill and paint the smiles on. I'm quite looking forward to seeing what Suzy looks like because I'll be able to tell whether she's been doing any work herself. By the way, don't let me sit next to Clive, and I'm relying on you to keep the conversation going."

"Here we are, Cheryl. Can you see her? Oh, I can. She's over there in the corner and she looks okay. Clive's not here yet."

"It would be really nice if he didn't turn up."

"No, we need him to turn up. Hopefully he'll go back to Dartmouth with her. Are you ready, Cheryl, put the smile on?"

"Hello, Suzy. It's nice to see you. Welcome to Holkamos. What do you think of this little island? Just a minute. I think that's Clive looking for us.

Okay, he's seen us."

"Thank you all for coming. It's so nice to see the three of you. Now what would everyone like to drink?"

I knew this was a bad idea, all this stupid chit chat, but thankfully Johnny's here to keep it up. No mention of Dartmouth yet, let alone the hotel. Just one reaction from Suzy when Johnny said he was going to spend the winter training to be a hairdresser. So that's given it away. She's here to get us to go back. We've all had a summer of fun and now it's back to Devon. Sorry, Suzy, that won't be happening for me.

"Here come the drinks and by the look of it the menus. What would you all recommend? You're the chef, Clive. Have you found it easy learning all the Greek dishes?"

"Yes, it hasn't been a problem. One good thing here on Holkamos is that the fish is so fresh and tasty."

"I agree. Nico and I hardly eat any meat these days."

"You're very quiet, Cheryl. What do you like to eat here? I expect you'll all miss it when the island trade closes for the winter months."

There, she's started. I just wish she would get to the point so we can eat and leave. Perhaps she doesn't know how to broach the subject so should I get in there first? If she hasn't mentioned it once we've ordered, I'm diving in regardless. My days of playing games are over, and it's rather uncomfortable sitting opposite Clive. Come on, Johnny, tell us some more stories about the salon. We need the atmosphere to be fun and light hearted.

"I think I better explain why I'm here although you've probably guessed that it's not just a social visit. Since you've all left the hotel, the place had gone downhill. There's been so many complaints and the reviews on Trip Advisor have never been so bad. As for refunds, well, the system has well and truly collapsed. I need you all to come back and help me. Once I realised that I wasn't capable of running the hotel, I spoke to my accountants with a view to putting it on the market. They've advised me that I need to get it back to how it was before you all left, otherwise I have no hope of selling it in its current state.

"Suzy, you've missed out a couple of very important things there. Firstly, you didn't mention the word 'please'. Neither was there any apology for the way you treated us all."

"But, Cheryl, you all worked for me and I paid you a good wage for it. Don't forget you all lived at the hotel so you didn't have to buy food or pay for gas and electricity. You were very well looked after."

"Excuse me, Suzy, but let me remind you that we worked a seventy hour week and got paid for forty. Are you actually saying that was fair? You really don't understand, do you?"

I want to leave. I really can't believe the nerve of the woman. She ought to be grovelling on bended knee, not that I'd ever go back even if she had apologised. She thinks we owe her something. How stupid can she be? I'm going now. I knew this was a bad idea. Why did I let Johnny talk me into it?"

"Okay, you might all have had to work a few extra hours now and then but that was because of Graham's death. He was good to all of you, and I think the least you could have done was to help me get over it."

"Get over it? You had a very strange way of doing that. I believe you were spending all his hard earned cash on a string of expensive holidays within a month of him dying. I really can't believe you have the cheek to come here and expect us to come back to the hotel like this. Come on, Cheryl, we're leaving."

"Hang on a minute, Johnny, I don't think you should be speaking to Suzy like that. Some of what she said was right."

"I don't know what you heard her say, Clive, but it must have been something completely different to anything I heard. Ready, Cheryl?"

"Yes, Johnny, but first, I'm sorry you've come all this way, Suzy, but I really have no more to say. Goodbye."

"Well, that's the end of that, thanks, Johnny. I just find it funny that she really doesn't seem to grasp it. She honestly believes we all owe her something. Come on, let's go and get something to eat and laugh about it."

"Laugh? I'm still fuming about all the unpaid hours I worked at the hotel. She's been the winner in all of his."

"Would you want to swap places with her, Johnny? What you and Nico have together is worth so much more than a hotel in Devon. She can keep the hotel. I've got a fabulous life, thanks very much."

Chapter 44

At least last night turned out to be a fun night after such a disastrous start. It was just like the old days, Johnny and I drinking too much and staying out late with not a care in the world. That said, I do need to find something to do for the winter months, but I'm sure something will crop up.

I've got a bit of a sore head today and I can't believe I've slept in until 9.30am. When did that last happen? Probably after we'd been out for a similar occasion. That phone sounds loud. I really do have a bad head. It's a text from Carla inviting Vangelis and me up to the villa for dinner tomorrow before everyone leaves and we can each bring a guest. It will be very informal so no need to dress up. I wonder whether Andreas would come if I asked him.

God, I look rough. I'm going to have to work hard on my appearance to even look half decent. I think today's a day for emails from home. I wouldn't want to go out and scare people looking like this.

Firstly, I need to put something together for this mystery wedding blessing, but where to start? Vangelis told me to create something that I would love. Well, for a start after the huge success of the large circular table, that has to be a must. Perhaps a plain and simple menu as I don't know what everyone's preferences are, but what should I put on top of the cake? This is a bit ridiculous really. How can I plan a wedding blessing without even knowing anything about the couple?

Eight more weeks before the restaurant closes and we've got twelve more weddings. I need to go through each wedding file to make sure everything's signed off, deposits are paid and tie up all the loose ends. I also need to fix a date to go over to Dissinos and spend the night with Moisis and Rhea. I think it'll have to be a mid-week visit. Oh, there's a text back from Andreas to say that he will come tonight, and also a funny text from Johnny.

"What happened last night? How much did we drink? I'm feeling so ill."

We did have a good time. I wonder how Clive got on with Suzy and whether he's agreed to go back to England. It was peculiar how he became so protective of her, and we don't know how long she's staying here for. I also need to phone home as it's all gone rather quiet. No messages from Julie or Dad. That can wait though. First things first. What do I wear for our visit to the villa tonight and I wonder who Vangelis will be taking as his guest?

Andreas will be here in ten minutes, so I'll just have to pick something. There, that will do, I've not worn this for months.

"You aren't fazed by any of this, Andreas! The fact they're superstars doesn't really matter to you. Everyone else on the island is so excited, but as far as you're concerned they could be anybody. That's such a lovely way to be, but are you ready for the paparazzi? The minute that this taxi stops at the villa gate, all the flash lights from cameras will look just like fireworks."

"Of course I'm looking forward to seeing Bella and Riven in real life, but it wouldn't bother me if I didn't. I don't mean that in a nasty way, but it's just that I've never been star struck by celebrities."

That's what I like about Andreas. He's so down to earth, just goes with the flow. I feel we're beginning to get back on track and putting Clive and the visit to Corfu with Vangelis behind us. When Andreas kissed me before we got in the taxi, it might not have been full of passion, but it was on the lips and when he pulled away the look in his eyes told me all I need to know.

"Cheryl, you're right. I can't believe how many photographers are here. What do they expect to see? Surely it's the same every day, the pair of them leaving the villa and returning later. It's all very bizarre."

"Hello. Thanks for coming, and this must be the artist you were telling Sharon and myself about. We love your painting, it's perfect for us. Just what the restaurant looked like the first time we came to Holkamos. So many happy memories come flooding back every time I look at it."

"Thank you. To me, it brings back memories of the time I painted it. I remember that summer very well."

"Hello, Cheryl. How are you? Hope your week's been less stressful. We haven't stopped talking about the wedding day, have we, Dad? It was so lovely."

"Thanks, Bella. Vangelis and I felt the same and we can't thank you enough for all the publicity you've created for the restaurant. We're so grateful. Oh, I'm sorry, I haven't introduced you. This is Andreas, the artist who painted the picture of the restaurant."

"Very nice to meet you, Andreas. We loved the painting. Here comes Mum and Riven. What can I get you to drink? This looks like Vangelis coming through the gate."

He's by himself. I was sure he'd bring someone with him. Now it will be an odd number. Lots of the female friends he's grown up with would have killed to be here with him tonight just to be able to stare at Riven.

"Here come the drinks. Thank you all for coming. It's been such a special week, not just because of Mum and Dad's wedding, but I've loved showing Riven my favourite place in the whole world. The wedding was the icing on the cake and now Mum and Dad have an apartment here, both Riven and myself will be popping back from time to time but hopefully without all the razzmatazz. If you'll excuse me, I'll go and see how the chefs are getting on with dinner."

"Hi, Vangelis. No date? I'm surprised. I would have thought you'd have some beautiful blonde on your arm tonight."

"I have, Cheryl. She'll be here any moment. Here she comes."

Carla's his date and just look at the way she's looking at him, not to mention how excited Vangelis seems to be. I'm jealous, but I don't know why? I don't want him and it's not as if I don't approve of Carla. She's lovely. How did I not notice this? They've been seeing each other all the time she's been on the island.

"Are you alright, Cheryl. You're miles away. Is anything wrong?"

"Sorry, Andreas. No, I suddenly thought of something I've forgotten to do at work, but it's not a problem. I can send the email tomorrow."

"Right, everyone take your seats, dinner is about to be served. Sadly, our last one here on the island for the time being."

"Before we begin, can I say a huge thank you on behalf of Sharon and myself to three special women who have made mine and my wife's wedding so special. Please raise your glasses to Carla for coordinating all the flights, transport, and this beautiful villa. Cheryl, you've worked so hard in all the planning for our special day and finally, Bella. If it wasn't for her, none of this would have happened."

"Thanks, Dad. That's very kind, but actually it was all down to Cheryl and Carla. Now dig in everyone before the food gets cold. So, tell me all about you and your painting, Andreas. Do you have a studio here on the island? What a fabulous place to paint."

"I was born and brought up here on the island, but came back from art college in Rhodes when my father died to help my mum run the family gift shop. I wanted her to sell up but she was having none of it. She felt that would be letting my dad down. So this year has been a bit stressful as I've slowly persuaded her to move with the times. She wanted to keep the shop exactly the same as Dad had it, but I've managed to get rid of a lot of the... let's say, not so

255

exciting stock and introduce more pottery, jewellery and art work to the place.

"It's been so successful, but I've got Cheryl to thank for encouraging me. The shop looks nothing like it did at the start of the season and now that's happened, my mum thinks she might sell up."

"That's exciting. Would that mean you could go back to college if she doesn't need your help?"

"I think I would just concentrate on my painting, yes. There's so many areas I want to explore and learn, so it could be a very exciting time for me."

What has he just said? Going back to Rhodes? I wasn't aware of any of this. He can't, the business is doing so well. Why can't he stay here and paint and have someone else run the shop?

This evening is turning into a disaster. First, I'd discovered I do have feelings for Vangelis. Now the one man I really want to be with is talking about leaving. I need to think of something to say. I don't want to hear any of this.

"Sharon, Brian, when will the new apartment be finished? It's very exciting for both of you."

"Yes, Cheryl. Hopefully we'll be able to move in next March. Bella and I have been on the Internet looking for furniture already. Brian's leaving all that to us, but as long as we get him a comfy chair out on the balcony, he'll be happy. Isn't that right, darling?"

"Whatever you say, Sharon. You know me, I'm happy with anything as long as I'm in the sunshine."

"That was a beautiful dinner, thanks so much, Bella."

"Don't thank me, Vangelis. I've not lifted a finger since I've been on the island. Why don't we move down to the little terrace for coffee and then the staff can clear up?"

"How long has this been going on, Vangelis."

"You sound just like my mother, Cheryl. Nothing's going on at all. We just discovered that we like similar things and we've spent a bit of time together."

"I see one plane taking off and another coming in."

"Do I sense jealousy in your tone?"

"Why would I be jealous, Vangelis?"

"I don't know, you tell me. By the way, you didn't mention that Andreas might be leaving the island. I hope you won't be going with him as I wouldn't want to lose my best employee. We're a team, we work so well together and everything's been so successful. We need each other to make this work. Yes, that's it. We're better together than apart. Don't you agree, Cheryl? We really are meant to be together."

Chapter 45

I wasn't feeling very well, but this time it's got nothing to do with either my head or stomach. It's my heart that's hurting. Why didn't Andreas tell me about his plans or even give a slight hint? Vangelis could tell that I didn't know anything about it and the whole thing about his date with Carla was a ploy to get me jealous. He knew very well that it would and yes, it worked.

This summer started out being my perfect summer, but now it's turning out to be one of the worst. I also need to start thinking about my future and what I'm going to do in October. Do I really want to be helping Mum and Dad settle into their separate lives? The bigger question is do I want to come back here next year. The way I'm feeling now, I regret coming here in the first place. Perhaps the answer is a life with Clive. He gave up his life in England to win me back. Should we go back and work for Suzy? To be honest, I think I should just give up on men and this whole wedding business.

As for the weddings, I can't believe how many more enquiries we've had. It's very kind of Bella and Riven to keep posting things about our restaurant on social media, but I'd really love to switch off from the whole thing. I deserve a day off.

I could go over to Dissinos and see Moisis and Rhea but that would mean discussing the situation with Andreas. I think I'll just have a day to myself with no phones, no conversations and no reading even the urgent emails or replying to the text from Johnny asking me to phone him as he's got some gossip. I'm not interested in gossip today. I'm switching off for the day. Normal service will resume tomorrow.

This is just what I need, a long walk up to Creakos through all the olive groves. It's just so lovely. One minute I'm under the huge olive trees and then all of a sudden out into the bright sunlight with hundreds of years' worth of stories. If only these trees could talk! I still can't get over how I feel so at home on this island. I'm so comfortable here that I can't give it up. I need to come back next year and earn enough money so that I don't need to find work in the winter.

Yes, I need to put down some roots of my own here. By next spring Vangelis will have given up all hope of us getting together. Perhaps I could rent something a little bigger, a small house or apartment and not just a holiday rental. Who knows, in a few years' time I might be able to afford to buy something. All those thoughts about regretting coming here are ridiculous. It's the best thing that ever happened in my life. This walk has done me the world of good and I know I have something exciting to look forward to when I get up to Creakos. It won't just be the fabulous view overlooking this stunning island, there'll also be food.

Creakos is special because it's not too touristy. It's a long way down to the beaches and so visitors would need a car but there's not many places to park down on Volmos. This little hilltop village is full of local people, mainly young families who travel down to work in Holkamos. The older ones have moved here for a quieter life. There's no gift shops aimed at the tourist trade. It's just businesses the village needs for everyone to live day to day, butchers, bakers, mini markets and lots of little taverns selling breakfast, lunch, dinners and coffee. I actually think I could live here. It's a lovely place to escape to after a day down at the beach.

Talking of coffee, this one's rather strong, but better than alcohol. I think the homemade biscuits help and the wondrous view. I feel so high up that I could easily touch the clouds, if there were any. It's perfect. The peace and quiet is lovely, just the odd car or scooter passing by.

"Hello, Cheryl, what brings you up to Creakos?"

"Oh, hello, Mrs Galanis. I just love it up here. It's the perfect place to come and think things over and put everything into perspective. Would you like to join me for a coffee?"

"Thank you that would be nice, but please call me Eudora. I agree it is lovely up here. I was actually born here, and without being morbid I hope to die up here as well. If you don't mind me asking, what do you have to put into perspective? You're not regretting coming here, are you? From all accounts you've done a fantastic job with the weddings and some people say you've managed to tame Vangelis. Personally, that's something I'd take with a pinch of salt. As long as young ladies keep coming to Holkamos, I don't think he'll ever change."

"Eudora, that's something we agree on."

"He's a hard worker and it's not his fault he was born with those beautiful eyes. His father was exactly the same. He loved the ladies right up until he died. I suppose it's some sort of family tradition."

"You're very amusing, Eudora, and yes, Vangelis is very committed to his business. I'll tell you something and that's he's a little scared of me. When I say jump, he answers, 'How high?' But I can handle him and I expect you're going to ask me whether I've fallen for his charm. The answer to that is no, I'm not going to be another name on his list of conquests."

"But, Cheryl, people are saying that since you've been working together, Vangelis has changed and that perhaps you've been the one to tame in. Anyway, Vangelis isn't the only one who's taken a shine to you, is he?"

"No, and if you're referring to Andreas, the feeling is mutual. But perhaps it's not to be. Things don't seem to be straightforward there either."

"I know I haven't made things easy for you, Cheryl, but you need to understand that I was the one who picked up the pieces when that woman did what she did. No one else saw what Andreas went through. I can't let that happen again. People here on Holkamos were very cruel, laughing and making comments. I don't know why they still feel the need to talk about it. Believe me, Cheryl, it was nothing to do with you personally, I'd have been the same with anyone who became close to Andreas."

"Perhaps it was all for the best. You're selling the shop and Andreas is moving away. I know it's none of my business, Eudora, but what's made you decide to sell the shop? A few months ago you wanted everything left as it was before your husband passed away, and now it doesn't seem to matter."

"I felt I'd be letting my late husband down if I changed things in the shop. It wasn't taking enough money to live off, but I didn't want to admit to it. I just wanted to keep it going in the same way, but when Andreas started to sell paintings and pottery I couldn't believe the difference.

"I thought to myself that if my husband had been in a position to change things he definitely would have done. I suppose if I'm truthful, I was scared of the future, but as the months have passed by I've come to realise that the shop isn't the right place for Andreas. He lives for his art and he's capable of making a good living out of it, so I need to let him go and do what his heart's telling him to do.

"While all these thoughts were going around and around, I was approached by a local business man who asked if he could buy the business. Apparently his daughter is an artist and wants it for a shop come studio, in much the same way as it is now. This time the first thing I thought of was what would my husband have done? He'd have grabbed the offer with both hands and taken the money. So I'm going to move back up here to where I was born and Andreas will be free to go off and pursue his dreams. Do you know, Cheryl, I'm not afraid to admit it, but I've been such a silly woman, trying to live in the past. I realise now that things change, life moves on."

"Yes, it does, Eudora, but the most important thing now is that you're happy and you don't have any worries about the shop. I'm so pleased for you and I'm glad that Andreas can go back to Rhodes and do what he loves the most.

"Before I came up here this morning, Eudora, I was ready to say goodbye to Greece forever. I've also been silly. Holkamos is my home now. I may have to leave it in the winter months, but I'll be back stronger and more positive than ever before."

"Why don't we have some lunch, Cheryl? I have a cousin just round the corner who has a little restaurant. Well, if you can call it that because it only has six tables and there's no menu. You just get what you're given, but I haven't heard anyone ever complain about that."

"That would be lovely. The good thing is that the way home is all downhill. I love using the word 'home' because, Eudora, after all these years, I've found somewhere I truly belong."

Chapter 46

What a lovely day I had with Eudora yesterday. God, she was right about the food, it was lovely, and the local Greek wine just goes down a treat. Lunch turned into dinner, how that ever happened I don't know. The time just flew by. It was so nice to hear Eudora talk about her life on Holkamos as a child, right up to the present day. Although Andreas featured in the conversation quite a bit, I could tell Eudora was avoiding it as much as possible. She's aware how much I like him so she was very tactful.

Today's another day and there's work to be done. First of all, I need to reply to Johnny. I can't believe the number of texts and messages he's sent over the last 24 hours. If it was urgent I would have replied sooner, but gossip can wait. I need to stop off at the bakery and get something to soak up all last night's wine, so I think I'll pop into the salon and find out what the gossip is. It's probably just hairdressing tittle tattle though. I also need to reply to Andreas. His text was quite funny: 'You got my Mum drunk. You should see her this morning, not a pleasant experience'. It wasn't my idea, it was totally Eudora's.

"Good morning, boys. Now what's so urgent that I need to know about it straightaway? Has someone's hair turned green? Has this Greek island run out of peroxide?"

"You may well laugh, Cheryl. I've a good mind not to tell you now and keep this exciting news all to myself."

"I'm only teasing you, Johnny, and don't be so loud, I've a bad wine head today."

"So that's why you didn't answer my calls or return my texts. You were out drinking. Anyone I know?"

"Actually I was out with Andreas' mum. We ate and drank too much and I'm suffering for it today. So, what's the news?"

"Only that one of your little problems has been resolved. You'll be glad to hear that a certain Clive isn't interested in you anymore. He has another interest."

"Really? How do you know?"

"Well, the night before last, Nico and I went for something to eat down in the harbour. It was late, about ten-thirty, and so by the time we were walking home it was well past midnight. We spotted a couple arm in arm. Well, you know me, I don't miss a trick, and I recognised the rear of a certain young man, namely Clive. So we slowed down but kept them in sight. The next thing I saw was the female turning towards him and they started kissing. I was gobsmacked, and you know it takes a lot for that to happen to me."

"So, he was kissing a girl. That doesn't mean he's not interested in me anymore."

"Ah, but the story doesn't end there, Cheryl. Nico's friend in the restaurant popped in to say that Clive's handed in his notice. He's leaving to go back and work in England."

"That's good news. One down, one more to go."

"Sorry, what do you mean, Cheryl?"

"Nothing, I was only mumbling to myself."

"Yes, that's the news, but don't you want to know the gossip? I saw the woman with my own eyes. Clive was snogging Suzy."

"No way. You must have imagined it, although he did stick up for her in the restaurant. I'll get to the bottom of it. We know where she's staying, I'll ask her."

"But why, Cheryl? If Clive's going back to England, we don't need to get involved. You don't seem very happy about it. You're not jealous, are you? Surely you're not interested in him after all this time?"

"Of course I'm not jealous. I just want to find out what's going on?"

"Okay, you find out, but none of it is of any

interest to me. Both of them are in the past as far as I'm concerned. Holkamos is my life now. I'll catch up with you later, darling."

Johnny's right, that is all in the past, but how can Clive go from declaring undying love for me one minute and then in the flick of a switch be snogging Suzy's face off? Am I jealous? Well, to be brutally honest, yes, I am, but I need to pull myself together. I was in such a good place yesterday, but now I feel like I've been trod on. Okay, I didn't want Clive, but I certainly didn't want Suzy to have him and whatever Johnny says, yes I do want to know what it's all about. Time for work now.

The view from this office is the perfect pill to calm me down. I'm blessed and I know that. Perhaps I ought to appreciate it a lot more. So many people would swap places with me, but I just don't need these three men messing around with my head. The stupid thing is, I'm just being silly for allowing it.

"Hi, Cheryl, are you free for a chat."

"Morning, Vangelis. How are you? Did you enjoy the evening at the villa? Bella and Riven have been so kind to us by dropping the wedding business into their social media posts. We've been so lucky with that, and the good thing is I've been able to judge the genuine enquiries from the fake, time wasting ones. At some point later we'll need to sit down and restructure some of the pricing though. I'm sure we can increase the price for certain things as you'll be able to negotiate better deals with some of the suppliers.

"Oh, by the way, were you able to spend some time with Carla before she left? She couldn't keep her eyes off you all night."

"I was waiting for you to bring that up. No, nothing really happened between us. It was..."

"You don't need to explain to me, Vangelis. It's no business of mine what you get up to."

"Don't be like that, Cheryl. I was just a little bit of

company for her amidst all the stress of organising everything up at the villa. All we did was have a few drinks together. Nothing happened, although she was a sweet girl.

"The night at the villa was lovely. One thing confused me though. When Andreas mentioned selling the shop and going back to art college, the look on your face was as if you didn't know anything about it. Surely he'd already discussed it with you?"

"What Andreas does with his life is his business. Now, was there anything else, Vangelis, because I've got a stack of emails to get through? Before you go, about this wedding booking you're dealing with. Have you got any more information because I'm finding it difficult to organise without knowing anything about the couple and what they do and don't like?"

"Just pretend you're in your fifties, and you're have a wedding blessing. Choose everything you'd want. I'm sure that will be perfect."

"Okay, but it seems rather strange to me."

"Cheryl, you know I'm always here for you and I'm sure the situation with Andreas is all for the best. He seems a little mixed up, and into the quiet things in life. You two are so different, but like I said, I'll always be here for you."

Sometimes I could just hit him. Vangelis certainly knows my weak points. He's right though, Andreas and I are like chalk and cheese and he does need to go and fulfil his dreams. Mine are here on Holkamos. I might not have a man in tow, but... no, there're no buts. Life's very good and I'm going to keep telling myself that until I truly believe it.

Now to organise this wedding blessing for the couple without a name. I'll christen them Fred and Ginger for now, and it will be a very glamorous do. Cocktails, canapés, all very sleek and romantic. Or should it be low key? This is so difficult. I'm going to forget about it for today. There's the phone now, a text. 'Hi, Cheryl. Do you have a couple of minutes to

266

spare? I'm just down on the beach a little way from your office. I promise I won't take up much of your time, but there's something I need to tell you, Clive'.

I know exactly what he's going to tell me. Should I tell him that he's wasting both our time because I already know or perhaps it would be better to see him grovel. I'll get this over and done with and say my goodbyes. At least I don't have to face Suzy.

"Give me five minutes and I'll meet you at Bar Volmos."

I need to play this cool and wish him well. Let him leave on good terms.

"Hi, Cheryl, thanks for coming. What can I get you to drink?"

"A large gin and tonic please."

"The waitress said she'd bring the drinks over. Now, I've come to tell you something. I'm going back to…"

"I know why you called me over here, Clive, and I'm pleased for you. You're brilliant at the job, and as far as the relationship, I wish you well with that."

"Cheryl, I don't know whether I'm doing the right thing, but I really miss Dartmouth. Not being there makes me homesick. I loved the job, but a large part of that was working with you, so it will be very different not having you around.

"I wasn't like you and Johnny though as the long hours didn't bother me so much. It was my kitchen and to ensure everything ran smoothly I was prepared to put in all the hours it needed. I don't have anything to lose by going back to England, do I? And on top of that Suzy and I have become quite close recently.

"After you and Johnny left us the other night, Suzy and I continued drinking and one thing led to another. Suzy does have a lot of issues, but she's very nice. Cheryl, do you forgive me for coming here and messing everything up for you? I know I've been a pain, but I did really think we should have been together."

"Yes, you have been a pain, but in some ways it was rather flattering to think you followed me here. Of course I forgive you, Clive. We've got far too many years under our belt to fall out. I wish you both well, I really do. No hard feelings. It's time for both of us to move on and see what the world has to offer."

So much for getting lots of work done, but at least Clive and I parted on good terms. How on earth he'll cope with Suzy is anyone's guess. Rather him than me. Saying that, she won't be there forever, but that's Clive's problem.

I'm not going back to the office now. The rest of the emails can wait until tomorrow as I'm just not in the mood for them. I'll take a walk into Holkamos, have a look round the shops and have a nice plate of moussaka. I might even call in on Andreas.

No, actually I've had enough of men for today. I'll go and have some food and then it's home to bed. Tomorrow I'll throw myself into other people's romances and making their dreams come true with the perfect wedding.

Chapter 47

I'm so glad I had that early night. I'm buzzing today and sitting at my desk at 6.30am. For once I don't need gallons of coffee to get me started and by lunch time every email will be replied to. That will give me the afternoon to plan this wedding blessing for Fred and Ginger. I'm going off the Fred and Ginger names though, and thought about calling them Pinky and Perky, but perhaps that's a bit rude.

It's lovely being down on Volmos beach before all the visitors settle for the day. I hope Suzy doesn't take advantage of Clive... Oh, I must stop wandering off the subject and concentrating on my work. I must phone Dad later though when he's at work so he'll be able to talk without Mum listening in. It would be nice if he had his own place by the time I go back to England in October. I could help him move in or do some labouring for him. That would keep me going until March.

All done. I said I'd get my work done by lunch time and I've beaten my target by fifteen minutes. The email inbox is empty. Now for something to eat and to get on with the mystery wedding blessing. Before I leave tonight I'm going to update the wall chart. Nothing else is going to be added to it, so I'm going to put the next three years' bookings up, so Vangelis will have to look at it. Oh, there's the phone.

"Hi, Cheryl. There's a lady down here in the restaurant asking if she can have a quick word with you."

"Thanks. Give me a moment and I'll be down."

"Hi, Cheryl. I thought I'd best come and say goodbye, and explain a few things. Is there somewhere quiet we can go?"

"Hello, Suzy. I'm glad you've popped in. Why don't we take a walk along the beach? If we walk towards the yachts, the beach gets a lot quieter." '

"You must be wondering why Clive and I got together. Before coming to Holkamos it didn't occur to me that there'd ever be an attraction between us, but something just clicked. Anyway, that's not the reason I've come to see you.

"I know you didn't have a lot of time for me and I understand why. When Graham died I didn't do anything to help run the hotel. I just left everyone to get on with it, but the problem actually started a long time before Graham died. When we both got together I wanted to help him run the hotel, but there wasn't a place for me. I didn't fit into the team. Johnny had the reception and all the bookwork organised. You and Clive had the catering. Graham was more than happy for me to be a lady of leisure but that wasn't really what I wanted. I was upset not to be involved in the hotel. Even when you all had the Friday management meetings, there wasn't even a chair for me to sit on, let alone join in with. It really did hurt.

"I knew exactly what the staff were saying. Apparently I was just a gold digger who arrived at the hotel with her belongings in a carrier bag. No one mentioned the fact that I also came with bruises. No one bothered to ask what had happened. No, I was the woman who was just going to jump into bed with the hotel owner, give him what he wanted and then spend his money. I wanted to be part of the team, but no one would give me a chance.

"By the way, those bruises were from a previous boyfriend who was unhappy that I didn't have any beer money to give him. That was the reason I walked out. I'd put up with the beatings for two years, and didn't even have a suitcase. I wasn't looking for a husband. In fact, men were the last thing on my mind. I just wanted to be safe.

"You were kind enough to give me a job and I appreciate that today as much as I did then. Graham made the first move, and for weeks I tried to put him off. When I eventually gave in and everyone found out about it, I was painted as some kind of scarlet woman. When Graham died and it became my hotel, you, Clive, Johnny and Debbie cut me out. I didn't have a clue what was going on and every time I asked one of you I got the same reply that everything was organised. All I wanted to do was be one of the team, but I was pushed away. No one considered the fact that I was grieving and needed help. All I could hear was 'the gold digger has got what she wanted'."

"I don't know what to say. Sorry doesn't seem enough. Graham did tell me that you hadn't had a good time before coming to the hotel, and he was determined to make it up to you. That's why you weren't involved. He just wanted to spoil you and for you to enjoy life. After he died, the people who worked for him felt that a way of saying thank you would be to keep things exactly as if he was still there. We weren't deliberately shutting you out, but he was such a good man to all of us we wanted to do our best for him. I'm so sorry that you felt like that."

"I just thought I'd best get all that of my chest before I go home. I don't know what the future holds for me or the hotel, Cheryl, but I want to learn about the business. Now with Clive taking over the catering side, I can concentrate on the front of house. If I can get to grips with the reception work, I might stand a chance of turning it around and back to the way it was before you left. I'm not doing this just for me, I'm doing it for Graham too."

"Suzy, you were the best thing that ever happened to Graham. All he ever had in life was the hotel until you came along and showed him there was more to life than work. You made him happy. He was very lucky to have you in his life and those of us who were close to him knew how happy he really was."

"Thank you, Cheryl, it's very kind of you to say that. I hope everything works out for you here on Holkamos, but remember if ever you come back to

England and are looking for work, there'll always be a warm welcome back in Dartmouth for you. The door will always be open."

Well, I wasn't expecting that, but Suzy was right in saying that we didn't involve her in anything. I'm happy for her and Clive. He'll take the lead and guide her through things. Perhaps that's just what he needs as well. In one way she's just like she was the first day I met her standing there with her carrier bags. Now, there're no carrier bags but a hotel. I know she'll succeed and in my heart I wish her all the luck in the world, I really do.

Now back to work and to put a couple of hours into Vangelis' mystery wedding blessing. I'll have it similar to Brian and Sharon's wedding with a circular table, but what about the floristry theme? Subtle or brash? Soft pinks or bright oranges? Now the phone's ringing. I'll never get this planned.

"Hi, Dad. How are you? I was going to phone you later."

"I'm good thanks. How's everything on Holkamos?"

"Oh, it's okay but a bit stressful. I'm trying to arrange a wedding blessing for a couple I haven't even spoken to. It's something Vangelis has given me to do and it's driving me mad as I don't want to mess it all up."

"There's no way you'll do that. Whatever you plan will be a success and I'm sure the couple will love it."

"Thanks, Dad. I don't share your confidence, but never mind that, what's going on with you and Mum?"

"Everything's pretty much the same, nothing new to tell you. I'll let you get on with your work. Just plan it as if it was your own wedding and I'm sure you won't go wrong. Hope you manage to get it sorted. Bye for now, darling."

Dad's still not saying very much. Perhaps he's waiting to tell me in person when I go back at the end of the season. It will seem strange having my parents living in two separate homes, but hopefully they'll both be happy that way. It's an opportunity for each of them to move on, but such a shame they didn't do it years ago because by now they could have been happy with different partners and not had to go through all that bickering.

Now, back to this silly wedding thing. Perhaps Dad's right, I should just arrange something I would want, and if it's not right Vangelis can take the blame for not giving me more information.

Chapter 48

It's now September. Where has the summer gone? Just four more weddings… Well, three and this mystery blessing thing that Vangelis gave me to organise. Then I'll be home, but with no indication on what Mum and Dad are up to. When I asked if I could stay with them it didn't seem to be a problem though. Looking at the catering agency websites, it looks like it will be quite easy to get some bar or waitressing work leading up to Christmas and if I'm willing to do split shifts and weekends I can take my pick of where I want to work.

"Morning, Vangelis. Just four more to go and it's all over with for this season. Just look at next year's bookings. I can't believe how many there are for one week in June. At this rate the beach café will be a permanent wedding venue.

"Yes, whoever would have thought it could have taken off like it has. It's such a lovely feeling and I don't have to worry about the winter so much. I can't go wild, but I will be able to take a little break without having to work in the olive groves or on a building site. All that's down to you, Cheryl, and I'll be forever thankful to you for it."

"We're a team, Vangelis, and that's why it worked. Fingers crossed, it will continue for many years to come. By the way, everything's finalised for the rest of the year and I'm making sure deposits for next year are paid before I leave at the end of the month."

"Thanks, Cheryl, you really do treat this as if it's your own business and not just act like an employee might. You put so much time and attention into it. To think this all started with your sister wanting a grand beach wedding! Whoever would have imagined it would turn out like this."

"Yes, Vangelis, but it was a gamble for both of us. You transforming your café and me giving up everything I had in England. We've both worked so hard, but it's been exciting watching it all pan out the way it has. Most of all we've had fun, don't you think?"

"Yes, everything's been really enjoyable. It's been one of the happiest summers I've had on Holkamos. Can I ask you something, Cheryl, and tell me to mind my own business if you like, but how are you and Andreas getting on?"

"I've only seen him a couple of times since we all went up to the villa. He's excited about going back to art college. Everything's very civil but it's just small talk with no mention of us, but then I've been just as cool about everything as he has been. It was nice while it lasted."

"I'm sorry, Cheryl and I know I didn't help the situation, but I don't think it's about you. He just loves art and his painting so much. I really don't think he has room for anything else in his life and as he won't have the worry of his mum or the shop he can pursue his dreams, and I believe he'll be successful."

"You're right, Vangelis. I think I was just expecting to have my dream job, this beautiful island and the man to go along with it, but I'll settle on two out of the three. I just want to go home to my parents, get the winter over with and then return here."

"As long as you're okay, that's all that matters. None of us know what the future holds. You might surprise yourself and come back and see your boss in a different way. Then it will be three out of three."

"Don't spoil it, Vangelis. Now, I have work to be getting on with, and I'm sure you have too."

"Okay, I get the message."

"By the way, you remember I'm going over to Rhea and Moisis on Dissinos for a few days next week, but I'll be back for the weekend wedding."

"Yes, no problem. Dissinos is just stunning. Have a lovely time and give them my love."

"I will. I'm really looking forward to switching off completely."

Vangelis never misses an opportunity. Surely by now he must realise that what we have is just a working relationship. He's right about Andreas though. Art is the love of his life and who can blame him after all he went through with Elpis. Hopefully we'll still be friends for many years to come as no doubt he'll be coming back to visit his mum. It would be nice if we could meet up for a drink from time to time.

A few weeks ago I was angry with all three men in my life. Now Clive's gone back to England knowing where we stand, there's no hard feelings over Andreas, and Vangelis and I are very good friends.

Chapter 49

"Good morning, Moisis. Thank you so much for inviting me over to Dissinos. I've been so excited about it. How's Rhea?"

"Hop aboard, Cheryl. Rhea's fine. We've both been looking forward to you coming over to the island. You know how quiet it was when you came last year, well, it's even quieter now. The season's coming to an end and we feel a bit like Robinson Crusoe on our own private beach. Sit back and enjoy the journey."

This is so perfect and what a way to finish off my first season in Greece. Okay, I've another couple weeks to work, but everything for those weddings is planned. All I'm doing now is updates on all next year's bookings, so this will be my leaving party with Rhea and Moisis. I'm sure the food will be excellent as cooking is their hobby and I can't wait to see their home. It looks stunning from the photographs.

"Nearly there, Cheryl. I've a quiet day, just have to go back to Holkamos once more this evening, so hopefully by eight o'clock you'll start to smell the delights of our kitchen. We're looking forward to cooking for others and not just ourselves."

"I hope you've not gone to a lot of trouble. I'm easily pleased, just being on the island is enough for me."

"No, we want to, it's our special end of season meal. I can see Rhea on the beach waving a welcome back to Dissinos wave."

"Hello, Rhea, thank you so much for inviting me."

"We're excited to have you here. Now I've just got to sort out the supplies which Moisis has brought back with him, so why don't you unwind by finding a nice spot on the beach? I'll catch up with you in a couple of hours if that's alright. Give me your overnight bag, Cheryl, and I'll take it back the house.

Enjoy the beach!"

They seem to be going to a lot of fuss just for me. I'm a little embarrassed by it, but Moisis said cooking for others? Why didn't he say cooking for you? I wonder if there'll be other people here. I hope not as I'm not in the mood to meet new people. Anyway, this is the perfect start to my couple of days off with the beach and beautiful blue sea.

Time to switch my phone off. There's just one text from Julie asking if I would like to stay with her and Richard when I come back for the winter. I don't think so. If Mum and Dad have split up, I'd prefer to spend my time between the two of them. The thought of girly makeover nights with Julie and her friends puts the fear of God into me. I'll reply later. Time for a dip in the sea first.

"Hi, how are you doing? Is it nice having a beach to yourself? Cheryl, do you fancy a cold drink and something to eat?"

"Oh, sorry, I must have dozed off. What's the time, Rhea?"

"We don't look at the clock on Dissinos, but I think you've been asleep for about three hours. It's getting hot out on the beach and I don't want you to burn. That's why I woke you up."

"Yes, I am hot. I might just have another dip. Shall I meet you up at the café?"

I can't believe I've been asleep so long. That's certainly enough sun for me today although I could stay floating about here in the sea for hours. I'm so lucky, and it's all down to Julie. If it wasn't for all her grand ideas about coming here for her wedding, I'd never have come to Greece. I suppose I'd still be in Dartmouth. Come to that, so would Johnny. Now look at him training to be a hairdresser and starting a new life with Nico. We both have a lot to thank Julie for.

I really hope the winter passes by quickly as I'll be

looking forward to coming back. It would be nice if I could find somewhere nice to rent. Vangelis' holiday apartment is lovely, but I can't really create a home there. Hopefully with all the contacts I've made here something will turn up. It doesn't have to be that big, just a lounge, kitchen, bedroom and bathroom will do me. Right, I'd best get out of the sea before Rhea comes looking for me thinking I've drowned.

"Sorry, Rhea, I just didn't want to get out the sea. It's so lovely."

"I know. I've been going in at least twice a day. I'm ready to close up here so let's walk back to the house. Just give me a minute. I don't know why I put everything inside really. It's not as if anyone's around to steal anything. That's it, follow me. We'll cut through the olive groves. It's only fifteen to twenty minutes away. Looking at these olive trees, that will be our next job once the holidaymakers have gone. It's hard work but all the islanders pull together and help each other working a few days in one place and then moving on to someone else's for a few days until all the olives have been harvested.

"It's nice to catch up with friends who have been working hard all summer. Just behind you is our little holiday studio you'll be staying in. That's another winter job for us. We're hoping to convert the other barn into a two bedroom apartment, but we've been saying that for the last three years so it probably won't get done this winter.

"The door's unlocked if you want to have a shower and get changed. Moisis put your bag in there earlier. I'll see you back at the cottage when you're ready. Feel free to help yourself to a drink from the fridge, or make yourself a coffee if you prefer."

"Rhea, you didn't need to give me the holiday let. I could have slept on your sofa and let you earn some money from the studio. Please let me pay something towards it."

"Don't be silly. It's yours to enjoy for a few days

and to come and go as you please."

"No, I've come to spend time with you and Moisis, not to do my own thing."

"Okay, Cheryl, we'll see. Come over when you're ready."

This holiday studio is so lovely, small but I love its rustic charm. Imagine staying here for a fortnight's holiday! I can see why it's so expensive to rent. It's secluded, but worth every penny.

Right, first thing is to have a shower and put my phone away in a drawer so no one can get hold of me. Vangelis has Rhea's number if he needs me for anything.

"Thanks so much, Rhea. It's really beautiful. I feel like I'm on holiday. By the way, I've put the other set of towels in the top of the wardrobe. I won't be one of those guests who uses every available towel."

"That's fine. Now come and have a look around the cottage. Not that we're ever in it for long. We cook, eat and live outdoors most of the time from March right through to October. We might need a fleece for the November evenings, but it's still quite warm."

"It's so beautiful. Can I do anything to help you, Rhea?"

"No, thanks, Cheryl, Everything's in hand. Moisis will be back later from his last trip of the day. How about we open a bottle of wine? I don't think it's too early, and you can tell me all about the wedding business and your plans for the winter."

"It's been really good, but the most exciting thing is the number of bookings for the next couple of years. A lot of that was thanks to Bella Lacywhite and Riven posting things on social media, and I've persuaded Vangelis to put his prices up."

"Talking of Vangelis, have you fallen for those eyelashes or that Greek charm yet?"

"Oh no, and to be quite honest he's got the message that nothing's going to happen. As for the winter I'm going back to England to live with my mum and dad, although they could be living separate lives by the time I get back. I'll work on wedding enquiries throughout the winter and then come back to Holkamos in the early spring. Hopefully next year I'll earn enough to see me through the winter so I won't need to go back."

"So what's happening between you and Andreas? I know his mum's selling the shop and he's going back to Rhodes, but surely you'll still be able to see each other."

"I don't think so. He's still got quite a few issues going on his head and I don't think there's enough room in there for me as well. I've come round to that way of thinking now and I'm quite happy about it."

"I've just got to pop indoors to finish off a few things. Enjoy the last of the sunshine and help yourself to more wine."

If I had enough money to not need to work, I could live here with a couple of dogs. It would be perfect here with no people around, but I suppose that's just a dream. I feel a bit lazy sitting here with my feet up while Rhea prepares everything, but I'll insist on clearing up after dinner. There's a phone ringing and it's not mine, thank goodness.

"That was Moisis to say he's just leaving Holkamos, so they shouldn't be too long."

"They? Is he bringing people who live on the island back, Rhea?"

"Oh, sorry, I forgot to tell you. We've also invited Andreas over for the evening."

"And I expect you forgot to tell him that I'd be here as well."

"You could be right on that. It's not a problem, is it, Cheryl?"

"Not for me, but I'm not sure about Andreas. This is a little bit like matchmaking."

"I really don't know what you mean. Would you like to help me lay the table, Cheryl?"

So this is the reason why Rhea's gone to so much

trouble. It's nice, but I think she'll be disappointed as both Andreas and I know where we stand. The plan isn't going to work, more's the pity but I know we'll all have a lovely evening.

"The table looks wonderful, Rhea. You've gone to so much trouble with all the candles and fresh flowers and I love all the lights in the trees. I think I might just pop back to my room and put a brush through my hair now it's dried, if that's alright."

"Yes, I'm going to change. I think I'll put on one of my summer dresses rather than my normal shorts and T-shirt."

That's Rhea's way of telling me to dress up and put a bit of effort into the evening. She's really thought this entire thing through. Thank goodness I brought my nice summer dress. I'm starting to feel nervous or could it be excitement? I don't really know. I don't want to look as though I've tried too hard, but equally I don't want Andreas to think I'm part of this plan.

I also regret having had three glasses of wine as the last one's gone to my head. I'll have to stick to water for the rest of the evening. Right, here goes, I expect Moisis and Andreas are here by now. I need to play it cool, but not overdo it, as that would look as though I'm not interested.

"Hi, Andreas. I think two people here have set a little trap for us. I'm sorry I didn't know you were coming here until a few minutes ago."

"Yes, I agree. I knew they were up to something because they mentioned bringing a nice shirt with me. Anyway, Cheryl, it's nice to see you away from the shop and all those weddings."

"Hands up! Yes, this was all planned, but if we'd have told either of you we weren't sure you'd both turn up. Things must be okay between you as there's no sulking or fighting, so take a seat at the table because dinner's about to be served."

So much for sticking to water, but then I'm not as nervous as I was before and as for the meal it was beautiful. I'm glad I've been allowed to do something, even if it is just carrying the dirty dishes inside.

"You're not angry with us, are you, Cheryl? We just thought it would be nice to get together. We'll go and sit down on the sofas at the bottom of the garden and Moisis will light the chimney. It's sheltered from the breeze down there and so very cosy."

"Let me top your glasses up. I know what I wanted to ask you, Andreas. Moisis and I were chatting and neither of us understand why you need to go back to the art college. Your paintings are selling well. Surely there's nothing else they can teach you there. I remember reading about an artist who said that too many technical skills take away an artist's passion and they begin to lose their unique individuality. You have such a brilliant take on things with your work and such great style that it would be a shame to lose it."

"I know what you mean, Rhea, but I feel I've still got so much to learn and..."

"...and it's a way to escape from Holkamos and the past. Why not just set up a studio on Holkamos, paint, sell your work and relax. Your mum's putting the shop behind her and moving on, so perhaps it's time to slow down and enjoy your life again."

"No one else could or would say that to me, but I'll let you get away with it, Rhea, and you're probably right about losing my style. Perhaps I'm just looking for the easy option."

"You don't realise how good your work is, Andreas. I think you'd learn more by not seeing other people's work, but what do I know? I only organise weddings. I'm not an art connoisseur, but I know what I like and your work's really good."

"Right I've said my bit and put you on the spot. Now it's time for dessert. Moisis, will you give me a hand, please?"

"I'm sorry, Cheryl, but I think between the two of them they've carefully orchestrated the whole evening, but I'm glad they did as I've enjoyed being here. I've missed you."

"And I've missed you too, Andreas, but they're right. They're saying it's time to put the past behind you. If you did stay on Holkamos, I know a certain lady would be very happy because she's missed not having you in her bed. The times she spent with you were very special and there's nothing more she'd love than to start all over again with you."

Chapter 50

"Good morning! So how did all this happen? Cheryl, I think we have a couple of people to thank, don't you? What time is it?"

"Yes, but not until tonight because if you remember, Moisis and Rhea have gone off the island for the day. That's a bit of a coincidence, don't you think? By the way, it's ten-thirty. I suppose that's okay, as we didn't get to sleep until around seven!"

"Rhea's had all this planned, and I'm so glad she did. Come here, I just want to kiss those lips again. It must be a few hours since I've done so! I have a lot of catching up to do."

"That's nice, very nice! Did you have anything else planned for us today, Andreas?"

"I have lots, Cheryl, and for the next couple of hours it doesn't involve a lot of talking!"

I can't believe it's two in the afternoon and we're still in bed. Well, technically Andreas isn't as he's gone to make some coffee. I can't believe how lucky I am. It's exactly what I wanted, but I never thought it would happen again.

"Coffee's ready. I've taken it out on the patio."

"Okay, give me two minutes. I'm just going to have a quick shower."

Oh, I wish I could get inside Andreas' mind. We've been here before when I thought it was all so perfect. He always has to analyse the relationship though and that's when he gets scared. I mustn't let that happen again.

Today I need to get some answers from him. I need to know where I stand. Do we have a future or are we just going to be dipping in and out of a relationship every few months? Rhea was right. He doesn't need to go back to college at all. He's learnt everything he needs to know. Now it's a question of creating his own style.

"Hi, sorry. I got under the shower and the time just flew by."

"Here's your coffee. You look so sexy with wet hair. Shall we drink this and go back to...?"

"No, as much as I'd like to, let's go and have a few hours on the beach before Moisis and Rhea get back. Shall we get something to eat? Rhea told us to help ourselves to food. How do you fancy me making us a couple of omelettes?"

"That would be nice. While you do that, I've a couple of phone calls to make and then we'll go down to the beach."

This is the first time I've cooked for Andreas. I'm nervous as his mum is probably the best cook in the world and my cooking will never match hers. Now, omelette. How does he like them? Firm? Fluffy? Or shall I put ham in them or even tomatoes? I wonder whether Andreas is a good cook. There's so much we don't know about each other. Oh, why am I panicking? It's only an omelette.

"Something smells nice. I could get used to having breakfast cooked for me."

"Breakfast? It's more like lunch, or even afternoon tea."

"This is lovely. My favourite! Tomato and ham topped with cheese. I'm spoilt, but then you did make me work up an appetite and we have all day to have more fun."

"Come on, eat up. Let's get to the beach before it's too late."

I can't believe there's no one else on the beach, but then I suppose Moisis isn't taking the boat to and fro today. Andreas and I still haven't talked, but how do I bring the subject up? The last thing I want to do is scare him off, but this is likely to be the last full day off away from Holkamos we'll have together before I go back home to England. After last night I'm not even sure I want to go, but I know for a fact there's no chance of me going to Rhodes with him. It will be a big house full of artists with no room for me.

"Cheryl, you're miles away. Tell me what you're thinking or should I tell you about the phone calls I made? I've told the college in Rhodes that I'm not coming back and also I've phoned Mum to say that I'm staying on Holkamos and I'm going to look for somewhere I can use as a studio."

"Why the change of heart, Andreas?"

"You know why. It's not just the feelings I have for you, Cheryl, but I believe you also feel the same way about me and this time I'm not going to mess it up. I think the college idea was a bit of a safety blanket and I would have used that for years. I do love my painting, but I need to have peace and quiet to develop that, not a busy college atmosphere. More than that, I want to be with you and your life here on Holkamos.

"There was a time when I was jealous of Vangelis, but I'm over that. The two of you do work well together, but when we were all up at the villa that night I realised that there was no spark between you. Then there was that silly situation with Clive. I want us to make a go of it together, Cheryl, and that means not putting any more obstacles in our path. From now on, it's all about the future."

"Are you sure? You had your heart set on going back to college."

"No, my only real aim in life was to get away from Holkamos because everyone looked at me with pity, but Holkamos is where my heart is and now they can all look at me with joy. I can hear them now saying, 'Oh, look. Andreas is happy again'. That's because I want you in my life, Cheryl.

"I'm going to put all those doubts and questions behind me. We've wasted most of the summer, and I don't want to waste any more time. I need to sit down with my mum and tell her she has to stop worrying about me. It's a new start with her selling the shop and it's a new beginning for us too."

"Andreas, are you sure, really sure? Do you need to give it more thought?"

"Give it more thought? I've never been so certain about anything in my life, but is it what you want, Cheryl? Would you be able to cope with a temperamental artist who has good days and bad days?"

"You'll have to put up with my working day being weddings, weddings, and weddings! Do you really want me coming home from work and talking about that?"

"I think I'd be able to cope. Oh, there's my phone, a text from Rhea. What a surprise, I'll read it to you, Cheryl"

'Hi, Andreas and Cheryl. Mosis and I are staying on Holkamos tonight, but I've arranged a little something for you both. You need to be down at the beach cafe at 9.00pm and no sooner, love Rhea xx'.

"I wonder what that's all about."

"I don't know, but like everything else these last two days, Rhea's put a lot of thought into it. It's nearly five pm now, so that gives us four hours. Fancy a little siesta back at the cottage?"

"I think you need to explain what you mean by siesta, Andreas?"

"I don't need to. I think you know what I mean?"

Second shower of the day and what a lovely day it's been so far. I wonder what Rhea's planned for us down on the beach. I want every day to be like today and I don't want to leave Dissinos. Saying that, look what I've got to look forward to back on Holkamos, a new future with Andreas. It's so exciting. I'm such a lucky woman as well as a hungry one.

"Come on, Andreas, it's nearly eight-forty-five. We can't be late. Anyway, what are you doing with your laptop? It's your day off."

"I'm only looking at a few things, but it's not work related. I just need to phone Mum. It will only take a few minutes. We don't need to start walking down to the beach until eight-fifty-five."

"About time too. How was your mum, by the way."

"She's okay, but I'll tell you about it later. Good job we have the torch while we go through the olive grove, but oh, look at the moon shining between the branches of the trees. Isn't it beautiful and look, there's candles leading to the beach café."

"Yes, Andreas, and there's a table laid out on the sand. It's set for dinner. Oh, how romantic is this."

"Hi, I'm hoping you're Andreas and Cheryl. I'm Maria, a friend of Rhea and Moisis. They've asked me to cook you a little dinner, so please take a seat and I'll pour you both a glass of champagne."

"Thank you so much. This is just like you see in a film or read about in a book. It's just out of this world. How special is this, Andreas? Thank you so much, Maria. I've got goose bumps. This is the perfect end to our couple of days here on Dissinos and we've got so much to thank Rhea and Moisis for."

"I hope you enjoy the meal. I've left some dessert in the fridge and some more champagne. Please help yourselves. I'm off now as I'm sure you don't want me here hanging around. Just one thing, could you put the table inside before you go? Here are the keys to lock up. Have a truly wonderful evening."

"Thank you, Maria. It was so kind of you to go to all this trouble."

"No trouble whatsoever. Have a lovely time. Goodnight."

"Your friends are lovely to do all this for us, Andreas."

"They're our friends, Cheryl. Moisis and Rhea wouldn't be doing all of this if they didn't think of you as a friend or if they thought you weren't the right person for me. They're very protective of me, I can assure you."

"Thank you, that's such a kind thing to say. I feel so very blessed."

"Let me go and get some more champagne from the fridge and I'll take some of the dirty dishes with me. I won't be a minute."

This is the perfect end to the day, a romantic dinner on a beach with no one else around. How lucky am I?

"Here you go, Cheryl, pass me your glass. I don't know how much Rhea thinks we drink, but there's another two bottles in the fridge. This will do us, I think, don't you?"

"I'm the happiest I've ever been in my whole life and it's all down to you. I fancied you the first day you came into the shop, and I can tell you something, after you left I thought to myself, 'If only you didn't have all that fake hair and those awful long red nails, you'd be the perfect woman for me'. Then it got even worse. You turned up at your sister's wedding with inches of make up on. I wanted to tell you that you didn't need all that. The woman I was falling in love with wasn't the one I was looking at, but the woman inside. She was the beautiful one. Imagine how I felt when all the hair extensions, false nails and make up disappeared. I had the perfect woman, the one I'm sitting with tonight.

"Cheryl, I love you with every bone in my body. Thank you for making me the happiest man in the whole world."

"I love you too, Andreas. You've made me the happiest woman alive."

Chapter 51

"Right, I'm off to the shop, Cheryl. Remember, don't be late. I'll meet you near the taxi rank at five o'clock. Love you!"

"Okay, I'll be there. Love you too, but in the week since we came back from Dissinos I don't know whether the love is wearing off because you won't let me get much sleep. Perhaps I need to start laying down some rules like sleep before two in the early hours and when the alarm goes off in the morning we get up, not stay there for another hour."

"I can always go back to staying at my mum's, if you'd prefer that."

"You know that's the last thing I'd want in the world. Go to work and I'll see you at five for whatever it is that you've planned."

I wonder what Andreas has planned. It's been a fabulous week but we haven't discussed the fact I'll be going back to England in a couple of weeks. Just two more weddings and I'll be gone, although something tells me I'll be cancelling my flight. There's no way either of us want to be apart and Eudora's been so friendly towards me. Every time Andreas mentions an art studio here on Holkamos her face has lit up.

Right, off to work, and a little chat with the boss. I hope he's going to be okay about it.

"Morning, Vangelis. Two more to go and then it's all over for the year. By the way, I've had the final numbers for this week's wedding. There're twenty-one adults and three children. The service will be earlier than normal at six-thirty. Do you have any more information about the mystery couple for next week's blessing?"

"Hi, Cheryl. I do, but it's no mystery. It's just that the couple wanted to do everything through me. There will be nine all together, but it has to be very special. Oh, have you got a date booked for going back to England. It's not that I'm in a hurry to get rid of you, but I wanted to be around to take you to the airport."

"That's something I wanted to talk to you about. Let's have a coffee up in the office."

"That sounds rather worrying. Go on up and I'll bring the coffees. Do I need a brandy as well?"

"No, I don't think so, but you might need to bring some champagne!"

"Here's the coffee. So what's the news? I hope you haven't decided to stay in England and not come back. If so, I'm not letting you go back for the winter."

"No, it's very happy news and I'm just hoping you'll be pleased about it too. Andreas and I are seeing each other again, and he's going to find somewhere on Holkamos to use as a studio instead of going back to art college. We're going to try and make a go of things and his mum seems to be fine with it all.

"I'd like your approval too, Vangelis. You know it would never have worked between us because a relationship is far more than just passionate sex. You and I have a special working relationship and we're best friends. I hope it will stay that way."

"I'm not surprised at all, Cheryl. You're made for each other and I know it will all work out well. I'm pleased for you both. Andreas is a lovely chap and as for you, you're a very special girl. That's why I carried on flirting and tried to impress you. I hoped you'd fall for me, but do you know what, Cheryl? You're far too nice for me. Like you said, our relationship is special and I really wouldn't want to jeopardise it. I wish you both all the luck in the world.

"Now, I'd best get on and go back down to the restaurant. One more thing, make the wedding blessing booking for ten, not nine. I think I made a mistake."

Well, that went okay. Actually it was lovely. I'm so

in love with Andreas, but I'm also happy to have Vangelis in my life as another best friend. Don't want Johnny to hear me say that though.

Now down to some work. I can't believe how many enquiries are still coming in thanks to Bella and Riven.

He moaned about me being on time, and look he's ten minutes late. Here he comes, but there's someone in the passenger seat. It's his mum.

"Sorry, we're late, Cheryl."

"That's not a problem, Andreas. Hello, Mrs Galanis."

"I think it's about time you started calling me Eudora, Cheryl. Get in, we're going on a little adventure. I'm so excited."

"Where are we off to?"

"You'll have to wait and see. All I'll say is that Andreas is driving us up to Creakos."

"We had lunch up there, didn't we, Eudora? I loved it and learnt so much about the hillside town."

I wonder what all this is about. Andreas is very quiet and it's as if Eudora has a new lease of life. I'm allowed to call her by her first name which is something I couldn't have foreseen ever happening. Driving up to Creakos isn't as nice as walking. You miss all the beautiful views out over the olive trees. I hope we're going for a lovely meal. Apart from the fact I'm so hungry, the views from the top are spectacular.

It doesn't look as though we're going to the top where all the shops and restaurants are. This lane's more of a dirt track and we're stopping in the driveway of an old, quite ramshackle old house. It looks like it needs a bit of love.

"Here we are, Cheryl. Come on, Andreas, you have the key."

"Mum, I think you need to knock on the door first. We can't just walk in."

"There, I've knocked and there's no reply. They'll

293

all be at work down in the harbour. Come on, Andreas, open up."

"Come through here, Cheryl. I want to show you the view. Well, if there is a view behind all these bushes and weeds. There, you can see the sea.

"Let me explain. This is the house where I was born and brought up. I lived here until I married Andreas' father and moved down to Holkamos town, but I still own it and rent it out to waiters who work on the island for the summer. When they go, we always say we'll stay for the winter but we never do. It does need a lot of work doing to it to make it into a proper home again."

"Mum, why don't you go into the garden and see...? Well, just go for a look around."

"Oh yes, sorry. I'll be outside if you need me."

"I'm sorry, Cheryl, this has gone slightly wrong. It wasn't the way I planned it. Mum wasn't supposed to be here with us, but it was her idea and as you can see she's very excited about it. You've been put on the spot. I didn't want that to happen and I'm very sorry."

"Andreas, the more you're talking, the more confused I'm getting. Slow down and tell me why we're here."

"The thing is, Cheryl, when I told Mum about us and that I've decided to stay on the island and get an art studio, it's her idea and like I said, I wanted to talk to you first, but..."

"Get to the point, Andreas."

"Mum thinks we can split the house into two, one half for her and the other for us. Our half would have this magnificent room as my studio. It does need a lot of work doing to it, but if she sold the house down in Holkamos that would pay for all the renovations. Would you want to be living next door to my mum, or more importantly would you want to be living with me, Cheryl?"

"Yes, to both questions, Andreas. I don't care

where I live as long as it's with you. I just want to hold you and kiss you, but seeing as I'm on your mum's good side at the moment, I don't want to push my luck in case she walks back in. She's so excited, and she's not the only one, Andreas. This is one of the happiest days of my life."

Chapter 52

It still hasn't sunk in even after a week. I really can't believe I'm going to be living here on Holkamos with the man I'm in love with as he doesn't want me to go back to England for the winter. I know he was only joking the other night to see what my reaction was when he said:

"What are you like with a paint brush, Cheryl? I don't mean art brushes like I use but larger brushes to paint walls, doors, ceilings? If you're any good, why not stay here for the winter and help me get stuck into creating our new home?"

Apparently the waiters are moving out next week and the builders will be putting in a couple of new walls, two new kitchens and bathrooms and then the two houses need decorating.

I said I was the best painter and decorator in Greece. I'm lying of course, as I've never really done anything like it before but as everything's going to be painted white it can't be too difficult. Since I've told Johnny all about it, he's been emailing me every hour with interior design ideas. Andreas wants it all to be plain and simple because it's an old house. We'll both be able to work from home as well as it can be my office throughout the winter when the restaurant's closed. The one thing neither of us will have any input into will be the garden. Eudora wants to transform it back into how it looked when she was a child, and I think that's a really lovely thing to do.

Back to reality and there's so many loose ends to tie up with next year's wedding bookings. Yesterday's was a great success, so there's just the one to go in a week's time. I also need to move out of Vangelis' holiday apartment and into Andreas' home, but that's not going to be straightforward as he's busy getting ready to move to Creakos.

As I'm not going back to the UK, I'll still be able to

use the office above the restaurant, and I also need to do a shopping trip up to Preveza with Johnny. I could do without that really, but he insists we all dress up for a dinner together to celebrate the end of the season. Why I don't know, and it's the night before the mysterious wedding blessing, the last of the season, although Vangelis thinks that will be over by 10pm. I thought Andreas and Vangelis would agree when I suggested going out the following night, but they both preferred to go out on the Saturday night. It's all a bit odd, but whatever! I've got so many other things on my mind now – new home, new life, new me.

"Johnny, do we really need to be going all the way to Preveza? Surely I could find something nice to wear in Holkamos."

"It's not all about you, Cheryl. I want something new to wear too, and it's nice for us to have a day away to ourselves. We don't see each other much now as there's always other people around, plus we can have a nice lunch somewhere. Come on, cheer up! The last time we were on this boat together it was all doom and gloom as we were off to Julie's wedding. Could you imagine that just six months later we'd be so happy here?"

"No. When I came here for the wedding I just wanted to get it all over and done with. What a day that was, Dad in his white suit, and me totally unrecognisable with my false hair, nails and make up. Yet if it wasn't for Julie's wedding, I'd have never started working for Vangelis and I'd never have met Andreas either."

"Come on, the boat's mooring up. Time to hit the shops."

One thing's for sure and that's there's no way Johnny's going to turn me into a Barbie doll again. I'm actually looking forward to the day, and I might treat myself to some nice casual clothes. I don't want to be lounging around with Andreas in my tired, scruffy old things.

"I know what I wanted to ask you, Cheryl? How did Vangelis take it when he knew you'd chosen Andreas over him? To think, neither of us actually got to find out what Vangelis is like in bed. Several women told me they had a very enjoyable evening in his company."

"I'm glad we didn't, as it would have ruined everything for both of us. Vangelis was fine about it. He gets on really well with Andreas, but then they have both known each other since they were children. Actually, the other night I noticed them whispering to each other about something, but changed the subject when I appeared."

"Right, come on, Cheryl. Let's get a taxi and hit the shops. First of all though, coffee and pastries. I can't shop on an empty stomach."

My feet are killing me. What a day! Shop after shop after shop, but at least I've bought something to wear which I approve of, something that makes me look like me instead of Barbie. It's a bit too classy just for going out in the evening, but I wasn't going to argue with Johnny. Saying I look classy, what about Johnny? His new outfit is more appropriate for a Royal garden party. Well, it is the end of the season and it will be nice to make an effort.

I wonder how many people will be there. I think I'll need an early night as tomorrow I'm moving all my things to Andreas' so that Vangelis can close the apartment block down for the winter.

This is the last night I'll be living as a single person. From tomorrow I'll officially be part of a couple. It's scary but exciting at the same time. How lucky am I!

Chapter 53

It's been such a bizarre few days. Here I am in Andreas and Eudora's house, unable to unpack much as in a couple of weeks we'll be moving up to Creakos. Today they're taking all their personal possessions out of the shop ready for the new owners to take over. Next week I'll have a whole day to myself with no wedding things to take care off. I've finished all I need to do with tomorrow's blessing, and hopefully Vangelis has also completed the tasks he needed to finalise. Apparently the numbers have gone up again, which will make it quite a tight fit around the table, but it will still work.

I'm going to walk up to Creakos and collect some keys from the waiters who are leaving today. Andreas wants me to spend some time looking around and seeing where things will need to go, but it's going to feel so strange as the house isn't divided into two yet. He thinks I'll be able to figure it all out in my head. Eudora has too much furniture to fit into her part of the house, so she says we can have some of it in ours. There's some beautiful pieces going back generations.

First, I need to phone my family and tell them I've moved out of the holiday apartment and in with Andreas. They knew I was going to, but I need to give them the landline number.

How strange! There's no answer from anyone either on the mobiles or home phones, not even Gran. That must be one of them calling back. No, it's Johnny.

"Hi, Johnny, how are you?"

"Fine thanks, but we've got a little problem in the salon and I wondered if you could help us for an hour today."

"You want me to come over and cut hair? Well, I've never done it before, but I'm always up for a challenge."

"Very funny, Cheryl, but no. It's just that our nail technician has lost her confidence. I won't bore you with the details, but if you have time today to let her do your nails for you for free, it would make her feel a lot better, I think."

"Okay, but I'm warning you now. I don't want those six inch claws you made me have for Julie's wedding. I'm going up to Creakos, but I'll come in afterwards."

"Thank you. Love you lots. See you later."

To think that this is going to be my walk to work every day, how fabulous! Walking through the olive groves looking down on Volmos beach, what a commute!

Looks like they're ready to go. How on earth will they fit into that little car with all the stuff they've already got in there? Here we are, the doors open but I want them to close it so I can open it with my own key – the key to my new home! My stomach's churning. Is it nerves, excitement or fear? A combination of the three, I think.

Hugs from three burly waiters, that was nice. Doesn't happen every day. Here goes! One door, one key and I'm shaking. Oh, there's a car coming down the lane. I hope it's not the builder as I really want to walk around by myself for a while. Now my phone's ringing. I'm going to ignore it. The car's stopping, but its fine, it's Andreas.

"This is a nice surprise, Andreas."

"I couldn't wait until tonight and I knew that Mum would want to come up as well. I wanted to be here with just you and me in our new home. I came here as a child, but I've never actually lived here, so it's a new adventure for both of us. Come on, Cheryl, open the door. Let's go in and run from room to room."

"There'll be no running around. You just need to explain which rooms are ours and which are your mum's."

"Cheryl, you're far too practical. I can see why Vangelis is scared of you."

Well, I've got everything straight in my head. It was good that Andreas did come up as I'd never have figured it all out for myself. Even when the house is divided into two it will still be very big. Andreas' studio is going to be so lovely. It's so light and airy with two huge windows for the light to stream in. Thank goodness Eudora is going to sort the garden out. I wouldn't know where to start with that.

"Cheryl. Calling Cheryl, are you with us? Gail's ready to do your nails."

"Sorry, Johnny, I was miles away."

"I noticed that. Hopefully it was somewhere nice?"

"More than nice. It was fantastic, and so beautiful. It was my new home."

Chapter 54

The day has arrived for the final wedding, but the least said about that the better. Then it's out to dinner with just about everybody. It's an awful thing to say but I couldn't really care less about either. I just want the builders to get stuck into the house so I can start the decorating. We've got such an exciting winter ahead of us and I'm going to be very disciplined with it all. Wedding paperwork on Tuesdays and Fridays, and the rest of the time working on the house. Andreas can't wait to get stuck into his art and he's excited about a new project on contemporary views of Holkamos. We're both going to be very busy, but exciting busy!

I don't need to be over at the restaurant until 11am. The first thing I want to do is try and get hold of Mum or Dad. It's unusual not to be able to contact them, but as Andreas pointed out, if there'd been any kind of family emergency, one of them would have got in touch with me.

"Hi, Dad. At last, I tried to get hold of you all day yesterday. Is everything okay?"

"Hello, darling. Yes, of course it is. How are you? Excited about moving up to Creakos?"

"Yes, Dad. Why isn't Gran answering her house phone?"

"Oh, she's gone away for a few days. That's why you couldn't get hold of us. I've taken her to visit some friends."

"What's that noise in the background, Dad? It sounds familiar."

"Sorry, Cheryl, I don't like to cut you off, but I need to go. Speak later."

Well, that's all very odd. Let's get today over with and then tomorrow I'll get to the bottom of it.

"I'm off now, Cheryl. I'm dropping Mum off at the hairdressers on the way to the shop so I'll pick you up from work and we'll go straight up to the restaurant to meet all the others. Do you want me to bring your change of clothes with me so you can get changed in your office?"

"Andreas, you're getting as bad as Johnny for fussing over everything. I really can't see what's so important about how I look and getting the timings right for today. Come to that, Vangelis is just as bad. It's a pity the three of you didn't adopt that attitude during the busy part of the summer. Yes, when you come back to change I'll leave everything I need on the bed. Have a lovely day in the shop. I love you, and try to calm down. I can't see what the fuss over tonight is all about."

"I love you, Cheryl. See you later. We'll have a special day, I promise you."

Right, let's get this show on the road. I'll get the restaurant set and make sure everything's in place and then the rest is down to Vangelis to charm the guests while I escape up to the office.

"Morning, Vangelis. What's all this?"

"What's all what?"

"You! You're all dressed up. Not that you aren't always smart for the weddings, but today..."

"Oh, it's just that we're all going out afterwards and I didn't think I'd have time to change. Now, what do we need to do first? Are you sure everything's organised?"

"Vangelis, I will just say one thing. When we organised Sharon and Brian's wedding, you weren't as anxious as this. Is there something I'm not aware of? I've got everything sorted, so why don't you take a walk along the beach and calm down? I know exactly what needs to be done.

"By the way, there seems a lot of staff here today. It's only a meal for a dozen people. We'll each have a couple of guests to serve. To be honest, just one in the bar would have been enough and both of us serving the food."

"I made a mistake with that, but it's not the end of the world. They might as well stay. Oh, and the cake's in your office and the flowers are in the kitchen."

"Vangelis, I won't say it again, but just let me get on."

I suppose I should count myself lucky that he didn't act like this for all the weddings, it would have driven be mad.

Table first and it will look lovely because the flowers and napkins are all in my favourite colours. Just what I'd choose for myself. The cake stand and knife are in my office with the cake. I can't believe Vangelis has gone out for a walk like I told him to. He's sitting on one of the rocks down by the edge of the sea, keeping out of my way. On his phone as usual, professing undying love to some unsuspecting holidaymaker I guess.

"Hi, Cheryl. Do you need a hand down with the cake? The table looks beautiful. Hope you've taken lots of photos for the website."

"Yes, Vangelis, I'm really proud of it. I hope the mystery couple like it. I'm a bit surprised, but I've just opened the cake box. It's lovely, but have you seen it? It says, 'FRIENDS, FAMILY AND NEW BEGINNINGS'. How odd."

"It's what they wanted. Now, we have an hour before they arrive. Do you fancy a drink to toast our last wedding of the season? To think it all started off with your sister's, which was a big learning curve, but look how it's all turned out! What a fabulous..."

"I knew when I was on the phone to Dad that the sound in the background was familiar. Why didn't I put two and two together? How stupid am I? Just answer me one question, Vangelis. You won't be giving anything away, but should I be wearing these clothes or should I be phoning Andreas to bring me my new outfit which I was planning on wearing tonight?"

"I think that might be a good idea, but first, Cheryl, take a deep breath and calm down. Most importantly, enjoy the last wedding of the season as it's very special. I'll go and take the cake down and you phone Andreas. I'll pop back up with a glass of something."

It all makes sense now. All that stupid business with the nails, having to go and buy an outfit and no one answering their phones, but most of all poor old Vangelis having to lie to me. Now I understand why I had to organise this my way. Today will be the icing on the cake, the end of my perfect summer in Greece.

"Come in, Andreas. You don't need to knock. Oh, it's you, Johnny, what are you doing here?"

"Vangelis phoned so I've brought your new outfit. I thought we could do just a little bit of make-up and you might just let me run a brush through your hair."

"Johnny, just hold me as I'm shaking like a leaf. I'm so happy I want to cry. Can you believe either of us could ever be as happy as we are? Do you ever pinch yourself just to see whether it's all real? I know I do."

"It is real, and no time for tears, Cheryl. We've only got twenty minutes to get you looking right. I have brought some hair extensions if you're interested. No, I haven't really, I'm only joking! There, that's better, it's put a smile on your face.

"It's been so difficult keeping all this a secret from you, but I think you need to relax and enjoy the day. It's a special day for your parents, but also special for us too. We came to this beautiful island unsure whether we'd like to stay here, but look how it's all turned out. We're very lucky. We didn't just fall in love with Holkamos, but don't you think, Andreas, Nico and Vangelis are very lucky to have us in their lives? Most importantly, we're all together as friends and that's so very special."

Right. Here goes! I look okay and feel quite

comfortable. It's now time to face the family. I wonder what's come over Mum. She's never had a good word to say about Dad. Someone's coming up the stairs. I hope it's Andreas.

"Hi. Can I come in?"

"Hello, Mum. You look lovely."

"Thank you, Cheryl, and so do you. Before all this goes any further, I do need to explain why it was here on Holkamos. When your Gran said about splitting up, I was upset. In honesty, we should have done it years ago. I don't think I loved your Dad. I wanted better than him. I just wanted the dream life, the house, the cars and everything. Anyway, when we got home after Julie's wedding, I realised that I wasn't a nice person and I hadn't been for years. I treated your father very badly and when I realised I couldn't have all I wanted, I tried to live my life through Julie, pushing her into the limelight. I did that for so many years and it was wrong. I thought I was better than everybody else, but actually I was the worse. All I ever did was spend your dad's hard earned money.

"I plucked up the courage to apologise to him. Actually, it was easier than I thought, although I was prepared to walk away with nothing. I realised just how bad I'd been. I'd broken his heart. After a few days of silence, he asked me how I felt now. I told him I felt sad because I knew what kind of a life I could have had for all those years and that I'd messed it up."

"But how have you got to this point, Mum? How did today's wedding blessing come about?"

"Your dad just asked me whether I felt differently about him now than I did all those years ago. For the first time, I did feel love for him so he asked whether we could just put all those years behind us and start again. That's why we're here today, Cheryl. We're going to start again. When we go back to England we're moving into a new house, but it won't be the grand manor house I always dreamed of. No, this will

306

be a nice little bungalow and we'll have enough money from the sale of the house to only work part time. I realise I've been given a second chance, Cheryl, and I'm going to make the most of it. I'm very lucky. It's a new beginning."

"Yes, Mum, I know all about new beginnings. Let's get this party on the way. This will be the wedding of all weddings on Holkamos. The end of a perfect summer in Greece."

Chapter 55

That's the formal part over with. I'm glad it was short, but very appropriate. So now the fun can begin!

I'm really pleased that Vangelis had extra staff in as it meant that we were both able to relax and enjoy the day. Gran's getting on really well with Eudora, and as usual Johnny is all over Richard. Even Nico's joined in. God help the poor bloke, but he takes it all in good humour. As for Mum and Dad, I've never seen them so happy. It's so odd. It's just as if none of us are here, they're in their own little bubble

"It's nearly time for everyone to sit. Cheryl, have you got a seating plan?"

"No, Vangelis. You'll remember that I wasn't involved with this wedding. Don't you have one?"

"Don't be silly. You know I wouldn't have a clue where to put people."

"Time to eat. There's no table plan, but being that you all know one another, please sit wherever you like. One thing though, after the starters, we'll all move round the table so that we're sitting next to different people. Likewise, we'll do that after the main meal and the dessert. By the time we get to the speeches, we'll all be back in our original seats. I hope that makes sense."

"That's a good idea, Cheryl, but there must be a reason behind it."

"Of course, Vangelis. You know me too well!"

"So, my darling, you don't wish to sit with me throughout the meal? This is a good start for us moving in together."

"Don't be silly, Andreas, although I know you're only joking."

I'm really proud of the table layout and décor. It's one of my favourites and what a way to finish off the wedding season. First move, I need to be sitting next to Julie. I have to say, she's looking different. The make-up has been toned down and she seems far more relaxed than normal.

"So, how's married life, Julie? Is it any different to when you just lived together?"

"People say it's no different, but I think it is. It's far better. Richard and I are really happy and the house is lovely. There's just one thing missing and that's a baby. We both can't wait to start a family. I bet you never thought you'd hear me say that, did you, Cheryl? I didn't either, but I offered to look after our neighbour's little boy after a family emergency. He's only eighteen months old. I ended up looking after him for a whole day and it brought me such joy and happiness in that short time that we've decided to try for our own baby. We've looked after him a few times since then, and it's the best thing ever. Hopefully, before too long you'll be an auntie. What do you think about that?"

"I'm so pleased for you, Julie. You'll both make fabulous parents, you really will"

"Thanks, Cheryl. It means a lot to me. What do you think about today's surprise?"

"It is a real surprise, but a nice one. Better late than never to see Mum and Dad getting on so well. If I'm honest, I wouldn't have thought it possible, but if they can put the past behind them, I think they're in for a lovely time."

"Yes, I'm pleased too. Gran and Mum are also getting on better now that Mum's being more respectful about Dad and has stopped snapping at him. So, what about you and Andreas? My money was on you and Vangelis. He was so keen on you."

"Oh, believe me he tried, and I was tempted, but no, our working relationship's great and I wouldn't do anything to spoil that. I know that once the lust and passion had passed, things wouldn't be so good and it would be awkward working for each other. It's different with Andreas. We're in it for the long run."

"Come on, Julie and Cheryl. Time to move round the table. I want to sit next to the granddaughter I don't see very often."

"Well, Gran, what a turn up for the books! After all these years Mum and Dad are actually getting on well. What's your take on it?"

"You know me, Cheryl, I have an opinion on everything and never miss an opportunity to say so, but not going to make any comment except to say that I'm very happy for both of them. Tell me all about your exciting news now. Eudora's lovely, isn't she? She's been telling me all about the new house. It sounds fabulous."

"Yes, Gran it is. I'm really looking forward to moving in and setting up home, but most of all being with Andreas. He's so kind. I'm so lucky."

"Cheryl, you make your own luck in this world, you really do. It's time to move around the table and I want to go and have a chat to Andreas. I need him to make sure that one of the first rooms he gets ready is the spare bedroom, so I can come over for a holiday."

"May I have everyone's attention please? Before we cut the wedding cake and get on with the speeches, we're going to have a fifteen-minute break. So if anyone would like a cigarette, you can go and have one while my staff clear the dirty glasses away. Is that alright, Cheryl?"

"Whatever you say, Vangelis. You're running the show today."

"You two get on so well, I'd have put my money on you becoming a couple, but what do I know? I'm only your dad."

"Come on, Dad. Let's take a walk along the beach for a few minutes and you can tell me how all this came about."

"There's not much to say really, Cheryl. After I returned to England after my holiday here, I realised that I did still want to be with your mum. Things were different. We weren't arguing, and we were getting on so much better. I suggested we move house and expected your mum to... Well, actually I don't know what I expected, but it was a real shock when she said we should look for a smaller property and release some of the equity. I wouldn't have to work so many hours then.

"The strangest thing is I've had to get used to your mum asking for my opinion on everything from food to furniture. That's never happened before. I do realise how difficult it must be for her to change like this, and so I just thought it would be great to put the past behind us and make a new start. Where better to celebrate than here on Holkamos with you. I hope you're not cross with me for not telling you earlier and causing this to be such a surprise."

"No, of course not. It's a lovely end to my perfect summer in Greece and far different to how it began. You and Mum look so happy together."

"We are, Cheryl, but you and Andreas look happy too. I've been talking to him and he's so in love with you. I couldn't be happier for the pair of you."

"Thanks, Dad. I didn't realise I could ever be this happy. Come on. It's time for the wedding cake and speeches."

"Has everyone got a drink? Please raise your glasses to Rachel and Dave. And for something completely different, the first speech will be from Rachel."

"Thank you, Vangelis and to your wonderful staff for making this the perfect day. I've just got a couple of things to say and I promise I won't take too long. Thank you all so much for being here today. Dave and I are over the moon you could share our day with us.

"There simply aren't enough words to express how much I thank Dave. Not just for today, but for the last thirty years. Why he ever stayed and put up with me I shall never know, but he's the hardest working person I know and the most loving father, son and husband. From the bottom of my heart I want to

311

thank him for giving me a second chance. I realise that I'll never be able to repay him for as long as I live, but I'm going to try. Thank you, sweetheart. I don't deserve you. I really don't."

I really believe Mum means that. It must have taken a lot of courage to stand there and say that. I'm so proud of her and Dad for hanging in there for all these years.

"Thank you, Rachel, and I wish you and Dave many more years together. Hopefully some of them might be spent here on Holkamos. There's just one thing I'd like to say before we put the music on and get into the dancing, so please bear with me for a few minutes.

"This has been my perfect summer, here in Greece. I'd like to mention how lovely it is to see my brother, Nico, so happy. That's all down to you, Johnny. You haven't only brought happiness to Nico's life, but also fun and joy to everyone you've met here on Holkamos. Also a huge thank you to Julie and Richard for starting the summer off by deciding to hold their wedding here. If it wasn't for them, we'd all have had a completely different summer.

"But my biggest thank you, and one that comes from the depth of my heart, is to Cheryl. Where do I start? She's turned my business around and if it wasn't for her, the staff wouldn't have their jobs. People see me in a far different light now. I'm not just Vangelis the café owner on Volmos. I'm now Vangelis, the owner of the most successful wedding venue on the island. None of this has been my own doing, but it's all down to the hard work and dedication Cheryl has put in.

"I'd also like to thank her for being my best friend and that's exactly what I needed – someone to kick me up the backside and tell me to grow up and stop acting like an eighteen-year-old. I will forever be grateful to Cheryl to that.

"Finally, I'd like to thank her for making one of the most genuine and nicest chaps on the island so happy. I really couldn't be more delighted for them both, so please raise your glasses to Cheryl and Andreas."

"That was really nice of him, don't you think, Cheryl?"

"Yes, it was, Andreas, but if you'll just excuse me, I want to nip up to my office. I'll only be a few minutes"

I wasn't expecting Vangelis to make a speech. What's that on my desk? Beautiful flowers and they're quite familiar. There's a card too but this time it has writing on it. It says: 'Thank you. The best man won'.

So it's the end of the summer and the final piece of the jigsaw. Vangelis was the mystery sender of the bouquets, not Clive or Andreas, and for some reason these flowers mean a lot more than the others. Why? Because they come with honesty. They come from the heart.

"Are you alright, Andreas?"

"Yes, I am now, Cheryl. How do you fancy a little stroll along the beach? It's getting dark and the visitors have all gone back to their accommodation. I love it here on Volmos when it's quiet. What a summer it's been and what an exciting winter we have to look forward to. Are you as happy as I am, Cheryl?"

"No, Andreas, I'm far happier than you could ever be."

"If that's the case, and you're so happy, perhaps I could end your perfect summer in Greece with a question. Cheryl, will you marry me?"

THE END

22280833R00181

Printed in Great Britain
by Amazon